LIVING STONES
THE PAST IN THE PRESENT

THE STORY OF UPPER DEESIDE'S PAST, ITS PEOPLE & ITS STONES

(From the source of the Dee to the Highland Boundary Stone at Dinnet, with one or two deviations if an interesting story is involved.)

Deeside:-
"Ground that sets the heart aglow
With great thoughts of long ago:
Soil that hides a sacred dust,
Earth that we must hold in trust."

Sheila Sedgwick M.B.E Ph.D

Glen Girnoc
6th September 2010. The anniversary of John Erskine, Earl of Mar raising the standard in Braemar for James Francis Edward Stuart, titular King James VIII & III in 1715.

Colour Photographs by Ken Cooper
Front cover, Ruins at Loinmuie by Gordon Bruce

Printed and bound in Scotland by Robertson The Printers, Forfar.

LIVING STONES

THE STORY OF UPPER DEESIDE'S PAST, ITS PEOPLE & ITS STONES

CONTENTS

LIVING STONES - THE THREAD OF LIFE

THE STORY OF DEESIDE'S PAST, ITS PEOPLE & ITS STONES

1. INTRODUCTION

"The story of those who lived in the past is not graven only on stone over their native earth, but it lives on, woven into the stuff of our lives".

Pericles

Deeside may have moved into the 21st century and consider itself in some matters at least to be up to date, but its attraction for locals and visitors alike lies in its scenery, its castles and old buildings, its connection with Royalty through the ages and its opportunities for discovering the past.

It is possible to find small specialised sections of information on Deeside's past but there is not a great deal available on the whole sweep of Upper Deeside's story and its vast quantity of stone, whether in ruin or in use. "Living Stones - The Thread of Life" is an attempt to supply the lack. A few years ago I spent some happy times with Ian Sutherland, journalist and author, exploring lost villages and re-discovering the past. I had the idea of writing about the stones of Upper Deeside and we planned to co-operate. Unfortunately Ian became ill and the project was shelved. Now, research on a slightly different line has gone ahead and the result is a consideration of the history of Upper Deeside, with particular reference to anything in stone, in the widest sense.

There are stones everywhere on Deeside, some as a result of glacial activity, many man-created. They all tell us something of the past.

Deeside and stone are synonymous. If there was no stone - and human ingenuity and skill to make use of it, Deeside would be without its castles and bridges, its monuments, and churches, - and few viable roads. If there was no stone we would know little of the dwellers in our area, - lords and paupers and everyone between, from the Stone Age to modern times. Without stone, Deeside's religious history would be poor indeed and for the story of Picts and Jacobites, scholars and crofters, we would have to rely on fallible human memory.

Together with its flora and fauna and its water, stone has made Deeside. However, much of the area's inheritance of stone is hard to find and often forgotten. Sometimes it lies in out of the way places or is difficult to put into historical context. Ruined castles or abandoned walls are not sad symbols of decline and fall, they are rather tributes to human skill and creativity. They are part and parcel of life on Deeside. Deeside has suffered from war and from social and economic problems. It has been, for over a century, portrayed as synonymous with the lives of sovereigns from Victoria to Elizabeth - Royal Deeside. That is only the modern part. Scotland's Kings, like Malcolm Canmore, hunted from Kindrochit Castle and he probably gave its name to Loch Kinord. The Jacobite connection is equally important.

Deeside's stones are being re-discovered, - from standing stones put up by people of whom we know little, to monuments in honour of many about whom we would like to know more. "Living Stones" is not a comprehensive history, - it is a starting point for the exploration and discovery of our rich and varied past. It follows the thread of life from the early days to the present.

The material is considerable, so only my own very subjective selection has been made.

On Deeside the past is ever with us. How did the people of this area live in the past? What were their hopes and aspirations? Was life difficult or were they satisfied with their lot? What can we learn about them as we look around Upper Deeside, visit some of the places where they lived and tread where they would have trodden? We can trace the lives of dwellers on Deeside from Stone Age settlements down to the present day.

II. THE RIVER DEE

"Rivers from babbling springs have rise at first".
Thomas Middleton

"Down rushes Dee
His cold clear tones
Fresh from the mountains
Ripple round stones"
Claude Colleer Abbott

Of Egypt in Biblical times it used to be said "Egypt is the Nile and the Nile is Egypt". The same saying could be applied to our area and the river Dee.

A small stream, the infant Dee, comes bubbling out of the ground in a wilderness area of stone and gravel on the remote plateau of Braeriach, over 4000' above sea level. A small cairn of white quartz marks the spot.

The hills are all around, row upon row. In this place where there is no shelter it is cold, even in summer. In winter it is a land of ice and snow. The plateau rises in one direction to the summit of Braeriach, in another to the cliffs circling the Garbh Choire and in another to the steep cliffs above Loch Einich.

Various little streams bubble out from springs on the plateau and join the original burn to form the Wells of Dee (OS 937988). Pink moss-campion abounds in summer. The augmented stream flows across the plateau for almost a mile until it reaches the cliffs of the Garbh Choire (the cold rough corrie) (OS 953985), where snow often lies all year round. The Dee falls in a foaming cascade for about 500 feet to form the Garrachory Falls. This rock formation is unique because there is no vegetation cover and no trees.

At the foot of the Corrie the Dee moves quickly through huge boulders. Before it reaches the Lairig Ghru it still has to drop 1000 feet. It flows through a little lochan only about 18m. across, the only loch in the course of the Dee's journey to the sea. It disappears underground, then, because the ground slopes considerably, it emerges in fast flow. Over rocks and into deep pools it continues on its way, among scenery as magnificent as any in the country.

The first tributary of any importance from now on is the stream flowing out of Lochan Uaine (OS 960980) which lies at an altitude of about 3000 feet. The water rushes headlong over the rocks to join the Dee. From the Garbh Choire to the Lairig Ghru is about 2 miles. The Lairig Ghru (OS 973012) runs north and south and is an old right of way from Rothiemurchus to Braemar. It was a drove road for sheep and cattle and there was much traffic between Upper Strath Spey and Braemar. At one time young girls carried eggs to sell in Braemar. The name Ghru may mean dark and gloomy, or, more likely, it derives from Druie, a river on the Rothiemurchus side of the pass.

The Braeriach branch of the Dee continues down the Braemar side of the pass. Another branch of the river rises at the Pools of Dee. Three pools lies just below the summit of the Lairig on the Braemar side at a height of over 2800 feet. Here the Lairig narrows, Ben MacDhui and Braeriach forming a V shaped cut through the hills. Boulders abound. The water of the pools is clear and because of the bottom 'paving' they glow with colour. The stream flows under boulders and when it emerges lower down, its flow is rapid and it is increased in volume by a number of small streams coming down the side of Ben MacDhui.

The branches join. The River Dee is born.

From the Lairig the Dee makes its way to the White Bridge, (OS 019885) just above the confluence with the Gelder. It succeeded an earlier foot bridge and ford. The river then flows on to the Linn and Inverey and then on to Braemar. The bridge may once have been painted white, but its name may have come from geal dhe, the White Dee, or Geldie. Midway between the White Bridge and the Linn are two larachs (foundations of old buildings). At the largest Bonnie Dundee probably stayed on his way to the Battle of Killiekrankie. An Sgarsoch (OS 933837) is a flat-topped hill with grassy slopes. It was a 'cattle halt' - a tryst on the march between Aberdeenshire and Perthshire. Here a cattle market was held, - Feill Sgarsaich. Eventually all the activity moved to Falkirk.

An old legend says that the Laird of Dalmore once hid his gold on Cairn Gelder and to mark the spot cut a horseshoe shape on a stone. Years later a shepherdess and a tailor thought they had found it and went for help. They could not locate it a second time, and it is still there! The old story says that as it was buried by a Mackenzie it will only be recovered by a Ruadhraidh Ruadh, a Mackenzie on both father and mother's side of the family.

The Dee is on its eighty-five mile journey to the sea.

River Dee

III. WHAT WAS THE VALLEY LIKE, LONG AGO ?

"Geology is the womb of history"

450 million years ago the area was mountainous, cut up by many rivulets, some of which were raging torrents. 400 million years ago the surface of the earth erupted and threw up molten granite. This red-hot rock gradually cooled, to form the Grampians and the Cairngorms. As time went by, they weathered and formed gullies and ridges as in the case of Lochnagar.

Around 2 million years ago, cold descended, - the Ice Age - but interspersed with warmer periods. By about 5,000 B.C. the ice had retreated, leaving behind great boulders and numerous 'kettle holes'. There are many to be found on Deeside. The hills and valleys as we know them were being created. The Dee glacier, hundreds of feet deep, formed a dam at Dinnet so that a great lake stretched back to the foot of Morven. Old lake-beds were reshaped by water-rolled stones and sand. The Muir of Dinnet was created. The river Dee, little by little, carved for itself its present channel. Some of the hills are not of granite but of serpentine or poryphry, and are heather covered. Examples are the Coyles of Muick and Morven.

Gradually it became still warmer. Trees grew, - birch, pine and oak. We have their descendants today. Craigendarroch, the Hill of Oaks, reminds us of the oaks. One ancient trunk of oak was found in 1890 in Ordie Moss.

IV. WHO LIVED ON DEESIDE IN THE EARLY DAYS?

"Time was unlocks the riddle of time is."

The earth is probably over 3,000 million years old, but man has been in the world for only a fraction of that time. For the first 2,000 million years the earth was a hot barren waste-land. The first living things were jelly-like creatures living in water. Very slowly, life forms developed, - fish and land plants and primitive reptiles like dinosaurs and pterodactyls (reptiles with wings). They were masters of the earth for 120 million years. When they became extinct over 70 million years ago mammals then appeared. The pace of evolution began to speed up. It was another 69 million years before man or "ape-man" appeared.

Imagine the history of the earth as a road you are walking along. The road is about a kilometre (1,000 metres) long. You would have gone two-thirds of a kilometre before you met even the most primitive "ape-man".

About half a million years ago a new kind of mammal appeared, with a larger brain than other mammals. He was short and thick-set, with a covering of body hair. He walked on two legs but he stooped and thrust his head forward. He had nails, not claws. Probably for the first 800,000 years of man's existence he was a hairy creature, very little removed from the apes, apart from the fact that he could use branches and stones as weapons. He wore no clothes and sheltered in caves or under bushes.

Over 8,000 years ago, towards the end of the Ice Age, large glaciers moved along Deeside, changing the aspect of the land and forming the valleys and hills that we know today. Gradually the climate became warmer and after many years the ice sheets melted. With increased warmth came bushes and trees. In time wild animals came north to the forest areas and hunters followed them. These men had weapons and primitive tools of bone, horn, wood and stone. Most of the artefacts that have survived are of stone, hence this period of history is

11

known as the Stone Age. For convenience, historians and archaeologists divide it into the Old Stone Age, (Palaeolithic), the Middle Stone Age (Mesolithic) and the New Stone Age, (Neolithic). Mesolithic incomers to Scotland were not settlers but wanderers. The Mesolithic period lasted for about 4,000 years and merged into the Neolithic or New Stone Age.

PEOPLE OF THE STONE AGE

"The flints and arrow heads of early man are fossil intelligence."

Henry Drummond

Early "men" ate whatever they could find - nuts, berries, roots, fish. Eventually they discovered how to chip stones and to sharpen points on wooden spears. Then they could hunt animals for food. In cold weather they made shelters of branches or found a convenient cave.

Life was difficult. They had to find enough food to stay alive, they had to protect themselves from wild animals and they had to learn how to keep warm. Slowly, over thousands of years, they discovered how to do these things. They made better weapons from wood and stone, and they cut up animals they had killed.

At the time when Britain was still joined to the continent men who were hunters moved across from Europe. They were tall and upright. They did not know how to grow crops or how to tame and keep cattle for food. Hunting, fishing and making weapons took up most of their time. They had no fixed homes but found shelter wherever they happened to be. Often they camped by lakes and rivers where they had water to drink and food to catch. It was perhaps not until the end of the Old Stone Age that the people made what was perhaps the most useful discovery, - they made fire. Fire kept them warm, cooked food and frightened away wild animals.

Following the Old Stone Age came the period historians call the Mesolithic or Middle Stone Age. Man learned to shape

12

stones, fasten them to sticks, make harpoons, flint knives and scrapers. He invented the bow and arrow and made animal traps. Failing a natural shelter, he made one from branches and leaves. Having now discovered fire he could shelter in caves for fire would keep out animals that normally lived there.

It was during this period that people first appeared on Deeside. So far nothing has been found in Aberdeenshire to show that people lived here before this period. Mesolithic settlers had presumably moved up from England and they lived in Scotland in 'camp-sites'. They were mobile on both land and river.

The early habitations, like the culture of the people, were very primitive. The occupants dug shallow pits in river terraces and roofed them with hide, heather or turf supported on branches. Obviously such dwellings have not survived. The flesh of the animals they hunted and fish from the river gave them food, supplemented by wild fruits and nuts. Clothes were made of animal skins. Perhaps there were as few as 100 families in the whole of Scotland. Very few people could be supported until crops could be cultivated and animals domesticated.

We know these early people were in the Dee valley because their pigmy flints, used as arrow heads, spears and as combs for dressing skins, were found at Banchory in 1905. More have been found since then in the gravel terraces of the Dee. There may even have been a 'factory' for producing pigmy flints which are less than 1/2" in length. They were probably used as arrow-heads, barbs or drills. West of Cambus o'May on each side of the A93 road local archaeologists have discovered evidence that Mesolithic people were here. Flint tools and waste from flint 'knapping' would indicate that hunter-gatherers were in the area around 6000 B.C. It is likely that only four or five families were involved at a time. This type of life persisted for about 2000 years.

These were a wandering people, hunters, not settlers, wandering from place to place in search of food. The community was small - it could only increase when cereals were grown and animals domesticated. Indeed, most of the time was spent making weapons and searching for food because they had no domesticated animals to kill for food.

While pigmy flints were being made, "strandloopers" appeared at the mouth of the Dee at Aberdeen. Their name comes from their habit of moving in dug-out canoes from one beach or river bank to another. They ate fish, berries, nuts, roots, deer, and wild boar and were helped in their hunting by trained dogs. They probably made expeditions up the Dee but left little to remind us of their presence. Life was hard. There was always danger from wild beasts. Nomadic people, they were absorbed by a more culturally advanced race who may have come from the Moray Firth area.

Roots, berries, seeds etc. were the basis of the family 'meals'. They may occasionally have come across a dead animal and that provided food for a while. They all huddled together for warmth but generally they had to spend a great deal of time looking for food, just to keep alive. The group never remained long in one place but wandered about in their search.

What more do we know of early dwellers or visitors to Deeside? We have to think of man's development, proceeding continuously, though not always improving or progressing.

Hunting

Men and boys had to face a great deal of danger when hunting. Their method was to hide in the bushes near water until an animal came to drink then hurl spears and kill the wounded beast with stone axes and spears. They often chased herds until an old or wounded animal fell behind. Then they surrounded it and killed it. To catch large animals they dug pits. Stakes were fitted on the sides and the bottom and the opening covered by branches. An animal was driven to the pit and when it fell through it was killed on the stakes. It was usually cut up on the spot and carried home on sledges made of wood and hide ropes. Small animals could be carried home over the shoulders or dragged by the legs. If hunting was poor these early 'Deesiders' ate roots, berries, and nuts.

They were now able to fasten sticks to stones in a much better fashion. Wood, stones and bones were the materials used for all tasks. Flint too was coming into use but was obtained by barter. They also learned to make and use with some skill bows and arrows and this meant having more to eat. Animal traps were perfected. Many things could be made from animal bone, including harpoons to add fish to the diet. Flint knives were used and scrapers to deal with animal skins.

It was the task of women and children to ensure the fire kept burning and to collect enough wood to keep it burning day and night. This was difficult, but fire meant that the family could keep warm, cook their food and frighten away wild animals. Women and girls cooked the food while men and boys went hunting and fishing. Meat could be eaten raw or cooked, - cooked over a fire or in water heated by red-hot stones. There was no wastage. The meat was eaten, - even the brains. The bones made tools, the sinews thread and the skin became tents and clothes. These skins were sewn together using bone knives and animal sinews. The whole family was involved. They did not know how to spin wool or weave cloth. They just used skins. After scraping off any meat and fat the skin was stretched on the ground to dry and then it was softened by rubbing in fat. At first the skin was wrapped round the body and fastened at the shoulder. When they discovered how to sew skins with bone needles and thongs of skin and sinew the garment was more useful. Both sexes made bracelets and necklets. Favourite materials were shells, teeth and fish bones.

The families were still wandering, moving from place to place as the fancy took them and as they looked for food. At first they crossed rivers by clinging to tree trunks as they floated downstream. Then they made rafts of logs. Later they used axes to hollow out tree trunks: sometimes a wooden framework was covered with skins. Boats were used for fishing. The family groups were mobile on land and river and established links with other groups.

Life went on as before during the period we know as the New Stone Age. People living at the eastern end of the Mediterranean had learned how to tame animals and grow crops. These herdsmen had flocks of cattle, sheep, pigs and goats. They grew wheat and barley and ground corn into flour. They wandered about Europe looking for more grassland and eventually some arrived in the south of England. They had to travel in dug-out canoes because by this time Britain was an island. Gradually they spread further north.

Men and boys spent a great deal of time guarding their flocks and hunting wild animals. They grew some wheat and barley but hunting and rearing cattle for meat, milk and skins was very important. Because of poor grass, most of the stock had to be killed off before winter. Every autumn, men and boys, with dogs, drove the cattle to a large "camp". This was made by digging two or three wide ditches round the top of a hill. Digging with stone axes and antler picks was hard work. The soil was put into skin "buckets" and thrown on the ground above the ditches. This made a bank and on top of this they built a fence. Cattle were driven into the spaces between the ditches and killed.

More food was now available than previously but there was still a winter scarcity and wild animals were hunted for food and skins. Deer and wild boar were shot with bows and arrows. Bears were trapped in pits. Fish were speared. There was still movement from place to place, searching for new land on which to graze their stock and grow their crops. Eventually men began to make polished stone axes, and towards the end of the period, to live by farming instead of by hunting. In order to farm families had to stay in one place so "home" became more permanent. Better shelters were made. Man learned to domesticate animals - sheep, pigs, cows and horses, and he used dogs to help him in his work.

Women grew the crops in small patches of land near the huts, helped by family members. The land had to be cleared of stones and small trees and bushes burned. The earth was broken up with antler-horn picks and stone hoes. Seeds of wheat and barley were scattered and covered over.

At harvest time the heads of corn were hand - picked or cut with flint sickles. Threshing separated the grain from the chaff. Some storage was in clay pots or skin sacks, to provide winter food. Flour was produced by grinding between two stones. Corn was placed on a bottom stone and another stone was rubbed over it. These were Saddle Querns. The bottom stone, worn down by use, produced a meal full of stone fragments that wore down the teeth. Women made small flat "scones" and cooked them in the hot ashes of the fire. Meat could be roasted over the fire or cooked in a pit lined with stones. This was the oven. "Stews" were made in clay pots by dropping red-hot stones heated by the fire into the water and adding the meat. Women and children collected berries and nuts to augment the diet.

Skins were cleaned by women and girls. After softenlng they were sewn together with bone needles. Buckets and sacks were also made.

The women and girls also made the clay pots for milk, water and cooking. Long strips of clay were wound round and round then fingers were used to smooth out the joints. Then came firing, not always successful.

Some homes were probably "tents" covered with skins or branches while others were shallow holes dug in the ground, with a roof of branches and heather. The centre of the roof was held up by a strong post and the roof edge rested on the bank.

Later, walls were made by weaving twigs and branches and covering them with mud to keep out the wet. The floor was often of grass and bracken and this is where the family slept.

While Old Stone Age hunters had made tools from bits of stone and lying flint, New Stone Age people dug better flints, polished them and fixed them to wooden handles. They also traded for flint, perhaps from the Peterhead area. Barter was common - flint for corn, meat or skins.

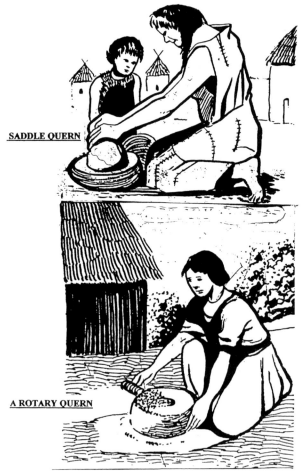

Grinding Corn

PEOPLE OF THE BRONZE AGE

Life went on and to some extent became easier. Man discovered metals, - first copper, then bronze and finally iron. The Bronze Age here probably began about 2000 B.C.

From about 1800 B.C. to 450 B.C. more warriors arrived in Britain from Europe, in search of land for their cattle. They fought with weapons made from the new metal, bronze, that did not break easily and retained its cutting edge better than stone, wood or bone. These people were herdsmen and hunters. They grew some crops but preferred to raise cattle and hunt. In winter they could still be short of food.

From about 1800 B.C. weapons and tools began to be made of bronze, a mixture of copper and tin, the latter having to come from Cornwall. Hence, it was expensive. This period is known as the Bronze Age. Tarland, Aboyne and the Forest of Birse have all produced bronze axes and a bronze spearhead was found at Loch Kinord.

The change over was gradual, with flint and stone tools in use a long time after the bronze was available.

Bronze Age people were also traders, some becoming wealthy. Their smiths made excellent bronze weapons. A Bronze Age sword is on display at Braemar Castle. Weapons and other bronze artefacts were exchanged for necklaces and jet and amber brooches. They bought sheets of gold and covered buttons and boxes. Not only did they trade in Britain but they had markets in Europe. Britain was becoming a trading centre.

Towards the end of the Bronze Age Celtic tribes arrived from Europe, armed with axes, swords, spears and circular shields. These Celts were also skilled farmers. They used ploughs pulled by oxen. Yield increased as did quality. Wheat and barley were grown in square or oblong fields and banks of earth topped with a fence kept stock in and wild animals out. Wheels had been invented and Bronze Age farmers used horse-drawn carts to move crops and goods. There was plenty of food. Once there was no longer need to search for food numbers increased. Families joined together in villages. Villagers joined to make tribes and chieftains ruled over them and led them into battle against "enemy" neighbours.

Making bronze tools was a skilled task. Smiths travelled around, selling their tools. "Hoards" were often hidden in times of danger so "finds" today reveal tools nearly three thousand years old. Bronze was dear so stone, wood and bone continued in use for hundreds of years.

Inside the home there was usually a hearth for the fire, with a hole in the roof for egress of smoke, a cooking hole and a stone platform on which to sleep. Houses were built in "villages" with a dyke to protect from enemies and animals. Throughout the years, construction improved.

Women had learned how to spin and weave and make clothes. Linen thread was made from stems of nettles and woollen thread from combings from their sheep. The thread was woven into cloth on a loom. There were two uprights with a post across the top. Warp threads hung from this and they were weighted at the bottom with lumps of clay. A weft thread was passed in and out of the warp threads, in front then behind.

Women and girls still made clay pots by hand. Patterns were more elaborate and a turn-down collar was often created on a pot. Both women and men wore jewellery and ornaments.

PEOPLE OF THE IRON AGE

Towards the end of the Bronze Age, at some time between 500 B.C. and 100 B.C. Celtic tribes reached Scotland, having originally come from France and Belgium. These people were armed with swords, daggers and knives made from a new metal, - iron. They had learned how to heat iron with charcoal and while still hot hammer it into shape. The resulting tools were harder than bronze and so much stronger. That meant these people were able to conquer those who used only bronze weapons and take their land.

Because tools could be made of the more durable iron

greater numbers of trees could be chopped down and more land cleared. These people had better ploughs that were pulled by oxen and so they were able to cultivate a larger area. In addition the soil was ploughed more easily and more efficiently so better crops were produced. They sowed oats and rye and raised short-horned cattle and sheep. In many cases there were pens near the dwellings where horses, sheep, pigs and cows could be kept.

These people also discovered that manure benefited the land so after the harvest had been gathered in the cattle were turned loose in the fields. The crops could be produced in the same fields every year. At harvest time the crop was cut with sickles, dried in ovens and stored in pits in the farm-yard. The corn was ground in stone querns. Some of course was saved for seed the next year and was wind and sun dried on frames and stored on little platforms.

This all meant that the farmers could remain in one place and not have to move on. Even though they still had to kill off most of the cattle before winter, nevertheless they had more food than their predecessors. There were years when they had enough fodder for feeding more cattle, to start new herds in spring. When necessary the farming folk could still augment their food supplies by hunting and fishing. Among Iron Age finds have been harness mountings and Rotary Querns that superseded the Saddle Querns. The top stone rotated on the bottom one, so grinding the meal.

Throughout this period hygiene as we know it did not exist although probably the area used as a latrine was some distance from the dwelling, to avoid the stench and the flies. Washing in the river was only necessary if covered by mud or after slaughtering an animal when hands and body would be covered by blood. Teeth were not cleaned but bits of meat or food were frequently poked out with a bit of stick.

Women's work was as in earlier times, with women and girls cooking, grinding corn, making pots, spinning and weaving while the menfolk worked in the fields, looked after the cattle and did a little hunting and fishing.

Some men were traders, so villages were built near tracks to enable goods to be moved easily. Trading was usually with other tribes as well as further afield.

When man invented writing he had the key to progress. Things could be written down and passed from one generation to the next much more satisfactorily than by word of mouth. This is really the beginning of history, for we can read about what happened long ago.

In 10,000 years - a mere fragment of man's life on earth, man has gone from a savage with nothing but stone, bone or wooden tools to a man who has walked on the moon. It took man about 800,000 years to discover how to make fire and only 54 years from the first manned aeroplane to the first satellite. The pace of progress is speeding up!

Spinning & Weaving

V. IN LIFE & IN DEATH

"Life is short, the occasion fleeting, experience deceitful and judgment difficult"

Aphorisms of Hippocrates

DWELLINGS

Houses occupied in the Iron Age were similar to those used by Bronze Age people. There was probably a fair sized community on Deeside.

Some farmers lived in thatched huts in little "villages" with a fence around as a defence against wild animals. Others lived on separate farms. The extended family lived in a building erected on a wooden framework. Building was simple. A shallow circular hole was dug. This was then surrounded by a tightly-fitting ring of stones standing on end. Another ring of stones was built outside this and the gap between the two was filled in with rubble and smaller stones to make a firm wall. The floor was paved with river washed stones or other available material so that a flat surface was obtained. Upright posts held up a roof of turf or heather that sloped down to the walls. Huts were bell-tent shaped, without windows or chimney and they had only one low door. Because the roof came down to ground level the house was fairly well wind and water-tight. The open hearth was in the centre of the floor. Sometimes there seems to have been a hole in the roof for egress of smoke. There was just one room inside, but it could be divided up with skins or brushwood partitions.

Remains of these Hut Circles are to be found in a number of places. Good examples are at New Kinord (OS 448999), with two large (40' to 50' across) isolated ones on the slopes of Cnoc Dubh. There would be a considerable settlement at Loch Kinord where the people grew crops but also hunted and fished. On the Nature Reserve around Kinord and Davan there are extensive remains of a settlement and field systems. New Kinord site is probably more visible, but at both Old and New

Kinord there are low stone-walled enclosures. They are bigger than those generally found and may have enclosed timber huts. The field systems have stone clearance heaps and low stone banks. They may have extended over several centuries until well into the early centuries A.D. The Dinnet area field systems also occupied reasonable farm land. In the Dinnet Nature Reserve there are at least three settlements, with enclosures that were probably stock pens, and fields with stone dykes and sunken pathways. One dwelling at Old Kinord had a paved floor and such places were probably occupied until medieval times. Another field system lies behind the Cambus o' May Hotel and there are many remains in Glen Gairn. At Tillycairn there are other cairns and the remains of a fair-sized settlement.

Bronze and Iron Age people wove cloth from wool and from a type of flax, so they did not have to depend on animal skins. There are of course no written records, but identification of pollen types and radio carbon dating provide our information. At Micras near Crathie there are also a number of hut circles.

Women and girls cooked, ground corn, spun thread, wove cloth and made garments. They also made pottery by hand. The results were more artistic than previously, with more elaborate decoration. They discovered how to coat their pots with a 'slip' that contained iron oxide. When the pots were fired this turned red and when polished gave the appearance of bronze.

Some of the Celts were traders, building their settlements where tracks intersected. Iron bars were used for money, probably in six lengths and values.

Their blacksmiths and carpenters were skilled. Round wooden bowls were produced decorated with flowing curves. Pots were still made by hand but these too had curved decoration. The warriors fought with iron daggers, broadswords and round wooden shields. They loved jewellery and usually fastened garments with brooches in lieu of buttons.

Bronze and iron were used concurrently for a long time. Celtic sculptured stones belong to the valley and one, the

Formaston Stone at Aboyne takes us from pre-history to recorded history.

Such are the early settlements. We would like to know more of these people who lived in the area, but they had little to leave us but the ruins of their homes. Habitations through the ages lie in close proximity, showing how from early times to the end of the nineteenth century sites had been continuously occupied. This is an outstanding characteristic of the area - the present develops from the past.

CRANNOGS

All Iron Age people did not live underground or in huts above ground. When geographical features made it possible they built crannogs - artificial islands in lakes, made of oak piling and stones. Enormous posts were then driven down to keep the structure in place. There was a wooden landing stage for unloading from canoes. The smaller island in Loch Kinord is an excellent example of a crannog. Oval in shape, it measured about 19m. by 22m. Successive layers of stone and earth were held together by intersecting mortised timbers and tethered by a girdle of piles. Dwellings were of wood, stone and clay. Stone, iron, bronze and timber items have been found. Among the latter were oak piles from the crannog and parts of a canoe.

Kinord's maximum depth is about 12' while Davan's is 9', but previously they were much deeper. The crannog dwellers also had fields to cultivate on the "mainland".

A peninsula, Gardiebane, was converted to a virtual island stronghold by the cutting of a canal across the narrow isthmus. The inside was defended by a ramp while on the landward side there were heavy earthworks. Communities would live on their island measuring 25 yards by 20 yards, about 250 yards off shore. In 1872 a plough turned up an underground structure, 21' long, up to 3' wide. There may have been a further loch that silted up to form the bogs of Ordie and the Black Moss. The people of the crannog used dug-out canoes and some have been recovered, as were bronze harness mountings known as terrets and rotary querns, an advance on Stone Age saddle querns. The top stone rotated on the lower one. Tree felling meant land could be cultivated: settled farming had arrived. Stone balls with elaborate carving may have been attached to leather and used as weapons.

The island to the west, known as Castle Island was a medieval fortress. King Malcolm Canmore, 1058-1093 was reputed to have had a hunting lodge there and Edward 1 may have stayed there while his army was encamped near by. James 1V was a regular visitor to Deeside. He stayed at the Castle on Kinord for the month of October 1505 and again in 1513. The Lord High Treasurer's accounts show money paid for transporting the King's dogs across the loch, payments to the boatman and a contribuion to a blind man. James V was also a frequent visitor to Deeside, travelling incognito as 'the gudeman of Ballengeich'. On one occasion when he was near Kincardine o'Neil he stopped, with his party, at a roadside croft at the east of the village. He was so pleased with the hospitality that he received from Cochran that he ordered that the property be given to the cottar, - hence Cochran's Croft, still there today.

The colony at Kinord was one of the earliest and most populous Iron Age settlements north of the Grampians. Some scholars believe it was the Devana referred to by the Latin writer Pompey, rather than Aberdeen, but this is unlikely.

Many wooden objects have been found in the Loch Kinord area, although in view of the time scale it is surprising that so much has survived. A three-legged bronze ewer 10" high with a handle and spout, was found near Castle Island in 1833. A bronze spear-head and part of the oak handle in its socket was also recovered. A second bronze spear-head is in the National Museum in Edinburgh. Beads and rings have also been found.

SOUTERRAINS

Houses occupied in the Iron Age by people at Old Kinord were similar to those used by the Bronze Age people. There is often a souterrain, usually covered by a stone slab. These souterrains or eird houses are underground tunnels of stone. The floor is of stone or pebbles and the sides are of stone without any mortar. The eird house was usually about 10' wide, 8' high and often up to 80' long and was entered by a series of steps. Tullich's eird house lies behind the old Kirk (OS 390975) on a slope of a hill. Its real purpose is uncertain. Too small for cattle and rather low for people to stand upright in comfort, it is likely to have been constructed as an adjunct to hut dwellings, probably for storage. Wonderfully built of stone, without mortar, it winds in a semi-circle for about twenty feet. No trace of any hut dwellings remain. There is another souterrain at Gardiebane (OS444990) Meikle Kinord, with a well preserved one at Culsh, Tarland and one at Milltown of Migvie. They date from around 300 - 100 B.C.

The souterrains or store houses would indicate greater control of crop distribution and storage

BURIALS

We learn most about these early people from burial remains. They buried their dead collectively in long cairns - vault-like chambers with cairns above, usually in groups. Some were elaborate, others no more than a heap of stones. Believing that after death the soul would need tools, knives, arrow heads and axes, these were buried with the bodies. Cairns were usually sited in places that had a commanding view of the surrounding countryside. The best examples are on Balnagowan Hill, Aboyne, - two big and about 900 small cairns, so it must have been a fair sized community over the years. There is another at Balnacraig: both were built on hills around Braeroddach Loch. Accurate dating is not possible and some may even be of Bronze Age origin, but they are likely to date from around 3000 B.C. Settlements would be near and pollen and sediment analyses show that livestock grazed and there was some cultivation.

In the parish of Aboyne, 1 mile east of Newton, on the summit of a ridge is Cairnmore. There is one large and several smaller cairns. The former was opened in 1818 but no record of any finds seems to exist. There are also sepulchral cairns at Glenmillan, Lumphanan.

By around 2500 B.C., when the Stone Age was coming to an end, new people came by sea, perhaps from Holland and the Rhineland. These people buried their dead singly, in cists or chests of stone slabs, so they are named the 'short cist' people. The body was placed in an embryonic position and given a 'beaker' or food vessel for the journey to the next world. Graves were about 3'8" long, 2'6" wide and about 2' deep. A flat cap-stone and earth covered the top. Short cists were always placed where drainage was good: in addition the floor was of clay or pebbles.

In the 1870's a short cist burial was discovered on Mulloch Hill (OS 323011) 2 miles N.E. of Dinnet, but it had previously been opened. The cairn is 56 yards in circumference, but no upright stones remain, just foundations. Mulloch was by tradition a Danish leader who fell in battle, but the cairn is unlikely to be associated with him, in spite of local legends. Another cist lies above Burn o' Vat. (OS 425996). There are numerous other mounds. Short cist people were given a clay mug or beaker for the journey to the next world, hence they were known as Beaker People. There were often tools and ornaments as well. In a lecture in November 1935 called "The Ancient Dead of Aberdeenshire" Dr. W. Douglas Simpson showed how streams of immigrants came to Scotland. One came in the Stone Age to our western shores from the Mediterranean area via Spain and Brittany. Dark faced and with long skulls, oval faces and refined features, this type survives in the west of Scotland. According to Dr. Simpson the short cist (stone box) people who came to our eastern shores from the Mediterranean via the Carpathians, the

Danube and the Rhine were those by whom Aberdeenshire was chiefly colonised. These people had round skulls, prominent eyebrows, hollow temples, broad noses and square jaws. He suggested that if a skeleton could be found from a short cist burial, covered with flesh and muscle and clothes of today, no one would give it a second glance as it walked along Bridge Street in Ballater. He suggested that the blood of these people still flowed in Deesiders and their racial characteristics lie at the base of our racial characteristics. A comparison of skull types shows that real locals of Deeside are descendants of these people.

For no reason that can be determined, cremation took over from burial. There were no immigrants: the same people changed their burial customs and the change was very gradual. The ashes of the dead were generally put in a pottery jar or cinerary urn around 18" high, with a narrow bottom and a wider mouth, buried and covered with stones and earth. Bronze Age burials have been found at Aboyne, Loch Kinord and Tarland. Round cairns were sometimes built over urn burials, like the Blue Cairn at Tillypronie. There is a ring cairn at New Kinord. At Tillycairn, Dinnet, urns were said to have been found with calcined bones, together with some bronze objects, but there is no documentary evidence. Cairns and hut circles lie in the fields near the old Glen Tanar Church, just off the South Deeside road.

STONE CIRCLES

Recumbent Stone Circles seem to have been built to a common plan, the name coming from the large flat stone usually towards the south west. Most are outwith our area. There were usually three concentric rings, of varying diameter. Standing stones, reducing in size towards the north, varied in number from six to eight or ten, while the height could be anything from 4' to 9'. Between the two tallest stones, known as flankers, on the south side of the circle, there was a Recumbent or Altar stone which could weigh up to 20 tons.

Sometimes these circles were thought to be pagan temples. Perhaps our best local example is the Stone Circle at Tomnaverie off the Aboyne/Tarland road. On a hill terrace with an open view, the circle is about 17m. in diameter. There is a recumbent, a flanker, a fallen flanker, 5 upright stones and a further fallen stone. They surround a cairn and there are slight traces of an inner kerb. There is another by the church at Migvie about 17m. in diameter.

Another circle is the Nine Stones at Mulloch Wood. It differs slightly from other stone circles in that the recumbent and flankers sit at the edge of an inner cairn while the remaining stones sit on an oval arc outside about 18m. by 15m. It may be that this was built later than most others. In the centre of the circle cremated bone was found in a funnel - shaped pit lined with slabs.

At Dam Wood, Glassel there is an oval circle, less than 6m by 3m. with 5 stones of slightly red granite about a metre high. A couple of metres to the south lies a boulder.

There are numerous smaller, often unrecorded stone circles on hills, in obscure places, as at Abergairn (OS 355974) and The Buailteach (OS 277933) and on the Sron Ghearraig (OS 263985).

Stone Circles were probably places of worship and often the illustrious dead were buried within the central circle. Small circular hollows cut into the stone, often called cup marks, are present on some stones and may have been used for libations. The remaining stone of a circle that used to stand at Potarch was known as the Worship Stone. Sacrifices may or may not have been performed, but the stones are more likely to have been linked with astronomical observations.

Urns were also buried near Standing Stones that are a feature of this period. Remains of Stone Circles are to be found in many places in the North East. Later Deesiders held the stones in awe, but farming necessities often meant they had to be removed. However there was a feeling that total removal would result in disaster so one stone was usually left standing. There are a few single stones that research has shown may be route markers. This may be the case with the monolith, the Scurrystane, (OS 358950) opposite Dalliefour Farm on the South Deeside road. It may have marked a route across the Muick and on to Glen Clova. From the Gaelic"sgur" to rub, for generations it has been a scratching place for animals.

A standing stone at Abergeldie Castle (OS 287953) was nicknamed Lady Portman after a lady in waiting when Abergeldie was let to the Duchess of Kent, (Queen Victoria's Mother).

The Scurry Stane

SCULPTURED STONES

The most important bequest to us from our early ancestors is their sculptured stones. With the inscription on one of them, the Ogham Stone, we can say we are leaving prehistory behind and advancing to the realm of recorded history. In St. Adamnan's Kirkyard, Formaston, outside Aboyne, which was the site of the early village and church, there was a stone with an inscription in Ogham, the Celtic alphabet. After a time at

West Lodge, Aboyne Castle, it is now on display at Aboyne Victory Hall. Ogham consists of a series of short lines of varying length, cut across a main vertical. A possible translation is "MacTail, son of Uorneht, descendant of Srobchenn". Presumably it is a memorial to a chief and is perhaps the earliest piece of recorded history on Deeside.

Sculptured stones have carvings of humans and animals and geometric designs. They are usually divided into three groups. The earliest, before 800 A.D. are rough stones, unshaped, and undressed. The symbols are incised. They are usually combinations of a V rod, a double disk often called 'spectacles', a serpent, an elephant-like creature, and a fish and a "horse". Sometimes there is a mirror, believed to convey female association.

A second group dates from 800 to 1000 A.D. and has stones that are roughly shaped. The Celtic Cross appears and groups of animal and human figures, or symbols, all in relief. The latest group comes from the eleventh to the thirteenth centuries. There are no symbols, and the Celtic Cross is more elaborate. Some have hunting scenes and Biblical characters or elaborate Celtic intertwined patterns.

Good examples of Sculptured Stones are at Tullich, which were in an enclosure at the Kirk, (Cill Nachlan) (OS390975). They were discovered in 1866 by the Rev. Grant Michie, one being used as a door lintel. In total there are 16 stones. It is probable that some of the stones were of pre-Christian origin, with Christian symbols added later. Missionaries built churches on sites that had been occupied by Bronze and Iron Age settlers because the soil there was cultivable. Some of the symbols were probably carved long after the stones were set up. The meaning of the symbols is uncertain, but they may have referred to social status or even have some ritualistic meaning. There is a pre 800 A.D. stone, almost 2m. high and $1/2$m. wide, with double disk, z rod, 'elephant' and mirror suggesting a female connection. It was probably wider but was reduced when used as a lintel, for that is where the Rev.Grant Michie found it in 1878. Col. Farquharson of Invercauld paid for the removal of this and other stones and placed them for protection against the north wall of the church, in front of the old doorway. The stone may be contemporary with Nathalan, the founder of the original Church at Tullich. A suggestion has been made that the stone came from the Correen Hills, near Alford, but there would appear to be no documentary evidence for this. Other stones, roughly shaped, with a cross, resemble Celtic stones elsewhere and are likely to be from 800 - 1000 A.D. while five stones are of later date, probably from the 11th century. Symbols may refer to social status or they may have ritualistic significance. With the stones is a baptismal font, hollowed out of a boulder, complete with drain hole. The men responsible for these stones had considerable skill and artistic ability. The function of the stones and the religious beliefs of the people are lost in the mists of time.

Modern living has caused problems with the stones and they were deteriorating. All the stones have been removed for conservation and are to have a new "shelter" constructed for their return.

In Tullich kirk-yard one can follow the course of history from Pictish times to the present day, something to make us re-live the past and ponder on the future.

One of the finest stones in the country, probably from the 11th century and group 3, is at Kinord, part of the united parish of Glenmuick, Tullich and Glengairn before the parish of Dinnet was created in 1881. The Kinord Stone is 6'3"high by 3' 1" wide and 12" thick, and is a wonderful example of cross ornamentation, five patterns being woven into a continuous plait. There are small scroll ends to the arms of the cross and lack of symbols would indicate this is a Christian monument from the very end of the Pictish period. Originally it may have marked the site of an Al or worship place. A tradition, with no documentary back-up says the stone was sculptured by Fumoc for his little chapel on Kinord shore but his date is at variance with the stone's eleventh century date. It is possible that the carving was executed later on an earlier stone. At one time it may have been used as a market cross near its original site. At the Reformation it was thrown into the loch. After it was recovered it was set up at Aboyne Cstle in 1820, then returned to the loch side, fenced in, among the broom.

The Pictish symbol stones are a link between the pagan Picts and Christianity. Symbols of a Christian cross alongside the pagan carvings show continuity of site through the ages.

We would like to know more of these early inhabitants of Upper Deeside, but all they have left us are the stones and the ruins of their homes. As time went by other settlements grew up close by showing that from early times to the nineteenth century sites had been continuously occupied. This is an outstanding feature of the area - the present develops from the past.

Tullich Symbol Stones

VI. CELTS, ROMANS & PICTS

"They who cross the seas change their sky but not their disposition"

(Said of a Viking raider)

The Celts were settling in Aberdeenshire and passing on their skills to the descendants of the Bronze Age people while in England life was changing. In 83 A.D. the Romans occupied a great deal of what was then England then moved north. In A.D.84 they gained a victory over the Celts at Mons Graupius, site uncertain, but suggestions have been made that it may have been near Stonehaven or perhaps near Keith, or even around Bennachie. The Romans failed to consolidate their victory and later retired behind their defences of the Antonine Wall, stretching from the Forth to the Clyde.

Between 208 & 211 A.D. the Romans again crossed the Grampians by the Elsick Mount under the Emperor Septimus Severus. They had a marching camp at Normandykes just south west of Culter that covered about 80 acres. Roman ships kept in contact by means of beacons. The soldiers marched up to the Moray Firth and no doubt there were numerous skirmishes. They did not stay long in Scotland and by 410 A.D. they had left Britain completely.

Some hill forts may have been built for defence, with the stone walls vitrified either by intent or by attackers.

It is doubtful if Roman forces penetrated to Upper Deeside, and the Devana of the Roman map is more likely to have been Aberdeen, for it is most unlikely that the Romans did not know it. The suggestion has been made that Devana was the Iron Age settlement in the Howe of Cromar and the inhabitants of Aberdeenshire were a tribe called Taexali who had a town called Devana. The map, anything but accurate, shows it as between Loch Davan and the Pass of Ballater. The Taexali would have been one of the many tribes in northern Scotland who later combined to form a group that the Romans called the Picts, towards the end of the third century A.D.

The Picts inhabited Pictland, Scotland north of the Forth except for Argyll. The name the Romans used for them came from the Latin for painted, because of the body designs coloured with plant dyes. The Picts were probably a mixed race of descendants of Bronze Age people, Beaker people and Celts. Their written language was Ogham - a line with short lines crossing or touching as in the Formaston Stone at Aboyne, although there are examples of round Ogham, like a wheel. The Picts were expert sculptors.

At the time of the Roman invasions Scotland had at least 17 independent tribes, usually warring against each other, but by the start of the eighth century A.D. they had been reduced to four. Eventually by 844 Pictland and Dalriada were under the control of Kenneth MacAlpin and by 1034 Duncan was the first king of 'Scotland'.

There was still a large area of Scotland outwith Duncan's control. Part of the northern mainland and the islands of Orkney, Shetland and the Hebrides were in the hands of semi-independent clan groups, like Macdonalds of the Isles, lordships who owed no allegiance to central authority and the Vikings who used their bases to raid the other parts of Scotland as well as England. Every summer the 'Summer Wanderers' under the sons of Eric-Blood-Axe went on their expeditions to Northern coasts, and they even attacked Aberdeen. Malcolm II eventually defeated them and as a result of a treaty then agreed the Norsemen evacuated all the north-east mainland. There was no permanent Norse settlement in Aberdeenshire. Sutherland, the southland, was the southern limit of Norse occupation. Between it and Aberdeenshire was the province of Moravia, almost independent of Scottish kings and causing endless trouble. As a result the king tried to ensure that Aberdeenshire was in the hands of loyal vassals who would support him in attacks from Moravia.

The rulers, kings and chiefs presided over a culture that was Celtic in origin. Celtic Scotland was based on the clan system but it was by no means a democracy. Everyone had his or her defined place. Mar, one of the four divisions of

Aberdeenshire was a Celtic province, probably dating back to the eighth century. It included all the land between Dee and Don and the upper and middle basins of both rivers. Its ruler was called a Mormaer. The Province was divided into districts, each having a strong place. These were Doldencha (Braemar) with its early "castle", Cromar with its "castle" at Migvie, Strathdee (Dinnet eastwards) at Aboyne and Aberdeen with Ruthrieston.

There were dynastic problems and constant marches and counter marches in the area, one of the most interesting being the episode that resulted in the death of Macbeth near Lumphanan.

Loch Davan

VII. RELIGION & LIFE

CHRISTIANITY COMES TO THE VALLEY
& PLACES OF WORSHIP ARE SET UP

"I saw them come from Dover long ago
With a silver cross before them, singing low.
Monks of Rome from their home"

James Elroy Flecker

The symbol stones are a link between the pagan Picts and Christianity. Symbols of a Christian cross alongside the pagan carvings show continuity of site through the ages.

The heathen Picts of Deeside were fairly late in being converted to Christianity. They may have heard of Christ as well as Mithras through traders who had contact with Roman soldiers but there was no organised attempt to preach Christianity to Upper Deesiders until the fifth century B.C. Even then it took almost another 500 years before the area was really Christianised.

Missionaries came from three areas, - Whithorn or Candida Casa by the Solway, Bangor in Northern Ireland and Glasgow. They stayed for a while, teaching and preaching, then moved on. Any early church building lacked permanence but often missionaries set up a stone as a preaching station. Missionaries were farmers, doctors and social workers as well as teachers. Their organisation was usually monastic controlled not by the Pope but by the "AB" or head. Unlike the Roman system there was no adoration of the Virgin Mary.

Ninian, Ternan, his disciple Erchard, Colm, Mochrieha, (Machar), Moluag, Marnoch, Manire, Mungo, and Nathalan were all missionaries to the area. St. Ternan was probably the first missionary to Deeside. From Kincardine o'Neil, of noble Celtic stock, at some unknown date he became a pupil of Ninian at Whithorn and then trained in Rome. He returned and set up his monastery at Banchory Ternan, of which nothing remains but a simple wheel cross. No doubt his influence was felt on Upper Deeside.

One of Ternan's pupils at the Banchory monastery was Erchard who eventually set up his own establishment at Kincardine o'Neil, presumably on the site of the present ruined church. He was said to have been buried in his church, at the end of the fifth century. Locals made a pilgrimage to St. Erchard's Well, still to be seen, on his festal day, 24th August. Shortly after St. Erchard, St. Machar or Mochrieha came to Deeside. On Balnagowan Hill, where there were long cairn burials, he founded a church. On the site is St Machar's Cross, a cone shaped stone with an incised equal armed cross and close by is a stone on which he is reputed to have sat, known as St. Machar's Chair. Nearby is St. Machar's Well. For many years Machar's feast day was observed on 12th November.

Another missionary from Whithorn in Wigtownshire was St. Colm, who came to Birse. Rome later re-dedicated his church to St. Michael. On Gannoch Hill is St. Colm's Well, once a centre of pilgrimage, especially on his feast day, 16th October.

Tradition says Christianity came to the Crathie area in the sixth century. Stirton, former minister of Crathie names Colm as the first missionary. Colm is remembered by a pool in the Dee where he baptised converts, Polhollich (Pol-Chom-oc) and by a fair, the Feill-ma-colm at Clachanturn (277947) on 27th February. (A bad time weatherwise!) Clachanturn, (stone of the kiln) was the scene of one of the earliest markets - cheese, wool, livestock, etc. and it continued all through the Middle Ages.

A chapel stood at Abergeldie, near Clachanturn, called variously St. Columba's or St. Valentine's. (Chapel Ma-Chalmaig) (OS 287946). Right through early records there is confusion between St Columba and St. Colm. This is probably the church said to be about half a mile up the Geldie Burn from where it joins the Dee, in Chapel Park.

From Cathures, Glasgow, where he founded a church in 567 A.D. St. Kentigern (Mungo) came to Deeside where he set up a centre at the junction of Dee and Gairn. According to early records Mungo's church was called Cill-Ma-Thatha, (OS 353970) the church of Tatha or Mungo. Tradition is the only evidence for Mungo's visit here in the 6th century but there probably was an early church near the junction of Dee and Gairn. He was long remembered by St. Mungo's annual Fair and Mungo's Well is near the later church.

The dedication to Mungo or Kentigern the patron saint of Glasgow may have been the work of Bishop Elphinstone, founder of Aberdeen University in 1494. Born in Glasgow and associated with that diocese, he placed in the chapel of the new University a statue of Mungo and ordered a hymn to be sung in his praise. It seems Mungo helped an indiscreet Queen who had given to her lover a ring presented to her by the King. As a result of Mungo's prayers the ring was discovered inside a salmon. This accounts for the fact that Mungo has on his banner a silver fish with a silver ring in its mouth, all on a blue background to represent the sea on which his mother had been set adrift when she became pregnant. It also appeared on Ballater Burgh's coat of arms.

Three of Mungo's disciples, Nidan, Finnan and Fumoc worked in Lumphanan, Migvie and Dinnet.

In the seventh century St. Marnoch established a church at Inchmarnoch, the island of Marnoch. (OS 424963). The ford over the Dee at Dalwhing used to be called Marnoch's Ford.

Later came St. Adamnan (Skeulan) who established his centre at Formaston, two miles east of Aboyne, site of the Ogham Stone. Ruins of a later church occupy the site. Close by was Skeulan's Tree, supposed to bring good fortune if a rag was attached to the tree on Skeulan's Day, 23rd. September. Nearby was Skeulan's Well.

St. Walloch founded a church at Logie Coldstone where, in the burial ground stands the Walloch Stone. Walloch's Fair was held on 29th January.

Lesmo, the hermit of Glen Tanar, is regarded as the founder of Glen Tanar but he probably exists more in fiction than in fact. The Hermit's Well is a reminder of him.

Nathalan set up his 'church' at Tullich, a settlement that

was the predecessor of Ballater - the civic and religious centre until the ferry failed to cope with visitors going across the Dee to partake of Pannanich Spa waters. For hundreds of years Tullich was the mother church and Glen Gairn and Glen Muick only daughter houses. An early church would have been of wattle and daub, lacking any permanence. Some walls remain of what was a post-Reformation reconstruction of a slightly earlier building. It measured $46^1/2$ feet by $22^1/2$ feet. Like the other kirkyards in the area, the churchyard was used for weapon practice, usually on a Sunday, as instructed by law. With the building of Ballater Bridge Tullich declined and Ballater developed. In Tullich Christianity started in the area and pre-Christian stones were 'Christianised'.

In the 9th century St. Manire was the last Celtic apostle to come to Deeside. Manire, Monire, Monar, Miniar - all versions are found - was a Bishop of the Celtic church, but he was not diocesan. Well-established tradition says another 'church' at Crathie was in later days dedicated to him.

Just after the 46th milestone on the Aberdeen to Braemar road, about three miles east of the present Crathie Kirk, between the Lebhal (OS 299961) and Rhynabaich (OS 302964) on a little rise in the ground on the north of the Deeside Road, is Manire's Stone. This is all that remains - an upright stone which tradition says is where the officiating priest put his manuscript when addressing the locals. Rhynabaich can be seen on the right, where are deserted dwellings of Easter Micras. One dwelling remains out of 17 "fire-houses" - houses with a hearth. All other structures of the time would of course be impermanent. This was likely to have been the site of prehistoric burials, for early missionaries were always in the habit of taking over pre-historic sites and using them for Christian purposes. There were burials in the area as late as the 50's of the nineteenth century.

Place names serve to provide a link with the past. A stream runs to the Dee near the site of the 'chapel' known as alt eaglais, the burn of the church, and behind is creag eaglais, the hill of the church, from the Greek ekklesia, a church. In late

Roman times the name was changed to the Church of the Hermites. A deep pool in the Dee nearly opposite Balmoral Castle, 'pollmanire', the pool of Manire is said to have been the place where he baptised converts. The pool was also reputed to have healing properties and folk suffering from a variety of complaints journeyed to the pool to take a dip in the hope of a miraculous recovery. Manire died about 824 and tradition says he was buried at his base at Rhynabaich as was the usual practice. His festal day is 18th December and for hundreds of years a fair was held in the vicinity known as 'Feill Manire', Manire's Fair. Tradition said, as it did of so many of the Deeside 'fairs', that if you were fit and well and did not attend, you would not live to see another 'Feill Manire'.

Another church was reputed to have been on the hill opposite Abergeldie Castle, between Torgalter and Wester Micras. There are a few stones, but who knows where they came from?

After 400 years Deeside was Christianised, - in name at least.

14th Century Doorway, Kincardine O'Neil

VIII. REMAINS OF PRE - REFORMATION CHURCHES

"The sons of the world and the sons of the church walked closely, hand and heart"

Medieval saying, source unknown

Where early tracks across the Mounth met a river crossing by a ford or later by a bridge, a settlement grew up. In these early settlements there was pre-Christian worship. Eventually, in these same settlements, early Christian places of worship were established. These early 'chapels' soon perished but legends survived, often elaborated.

By the end of the 13th century the Celtic Church had been absorbed by the Church of Rome and run on parochial lines. Some buildings had gone: many had been re-dedicated to Roman Catholic saints. In many cases hallowed ground was used for new churches and more elaborate buildings erected. Ruins of two of the Roman Catholic churches remain on Deeside, - the kirk at Kincardine o'Neil on the site of the building erected by Alan Durward of Coull around 1240 and St Nathalan's at Tullich

During the eighteenth and nineteenth centuries many of the churches that had been adapted for Roman Catholic worship were pulled down and new parish churches built. Some were on the original site but many had new sites, although the old graveyards continued in use.

KINCARDINE O'NEIL CHURCH

Although Kincardine o'Neil falls outside the boundaries of the area being considered, it is a link with the past and so justifies inclusion.

Tradition says that Erchard was born at Tolmauds near Learney Hill and ministered to the people of the area. Erchard's Well is now enclosed by a 'box' and there is a lion's head water spout, probably created about 1860.

The ruined church dedicated to St. Erchard then to the Virgin Mary is linked to the hospice built by Alan Durward (Door Ward) for the benefit of travellers using the bridge erected by his father Thomas, linking their territory with the Cairn a' Mounth Pass. Although the date of the foundation is not known for certain, in 1230 it was erected into a prebend of Aberdeen Cathedral. This was further confirmed by a charter of Duncan, Earl of Mar, in 1238. According to the Registrum Episcopatus Aberdonensis in 1511 a royal charter created the ecclesiastical lands into a barony in favour of the Rector Elphinstone. The kirkyard was a busy place: in accordance with medieval practice, goods were sold and trading done, often on the flat headstones.

Eventually the Kincardine o'Neil church became a parish church and served in this capacity until 1773, when the roof thatch caught fire. (This was a fairly common event in the area). The roof was then slated. It was repaired again in 1799 and doors and windows repaired but by 1859 the building was considered unsafe. Across the road a new church was opened in 1862 and the roof of the old building removed. In 1869 the old church was divided into private burial ground for Heritors and Ministers.

In the early 1930's the ivy that had covered the walls for almost a hundred years was stripped off and interesting pre-Reformation features were revealed. The north door had been walled up, covering beautiful molding and a buttress that had been added in 1830 obscured much of interest. Among other things was the "Early English" doorway of mid 14th century date which is a particularly fine specimen. Sections of molding were restored to their original position. The buttress was removed and re-erected by the doorway. A small basin, probably to hold holy water, was repaired. A little recess near the door may have been to hold a closure bar. A small inner doorway, date undetermined, was replaced in its original position. It was discovered that the west gable had had two tall lancet windows before the insertion of the round-headed windows and door.

William Robertson writing in 1725 said the building was shorter then by half than it had originally been. Now nothing remains of the earlier walls he mentioned but foundations extending eastwards for 73'. Although the building was originally twice as long as at present it would be unlikely that both ends were used as a church if there was a thick dividing wall between. The east gable has two upper windows looking into the ruin as well as, below them, the two lancet windows looking out of the ruin. The upper windows are of granite, roughly dressed. The lower ones are of carefully dressed freestone. Three niches are visible on the outside of the east gable. It would appear that the east side of the building had an upper floor with two windows looking into the church, so that the sick in the monastery buildings could see what was going on in services in the church. This was quite a usual practice. Later the east part had been pulled down and the lancet windows inserted in the gable, old moulded windows from the eastern section being used. We know that in 1233 Alan Durward had founded a hospice at Kincardine o'Neil and this may have been at the east end of the church, with windows looking in.

The granite belfry dates from about 1640. The bell was transferred to the new church.

TULLICH CHURCH & PEOPLE

Tullich is Ballater's past.

Tullich lay at the junction of the east to west route, Aberdeen to Braemar, and the north-south route from Donside, round the shoulder of Culblean, across the Dee at Tomnakeist (Hillock of the coffin) (OS 400981) site of an old graveyard, and south by Glen Muick and the Capel Mounth to Clova. Where road and river routes met, there was always a community. Tullich was once the headquarters of religious and civil life on Upper Deeside

The most important missionary for the area was Nathalan

who founded his church at his reputed birthplace, Tullich, in the seventh century, probably about 678 A.D. When Nathalan put his church on the knoll it became the knoll of Nathalan, or Tulachnathlak.

Nothing of Nathalan's building remains. The name was in use until the sixteenth century, when the saint's name was dropped and the place was known as Tulach or Tullich. The area had another name frequently used in records - Dalmuickeachie, the field of pigs. The name was also used for the ferry that ceased to operate about 1890.

Celtic missionaries selected sites with outstanding views and at places where there were earlier settlements. Their Christianity was a missionary Christianity, but the monks were agriculturalists as well as missionaries. They were teachers, doctors and social workers. Tullich, the Mother Church, served a wide area. Missionaries did not expect native Picts to travel to them, so they built churches on sites where Picts lived, - sites that had been occupied in the Bronze and Iron Ages because the soil was cultivable. This continuity of usage is seen everywhere on Deeside.

As is the case with most of the early saints, legends about Nathalan abound. On one occasion he cursed the weather when it seemed that the harvest would be ruined. The weather improved: the harvest was saved. By way of penance, he locked his hand to his leg and threw the key into the Dee, vowing not to remove the chain until he had been on a pilgrimage to Rome. We still have a Poll-na-hiuchrach, (Pool of the Key) (OS394969) below Tullich Kirk. The 'miraculous' story says that after Nathalan bought a fish in Rome he found the key inside, and unpadlocked his hand. He then returned to Tullich. The legend of the key provided one of the symbols on the coat of arms of the former Burgh of Ballater.

Another story also involved Nathalan's agricultural activities, for, although of noble birth and having a liberal education, he personally cultivated the fields. Having given away all his seed corn in time of famine, he was told by God to sow sand. He had a good crop in a field west of modern

46

Ballater, still called Sluievannachie, "The Moor of Blessing" or Moor of the White Field (OS 361959)

Such stories are only legends and documentary evidence is meagre, but in Bishop Forbes' "Kalendars of Scottish Saints" there is a reference to Nathalan as given in the "Aberdeen Breviary". "Nathalan (Nachalan) the great saint of Deeside in north parts of Scoti was born and buried at Tullich in the diocese of Aberdeen". The "Irish Annals" say Nathalan died on 8th. January 678, although some traditions make January the date of his birth. After his pilgrimage to Rome Nathalan returned to Tullich, settling and using it as a base for his missionary activities. The details of the stories are unimportant, but behind all the 'trimmings' can be seen the purpose of the 'fable-spreaders' of the Middle Ages. They were trying to show that even at an early date the Pope, as representative of the Roman Church, had influence in Scotland. They were aiming at denigrating the early Celtic Church that they eventually superseded. It was religious propaganda.

Nathalan's church of wattle and daub lacked permanence, while a much later church on the site was mutilated at the Reformation although a 14th century doorway remains and the symbol stones. The circular wall was erected because of the belief that the Devil would not cross a circle, there being no corners in which to hide.

By the end of the 13th century the Celtic Church had been absorbed by the Church of Rome and run on parochial lines. Some buildings had gone: many had been re-dedicated to Roman Catholic saints. In most cases, hallowed ground was used for the new churches and more elaborate buildings were erected.

The Knights Templar had in 1187 been granted lands that included Tullich and their successors the Knights Hospitaller, inherited them. Later the Earl of Mar, Gordons and Farquharsons were feudal superiors. Written records go back to 1275 when a valuation roll of ecclesiastical property was drawn up, known as "Bagimont's Roll"- Boiamund de Vicci's valuation roll. It records details of Tullich, owned by the Knights Templar.

By a 1663 Act of Parliament revenues of Tullich passed to King's College, Aberdeen. Records of 1898 tell of traces still visible of a 13th century fort built around the church by the Knights Templar. It can not now be identified with any degree of certainty.

Plague had hit the area in 1350 and again in 1362, when considerable numbers died. Children seem to have been particularly vulnerable in Tullich. Communal graves were used, outwith the kirkyard, probably in the Pass, and behind the present "fishery."

Tullich, the Mother Church of the area, kept sacred relics until the Reformation, and these were supposed to have had healing powers. Local tradition says the Reformers threw bones, etc., reputed to be those of Nathalan, into the Dee near the Church.

The present Ballater dates from the end of the eighteenth century. Before that Tullich - probably a Royal Burgh - was the civil and ecclesiastical centre of the whole area. It had its Market Cross, Tolbooth, and Barony Inn. The church building, in a poor state at the end of the eighteenth century, was allowed to decay when the Centrical Church was opened in Ballater in 1800 to accommodate people from Tullich, Glen Muick and Glen Gairn. Once its thatched roof went, deterioration was rapid. It was probably a wise move to close the three existing churches and have everyone worshipping in Ballater but an historic building became a ruin.

The ruin that remains today is rectangular, 25m. by 9m. and the walls are 1m. thick. Inside it is divided up into burial spaces for local landowners and other burials are all around, outwith the church. The newer section of the burial ground is still in use as Ballater and district burial ground. Names on stones tell of the more recent history of the area. There are older stones bearing the skull and crossbones, Old Father Time, an hourglass and a coffin.

INCHMARNOCH

Because they were so poor the Inchmarnoch/ Glen Tanar parishes were split. Inchmarnoch disappeared into Glenmuick, Tullich and Glengairn, while Glen Tanar was linked with Aboyne. Glen Tanar kept its own services until 1763. The ruins of this Kirk, in its own burial ground, stand below the former Glen Tanar school building.

The chapel at Inchmarnoch was on an island in the Dee, the island of Marnoch, (OS 424963) nearly opposite to the road leading to Ballaterach. Tradition says Marnoch, the local saint, was buried on the island and indeed ruins of the chapel and graveyard were to be seen until the 1829 Muckle Spate. A number of years ago a stone font, probably from that chapel, was found there and taken to Ballater Roman Catholic Chapel.

Elderly local people speak of annual games held there known as "haudan (holding) their Marnan". An alternative name was "the Marnoch shooting".

Tullich Burial Ground

IX. ANGLO-NORMANS

"The Norman is a gate. What entered by that gate was civilization."

G.K.Chesterton

King Malcolm married Margaret who reformed the Celtic Church to bring it into line with the Roman Catholic Church in England. She tried to stamp out the Gaelic language, believing it to account for Scottish 'backwardness' and introduced the use of English. Foreigners and Anglo-Saxons who had fled from William the Conqueror flocked to the Scottish court, so further bolstering 'English' ideas. During the reigns of her sons Scotland became a feudal monarchy following Anglo-Norman practices. Between 1057 and 1289 there were vast changes in national and social life.

Mar was a buffer state involved in clashes with forces in the north. The Mormaers of Mar eventually adopted the Normanising policy of the crown and the Celtic Earldom became a feudal Earldom.

We know very little of the lives of people on Deeside during this early period but once feudalism was established we know a little more. People had very little say in the ordering of their lives. The feudal system clearly defined everyone's duties and obligations and the rank and file had to obey their Laird's orders as he in turn had to obey his Feudal Superior.

X. FEUDALISM - & AFTERWARDS

By the end of the 13th century feudalism was established on Deeside with Normanised Celts and Anglo-Normans in control. The old Celtic line remained in Braemar but elsewhere there were 'incomers'.

Aberdeenshire was divided into the Garioch, Buchan, Strathbogie and Mar. Deeside was part of the Celtic province, later the Earldom of Mar, the most important stronghold being Doldencha (Braemar). Mar included all the land between Dee and Don and was in existence in the 8th century. The chief was the Mormaer who divided his land into districts, each with a strong place - probably no more than timber and earthworks.

Malcolm Canmore (1057 - 1093) was probably the first real King of Scots who was more than a name. With his second wife Margaret he and his sons and successors changed the face of Scotland and transformed the social structure of the land.

Feudalism was introduced on Norman French lines and Scotland between 1057 and 1289 was totally changed. Margaret wanted unity, with everyone to conform to English ideas gleaned when she had spent years in exile at the English court.

Meanwhile Mar territories were a buffer state between south and north and a base from which the king could launch attacks. Donald, 7th Earl of Mar, the feudal Superior, was involved in the politics of his day. Deeside played a prominent part in national affairs.

The structure of medieval society developed under the Canmore dynasty. Two centuries witnessed changes in military organisation, the church and trading arrangements. The adoption of Norman practices was a deliberate attempt to extend the authority of the monarch.

The castle may have been a very obvious sign of the feudal regime but it was not the only one. Following Norman practice, territory was divided into parishes. Part of the revenue was allocated to the Church so castle and church were usually found in close proximity. The baron had vast powers, including those of 'pit and gallows' and such powers continued until feudal jurisdiction was abolished by an Act of 1747, following the Jacobite activities of 1745. There was usually a gallows hill attached to the feudal barony and a 'hangin' stane. One survives at Dess while the Gallows-Tree of Mar stands pathetic and supported on the Braemar/Inverey road.

The king did not give out to his barons large stretches of land quite free of charge. No money changed hands but military service had to be given. The amount depended on the size of the land but 416 acres, called a davoc, was the basis of calculation. According to the computation, fighting men had to be provided when required, so the king was assured of an army. The barons in their turn gave land to their sub-tenants who had also to swear loyalty and undertake military service with their followers if demanded. The sub-tenants let out land to their men, freemen and villains. Their rent was not paid in money but in farm produce - grain, poultry, sheep and also by working for the Superior on an unpaid basis.

In feudal times ordinary people were of little consequence. They may have had status under the old Celtic clan system, but all that was gone. They had no rights. They belonged to the land where they had been born and were not allowed to leave. They were the lord's property. They were serfs, - virtual slaves with an assessed value of a pound of wax. However, surfdom died out in Scotland earlier than anywhere else in Europe and it had gone by the end of the fourteenth century.

Bishops, parish priests and monks were often incomers from England, to the annoyance of 'locals'. Trade however increased. Gradually English language and English ideas became dominant and the customs and ideas of the Celts were replaced. It happened gradually, with the native language being spoken at home and English used on other occasions. Gradually the native tongue died out and only survived far up the valley, although many Gaelic place names remain. Little by little the clan system disappeared, save in the remote areas, and the jurisdiction of the chiefs was finally abolished after the '45.

The changes were gradual, taking place over many years. The ordinary people in most cases kept their holdings as sub-tenants of the incoming landlords. However, the gap between common people and their overlords increased. It all helped to encourage support for those who aimed at achieving independence from England after the Wars of Independence.

Burghs were created. Tullich was the oldest burgh in our area and may even have been a royal burgh, but documentation has long since been lost and even the date of its creation is unknown.

Permission was granted to hold weekly markets and an annual fair, usually named after the local patron saint. In return for privileges villagers had to arm themselves and follow their superior to war. Weapon training, known as 'wapinshaws' or weapon shows, was held regularly, often in or near the Kirk yard. Absentees were fined.

The early burghs were a straggling collection of huts, but by virtue of burgh status they all had three things in common - the inn, the tollbooth or prison and the market cross.

The inn served the function of a community centre. Inns developed from the 'hospice' that sheltered travellers over the Mounth. These spitals were essential for travellers in medieval times. The first one had been erected in Kincardine o'Neil by Alan the Doorward (Durward) in 1233 and this is likely to have been the first 'hotel' in the valley. Barony inns did much more than the hospices. They did accommodate travellers but they also catered for those taking part in markets and fairs. They were too the place where barony courts were held. A burgh inn was further up the social scale than an alehouse, many of which seem to have been rowdy places. Barony inns were inspected and only if they reached the required standard were they allowed to bear the baron's name and display his armorial bearings.

The tollbooth was the burgh prison. It took over from the 'pit' in the baron's stronghold. Early ones were stone huts with heavy doors and iron bars. Criminal cases were tried in the castle or in the market place but in time a court-room was added to the tollbooth. Aboyne had one where the War Memorial stands and Braemar's is the site of the Invercauld Arms Bar.

The centre of all activity was the market place and here stood the cross. It represented both religious and secular authority. Originally of wood, many were rebuilt in stone. Usually there were three parts to the cross - the base, the shaft which varied in shape and the head with carvings of religious scenes, the King's arms and the baron's arms. Because the church, the crown and the baron were represented, the cross stood for honesty and integrity. All goods had to be of first class quality and it was considered that transactions there were binding before God and man. Buying on the cheap before the market was an offence.

From the cross proclamations were made and public notices displayed. Criminals were sentenced here and put in the 'jougs', - often chained by the neck to the cross. The cross was also the centre for public rejoicing e.g. after victory. Once the ideas of the Reformation really took hold, the cross ceased to have religious significance. An Act of 1581 condemned the crosses, so many were pulled down or the religious symbols defaced. About 1857 Tullich's cross was smashed up for road metal.

The Reel of Tullich tells the story of the minister delayed and the impatient congregation taking steps to keep itself warm. Whisky was brought from the inn, the Style o'Tullich and the reel began. When the minister eventually arrived he condemned the sacrilage and said death would come to the participants within the year. And, we are told, it did!

The clachan of Tullich probably had some written charter rights, but it seems that Sir Walter Scott was given them by William Farquharson, a close friend, to take to Edinburgh when George 1V visited there in 1822. The two men were both members of the Royal Company of Archers, the Royal Bodyguard in Scotland. One of William Farquharson's letters still exists, asking a friend to hand the documents to Sir Walter Scott to convey them to the King. The aim was to transfer the charter to the newly created Ballater. Unfortunately Scott lost the documents and they have never been seen since.

How the land was held
(Simplified diagram of 'Feudal Duties')

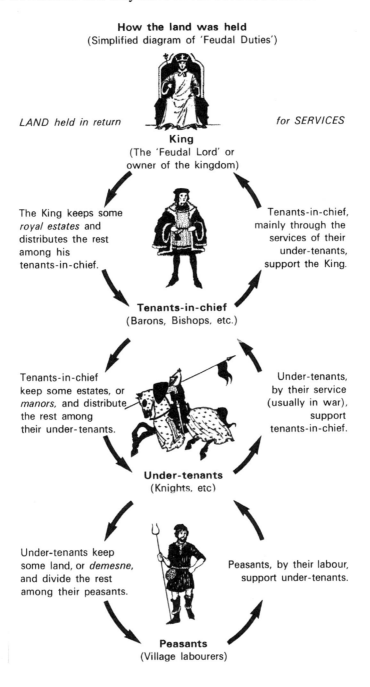

LAND held in return   for SERVICES

King
(The 'Feudal Lord' or
owner of the kingdom)

The King keeps some *royal estates* and distributes the rest among his tenants-in-chief.

Tenants-in-chief, mainly through the services of their under-tenants, support the King.

Tenants-in-chief
(Barons, Bishops, etc.)

Tenants-in-chief keep some estates, or *manors*, and distribute the rest among their under-tenants.

Under-tenants, by their service (usually in war), support tenants-in-chief.

Under-tenants
(Knights, etc)

Under-tenants keep some land, or *demesne*, and divide the rest among their peasants.

Peasants, by their labour, support under-tenants.

Peasants
(Village labourers)

XI. THE CHURCH IN FEUDAL TIMES

There had been a headlong collision between Celtic Christianity and the Roman form of Christianity brought to England by St. Augustine. After the Synod of Whitby in 664, Roman Christianity was supreme.

With the coming of Queen Margaret to Scotland as the wife of Malcolm Canmore the policy of reforming and 'Anglicising' the church began and was continued in the reign of her sons. Abbeys and monasteries were built for members of European Orders. The country had been split into parishes and these were arranged in dioceses with Bishops in charge. Some parish churches replaced earlier missionary churches, while others were developed from the chapels attached to the baronial castles. The Canmore family was helped in its Anglicising policy by the Anglo-Norman newcomers, - the 'white settlers' of their day.

Descendants of the original Celtic dynasties opposed the spread of feudal ideas but, supported by Anglo-Norman barons, Margaret's sons were victorious. Feudalism changed the face of Scotland. By about 1250 the last remains of the Celtic Church, the Culdees at Monymusk, had been wiped out and replaced by the Order of St. Augustine.

Many of the early chapels built by missionaries and their successors had perished. Often only legends survived. Frequently the name of the saint to whom the original establishment was dedicated was changed. Deeside still continued to be a buffer state. The Knights Templar were granted more land on Deeside at this time. By the end of the 13th century the Celtic Church was Romanised and organised in parishes. The money for the upkeep of churches came from teinds and tithes, not from gifts or offerings as previously. Whereas the Celtic Church had been supported by the equivalent of 'free-will' offerings the Roman church was endowed by tithes and tiends, in money or in kind, by wealthy landowners. A steady income might be good, but it led to impropriation, the unsatisfactory situation of placing church lands in the hands of laymen. Ultimately, this was one of the causes of the Reformation. Initially, from the endowments of landowners, churches were redesigned on Roman models, or replaced. Nearly always, the earlier hallowed ground was used.

In the beginning, when money was available for building, the original churches were allowed to decay while new ones were constructed on the Roman Catholic pattern. Early sites hallowed by years of worship were still used for the new more elaborate buildings. Four ruins of these buildings remain, - the Templars church at Maryculter (c. 1288): Alan Durward of Coull's church at Kincardine o'Neil (c.1240): St. Mazota's at Drumoak (c.13th century) and St. Nathalan's at Tullich.

The Church in Feudal Times

XII. THE CHURCH - THE REFORMATION & AFTERWARDS

"Erasmus, the solitary monk that shook the world"

Robert Montgomery

During the 16th century there were great religious changes. Parliament met in Edinburgh in 1560. Protestantism was established. Mass was abolished together with Papal authority. Many Roman Catholic clergy had been ill-educated and neglecting their duties, even living lives of debauchery. Abbeys were in the hands of lay people, using the revenues for their own purposes. As a result of the new regime, noble families gained control of church revenues. At first there was little change in Aberdeenshire and no changes were made in services although systems of church organisation and practice sometimes clashed. In other parts of the country the teachings of Martin Luther and John Calvin were being introduced. There was a clash of ideas. Some landowners had become Protestant but apart from changes in land ownership there were no laws to change services in church until the second half of the sixteenth century.

The Presbyterian Church was organised with a General Assembly, Kirk Sessions and Elders and plans for Education, - a school in every parish - that never materialised because of lack of money.

The religious struggles continued with clan rivalries adding to the problems. Many of the local Lairds adhered to the old faith and the locals knew little or no change.

On Deeside at the time of the Reformation there was a shortage of Protestant ministers to fill the former Roman Catholic charges. Because one minister sometimes had the oversight of seven parishes, a Reader was employed. Scott's "Fasti Ecclesiae Scoticanae" records a Lawrence Cowtiss (Coutts) as Reader from 1567 - 1580, at a stipend of £20, £4 more than usual. He served in Tullich, Glenmuick and Glengarden (Glengairn).

Many people of the glens were adherents of the Old Faith and the Kirk Session of the joint parishes, united in 1618, was powerless to act against the 'offenders'.

After the Reformation, Protestantism spread very slowly in Tullich. Well over a hundred years later, in 1704, Session Records indicate that Calum Grierson, alias McGregor of Baladar, "erected a high crucifix on a little hill near his house, to be adored by neighbours" and James Michie "built a particular chamber for Popish use."

The Kirk Records are full of condemnatory references to Roman Catholics and there was a great deal of intolerance. In fact, in the seventeenth and eighteenth centuries, Tullich folk were a headache to the Kirk Session. Moral offences were more numerous than in neighbouring parishes and at practically every service held in Tullich, at least one person appeared in sack-cloth, facing the congregation from the Stool of Repentance. Tullich folk seem to have been less in awe of Session worthies than other parishioners. No doubt, being Roman Catholic, they were less willing to submit to the discipline of the Established Church. Often, because of storm, the minister was unable to get over the Dee from the Manse by the Muick to Tullich. Tullich parish was Roman Catholic in spirit and residents there were "receptors of popish priests"

The Gordon Earls of Huntly were the great Roman Catholic champions of the area. In Tullich, the authority of the Pope might not always have been openly acknowledged, but it was obvious where loyalties lay.

After the Presbyterian settlement of 1689 the preaching of the word took precedence over the administration of the sacrament. The pulpit was in a central position and churches had a pleasing simplicity. A good many of these kirks were built in existing burial grounds on earlier foundations.

All the burial grounds on Upper Deeside were close to a kirk, scenically sited and near to a river. The kirk yards were not always quiet places. Markets were held here, with goods displayed on the flat gravestones.

Medical education and research in the 18th century

created a demand for corpses so many churches had mort safes and some had watch- towers. Fortunately Upper Deeside was just a little too far away from Aberdeen Medical School to make the risky journey to pick up a body worthwhile.

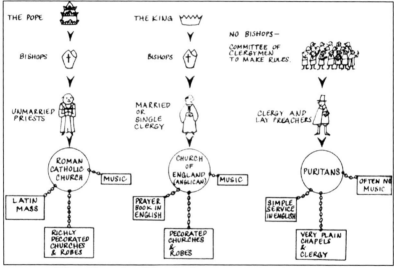

The Church - The Reformation & Afterwards.
What Roman Catholics, Anglicans
& Presbyterians wanted

XIII. DEFENSIVE STRUCTURES & CASTELLATED & IMPORTANT BUILDINGS

"This castle hath a pleasant seat"

Shakespeare

"Farewell then, ancient men of might,
Crusader, errant squire and knight"

Thomas Hood

"Gunpowder rendered feudal fortresses useless, gave strength to masses of plebean soldiers and created the necessity for science in battle as well as tactics and valour"

Lord's Modern Europe

The early defensive structures in the valley, like hill forts or crannogs were places of safety for Deesiders and have no relationship to the later strongholds of barons.

Early strongholds were of the "motte & bailey" type, of earthwork and timber, easily set on fire by blazing arrows fired by the enemy. The motte was a steep flat- topped mound of earth, easy to defend, with a wooden palisade inside of which stood a timber tower. The whole structure was surrounded by a ditch. Often a second mound of earth, not as high as the first, was attached and this was the "bailey". The whole structure was also surrounded by a ditch and had on it a palisade where were the subsidiary buildings necessary for the functioning of the castle. The mound could be a natural hill, or even an earlier Iron Age structure. Only the earthworks remain nowadays, as the timber structures have disappeared, but some can still be seen at Lumphanan, Auchlossan and Coldstone. No doubt there were others and the name 'Castlehill' may be an indication of a site. In some places motte and bailey structures may have still been in use well into the 14th century.

The feudal barons' homes were the headquarters from which the area was governed. Officials enforced the law and the baronial court tried offenders. Castles were strong bases from which to quell opposition and before the introduction of cannon gaining control of a castle meant victory or defeat. The castles provided protection and were the assembly point for forces setting out to fight. Because of their vital role, castles had to be well situated, to guard strategic routes.

Some stone castles were built in the county in the thirteenth century, like Kindrochit in Braemar, but earthworks and timber continued to be used for some time. Castle building developed with the use of stone and towers for defence. The baron owed military service to the Earl or the King as Superior. He and his family lived in the castle with nearby mensa or table lands supplying food. A barony existed where one finds the name "The Mains". Every castle had its "doocot". It was useful for providing pigeon pie but albumen and shells were an essential ingredient in mortar used for building. Often the "doocot" and the mill near by were the perquisite of a younger son.

Malcolm Canmore (1057 - 1093) and his wife Margaret introduced a Normanising policy that resulted in a change in social and national life. The parish system was introduced and often church and castle stood side by side, representing ecclesiastical and civil power.

With the passage of time, more stone castles were built. The great courtyard castle of Kildrummy was the model for others. The ruins of a late 12th or early 13th century castle of Coull, stronghold of the Durwards, sits on a knoll with a view of the surrounding countryside. It was an "enclosure" type with high stone walls and flanking towers enclosing a courtyard. This, the only example in our area, was destroyed in the Wars of Succession & Independence. One of the towers generally contained the water supply and was in effect the castle keep. Dr. A. Marshall Mackenzie did some excavation in the early years of last century. He discovered a wall 12' high and 30' long and 8' thick with a circular tower 20' in diameter, with doorway. Another wall ran at right angles, 70' long, with doors and windows. Doors and windows are of Kildrummy freestone and mouldings belong to the transition period between Norman and Early English. These would be the enclosing walls of the courtyard and inside would be the inner building. Migvie may also have been of this type. First mentioned in 1268, it was one of the Deeside strongholds of the Earls of Mar, for it controlled the routes from Don to Dee. Today it is no more than grass-covered mounds.

In the early 14th century, because of the previous Wars of Succession and Independence the country was impoverished so few castles were built.

A new type appeared in the post-war period, modelled on England's Norman keeps. They appear to have been grim places with rectangular keep towers of up to six storeys, built of stone. Walls could be up to 12 feet thick with the parapets machicolated to enable missiles, - pitch, boiling oil etc. to be hurled down on attackers. The long bow was the usual weapon. Within the defensive parapets were rectangular buildings with crow-stepped gables and stone slab roofs. The entrance was always at first floor level by means of a stairway that could be drawn up in time of trouble. Defensive walls with angle towers surrounded the castles to make courtyards where were the buildings necessary for the functioning of the castle. Such a castle was virtually fire and siege proof. Accommodation was usually provided in the form of one room to each floor, accessed by a stone stair built into the thickness of the wall. The castle well, vital in time of siege, was in the basement. Drum Castle is the best surviving example, and Kindrochit and probably Clune and Maud are from this period.

By the end of the 14th century prosperity was returning to Scotland. There was a desire for better living quarters yet without compromising defence. This was done by adding a wing to one side of the keep tower so producing an 'L plan' building. This meant at least one more room on each floor and assisted the defence of the entrance, now at ground floor level. Arrow slits were still necessary for the long bows and the L plan assisted cross-fire. This type of castle continued until the beginning of the 17th century.

Firearms were introduced in the 16th century. This meant cross-fire was more important so 'double towers' were built.

Gun loops replaced arrow slits. Abergairn and Abergeldie are good examples.

Later in the 16th century Z plan castles appeared. The main section was flanked by two towers, usually round. Scottish Baronial architecture of the 19th century followed the same principles with a stress on decoration rather than defence.

A Motte & Bailey Castle

ABERGAIRN or GAIRN CASTLE
(OS 359974)

Behind Abergairn, where there was once an inn, are the ruins of Gairn Castle. West of Balmeanach on a site overlooking the Pass of Ballater are the remains, possibly of 15th century origin. It is referred to in a bond of manrent dated 1468. Like Strathgirnoc this was originally yet another Forbes stronghold and it lay in close proximity to "enemy" Gordon possessions.

In 1614 Lord Forbes sold some land to William Gordon of Abergeldie and a small fort is referred to in the documents.

The walls that remain are no more than four feet high, but the building probably had three storeys. There was a stone stair in the tower, as at Knock. It had a rounded angle wall which could be clearly picked out in the 1930's and the mortar used was still in a hard state.

Some excavation was undertaken in the 1930's but very little was found. There was nothing more than some rather uninteresting pottery.

The Castle is on private land.

ABERGELDIE CASTLE
(OS 287953)

Pink-washed Abergeldie Castle was built in mid 16th Century. Built on the link plan, it represents an intermediate stage between the medieval keep and the L plan Renaissance tower house. There was a rectangular building, four storeys high and double the width of the single keep. There were crow-stepped gables and a round stair tower. At a later date a clock and copula had been added. In the basement is a vaulted kitchen. The hall is above.

The family of Gordons have owned Abergeldie estate since 1482. The castle dates from shortly after. The castle was rented by the Royals in Queen Victoria's reign and later. Some early 19th century extensions by James Henderson were removed in the 1980's

Some of Abergeldie lairds have been colourful characters. "Black Alister" Gordon fought at Corrichie in 1562 and was imprisoned afterwards. Pardoned, he became a loyal supporter of Queen Mary. He and following Gordons were involved in feuds with the Forbes. Abergeldie Castle resisted an attack by the Mackintoshes in 1592.

The seventh laird was a Royalist in the Civil War. When Deeside fell to the Covenanters, Abergeldie Castle was to be razed to the ground but the order was never carried out. The castle was again involved in the struggles between Jacobites and the Government represented by General Mackay in 1689. A 70 strong garrison was left in charge but John Farquharson, the Black Colonel, cut off their supplies. Mackay then reported that he burned 12 miles of territory and twelve to fourteen hundred homes in the area.

Nearer home, there were feuds between the Gordons and the Forbes.

The present laird, John Howard Seton Gordon lives in the Castle which is not open to the public.

Abergeldie birch trees are superior to those at the Aberfeldy of Burns' song, "The Birks of Aberfeldy." Birch wine was famous throughout Deeside and was said to be superior to champagne. Its last recorded use at the Castle was at the laird's funeral in 1831 but it was still being sold at Birkhall in 1845 for was a shilling a bottle.

The area was noted for "witches" and Abergeldie had its own witch, French Kate, who was burned on the hill opposite.

Abergeldie Castle

BALMORAL CASTLE
(OS 255951)

The name Balmoral may come from the Gaelic balmhoral - perhaps a settlement by the river, but there is no certainty.

The lands of Balmoral were part of the ancient province of Mar whose chiefs can be traced back to 1014. The Celtic province later became a feudal Earldom. Balmoral, on the south side of the Dee first appears in records in 1451 as Bouchmorale and in 1484 Balmoral is recorded as a Barony with the Earl of Mar as Feudal Superior. In 1539 the Exchequer Rolls mention John and Alexander Gordon as tenants. The Gordons had lived in the area since the fifteenth century, as had the Gordons of Abergeldie. It was the Gordons who built a simple fortified tower-house surrounded by a courtyard. By 1629 James, son of Gordon of Abergeldie had Balmorall which was valued at £88 Scots. When Anne Gordon married Charles Farquharson, second son of William Farquharson of Inverey, Balmoral passed to the Farquharsons of Inverey. Probably the most famous Balmoral Farquharson was James, Balmoral the Brave, son of the Black Colonel of Inverey. He was an ardent Jacobite and was badly wounded at Falkirk. He was later pardoned. Balmoral itself was forfeited. In 1798 it was acquired by Duff, Earl of Fife. The family never lived in it during the 54 years they held it.

The next occupant was Capt. Jame Cameron of Speyside who leased it from the Earl of Fife from 1818 - 1830. It was then leased for 5 years by a diplomat, the Rt. Hon. Sir Robert Gordon, 5th son of the 3rd Earl of Aberdeen and brother of the Prime Minister, Lord Aberdeen. The lease was renewed in 1835. Sir Robert retreated to Balmoral when not away on diplomatic duties. At that time most of the original castle had survived. He altered and enlarged it and laid out the gardens so that even at that time Balmoral was considered to be a highly desirable mansion. The castle stood on a slight elevation bounded by the Dee and surrounded by birches. Sir Robert had the place almost rebuilt by the architect John Smith of Aberdeen, "Tudor Johnny" in 1835 and it survived until 1856. A painting by W. Wyld and a George Washington Wilson photograph taken in 1855 show an original fortified tower-house of the link plan with a round tower and a large 16th century keep. Sir Robert came back from the Court of Vienna in 1846 intending to retire permanently to Balmoral. He was in fact leasing the old Gordon family property after 200 years His totally unexpected death the following year, with

27 years of the lease still to go, changed the whole situation.

After a month's stay at Ardverikie on the shores of Loch Laggan in Autumn 1847 Queen Victoria wrote in her diary "The country is very fine but the weather is dreadful." Their visit had been in the nature of a reconnaissance, to find a Royal Home in Scotland. While the west had been drenched in rain, Deeside had been enjoying glorious sunshine. The Queen's physician, who was also her mother's, Sir James Clark, told her of the health-giving qualities of Deeside where his son was convalescing at Balmoral, a guest of Sir Robert Gordon, leasee of the castle. A report was prepared, showing the valley as one of the driest places in the country.

On a September day in 1848 Queen Victoria and Prince Albert first came to Balmoral. Welcomed all along the route by garlanded arches, they travelled by the North Deeside Road to Ballater then to Balmoral by the South Deeside Road. Victoria's impressions are recorded in her 'Journal of Our Life in the Highlands'. The visit lasted only three weeks, but it convinced the ouple this was the place for them. She fell in love with the scenery and Albert with the prospect of great deer-shoots. The royal couple came again in the three following years.

James Giles, R.S.A. prepared sketches for the Queen - the usual practice before the days of photography. It was now possible for Royals, in the 10th year of the Queen's reign, to take over the lease and four years later in 1852 Albert bought the property from the Earl of Fife's Trustees for £31,500. He gave it to the Queen so it is the sovereign's personal property. A cairn on Craig Gowan celebrated the purchase, a precedent followed in celebration of many family joys and sorrows.

When they first came to Balmoral in September 1848 the Queen described it as "A pretty little castle in the Scottish style. The view is charming." Although the Queen had a great liking for it, the Castle was not adequate for Royal requirements, so a new building was planned. Numerous additions had been made for Sir Robert Gordon between 1820 and 1847. William Smith, son of the architect who carried out

68

most of the additions was the architect employed to build a new home on traditional Scottish lines. He worked with Prince Albert to design the new building. The foundation stone was laid on 28th September 1853. By 1856 part of the new building could be occupied, and soon the family was in residence. The castle was built of grey Invergelder granite from the estate in Scottish baronial style. The slates came from the Foundland Quarries. There is an 80' clock tower from which flies the Royal Standard when the family is in residence.

The chief entrance is on the south side with a porte-cochere and Albert placed his family crests and armorial bearings on the wall. The old Royal Arms of Scotland are also displayed. It is interesting that Prince Albert's funeral escutcheon displayed over the porte-clochere is the last time this custom was observed on Deeside. The old building was demolished. A tablet marking the site of the demolished castle reads:-

"This stone marks the position of the front entrance door facing the south, of old Balmoral Castle taken down in 1855".

Balmoral's interior was a mixture of Gothic and Scottish baronial, with generous use of tartan. Designed as a home, not a royal palace, it is a family meeting place. Throughout the years Victoria's "Dear Paradise" has remained in the affections of the Royals and visitors alike and is probably one of the best-known castles in the world.

The extensive policies were landscaped. They are well maintained and there are many trees, - pines and poplars, planted by the family and distinguished visitors.

There are many monuments in the grounds.

Queen Victoria's son and successor, Edward VII determined to erase the memory of John Brown. His statue was moved from Garden Cottage to behind the dairy, now hidden by trees. The statue by Edgar Boehm shows something that does not appear in paintings - his lucky 3d piece hanging from his watch-chain. He is also wearing the two medals bestowed by the Queen - the Faithful Service Medal and the Devoted Service Medal. The inscription on the base reads

"Friend more than Servant, Loyal, Truthful, Brave, Selfless, Dutiful even to the Grave."

The South Deeside road that passed from Abergeldie to Balmoral and on to Ballochbuie Forest and the Old Bridge of Dee was closed to secure privacy for the Royal Family.

BIRKHALL
(OS 349936)

The lands of Birkhall had been a pendicle of Abergeldie. Originally called Sterin - stairean - stepping stones, it took its name from a ford over the Muick that had stepping stones.

The original rectangular hall-house was built by Rachel Gordon in 1715 and her husband Charles Gordon. She was 10th Laird of Abergeldie and their initials appear over the door- 17. C.G. R.G. 15. On Rachel's death her third son Joseph, an ardent Jacobite, inherited Birkhall. Joseph Gordon of Birkhall hid in the Coyles of Muick after the '45 at a place known as The Laird's Bed. A father and son, the Ol;iphants of Gask, friends of Joseph Gordon and his wife Elizabeth sought refuge from Redcoats at Birkhall after Culloden. Under the names of White and Brown they escaped to Sweden.

The property reverted to Abergeldie. In 1848 Michael Francis Gordon proprietor of both Abergeldie and Birkhall became bankrupt and sold Birkhall to the Royal Family for the Prince of Wales. He stayed only once and in 1885 sold it to his mother, Queen Victoria. During the rest of her reign it was used by family or distinguished visitors. It was there that Florence Nightingale worked out a plan for an Army Medical Service and persuaded Lord Panmure, Secretary of State for War to agree to the formation of the Royal Army Medical Corps.

A north wing was added in 1890 and a south wing conversion undertaken by Graham Henderson in mid 1950.

The heirs to the throne - later Edward V111 and George V1 and other Royals including the late Queen Mother, The Queen and Prince Charles have had close associations with Birkhall.

BRAEMAR CASTLE
(OS 156924)

The ford river crossings of Dee and mountain track met to the east of Braemar Castle. The mound on which the present castle stands had from early times been a place of great importance. In the 8th century at Doldencha (dail-dun atha) the fort at the haugh ford, the King of the Picts, Hungus MacFergus met Acca, exiled Bishop of Hexham. A simple chapel dedicated to St. Andrew was erected in what is now the present burial ground of Braemar. This was likely to have been before the place we now know as St. Andrews was dedicated to that apostle. Doldencha was one of the strongholds of the Celtic Province of Mar. Like other 'strong-points' of the time, the 'castle' was a simple structure of earthwork and timber.

When the Erskines had their lands returned, John Erskine, Earl of Mar, High Treasurer of Scotland as well as Guardian of the young king James VI (1556 - 1625) built at Braemar a new fortress in 1628. Ostensibly a hunting lodge, it was a fortress to counter the rising power of the Farquharsons. It is an L-plan tower house with a circular stair in the re-entrant. A contemporary described it as "A great body of a house, a jam and a staircase."

During the brief rising in 1689 it was burned by the Black Colonel, John Farquharson of Inverey, to prevent government troops using it as a base. There were plans for upgrading in 1689 and again in 1715 but nothing was done until much later.

John Erskine, Earl of Mar, "Bobbing Jock" because he frequently changed his political allegiance, lost his office of Scottish Secretary of State when Hanoverian George I ascended the British throne. He joined the Jacobites and planned the 1715 Rising. After the defeat at Sheriffmuir his lands reverted to the Crown. John Farquharson of Invercauld bought some of the sequestered estate and gained Braemar Castle. He managed to stay clear of any imvolvement in 1745 but the Jacobites did destroy some of his property. Perhaps as a result he leased the castle to the government for 99 years as a garrison base for £14 per annum, to keep the area quiet after the '45, as well as to put a curb on whisky smuggling. With the castle went 14 acres of land. The pacification of the Highlands included road and bridge building and the old Invercauld Bridge belongs to this time.

The castle was then repaired and reconstructed and the defensive walls - star shaped, were erected. John & William Adam of Robert Adam's famous architectural family were already working on Fort George and they were responsible for the upper part of the castle. Plans for the work still exist in the British Museum. The "Red Coat" garrison consisted of a captain, a subaltern and 56 men. The first captain to take over the command was Capt. Esme Clark. The castle remained a Government outpost. We know that the soldiers grew potatoes in the field adjoining the Castle and frequently gave the locals a treat of a few potatoes which were duly cooked and enjoyed at local 'parties'. By the nineteenth century Jacobitism was dead but whisky smuggling was rife. Between 1827 and 1831 a detachment of the 74th Foot regiment was based in the castle to check this. The garrison occupied the castle until 1831. The soldiers left a small cairn on the north west shoulder of Creag Choinnich The inscription on the south side of the cairn reads

> "Erected by
> Edwin Ethelston
> Ensn. 25 Regiment
> A.D. 1829

Presumably it was as a commemoration of their stay or to while away hours of boredom. There are also earlier crudely carved names on the Castle window shutters, one by Drummer I. Skeaf in 1753 or 8, another by Corporal William Dix, 1757, of a Captain Lumsden's Company that eventually became the Green Howards. In 1762 Ensign B. Sullivan Suthers of the Sutherlands carved name and date, 1762, and another soldier of the XXII Regiment dated his 1771. Sgt. Robert Fishley of the 43rd Regiment dated his carving 177? and Sgt. John Chestnut 1797.

When more peaceful times came and the troops departed, the Farquharsons were left in possession. James, 10th laird of Invercauld improved and extended the estates. Braemar Castle was restored as a family home. His surviving child Catherine married James Ross who took the Farquharson name and their son undertook further restoration.

The building suffered from age and damp but has now been taken over by a Community Group and is being restored gradually to its old splendour.

Here at Braemar Castle is stone of many facets, shaped for war and for family life.

CAMBRIDGE COTTAGE
(OS 370960)

The house is on the east side of the Church Green in Ballater. A feu had been granted to Donald Cattanach in 1820. In 1833 there was permission to Charles McConnach to take stones from the North Craig of Ballater to build a dwelling house. In 1841 the property was sold to a Farquharson of Alford but by 1848 he was bankrupt. By 1856 a Ballater merchant called Haynes was in possession and it remained in the family until in 1930 when it was sold to the Church of Scotland Trustees. It was the Glenmuick Manse from 1930 to 1954.

Originally a single storey cottage, a floor had been added. Behind the feu is a little cottage, perhaps even older.

The Church sold Cambridge Cottage and it passed through several hands until it was bought in 1979 by Douglas Glass of Deecastle for his future retirement.

CAMBUS o'MAY HOTEL
(OS 421978)

This was originally a fishing lodge, a gift from William Cunliffe Brooks to his daughter Amy, about 1874, and known as Cambus House. The front has three gables and the building is entered through classical columns.

CORNDAVON LODGE
(OS 228021)

Corndavon Lodge (Coire an da Bheinn, the corrie of the two hills) a rather splendid granite-built shooting and fishing lodge lies at the top of Glen Gairn. Behind it rises the hill of Culardoch.

Built around 1810 on an earlier foundation, the house was extended considerably. When Queen Victoria came to Balmoral it became fashionable for many noble families to come to Deeside to enjoy the hunting and fishing. Together with shooting and fishing rites, wealthy families leased the property for the season. They arrived just before the season started with servants and much household equipment. Lord Cardigan, of Crimean fame was a tenant for a number of years and George VI shot over the moor. Local stories tell of tartan draperies reputed to have come from Culloden.

The glory has departed. The Lodge was gutted by fire and only a shell remains, although one corner is almost intact. On a wall of the room, there is a vast mural depicting grazing deer and local scenes. This was painted in 1968 by Major Philip Erskine of the Scots Guards, garrisoned in the Victoria Barracks. Unfortunately some years later vandals gained entry and vandalized the mural. By this time Philip Erskine was living in South Africa but he returned to Glen Gairn in 1998 to repair the damage and to freshen up his earlier work. The room is still used by parties from Invercauld estate.

Like any building of this period, it is reputed to have its ghost.

What was once a staff house is now a bothy for hill walkers. Close by are the former dog kennels. Once a stalker, Donald McHardy lived here with his family. Lodges of this period were usually only occupied in summer and autumn. Snow was a problem here and the keeper had often to cut a snow tunnel to reach the dogs for feeding. The wealthy tenants had of course returned home. Apart from earning a little extra as ghillies or keepers and beaters when the shooting lodges were occupied there was little to support large families in Glen Gairn. Earlier many had gone over the hills to Angus for harvesting but when demand for labour ceased due to advanced techniques, many sons on reaching adulthood emigrated to Canada, Australia or New Zealand, where they usually did exceedingly well.

Making whisky and smuggling it to market helped to make ends meet and there was the added thrill - almost a bounden duty- to outwit the excise man. Supplies were retained for home use but much was put into kegs, slung over ponies and taken south. Most homesteads in the area were involved.

Just before the Lodge a dam was planned to power a mill and a channel was cut. The task was never completed.

CRAIGENDARROCH HOUSE
(OS 366964)

In 1868 George Hall, a builder, built a house for himself on Braemar Road. His father has purchased sites for houses just before he died. George Washington Wilson photographed it in 1868 and there were no trees. There was only one other house, Aspen Lodge.

The Halls were stone masons They erected a three storey L shaped house. By 1920 they had acquired more land at the back and enlarged the house by adding a rear wing. At the front they added a square tower and an archway entrance and a turret. The granite was from the newly demolished Union Bridge in Abedeen.

Local information suggests that the granite stag's heads came from Braickley (Glenmuick House.)

The house was a summer residence and the family spent the winter months in the Aberdeen area.The Halls were in occupation until the late 1960's but the two remaining ladies let the place fall into disrepair and the garden became a wilderness. After they left the house was derelict for a few years. In the early 1970's it was bought by a tea planter, Tom

75

Forsyth who did a great deal of restoration, as did later purchasers. He sold the property to Mr. & Mrs. Begbie in 1983 who did many repairs and alterations and landscaped the gardens. The next purchaser, Mrs. Strachan, ran the place as a guest house. This did not last long and in 1994 it was bought by a Russian lady, Tatanyana von Rotterstall (Mrs. Poole). It then became the home of a local family, the Bruces, and stands proudly as a beautiful property representing modern comfort and a link with the gracious days of the Victorian Era.

CRAIGENDARROCH (HILTON)
formerly MORVEN
(OS366965)

The land on which the house was built was originally Gordon territory. In the 1880's the Marquis of Huntly needed money so he sold 10,000 acres with shooting and fishing rights to John Keiller of Dundee, the "Marmalade King." This was "new money" coming to Ballater. When here for the season the Keillers were in Morven Lodge. The young Keiller with a young family decided in 1891 to build a new home.

The Dundee architects did not use local granite but red sandstone which came by rail and then was hauled up the hill in carts. Unfortunately, Keiller did not have long to enjoy his new mansion. He was a sick man and had to spend much time abroad. He died in 1899, leaving as his heir 9 year old Alexander.

Alex served in the Flying Corps in World War I and afterwards flew his own bi-plane on Deeside. He developed an interest in aerial archaeology. He was also interested in racing driving.

The days of splendour were over. During World War II Glasgow evacuees were there then soldiers on training exercises in the hills. The house suffered badly. After the war the Keiller family decided to sell. Much land went to Dinnet Estates while house and fishing rights went to a Mrs. Montgomery from St. Andrews. She sold the land to Cordiner the timber merchant who did much felling. He then sold the property to the McLean family with interests in the bakery business. One member of the family ran the place as an hotel while another ran the Fife Arms in Braemar. In 1960 they sold to the Schofields.

I knew the place well from this time on. Mrs Schofield had a wonderful collection of antiques, many on view.

Private ownership ceased. The Craigendarroch became part of the Hilton organisation and continues so, after many alterations and additions to the building.

DARROCH LEARG HOTEL
(OS 361963)

The building was erected around 1880 but there is no certainty as to the architect.

This was the last building to be erected before the hill became too steep. It was a two storey building in a more Tudor style than its neighbours. The building is of granite on the ground floor while the upper level is of wood with the gables covered with fish-scale tiles.

The windows are all different. Because the building was above the main water level a private well had to be sunk. Originally hand-operated, a new electric pump was installed. This was further improved in 1961 and at times since.

On the other side of the road a building was used as stables then it became garages then a house sometime in the 1970's.

The first owner was Joseph Alexander who possessed it until 1909. It was purchased by Dr. Alexander Hendry who became Royal Physician and he remained there until 1917. He is linked with Glenmuick (Ballater) Parish Church for in the entrance is the bell he donated for the steeple of the Free Kirk, now the Auld Kirk Hotel.

A shipbuilder, Walter Jamieson was the next owner until 1925. He was followed by Henry Gibson Anderson. He used it as a base for fishing, shooting and golf. The Mackenzies of

Braichlie (Glenmuick House) were frequent partners or opponents and the families indicated they were free for one of their sports by running up a flag on their flag-poles. He made many additions to the building and improved the interior. He had "local"connections for his mother Mrs.Anderson, was at nearby Oakhall.

The Andersons sold the property to an accountant from Edinburgh called Atwell who worked for the Hong Kong and Shanghai Bank. During the war the house was a Royal Navy Convalescent Home. The Atwells then opened Darroch Learg as an hotel. The owner was somewhat eccentric. A local name for the hotel was "The Kipper Hotel"- typical of local humour.

The Atwells sold the property in1961. Douglas and Helen Franks ran a successful hotel and catered for skiing with a resident instructor.

Additions and improvements were made. Nigel and Fiona Franks took over the hotel in 1988, made improvements and added a conservatory.

DEE CASTLE
(OS 438967)

One of the important Mounth passes went from Candecaill (Ceann-na-Coille - head of the wood), the modern Deecastle to Invermark in Glenesk. Deecastle was a dramatic name for a hunting lodge.

It was at Candecaill in about 1600 that the 1st Marquis of Huntly built Dee Castle as the principle family home. Unfortunately it was burned to the ground in 1641, to be replaced some time later by a less splendid shooting lodge. It was at one time used as a Free Church after 1843. It is now a private residence with an adjoining farm and steading some of which dates to the 17th century.

FASNADARACH
(OS 461981)

This "fishing-lodge" was built in 1896 for Sir Ian Cecil, a cousin of Cunliffe-Brooks and a descendant of the Elizabethan minister, Cecil, Lord Burleigh.

There are rooms on two floors and the setting on the river bank is most attractive.

THE FIFE ARMS HOTEL, BRAEMAR
(OS 150915)

This was a large purpose built hotel for the "carriage trade." Built of grey granite, it has three storeys and attics, bay windows and an interesting porch. It was built about 1880 but was given a new frontage by Marshall Mackenzie in 1898. It was extended in 1905, with the porch area being doubled

GAIRNSHIEL LODGE (GARDEN SHIEL)
(OS 294007)

At the Gairnshiel Bridge the road divides. Ahead lies Crathie and stunning views of Lochnagar. Over the Gairnshiel Bridge the narrow road leads eventually to Tomintoul. On the left is Gairnshiel Lodge, now an Hotel, but built as a Shooting Lodge. Originally it was called Garden Shiel (a Shiel is a summer resting place). The Lodge was built or extended by Mr. Garden of Troup. and named after him, and not after the river. Glen Garden was the old name for Glen Gairn.

A nearby stone bears the date 1746 but its origin is unknown. It is likely to have Culloden associations.

GLENBARDIE

One of the most interesting houses on Braemar Road is Glenbardie. Ballater was growing and feu charters were being granted. The Invercauld Laird, James Ross Farquharson, granted a charter to James Proctor from the Aberdeen area. The feu duty was £14. 8s. per annum, starting in 1869. By 1881 he seems to have been unable to continue the payments. Alexander Haldane Farquharson succeeded as Laird and a new lease was arranged with a John Rennie who, according to Invercauld records, paid the outstanding debt plus interest. In 1806 he was granted an acre of land "bounded on the west by Aspen Bank and on the east by land feud to Dr. James Neil. (This was later to become the Manse, Fasnadarrach.)

Glenbardie was probably erected around 1807. It was named after a summer shieling in Glen Gairn.

The new owner, John Thompson Rennie was an Aberdeen shipping magnate owning the Aberdeen White Star Line. His best known ship was The Thermopylae, a China tea clipper.

As a ship owner, Rennie built the traditional "Widow's Tower" - originally a lookout place from which a wife would look for her husband's ship returning

There was a succession of owners - Principal Stewart of Robert Gordon's College, McCormacks, Mitchells, Littlejohns and Campbells. Hugh and Isobel Craigie were the owners in 1974 and they ran a very popiular Guest House.

In 1987 Duncan and Audrey Macrae purchased the property and ran it as a Guest House until 1999. They then sold the property.

THE HOUSE OF GLENMUICK

Present house -(OS 372946)
Former house, now demolished (OS 358938)

The lands of Glenmuick were originally part of Gordon territory, but after the settlement of entailed estates following the Jacobite Rising of 1745, the territory was acquired by John, 9th Laird of Invercauld in 1749. It remained in Farquharson hands until 1868 when the 13th Laird of Invercauld, Col. James Ross Farquharson sold the south-east side of Glen Muick to James Thomson Mackenzie, son of an Aberdeen merchant who had made his fortune trading in silk. James Mackenzie was created Baron Glenmuick in 1890..

There was near the site of the present Glenmuick House an earlier dwelling, Brackley, the site of a murder involving a Gordon Laird, the local Baron of Brackley and Farquharson of Inverey. The murder is celebrated in song and legend, but two separate incidents have been amalgamated.

Sir James Mackenzie built a house in 1868 - 1870 to the design of Sir Samuel Morton Peto who had achieved fame for his work in connection with the Great Exhibition at the Crystal Palace in 1851. The massive building was of granite: it formed three sides of a square with a 75 feet high tower. Records of 1881 show that it had 52 windows - one for every week of the year. People in the area loved or hated the house.

We know that in the 1880's 49 year old unmarried Mary Lewis was the Housekeeper. William McKenzie with his wife and family looked after the grounds and had a house in the Stable Yard. East Lodge was in the 1880's occupied by James Coutts and family, then later by Alex Jameson. By the early 1890's Alex Grant occupied West Lodge.

Sir James' son, Sir Allan, extended another house, Brackley or Braichlie House, in 1898. This was planned by Daniel Gibson and the landscape designer was the famous Thomas Hayton Mawson.

The Mackenzies mixed with the high society of the day and entertained guests like the Shah of Persia and the Tsar of

Russia. They frequently entertained the Royal family.

Time moved on and with it came many changes.

Sir Allan's son Lieut. Allan James, died in Nigeria in 1903 and was buried with full military honours in the family burial ground at Glenmuick. His brother, a Captain in the Grenadier Guards, died on the Somme in 1916. Brother Victor became third baronet on his father's death in 1906. He served as a Colonel in the Scots Guards in 1914 - 1918. A bachelor, he wandered round Ballater in his kilt and was often an escort for Princess Mary, the Princess Royal, later Countess of Harewood. His sister Lucy, a noted beauty, married Lord Kilmarnock, heir to Lord Errol and their son succeeded his father. Because of his fast life he had to leave the country and joined the loose living "Happy Valley" set in Nairobi. He was shot, presumably by a jealous husband. A film, "White Mischief" deals with the events. His mother Lucy was a charming old lady who often visited Ballater. She died in 1957. A young son of Sir Allan was also a Scots Guards Colonel. He inherited in 1944 and was often to be seen in Ballater in his kilt, with his chocalate Labrador, Dee.

Death duties took their toll as did a great deal of litigation and involvement in a divorce suit. Eric had to sell up. He retired to Mull and married late in life. In 1972 Colonel Eric Mackenzie, CMG. CVO. DSO. was buried quietly in the family ground. The present holder of the title now lives in Devon.

The original Glenmuick House had been used by various branches of the forces during the war of 1939 - 1945 and suffered a great deal of dilapidation. It was demolished around 1948 and some of the granite blocks used for building the "council houses" being erected after the war.. When demolition took place the house known as Braichlie was re-named The House of Glenmuick and that is today's "Big House".

The Walker-Okeovers followed the Mackenzies as owners of Glenmuick House.

THE INVER HOTEL
(OS 233938)

Although by no means as splendid as some of the previous buildings, nevertheless the Inver is worthy of mention.

It was a coaching inn built in the late 18th century by the Farquharsons of Invercauld, in the neo-Tudor style It was from a design by Peter Roberts of London. The chimneys are from the 19th century. The interior was changed after a fire in 1978.

INVERCAULD HOUSE
(OS 174924)

(Although a family home, Invercauld has all the architectural features of a castle.)

The stone coat of arms above the door of Invercauld depicts the clan badge, - a fir tree growing from a mound. In early times twigs of fir were worn as a clan badge in time of war. Also remembered are the achievements of Finla Mor, standard bearer at the Battle of Pinkie in 1547. The cat supporters of Clan Chattan, of which the Farquharsons were part, are in evidence.

Invercauld House stands on a green haugh (level ground on the banks of a river) about 3.5 miles from Braemar, overlooking the Dee and viewing the towering heights of Ben Avon and Beinn a Bhuird, often snow-covered. Not far off is Braemar Castle, a fortalice converted by the Hanoverians to keep the Highlands in order.

The date of the original building of Invercauld is uncertain but the oldest part, a rough hewn vaulted chamber which can be approached by steps from the long back-door corridor certainly goes back to the reigh of James IV (1473 - 1513) and may be earlier.

Originally there were several buildings eventually linked together. Invercauld is an extended Z plan building with three storey and attic wings and a square tower of six storeys.

The house is in the baronial style with wings radiating

from the 70 feet high central tower. The exterior is plain and simple without over-elaborate decoration. Inside a wide entrance reveals a magnificent staircase with rooms branching off at many levels.

Considerable alterations had taken place in the 17th century and again in the 19th century. Additions were made in the 1820's and the gables added in 1847. There was considerable re-modelling in 1875 by the London architect J. Wimperis when the tower was raised.

The Drawing Room was in the past the show-piece of the house with gilt furniture, chintzes and Regency style sofas covered in claret, jade green or amber. The walls were very pale, showing the furniture to advantage.

Off the Drawing Room is a little boudoir, used by the present Lairds's grandmother, a daughter of Musgrave of Edenhall, Cumbria. A noted beauty in her day, her portrait was painted in the early 1900's.

In the older section of the house is the Dining Room, pine panelled and with a number of stag heads. The magnificent 18th century table takes twenty place settings. Sconces on the walls hold candles that give an air of mystery but on important occasions silver candelabra sat on the table. They had designs of grapes and vines and silver deer.

The Library, well stocked, used to be used as a gentleman's lounge in the shooting season. It was in this room that an attempted murder was avoided.

Upstairs there is period furniture. In many rooms there are tester or four-poster beds. There are Summer and Winter bedrooms with different outlooks. One room is known as the Prince's Room because Queen Victoria's husband Prince Albert stayed as a guest. The bed frame was made of guilded metal and the bed had a carved canopy.

The house was always lived in and enjoyed. Everywhere there were portraits and engravings of family members. There was a portrait of Francis Farquharson of Monaltrie, the "Baron Ban" (fair haired) near the desk that was given him when he was a prisoner in England.

A table made from a church seat carried an inscription about the Farquharsons of Achriachan, another branch of the family. They too were descended from Finla Mor. A carved box used to stand on it. It once belonged to Mary Queen of Scots and may have been a gift to the Queen from the Holy Roman Emperor. The Queen gifted it to Beatrix Garden, Findla Mor's second wife. She was a skilled harpist and sang at the Scottish court.

There were swords and shields of family members. The dirk, targe and basket-hilted broadsword of the Black Colonel who fought under Bonnie Dundee in 1689 were there, together with other broadswords. There are dents on the targe that legend attributes to the Black Colonel summoning his ghillie by firing at it.

Over the years there were souvenirs of Royalty and of the family's Jacobite connections. They included a medallion of Charles I and a miniature of Bonnie Prince Charlie together with other memorabilia including the Order of the Garter ribbon he gave to Lady Ann Mackintosh daughter of the 7th Laird of Invercauld when she saved the Prince from capture at Moy Hall. They are now in safe keeping.

The ambience of the house is one of welcome but ever present is the link with the past.

The house is now leased.

FORMER INVERCAULD GALLERIES, BRAEMAR
(OS 150915)

Built as a village hall for the Castleton section of the village, this two-storey granite building has very large windows at the top level and horse-shoe arched windows at the lower level. It was designed by J.B.Pirie about 1880.

Auchendryne had its village hall built by the Duke of Fife to rival the Farquharson building and to cater for the Auchendryne dwellers, many of whom were Roman Catholics. It is an entirely different style of building with red timber cladding, white bargeboards and drooping eaves.

85

THE CASTLE OF INVEREY
(OS 033393)

John Farquharson 3rd Laird of Inverey, the Black Colonel, is particularly associated with his home. Stones are all thart remain. In 1666 on 7th September he was accused of involvement in the murder of John Gordon, Baron of Braichley. As a result, he was outlawed. Many of the stories involving "The Black Colonel" are the stuff of legend.

At the end of April 1689 Dundee came to Deeside to raise the clans for James VI & I. To prevent Dundee and his Jacobites from escaping over the Mounth the Earl of Mar was ordered to garrison Braemar Castle. Mar died before completing the task. The Master of Forbes was sent to carry out the instructions but he was out-manoeuvered by John Farquharson who burned the Castle to prevent government troops from occupying it. Abergeldie Castle was garrisoned instead.

The final clash came at Killiecrankie in July 1689 with a Jacobite victory but the death of Dundee. The Black Colonel "lurked" on Deeside, often at his home in Inverey Casrtle. He was hunted by Government troops and on one occasion is reputed to have escaped by climbing on horseback the steep slopes of the Pass of Ballater.

Tracing the Colonel one night to Inverey, Redcoats attacked the Castle. Having been warned, with little time to spare, John Farquharson escaped under cover of darkness and hid in Glen Ey, in a gorge still known as "The Colonel's Bed". The Castle was burned. John survived. Food was brought to him by his faithful "Annie Ban". He died around 1698 and was buried in Braemar, in spite of his wish to be interred in the Chapel of the Seven Maidens in Inverey. (OS 087894). According to the story, three times the coffin appeared on the surface and three times it was re-buried. So it was taken up the Dee by raft and buried as requested.

A little to the north west of the ruined castle lies the burial ground of the eleven Farquharsons of Inverey.

James Duff, 2nd Earl of Fife, acquired Inverey in 1798.

KINDROCHIT CASTLE, BRAEMAR
(OS 151913)

Since early times Braemar has been visited by kings and nobles.

The Castle of Kindrochit stands in the middle of the village of Braemar, beyond the car park. The ruin lies on the east bank of the rocky gorge of the Clunie, while on the other side is the old mill-lade. This was a well-defended site and the fortification was important in the defence of the north-south routes over the Mounth.

One tradition says there was a fortification of some sort in the days of Kenneth II, 971 - 993, and Creag Choinnich or Kenneth's Hill is said to be named after him. Races were reputed to have taken place up the hill. Another tradition links the area with Malcolm III, Canmore.

There is no documentary evidence of a castle having been built at Doldencha before 1390. One must assume that any charters granted by Robert 11 from 'Kyndrocht' refer to the stronghold at Doldencha which had adopted the name 'Kyndrocht'. Some of the entries in the Register and Rolls when Robert 11 was in 'Kyndrocht' show an annual award of 20/- out of the rents of Aberdeen to John Barbour, author of "The Brus", and expenses for transporting wine and for provisions from the baker, all for the King's use. In 1388 the king in Braemar summoned Parliament to meet him in Aberdeen to plan an invasion of England which resulted in a victory at Otterburn. It is likely that there was a timber bridge over the Cluny this time. There was a narrow rocky gorge about 3/4 of a mile above the old stronghold of Doldencha and the bridge would be a help to travellers over the Cairnwell and the Tolmounth. Known as Ceann-drochaide, "the bridge head", it gave its name to the district.

Robert III (1390 -1406) gave a special licence on 10th November 1390 to his brother-in-law Sir Malcolm de Drummond, brother of the Queen, to build a fortalice at the bridgehead. The tower of Kindrochit was the fifth largest in Scotland.

In 1402 Drummond was beaten up by persons unknown and died as a result. The likely murdered was Alexander Stewart, illegitimate son of the "Wolf of Badenoch" fourth son of Robert 11. He forced the victim's widow, Isabella, Countess of Mar, to marry him, so he became Earl of Mar. It is probable that the Earl of Mar then completed the building, using prisoners from East Prussia, captured in a pirate foray. There was probably a mote where today's car park is sited.

The first record of a castle Keeper was in the early 15th century when Alexander Stewart held office. He was dead by 1455 when his widow was claiming her "terce" (life rent of one third of her husband's property.)

We know that towards the end of the reign of James VI, 1567 - 1628, Kindrochit was in ruins. John Taylor the "Water Poet" was entertained by John Erskine, Earl of Mar in 1618 at the ancient site at Doldencha. He gives no description of the building preceeding the present Braemar Castle built in 1628, but he does say that Kindrochit Castle was in ruins. He wrote about it in his 'Pennyless Pilgrimage' published in 1630. Since that time the building has steadily disintegrated and it was at one time used as a quarry for building stone

Pestilence came to Deeside on a number of occasions and the Gala Mhor or great plague visited Braemar. To prevent the sick from leaving the Castle precincts and spreading the infection, standard policy was followed. Cannon were brought from Atholl, over the Cairnwell and, from the hill overlooking Braemar, the Castle was reduced to a heap of rubble and the inhabitants buried inside.

English troops were stationed at Kindrochit Castle to keep an eye on Jacobites and likely troublemakers. Tales of hidden treasure had been told for many years, but little had been done to find it. However curiosity and greed made the Redcoats act. After throwing stones down what appeared to be a flight of steps, one of the soldiers was lowered down by rope into a vault under the rubble. When he was pulled back he was terrified. He reported that he had seen a dreadful sight, - a company of skeletons wearing odd clothes now reduced to rags, seated at a table. There have been many attempts to rediscover the skeletons and the treasure - including mine - but all have been to no avail. Tradition says there are a number of vaults and stables and a subterranean passage for watering the horses in the Clunie without leaving the Castle.

Time moved on. A family living in Castleton (Braemar) who were reputed to be fairly wealthy, cleared up the site, finding coins, drinking horns and animal bones. Before they finished a little man in a red cap was supposed to have told them to stop if they wished to stay alive. They did.

Dr. Douglas Simpson excavated the site in 1925/26. The treasure he found was an early sixteenth century silver gilt brooch with an inscription "Here am I in place of another". Was this once a romantic momento of love? It was found in the prison. An excellent example of a highland brooch, it measures $3^3/16$ inches in diameter. The silver was probably originally gilded. It is now in the National Museum of Antiquities in Edinburgh. A replica of the brooch was presented by Capt. A.A.C. Farquharson of Invercauld to highland dance winners at Braemar Games.

According to legend a huge monster lived among the rocks of the Clunie, known as Tad-Losgann. It lived on cattle belonging to locals, supplied on a rota basis. Close to the Castle lived a poor family called McLeod. McLeod senior died, leaving a widow and son who eventually married and had a son of his own. Widow McLeod's one cow was selected as the next 'food' for Tad-Losgann. Her son Sandy was indignant and decided to take action. He hid in a hollow and when Tad-Losgann appeared shot it through the heart with an arrow. Sandy was arrested and faced the death penalty, - death by hanging.

This was a great public occasion attended by local barons and according to one story, by the king himself, Malcolm Canmore. The distraught mother and wife went to Canmore and pleaded for Sandy's life. The king had heard that Sandy was an excellent archer, - after all that was how he had killed Tad-Losgann, and good bowmen were at a premium - so he decided to offer Sandy a chance of staying alive. Sandy's wife and child were put across the river. A peat was put on the head of the little boy in his mother's arms. Sandy, on the opposite side of the river, picked up his bow and selected three arrows from his quiver. He fitted one to his bow and after a brief hesitation, he fired. Away went the arrow. It was embedded in the peat. The bystanders cheered.

The king asked Sandy why he had selected three arrows. Back came the reply "If I had missed or hurt my wife or son, I would not have missed you". As was to be expected, the king was furious. However, the realisation that here was an excellent archer outweighed his anger, so he offered the young fellow a position in his personal bodyguard. The proud young McLeod replied that he could never love the king enough to fight for him after the ordeal to which he had been subjected. True to his word, the king set Sandy free, saying "As you are such a hardy fellow, your name from now on will be Hardy". There are still descendants of Hardy living in the area, the sons of Hardy being McHardy.

Ruins are all that remain of a great castle that played a part in local and national history. The story of Kings and nobles, prelates and peasants may not exist in writing, but their spirit lives on in Kindrochit Castle. Go there as dusk gathers and the past is all around you and with you.

Kindrochit Brooch

KNOCK CASTLE
(OS 353952)

The outstanding late 16th or early 17th century castle ruins on Deeside are those of Knock - Cnoc - a hill, hence a castle on a hill.

On the north side of the South Deeside Road (A973) west of Bridgend of Muick a substantial ruin stands proudly on The Knock, built on land that was not originally as thickly afforested as at present. It has a commanding view over the surrounding area, surrounded by trees, not far from the confluence of Dee and Muick and overlooking the drove road to Clova and the South.

Knock, a Durward stronghold or simple fort, existed in the time of Wallace and Bruce. The Durwards also had a stronghold at Abergairn. Legend says there was a secret passage between the two, but common sense would say that the distance was too great. The Durwards probably held the Royal Commission to check unrest on Deeside but by the time of James IV the Gordons were carrying out the duties. Huntly gave the command to his son but both father and son were killed at Flodden in 1513. The duties then became the responsibility of James the Gross, High Chancellor to James V. He gave the lands of Knock to a brother of Abergeldie.

Alexander, 3rd Earl of Huntly gave one of his sons the command of an early castle of Knock, while George, 4th Earl (1513 - 1562) granted castle and lands to another Gordon, Abergeldie's brother. Family feuds spanned the generations, and they were particularly bitter between the Gordons of Knock and the Forbes of Strathgirnoc, further complicated by the fact that Strathgirnoc at the foot of Creag Phiobaidh (the Hill of the Piper) was a 'buffer' area lying between the Gordon property of Knock and the Gordon castle of Abergeldie.

After the Battle of Corrichie in 1562 the two clans were involved in a fight that resulted in the Gordons capturing the leader of the Forbes and imprisoning him in a Gordon stronghold of Glenfiddich. Even when he was set free, relations between the two clans were little improved. One story tells of a Forbes returning to Strathgirnoc from a foray to find the Gordons in occupation. Matters went from bad to worse when Henry Gordon of Knock was killed in a Forbes raid. He was succeeded by his brother Alister or Alexander who repaired or rebuilt Knock Castle around 1600, the ruins of which we see today. It was obviously prepared for defence purposes against the Forbes.

There were more localised differences, such as access to a peat moss for their tenants and the "poinding" of stock.

The Forbes stronghold was at nearby Strathgirnoc, at the foot of Creag Phiobaidh, the Hill of the Piper.

Animosities continued. However, human nature being what it is, in spite of all the hatred and bloodshed, Francis, the third of old Alexander's eight sons fell in love with the only daughter of Forbes of Strathgirnoc. She was a noted beauty, her father's only daughter, and she could have married well. Her father had planned for her to marry a young relation, Forbes of Skellater on Donside, to continue the family name, but it seems the lady was not in agreement with father's wishes. Old Forbes was a very irascible man and he distrusted any Gordon, young or old. He may have feared treachery, or he may just have been unwilling to give up his daughter because he had plans for her. It may of course have been a Gordon attempt to bring the feud between the families to an end, but this seems unlikely. Arrangements were made by the Baron of Braichlie, as a neutral party. Finally the lad went to call on his future father-in-law. The character and temper of old Forbes were well known: he had the reputation of lashing out at people. The interview took place but did not seem to be going in favour of the young lad. The old man lashed out at the suitor with his sheathed sword. Off flew the scabbard and off too came the head of the young Gordon. Tradition says the old man commented "They wanted a wedding, now they can have a funeral".

The fate of the girl is not recorded, except that her ghost is reputed to wander round the Strathgirnoc area searching for her lost lover!

Forbes went into hiding, fearful of reprisals but still determined to continue the feud against the Gordons. So, as might be expected, that was not the end of the matter. More bloodshed was to come. The seven remaining Gordon sons were one day casting peats. Totally unaware of danger, they were attacked by a band of men led by Forbes of Strathgirnoc and his henchman, Wattie McGrory. Their heads were cut off and stuck on their flaughter (peat-cutting) spades. A Knock servant arrived at the peat moss with food for the seven young men and was met by the grisly sight. He rushed back to tell Alexander of the fate of his sons. The old man was at the top of the spiral stone stair in the Castle. Whether he had a heart attack or was just overcome by grief we will never know, but he fell down the stone stair and broke his neck. That really was the end of that family of Gordon. The Forbeses had triumphed. Old Alexander Gordon had no heirs to carry on the family name.

The feudal superior and law administrator for the area was "Black Alister" Gordon of Abergeldie, Baron Baillie of the area, who had also a family interest in the atrocity. Representative of justice and Alexander's relation, he hanged Forbes at his own house of Strathgirnoc and took over the property, granting it to another Gordon. It is said that a clump of rowan trees marked the spot. Nothing of the original Strathgirnoc remains. A later building occupies a similar site, but a few scattered stones may date back to the period of conflict.

Passing years have no doubt led to the embroidering of the story but there is no doubt that Alexander had sons who were killed and that Forbes of Strathgirnoc was punished.

The castle of Knock was later occupied, according to tradition, by a lady called Graham, but there seems to be little documentary evidence. There is evidence of a fire. The castle is now a splendid ruin, rousing particularly evocative memories when seen by moonlight. Strathgirnoc has gone, a more modern house standing further back.

Go to the ruins of Knock Castle. Go by moonlight. The ghost of Alexander Gordon may be there, cursing the name of Forbes that put an end to his family. So may the young Forbes beauty, searching for her lost lover. It was a bloodthirsty age.

Knock Castle

LOCH BUILG LODGE
(OS 188027)

Further up the glen than Corndavon Lodge and about 3 miles to the west, is Loch Builg Lodge, by no means as splendid as some of the other Lodges, yet another mute reminder of the past. Once a stalker, Donald McHardy lived here with his family. The roofless ruin is in Aberdeenshire but Loch Builg itself, only a few yards away and home to mountain char, is in Banff. Towering over the area is the 1172m. Ben Avon, habitat of many rare Alpine flowers.

There is a story of a keeper, name unknown, who lived here. He found many semi-precious gem stones and made a

94

considerable amount of money, much of which he kept in the house, so he was always wary of strangers. The money was kept in a hole in the wall. A tink came to the door, begging for food and refused to go away. The keeper threatened to shoot if he returned. The tink came back again during the night and attempted to break into the house. The keeper fired through the door, intending to deter him, and went to bed. In the morning he found the dead tink outside the door. He buried him on the moss and said nothing. The keeper kept silent until he was dying and then the body was found and given proper burial.

The Loch itself, at the NE base of Ben Avon is 1586' above sea level and is in Banff. About $^1/_4$ mile wide, it is at its longest $^3/_4$ of a mile long. Probably the name comes from the Gaelic "balg", a bag, because it is said to resemble a sack or bag ready for tying up. The old road from Deeside to Tomintoul ran along the east side of the loch. On a very frosty day a tramp came along the road that can still be traced among the heather and stones. He lost his way but later picked up the track again. While in the inn in Tomintoul he was in conversation with an old shepherd familiar with the road when he was driving his sheep. The tramp told him he had lost his way in the darkness but found it again after going over a large area of very smooth and slippery ground. It seems that the tramp, without realizing it, had crossed over the loch, frozen solid.

MAR LODGE (DALMORE)
(OS 096899)

Where the Dee and the Quoich meet are the lands of Dalmore, Dail Mhor, the big field, the old name for Mar Lodge. In the 15th century James IV granted the land to Kenneth Mackenzie, son of his friend Mackenzie of Kintail. Young Mackenzie built a house soon after obtaining the land and the family became foresters to the Earl of Mar. He married Beatrix, daughter of "Findla Mor" by his second wife Beatrix Garden.

In 1715 both Kenneth and his son were present at the

Raising of the Standard in Braemar. After the Rising of 1715, the Mackenzies had financial difficulties. Dalmore was sold to Lords Grange and Dun. It was then acquired by the Duffs who also purchased Alanquoich, Auchindryne and Inverey from the Farquharsons.

Old Mar Lodge was built by William Duff. About 1732, slightly behind the present building, he erected a new dwelling. It was quite a simple building - virtually a hunting lodge. Nearby were a number of 17th century homes but by 1770 the Earl of Fife had cleared them off to give himself privacy and clearer views. William was created Lord Braco and Earl of Fife. In 1798 he purchased Balmoral. Mar Lodge was badly damaged by the "Muckle Spate" in 1829 and was later demolished.

Another Mar Lodge, known as New Mar Lodge or Corriemulzie Cottage was built on the south side of the Dee between 1885 and 1888 for the Duke and Duchess of Fife (Princess Louise, Princess Royal, eldest daughter of Edward VII). The architect, Marshall Mackenzie of Aberdeen created a pseudo-Elizabethan mansion with half-timbered gables and a red tiled roof. It burned down in 1895 leaving only a game larder and a keeper's cottage. The Corriemulzie ballroom had a vast number of stags' heads which were saved from the fire.

A new Marshall Mackenzie Mar Lodge was built in 1895. The style was entirely different. It was a two-storey pink granite building with timbered gables and an orange tiled roof. It passed through other hands and then again suffered as a result of fire when repairs were being carried out in 1991.

Luckily most of the original furniture had been removed to facilitate alterations.

When repaired Mar Lodge was sold to the National Trust for holiday apartments.

MONALTRIE HOUSE
(OS 376927)

James Robertson built this low, two storey building for Francis Farquharson of Monaltrie about 1782. He was the son of the laird of Monaltrie and factor to his uncle John Farquharson of Invercauld. The original Monaltrie House at Crathie had been burned by Redcoats after the '45 and when Francis eventually returned from English "house arrest" and recovered some of his land, he need a home. When he first returned he stayed with friends and then Ballater House, later called Monaltrie House, was built. It was a long low house, with small rooms. There is no evidence that Francis Farquharson actually residerd there and none of his letters are addressed from the house. It became the residence of his nephew and successor, William.

Many letters are dated from "Ballater House" but when the son of Lord and Lady Cochrane, Thomas Alexander, was born and baptised there on 10th April 1851 the Baptismal Register records the place as Monaltrie House. Presumably they leased it.

The house was badly damaged by the troops quartered there from 1939 - 1945 but now it has been restored.

MORVEN LODGE
(OS 338030)

Morven is the big hill, Mor Bheinn. Oblong in shape, 872 feet high, it can be approached by a number of routes.

A rough track from Lary Farm goes to the ruins of Morven Lodge. The Lodge stood in a green hollow, sheltered by a little belt of trees. The path from Glenfenzie goes through them.

In the days of its Victorian splendour it was an up-market shooting lodge. A shepherd's cottage lay behind. Children from here had a 10 mile round trip to school every day. On Sundays about 17 young men from here went to church in Ballater.

In an open area in front of piles of stones a duel had taken place between a Donside Laird and the Laird of Braickley. The son of the latter, a herd, deputised for his father and introduced himself as a herd. The Donside laird deputised one of his followers, also a herd. Realising that Bracklie's lad was a skilled swordsman, he stepped in. Young Bracklie defeated him and he was carried off, badly wounded.

Towards the end of the 19th century the owner was the Dundee marmalade king, Alexander Keiller. It was a busy place particularly during the shooting season, when society folk were entertained. Their presence gave some locals employment as ghillies and beaters.

In 1891 Keiller built himself another Morven in Ballater, now known as the Hilton Craigendarroch, and demolished the original dwelling. The pillars of the gateway can be seen, sad reminders of a departed age. Only scattered stones remain to remind us of its activity and social cudos, but the laundry and stables are still there, together with the keeper's and shepherd's house.

All around the track to Morven Lodge are ruins of earlier settlements. Most of them were fairly primitive and lacked comfort.

OAKHALL
(OS 366965)

Yet another example of "Balmorality" is Oakhall. The architect is unknown but it was typical of the work of Kinnear and Peddie who were designing in Aberdeenshire at the time.

It has all the usual castle features - two round turrets, crow-stepped gables, pediment dormers and a "sitooterie" and a castellated terrace. In its original state there were iron railings and gate and steps to the door. Internally it had oak floors, a pine stair and ornate plaster work.

Oakhall's first owner was the Headmaster of Robert Gordon's College in Aberdeen, Dr. Alexander Ogilvie. He bought land across the road which at one time was landscaped and later on supported large greenhouses. The Ogilvies sold the house in 1896 to an Anderson family from London who spent the summers here. They added a wing and an annex for cars and staff. The Andersons were involved in overseas banking and Henry Gibson Anderson was president of Ballater Golf Club. Mrs. Anderson gave Communion Plate to the Kirk in her husband's memory.

After her husband's death in 1913 Mrs Anderson remained in Oakhall until the 1930's. One of her sons owned the next-door Darroch Learg.

Big houses were requisitioned during the war. This time it was The Royal Veterinary Corps in Oakhall. In 1947 the owner of Oakhall was Florence Muir from Edinburgh. It seemed she planned to use the building as an hotel. Something went wrong and the land across the road and the annex were sold. In 1949 Winifred Milne (Mrs. Winifred Thornton) bought Oakhall to run it as a Children's Hotel. When she married she continued the Children's Hotel until the early 1960's. Numbers reduced, the Hotel closed and she went abroad. She died in South Africa in 2005.

When the annex was sold and made into flats, Captain Frai bought the chauffeur's flat and ran a walled market garden with greenhouses. He sold the produce in a Garden Shop at the Station.

In 1962 Oakhall was bought by the Franks who ran it as part of the Darroch Learg Hotel.

SLUIEVANNACHIE
(OS 361959)

Sluievannachie was the Moor of the White Field or, from the legend of St. Nathalan, the Moor of Blessing. The old farmhouse is neither beautiful nor distinguished architecturally but it is typical of its period and has impressive chimney stacks, diamond coped on square bases.

A single-storey and attic house was built for Peter Mitchell about 1836.

Local tradition places a long-gone religious building on the site but to date nothing has been found. On the other hand the cellar walls appear to come from an earlier date.

Peter Mitchell, a farmer and builder came to Ballater when buildings were being erected in the village. He married in 1826 and presumably resided in an early dwelling. In 1836 he leased the farm land of Sluievannachie and built a house. The land with the house included what is now the golf course. When they moved into the house their seventh child, Alexander, was born. There were eleven children in all. About 1852 five of them left with an uncle and his family to make a new life in Australia.

Alexander eventually inherited the farm. He does not seem to have been a builder like his father. Instead he hired out horses and carriages. Some of his wooden buildings remain to this day.

The golf course was developed in 1892 on some of his rough land. Over 10 years later the golf club decided to extend and as a result Alexander lost most of his land after much argument and disagreement. Alexander, known locally as Old Sluie, died in 1922. His widow, a keen gardener, was a member of the Royal Horticultural Society, and had Press coverage for her beautiful garden and Royal visits.

Hay's Lemonade depot took over the farm steadings and held them until the land was used for housing.

When Alexander's widow died in 1938 the leased house passed to a family member and was used as a holiday home. It passed through the generations until the 1970's when it was purchased from the owners, Invercauld Estate, together with the remaining land of about 2.5 acres. In 1999 the present owners purchased house and land, so it remained with the Mitchell family. Some internal improvements have been carried out but externally the house remains the same.

TULLICH LODGE
(OS 390985)

This was another Marshall Mackenzie building erected in 1897. It was a T plan house built for the Aberdeen advocate, William Reid. The tower was added in 1910 and there were further additions in 1923 by Vincent Harris.

XIV. THE DEVELOPMENT OF THE HOUSE

"The house of everyone is to him his castle and his fortress"
Sir Edward Coke

Hut circles of the Bronze Age were the proto-types of the familiar later 'but and ben'. Rectangular huts succeeded round ones, but angles were rounded. Often there were two rooms, separated by a wooden partition and on occasion a tiny window, unglazed, of course.

Houses were simply made. Walls were of rough stones with divots and clay infilling. There was no cement and very little lime at first. The roofing couples were entirely of wood, embedded in the walls at the bottom and fastened to the short cross bar with wooden pins. The roof-tree ran from end to end of the house across this bar and between the points of the couple legs. Saplings, sawn up the middle, were placed horizontally down the ribs of the roof and then over these, transversely. Small sticks were split with a wedge and they carried the divots, then the 'thak' was fastened on with 'strae ropes.' Over this structure was a roof of heather or fails (fails were root-matted turf) - made watertight by clay. The barn was of similar structure, with the roof also tied on with straw ropes. Poor houses had only one room, with a waist-high partition separating residents from animals. There was no chimney to let out the smoke from the peat fire on the hearth.

Peat and wood were burned on the fire: coal was too expensive for all but the Laird. Originally the fire burned on a hearth-stone, then in the gable end a wide open fireplace burned the peat and wood. Traditional building was still followed. Two rooms with a wooden partition had on each side a box bed that could be closed off. Each room had a fireplace of stone. In the but or 'kitchen' was a large one, complete with swey, while there was a smaller one in the ben or parlour. Usually windows were in the gable ends. Often planks were laid over the earth floor. The roof was of heather, or broom, and occasionally of divots. Ruins of this type of building can be seen in many glens.

In the 14th century a hall or ha'toun was the name for a tenant farmer's house while cottars' dwellings were cot-touns. A baron's dwelling was a fortalice.

As time went on some of the better houses had a But and a Ben. The Ben, rarely used, was for entertaining the Laird or the Minister, or at times of funerals. The house walls were not plastered and rushes or heather or sometimes straw covered the floor. Annual 'refurbishment' helped to take away the 'foosty' smell, but everyone was accustomed to the odour! The But was an all purpose room, - for living, eating and sleeping. Bedding was usually heather covered by a blanket. The space between the two rooms, if there were two, was the Spence. This was a 'pantry', or a storage place for meal, ale or milk. On occasion it did duty as the children's bedroom. An overflow of young sons could use the barn. Privacy in the home was limited! This probably accounted for the high rate of illegitimacy. Lack of privacy also accounted for the fact that the daughter of the house often bore an illegitimate child fathered by the farm servant. Incest too was at a high rate.

Over the fire was a sway, - a metal rod hanging over the fire often on tripod - like legs on which pots hung. Smoke went out of the windows that in the early days had no glass.

Stirton, writing in "Crathie & Braemar" described homes on Deeside, with dried mud on the walls and thatch of heather or broom. Rooms were generally divided by a partition.

Food had to be cooked simply, - boiled or 'pot roasted' or made on the girdle, hence bannocks, oatcakes, scones, brose and porridge, and boiled in the cloth puddings like 'clootie dumpling', - and even haggis! Even earlier a flat stone was a girdle and a clay pot boiled water.

Furniture, basically a table, chair and bench, and a chest, was the work of the local carpenter.

Willow baskets were used for carrying and for storage. A creel was strong and light and went through doorways without difficulty. It could be carried on a person's back or on a packhorse. A creel could be made seed proof, meal proof or bee proof by edge-joining tightly coiled tubes of bent grass. Willow and hazel were also used to form partitions in houses, to separate the inhabitants from their animals.

Plague ravaged the country from 1349-50 and it came again in 1362, killing up to a third of the population. Famine was present, as a result of harsh weather and farming improvements. Uncontrollable circumstances often meant enforced removal from buildings, the linking of little farms or the land being turned into a parkland to give the Superior a better view or to have larger 'policies' around the house. The land could be turned into grazing for sheep or into a deer forest. Whatever the reason, by mid to late 18th century, there was a rapid decline in population

With the coming of improvements in farming the old-style house changed. Previously the roof, thatched with heather or straw, could be ripped off and used as manure. Improvements meant that houses were rebuilt using stone and slate. Gone too was the simple bed of stone in the middle of the floor to hold the fire and to sleep around. Eventually proper chimneys were built in, known as "hingin lums", looking like a wooden box measuring about five feet long, with open sides. It was smothered with clay and tied with ropes of straw on the outside, the whole structure being liable to burn and to ignite the roof.

Lofts were built to give greater accommodation.

A Typical House

XV. INTO MORE MODERN TIMES

*"The old times are gone and progress there must be, but
the old days, the old ways and the old folk have left memories
behind them"*

Source unknown

Although the history of early man is interesting it does not
seem to have had much direct effect on the way people lived
their lives here. However, the Greeks, Romans, Saxons and
people of the Middle Ages played an important part in shaping
our lives - in language, customs and even government. Even
so, their homes, customs and ideas as well as their knowledge
of the world, were very different from ours. The history of the
last 400 or 500 years or so shows lives that were more like
ours.

Modern history began in the second half of the fifteenth
century when discoveries were made that changed life for ever.

Deeside was in many respects cut off from the rest of the
world and changes came slowly.

In the Middle Ages there were two classes of people here,
- powerful Highand Lairds and poor overworked peasants. The
Lairds were generally a law unto themselves, often defying
even the power of the King. But in the 15th century the use of
gunpowder and firearms meant that no castle was impregnable.
Armour that had withstood arrows was no match for bullets.
Once the printing press had been invented ideas could be
disseminated. By the end of the 15th century men were
exploring their world and bringing home new ideas and new
goods. Religion began to be questioned. The King was still
ruling as he pleased - as far as unruly barons permitted.

COUNTRY LIFE

"Work is the conquest of the environment for the present needs"

Grenville Macdonald

Life on Deeside changed very little from Stuart times to the middle of the nineteenth century, but when life did change, it changed fairly rapidly. For hundreds of years life was a struggle, with poor harvests, famine, stones and bog. Folk were born into that type of life, their expectations were low but in spite of difficulties they lived full lives, with their joys and sorrows shared.

LITTLE COMMUNITIES

People lived in little communities, - collections of cottowns, made up of anything from four to a dozen dwellings in a group, some with a barn or byre. There was no attempt at orderly lay out, but the settlement was generally near a source of water, possibly some grazing, and perhaps some flat reasonably fertile land for a little cultivation. Because of these requirements, the place was often beautifully sited although remote. Every house had its kailyard to grow some kale and cabbage and perhaps some greens for family use, including syboes (spring onions), although in the early days there were few vegetables. Near the dwellings was often a bourtree (elder) and a rowan or mountain ash, to keep away the witches and to enable folk to put crosses above the barn door on Hallowe'en.

As well as those who worked for the Laird or for the local farmer there were in the little settlements artisans like the miller, weaver or wabster, carpenter, tailor, cooper, pewterer and horner and sometimes a tinker. Later there was a blacksmith and a shoemaker, although shoemakers were at first un-necessary. People went barefoot in summer or wore untanned leather or skin of their own fashioning.

The miller was an important man in the economy. There

were many mills in the Glens. By an Act of Parliament in 1284 querns were to be superseded by water-driven mills. Everyone was "thirled" to their mill, forming the "sucken". There was no choice. Grain had to be ground there and the mill multure paid. Both laird and miller gained. In actual fact, some querns were still in use in Glen Muick down to the end of the 18th century, - on the quiet, unknown to the laird or the nmiller. When needed, a new mill-stone had to be tramsported - a risky business. It was sometimes trundled on its edge, with a long pole through the hole in the middle and men to steady it. A wooden frame was built over it and the whole thing was pulled by a team of horses or oxen. Considering the state of the roads, it was a long and dangerous job, especially if the stone had to be brought from Aberdeen. Going down hill was certainly hazardous. A Kirk record tells of a stone being dragged on a sledge and the unfortunate "escort" being killed. A further inconvenience was the clearing of the mill-lade, particularly at times of hard frost. The miller was often disliked - because he had to be paid, often in kind.

The miller's job explains itself, as does the weaver's. The carpenter made household furniture and did various repair jobs around the farm. A 'stan' o' shapit claes' usually required a tailor although many cottars could not afford such things. He worked in customer's homes, staying until the job was finished. That was how the local gossip got round the glens. The cooper made cogs, wheels, ladles, utensils. The pewterer made items from pewter like plates, mugs and containers. A great deal of his trade was outwith his local community. The horner was closely allied to the tinker, but probably more 'respectable'. He made plates and spoons, the latter by cutting and partly dressing horn, heating it to make it pliable, and moulding it on a wooden 'caum' to shape it. Tinker families followed in the same occupation for generations. Tinker 'cairds' were wanderers, often homeless, unlettered, but with considerable technical knowledge. They mended pots and pans. They were talkative, usually respectful, loved music and dancing and whisky. In the hamlet there was sometimes a packman or chapman. He was in effect a travelling merchant with a pack, and frequently such men had more ready cash than most farmers. He supplied goods and accessories not readily made at home or in the glens.

Every farm had its 'cottown' or 'fairm toun' where the farm servants lived. They sometimes kept a cow or a few sheep and farmed their little bit of land, but most of their time was spent working for the farmer.

A working day was long with a 5 a.m. starting time to thresh grain. Breakfast (referred to as pottage) around 5.30 a.m. was brose and milk and oatcakes without limit. At mid-day, or just before, dinner (lunch or sowens) consisted of vegetable or kail broth, and when potatoes became available, chappit tatties or sometimes stovies. Salmon (complaints if it was served too often) was available, but little meat. There was plenty of milk. Supper was brose with milk or whey, with cabbage, kale or turnip or nettles (mugworts). Once again, there was a plentiful supply of oatcakes and home brewed ale. The malt had been dried with peat or turf so that the ale had a pungent taste and was probably not particularly appetising. Sunday food was often special, with a treat of tea to drink and butter with the oatcakes. For an extra special treat, there might even have been herring. There was very little bread made of flour. Those who lived in a bothy made their own meals, usually little more than brose. On Sunday they pooled resources and got the kitchen 'deem' to cook a meal.

Clocks and watches were rare until the end of the 18th century. Light and dark governed activities. Sometimes there were fir 'caunles'- sticks of pine containing roset or resin that gave light when essential and the pith of a rush supplied the wick for the cruisie of oil, but firelight usually sufficed. Matches could be bought from the packman. Early rising and early to bed was the usual habit.

After 1725 there was an increase in tax on the grain used for brewing ale, so it became less popular and whisky took its place. To make ends meet many households resorted to 'smuggling'. This meant distilling and delivering illicit whisky.

Ponies transported the liquid to the south. It was considered a duty, and even honourable, to outwit the gauger. Smuggling was part of the life of the Glens. Stills were numerous, carefully concealed. Smuggling on Deeside was supposedly suppressed - officially, at least, during the 1820's.

MONEY

Estate records of wages and prices given in the equivalent of £s Sterling are interesting. Men could earn £2 - £2.10s. per annum, women £1 - £1.5s. Masons were on day wages, 6d. -8d. as were wrights (carpenters). Day-labourers and tailors earned 3d -4d per day.

A horse cost 60/- to 70/-, a cow 30/- to 40/-, a sheep 5/- to 6/-. Surprisingly pigs were cheap at 6d.-8d. Pork was never popular here and my Granny and Great-Granny would never touch it. A hen cost the same, with a duck 1d. cheaper and a goose three or four pence dearer than a pig. Of course items of food etc. had to be balanced against these prices. A loaf cost $^1/_2$d. A chicken was 2d., the same price as 1lb of beef. Milk was $1^1/_2$d per pint as were 14 eggs. Ale was 1d. per pint and a load of peats 6d.

Scots money was in use until about 1788 when a change was made to sterling. Folk did not like change and tended to go their own way. Scots money was one twelfth of the value of sterling. A doyt or Scots penny was $^1/_{12}$th of the value of 1d. Two pennies were a bodle or $^1/_6$th of 1d. sterling. Two boodles were a plak worth $^1/_3$rd of 1d: 3 bodles were a bawbee or $^1/_2$d. sterling. Two bawbees were 1/- or 1d. sterling. A silver merk was 13/4 or 1/1 sterling. 20/- Scots was about 6p in modern money.

Most Scots names for coins were derived from the French. A bodle was named after a coiner called Bothwell, although its alternative name was a turner, after a place called Turnois. Bawbee was from bullion or base bullion, plack was a plaque and a groat took its name from gros.

AMUSEMENTS

The traditional religious holidays were not those we keep. There were Fast Days and Preparation for Communion and then the Thanksgiving Monday the day after the service. Christmas was not kept as a holiday period but the three days around the New Year were. Whenever possible people returned to parents or the home of their youth, usually on the middle day of the three day period.

Cockfighting was very popular. There was always a cockfight on Fastern's Eve (Shrovetide, the night before Ash Wednesday and the beginning of Lent). Children had a holiday and the schoolmaster supplemented his income by getting carcasses and 'fugies' - those birds that would not fight. There was an annual football match, a free for all like some traditional 'Uppies and Downies'. On this occasion it seems to have been contained by the field and the river. There was always a three-day holiday period at Yule, so the match was held then. The weather of course could not be guaranteed. There seems to have been have been little provision for refereeing.

Wrestling was another popular sport. There was also 'wad' shooting with a single barrelled flint-lock musket and pellets, the wad being the prize. Whether this was money or goods is unknown, but it is very likely to have been the latter. Bullets were made by the competitors, of molten lead in a 'camb' and were frequently not of the correct bore and the amount of powder was just a guess. An entry fee was taken, a bonnet was put on the dyke as a rest, and the target, 100 yards away, was aimed at. It was an old door with black and white rings. Markers stood at least 50 yards away, probably a very necessary precaution, because one year a spectator received a free gift, - some shot in his rear. Wad shooting went on all day. Only one or two competitors ever got close to the bull's eye.

Entertainment was 'home produced'. There was dancing on the grass or in a barn, to pipe or fiddle; ceilidhs; ball games; racing; tossing a 'caber'; throwing a weight; wrestling.

110

Fairs were a great attraction. They had started in the Middle Ages under the jurisdiction of the monks, and permission had been granted by King or overlord to burghs of barony to hold a fair and some markets. Details of the coming attraction were announced on the church door. The Church was the centre of all activity. A local expression about something known by all and sundry was 'like a cried fair'. There were always fights or athletic competitions at the close of the fair - and problems for the Kirk Session to deal with illegitimate children nine months later! A well-known fair was held at Clachenturn and another at Tullich.

At the fair there was livestock, - cattle, horses, sheep: household furniture (chairs, stools): kitchen equipment like ladles, cups, 'bowies', creels shown by coopers and ploughs and harrows by ploughwrights. There was wool spun into yarn at home and converted into webs of 'fingrams' by the weaver. Merchants bought these webs and sold them in town or abroad. There were knitted socks. There was moleskin for trousers, and bed ticking was available. Chap-book literature could be had, as well as 'carvy' (sweets with caraway seed) and coriander sweeties for young men to treat their girls. There were shows and amusements, pipers and dancing, and 'slicht o' han' men' (magicians). Almost anything could be found. Refreshments were served and home brewed ale consumed in quantity. Men wore their home-spun, women their 'braws' (best clothes, if they had any), and mutches (shawls).

There was no 'Social Security'. 'Gangrel bodies' - often women whose husbands had died in continental wars, - travelled the country, peddling wares from farm to farm, staying in an area for a week or so at a time.

The weekly newspaper, the Aberdeen Journal, cost 3d, including the 2d tax stamp. Five or six families joined and had a day each. The largest contributor, usually the farmer, got day one. The last man kept the paper and copies were shared out half-yearly. In 1876 the paper became a daily.

HYGIENE

Baths were late in coming to the area. A wash in cold or hot water had to suffice, or a dip in the river. Teeth were rubbed with mint to freshen the mouth and twigs could make tooth-picks. Toilets were certainly not convenient - a bucket on top of a box with a hole, some distance from the house. A number of families shared at first. Sometimes a hut was built around the 'box'. Better off families had their own facilities.

DOMESTIC INDUSTRY

'Domestic industry' was vitally important. Aberdeen merchants sold the work of the women in the city or abroad, usually to the Dutch. Stockings, of a rough or 'tarred' wool were made throughout the 17th and 18th centuries. A woman could make 2/- to 2/6 every week, and it always helped to pay the rent. Some women were experts at knitting, producing stockings in plain knit, ribbed or in squares, to please the Dutch. These stockings sold at 1/- to 1gn per pair, with the very fine ones for the gentry selling at 5 gns. A pair like that could take three or four month's work. Such stockings were knitted on exceptionally fine brass needles that cost up to £4 sterling, but these were provided by the merchant, on a loan basis for particular jobs. Unfortunately, the Dutch market collapsed.

Wool was a very marketable commodity, both in the cities and abroad. Obviously family requirements had to be met before the surplus was sold. Wool was cleaned and spun at home then often made into 'hodden grey' by the local weaver. People had few clothes. Men wore the coarse woollen homespun, tailor or home made, and often, if poor, little underwear. A bonnet was usually worn. Both men and women wore plaids. Ordinary folk and children went barefoot.

Women also spun flax for the merchant, and blue or tartan webs of their own cloth sold at 2/- to 2/6 an ell. An ell was 37 inches. The women spun at home then the yarn went to the weaver. Plant and vegetable dyes were used to enliven the cloth. There were laws to maintain standards. It seems one subterfuge was to thicken cloth with batter to hide faults and variation in thickness of thread. Authorised stampers used the initials of the district when they checked production.

The coming of power-driven machinery put an end to the cottage industry so a supplementary income was lost to the people of the Glens. By 1870 there were no more home produced goods.

FARMING

The feudal system had produced two grades of agricultural worker, - cottars who lived in cot towns and rented anything up to 9 acres of land, and farmers or husbandi. These latter rented a husbandland, made up of two oxgates (13 acres) so their holding was 26 acres. Usually 4 men formed a 'commune' with a holding of a ploughgate, -104 acres to farm. Disputes, personal and over land, were in early times settled by an arbiter, a 'birley man'. "Birley Crofts" - the name for their dwellings, still exist on Deeside.

The land the folk had to cultivate had many stones and much bog. Proper rotation of crops was introduced very late. The land had been used so much, without manure or general husbandry that it was exhausted and produced poor crops. Tillage was as for previous generations. The soil was worn out.

POOR WEATHER

There were years of dearth. 1693 to 1700 were 7 years of bad seasons, known as 'King William's Dear Years'. Summer and winter were cold. There were no insects and even clegs had died off. Shearing was in November and December and some even in January and February with the result that sheep died from frostbite after shearing. Crops rotted in the ground. Many people died as a result of the famine and there were problems with burials. Folk in the Glens were desperate.

Farms were deserted, so some owners converted them to sheep runs. 1740 was another scarce year. There was frost, snow in early spring and a bad summer. Day labourers were prepared to take 1d per day, to do any job. There was an exodus of men to the city, to the army and overseas.

Further bad winters meant tenant farmers were impoverished. Sometimes the laird stocked the farm - cattle, implements, etc, and the tenant had to return articles equal in quality and quantity at the end of the lease. This arrangement was called 'steelbow'. Farmers' holdings were extended by joining adjacent farms, and some arable land was allowed to go back to nature.

1782 also saw a late harvest, the worst on record, followed by a really hard frost. Again there was famine! The Government released peasemeal at a reduced price then the Kirk Session uplifted £24 that was at interest and bought some peasmeal. There are records showing that Invercauld bought supplies and gave them to his tenants. Many crofts were abandoned, so it was in the interests of the Superior to encourage good tenants. Gradually leases longer than 19 years were granted. Once a farmer's tack or lease was put on a longer term basis, he was in a position to employ more farm servants for a term of work, - to 'fee' them.

No longer was it compulsory to use the laird's mill, paying for that as well as the dues to be paid to the miller. 2% could be added to the rent. Millers had always been plentiful and in the first 30 or 40 years of the 19th century many "out of work" millers left for the colonies. A form of 'Clearance' had already started and numbers moved away because they could no longer exist at home.

In the early days, wages were paid not in money but in kind. The end of the 18th century saw an improvement in standards generally - standards of living, of diet, and of wages.

PLOUGHING

Cultivation with ploughs drawn by animals had been going on since the Bronze Age. Ground was generally ploughed with a twelve oxen plough. If the plough encountered a big stone, the ploughman was easily upturned or the plough smashed.

The timber 'twal ousen' plough was often in joint ownership but each of four men had to provide three oxen to pull it. Harness for the oxen was of rushes or straw, twisted together, or sometimes of woven material. Besides the man guiding the plough a man or boy often had the job of keeping the plough from getting choked with weeds, roots or stones and he had to adjust the cut when necessary by leaning on the beam. The gadsman or gaudsman would go up and down the team urging on the oxen with a whip or generally prodding them with a stick. At the head of the team, often walking backwards, was a man or boy to lead the beasts. The ploughman was often expected to whistle a psalm tune to the oxen. S shaped furrows were produced because it was difficult to turn oxen without making a wide sweep. These furrows can still be seen. The best oxen for the ploughing job were 6 or 7 years old. This type of ploughing was in general use in the area as late as 1884, when oxen were superseded by horses.

The 'villagers' shared land, so it was divided into sections known as rigs. Between them were never cultivated baulks, harbouring all types of weed. Rigs were in all parts of the farm so each man had some good and some bad land. Frequent re-allocation killed the initiative to improve the land. Known as run-rig farming, it was anything but satisfactory.

LAND MEASURES

The old land measures were based on ploughing. An oxgate was 13 acres, considered to be as much as oxen could plough in a day. Two oxgates or 26 acres was a husbandland. Four husbandlands (104 acres) made a ploughgate while four ploughgates made a davoc of 416 acres, the basis on which medieval military service for knights was calculated. A Scots acre was 6150.5 square yards

INFIELD & OUTFIELD

Attempts at farming were made difficult by large stones that had to be cleared and by lack of drainage. As in medieval times there was an Infield and an Outfield. The Infield, nearest to the farm, covered as much as a fifth of the land and was cultivated annually. Two thirds produced oats, the rest an inferior barley or bere. One part was manured each year. The yield was poor. In the Outfield were faughs and folds, each split into ten. Every year a divot dyke was built around one part of the fold, to retain animals grazing. So each bit had some manure every ten years. For five years after manuring, oats were grown, then grass for five years. Faughs never had any manure. The crops were often too poor to harvest and too full of weeds for animal food. In fact by the end of the 18th century, agriculture was in a period of stagnation. When duties due to the Laird had been performed, - (carting for him was in force as late as 1866), helping to repair the church and later the school, little time was left.

ANIMALS

The land was really better suited to sheep than to cattle, but in the early days small black cattle were raised and sold at southern 'trysts.' There was no provision for either breed during snow: no hay or straw: no enclosures to shelter from the

116

cold spring winds. As there was no good hay, and turnips were late in being introduced, boiled chaff and bruised whins (gorse) were the usual cattle food. Many beasts had to be killed off in November and the meat salted. Beasts that did over- winter were often so weak that they had to be carried out to pasture in spring. These small beasts went south via the Spittal and Glen Clova which was the route by which other cattle from more prosperous areas went to the trysts.

After the Act of Union in 1707 there was an impetus to trade with England. At first grazing stances on the way down were free but an account of 1723 speaks of the free grazing on the way down being gradually stopped, so Falkirk took over from Crieff as the market centre. Droving was difficult. There were no fences and few bridges. Drove roads were usually grass tracks with water available. If hard roads had to be covered for any distance metal plates were nailed on feet, but injury was frequent when cows were on their backs. 10 miles per day was the distance aimed at. Before Ballater existed as a village there was a Stance by the river. To avoid paying bridge tolls, cattle were taken across rivers at fords. Once over the Dee, a Mounth Pass was used. Droving was still going on until around 1830. Cattle gradually improved in size and quality and demand for butcher meat increased. Turnips were used for cattle food and by 1810 the weight of the beasts had doubled.

Cattle thieving was a real problem from early times. The stories of the Glenesk men and the burials at Glenmuick Kirk and the lifting of cattle in the Ballad of Braickley are true to life. A company of men was formed in 1724 to deal with the problem. They wore a black tartan, Reiendan Dhu, - the Black Watch. In 1735 they became a regiment in the British Army and were sent abroad. Significantly, cattle lifting increased.

Sometimes cattle pulled farm implements before being slaughtered. Humlies were small, black cattle and had no horns. They lacked stamina and only the very poor used them for ploughing. The long-horned breed was more successful. The problem was that there was not enough food for oxen, for even the ordinary black cattle had not sufficient. In spring the pasture was poor, so the cows and oxen were in May or June sent off to the hill grazing, coming home in September, the latter ready for work. There was a great deal of movement by men, women and children. The migration of livestock and people to summer grazing is known as transhumance. This annual movement of stock to the richer hill grass had been going on since the 15th century. Grassland at lower levels was given a chance to improve. Everyone looked forward to the annual 'migration' to the hills. Life was simpler and friendships could be renewed.

Small native breeds of sheep were reared, then blackfaced sheep were introduced towards the end of the 17th century as the most likely breed to survive. Cheviots appeared, in no great numbers, after 1791.

IMPROVEMENTS IN FARMING

At the beginning of the eighteenth century farming was still being carried on in the same way that had been done for centuries. Implements were poor, land was not well manured or even drained, weeds were rife, stones were everywhere, little of the land was enclosed and old methods like the run-rig system were still in use. There was little knowledge of the proper rotation of crops, the old Infield and Outfield system still being used. Improvements needed money and few farmers had any. There was too all over the area an inbuilt resistance to change that seems to be part of the local character.

When farming improvements eventually came, bigger farmers employed landless men and their families as full time farm workers. As a result, tenant farmers became a special class, fairly well off. Staff were engaged at the feeing markets. There were many skilled cattle men available. A good byre woman was a great asset: she could earn as much as a ploughman.

Living conditions for staff could be primitive. The chaumer (chamber) was often a rough hut with a damp floor and no fireplace. Planks led to a bed. On the other hand, some accommodation was good. 'Feed' men were often in the stable loft above the stock. It may have been warm but there were rats in the straw.

However, there were some landowners making improvements, particularly Sir Archibald Grant of Monymusk. He made roads and planted trees to shelter his fields. He, like others, tried out crop rotation and planted clover and turnips for cattle food. Some enclosing of fields was started by various lairds. Other improvers were James Farquharson of Invercauld and the Earl of Aboyne who built miles of stone dykes.

Vast acreages of land were held by a number of Lairds and they usually had their residences at the centre. These had been built up over centuries by inheritance, wise marriages and purchase, particularly from the Commissioners of Forfeited Estates after 1745. The Earl of Fife in this way acquired Dalmore (Mar Lodge) and Braemar. In the 19th century deer forests of Upper Deeeside and the fishing on the Dee became fashionable for patrons from the south. Prince Albert improved Balmoral. Glentanar estate owes its improvement to Sir William Cunliffe Brooks who had an individual style.

'Improvements' had all been tried in England as well as in the south of Scotland. To teach farmers new methods 'Improving' Societies were formed. They gave grants to farmers to grow clover and ryegrass but the local farmers were slow to take up the offers. However, in some places the infield and outfield were done away with and clover, ryegrass and turnips grown. The three year rotation of oats, oats, barley was changed to a seven year rotation, with peas, barley, grass, grass, grass, oats, oats. Later turnips made an eighth year rotation. Agricultural production increased but many tenant farmers were displaced when farms were amalgamated.

In some parts of Scotland the quarrying and burning of lime as a fertiliser began in the 17th century, but generally it was after the middle of the eighteenth century before farmers in the area had begun to use lime in any quantity. It is surprising how many lime quarries there were. Cartage was often a problem as only small amounts could be carried in creels. Lime kilns were usually free standing stone structures.

Changes may have started but they were slow to take hold. At the close of the eighteenth century the area was still very backward as far as farming was concerned. The old fashioned ways continued with old fashioned implements. Only a few horses were used for harrowing and carting. Skill was lacking so frequently an experienced ploughman had to be brought in from another area.

Carts had wooden wheels. They were small and unable to carry a big load. Time was short too, for some unpaid work was still done for the Lairds.

Improvements in farming really came in the nineteenth century. Land was drained and enclosed, the infield and outfield were no longer used, stones were cleared, the runrig system was abandoned and implements were improved. Most of the work was done by tenant farmers. By 1875 the cultivated area had doubled. Turnips, clover, ryegrass and potatoes were grown. A six year crop rotation was common, with more turnips and sown grasses.

Eventually most of the ploughing was with horses, with an improved type of plough.

At the beginning of the nineteenth century the sickle was still used for harvesting but it was superseded by the scythe. The sickle had been used by women but men now used the scythe while the women gathered in the cut crop. Threshing with a flail continued on the 'sheeling' hill, until the beginning of the 19th century and on many farms it was used for another 100 years. Eventually threshing mills and engines went from farm to farm, pulled by horses.

Beside a river, mills were driven by a water wheel. If no water was available the mill could be driven by a horse, or oxen, walking continuously in a circle to turn the wheel.

More use was made of farmyard manure. Lime was used in quantities. Some farmers burned the lime in kilns then spread it. Powdered bone as a fertiliser increased turnip yield. Guano from Chile and nitrate of soda were fairly general but not much used in the area. Because food stuff improved, cattle improved and Aberdeen Angus and Shorthorns were bred solely for beef. Such cattle could not walk to trysts so droving stopped. Transport by sea or rail became available.

Around 1840 the average rent of arable land was £1 a Scots acre. Some farms were of 20 to 50 acres, but a good many were crofts of up to 15 acres. The smaller the farm, the higher the rent, for there was demand from farm servants who had saved enough to rent and stock a small-holding.

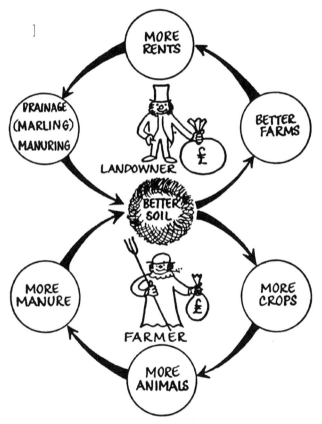

Farming Improvements

XVI. WARS & RUMOURS OF WAR

CIVIL WAR & COVENANTERS

When Scotland became Presbyterian it was organised without Bishops, with Christ at the head of the church, not the king. James VI, with an eye on the throne of England, liked the idea of Episcopalianism. By the Black Acts in 1584 he declared himself head of the Church and insisted the General Assembly only met at his summons. Eight years later he relaxed the position.

In spite of everything, and Scotland being officially a Presbyterian country, this was not so in practice in all of Aberdeenshire, particularly in Tullich and Glengairn. There were plots and counter plots until in 1597 the Catholic Earls of Huntly, Erroll and Angus publically accepted the new faith.

Before going to London as King in 1603 James planned to introduce Episcopalianism and appointed 13 bishops. Penalties for attempting to hold a General Assembly were exile or imprisonment. James' son Charles I determined to make the Church in Scotland identical to the Episcopalian Church of England. A book known as Laud's Litergy was to be followed in services. When it was first used in St. Giles in Edinburgh there was uproar.

An agreement or Covenant was signed to stop Bishops controlling the church. Signees were known as Covenanters, opponents as Royalists. Copies for signing were distributed. Aberdeen was happy, with support from Church and University. Deeside was not and there was little interest, particularly from those on Huntly and Gordon estates.

Meanwhile, both sides got ready for war as the years went by.

THE BATTLE OF TULLICH, 1654

On a snowy day, the 10th February 1654, the long-bow was at Tullich used for the last time in a British battle.

Royalist forces supporting Charles II had occupied Kildrummy Castle and moved to the east end of the Pass of Ballater. Roundheads led by Col. Morgan came from Aberdeen. On the swampy ground below Tullich Lodge they lined up.

Royalists controlled the Pass so Morgan's men forced a fight on the northern slopes of Craigendarroch. Royalists were soundly beaten, with 120 killed and many captured. No stone commemorates the event.

Civil War had raged from 1639 to 1654 with varying success. After the Royalist defeat at Tullich in 1654 the end of the struggle came for Aberdeenshire but the support for the Stuarts and for the Old Faith was still strong and led eventually to the Jacobite Risings.

THE JACOBITES

James VII of Scotland and II of England tried to restore Catholicism and became so unpopular that he had to flee to France. The crown went to his sister Mary who was joint sovereign with her husband William. The Scottish Parliament accepted them as sovereigns but there was still support for James and the Stuarts. Support for Jacobites (from the Latin for James) was strong on Deeside.

During the summer of 1689 Bonnie Dundee (Graham of Claverhouse) was in Aboyne, collecting forces. William's forces were under General Mackay who ordered the Earl of Mar to garrison Braemar Castle to prevent the Jacobites from going south. The Earl died before carrying out the order, but the Jacobite 'Black Colonel', John Farquharson of Inverey burned it to prevent its use by Mackay's troops.

Dundee defeated the Royalists at Killiecrankie but was killed there, and soon afterwards, without his leadership, his men were defeated at Dunkeld.

James VII died in exile in 1701. His son was known as The Old Pretender. (French 'pretendre' means to claim). Attempts backed by France to put him on the throne were unsuccessful.

Queen Anne died in 1714, to be succeeded by a cousin George of Hanover. This had been arranged by the Act of Settlement in 1701, without the consent of the Scottish Parliament. Plans were made to replace George of Hanover by The Old Pretender, the Marquess of Huntly being in the lead. Bobbing Jock, Earl of Mar had varied his allegiance but finally supported the Jacobites. Summoning leading men to a tinchal or hunting party, the guest list included all leading Jacobites. Farquharson was forced to join his feudal Superior, against his will. In Glen Quoich they drank whisky from Mar's Punchbowl to the success of the Rising.

On 6th September the standard was raised in Braemar, although when the gold ball fell from the top superstitious Highlanders were worried. Forces gathered as the march south continued. Mar was no general. The Battle of Sheriffmuir was indecisive. The Old Pretender was too late in coming to Scotland. The opportunity had gone and the forces were disbanded.

The Jacobites were punished by execution, imprisonment, or by being sent overseas as slaves. Castleton of Braemar and part of Kildrummy Castle were burned. Jacobite Lairds' estates were sold.

An abortive attempt to return the Stuarts to the throne in 1719 was backed by Spanish soldiers. They were defeated in Glenshiel.

In 1745 the Old Pretender's son Prince Charles Edward Stuart raised his standard in Glenfinnan and collected an army, mostly Roman Catholic clansmen. They beat the Royalists under Sir John Cope at Prestonpans. There were various skirmishes. Prince Charles invaded England but support was disappointing. The forces reached Derby then returned north. They did win the Battle of Falkirk but continued their northwards withdrawal, followed by the Duke of Cumberland.

On 16th April 1746 the Jacobites were defeated at Culloden (Drumossie Moor.) No mercy was shown to the wounded.

It was made illegal to carry arms, wear the tartan or play the pipes. The clan system was abolished.

Houses and lands were burned and plundered. Owners 'lurked' or fled overseas. This was not new for the area. Over a long period Deeside had been involved in "military" action. The largest islet in Loch Kinord, probably partly artificial, was the site of a "castle", built, according to tradition, by Malcolm Canmore, while on another island there was a tollbooth (prison). Edward 1 and his army encamped twice on the Moor of Dinnet and the King is reputed to to have stayed at the island castle on the loch. After the Battle of Culblean Atholl's followers sought refuge there. James IV stayed for two nights in 1504. In 1647 it was captured by the Covenanters and a garrison stationed there. - a little Covenanting island among strongly Royalst landowners and tenants. Parliament passed an Act in 1648 ordering the fortifications to be "slighted." The demolition was well done. The wooden causeway was utilised in the construction of Ballater's Bridge in 1783.

Loch Davan too had its fortalice at the Ha' of Ruthven, and it too had been involved at the Battle of Culblean in 1335.

AN EIGHTEENTH CENTURY LETTER

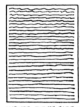

WRITE FIRST SIDE—
SMALL WRITING
CLOSE TOGETHER

WRITE SECOND SIDE
AND FILL IN
ADDRESS

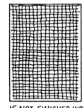

IF NOT FINISHED, WRITE
ACROSS ORIGINAL
WRITING ON FIRST SIDE.

FOLD INTO THREE
AND SEAL WITH
SEALING WAX.

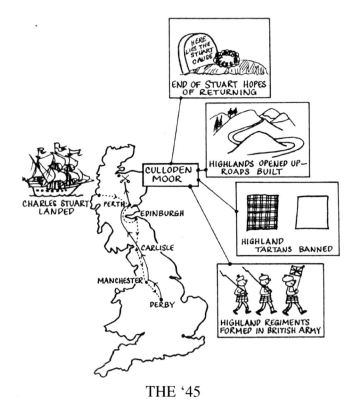

THE '45

XVII. CHANGES & DIFFERENT ATTITUDES, 18TH & 19TH CENTURIES

"We know what we are, but we know not what we may be"

Shakespeare

Before the end of the seventeenth century and the building of the Bridge in 1783, Ballater of course did not exist. Tullich was the civic and ecclesiastical centre of the area, the mother church of Glenmuick and Glengairn.

With the coming of the "Revolution" in 1688 there were great ecclesiastical changes. Presbyterianism was established. A manuscript, "Gideon Guthrie: A Memorial" deals with the period of the Revolution of 1688 and records the activities of the minister and his brother David at Glenmuick. It throws light on the unsettled state of the parish. There are constant references to "Highlanders", and "loose men", "two armies in the parish" and "the burning of McKay". So serious was the situation that the people were prevented from assembling for worship on a number of Sundays. The minister's brother David who often preached for him, was a rabid Episcopalian and a determined Jacobite. Ministers had to take an oath of allegiance and submit to Presbyterian rule. He would have no part in William and Presbyterianism. Gideon however, with a wife and family to consider, conformed to the requirements of the time.

When Gideon Guthrie died at the age of 39 years he was succeeded by the Rev. James Robertson with aristocratic connections and a taste for Episcopacy. During his period of office he managed to have necessary repairs made to the Bridge of Muick and he petitioned the General Assembly as early as 1726 to authorise a collection throughout Scotland to raise money to build a bridge at Ballater. Success was not achieved until 1783. The '15 Rising, origination in Braemar, caused some trouble in the area. The minister refused to read "Rebellious Proclamations" and offered prayers of thanksgiving after Culloden. The Rev. James Robertson died in 1748 after 49 years as minister. Surprisingly, there seem to be no records for the second half of his ministry.

The new minister, the Rev. William McKenzie, was opposed at first but was soon accepted. He seems to have been somewhat lax in attending to his duties and was very much a law unto himself. The moral life of the community seems to have improved about this time but it had its down side. Penalties decreased so there was little money to support the poor. By 1784 so many people were starving as a result of harvests ruined by frost and snow that the Session withdrew money to buy peasmeal. At this time too, perhaps because people were poor but had not the courage to pass the collection plate, a great deal of counterfeit and foreign coins appeared in the church collection. To avoid re-circulation, it was sent to the Infirmary in Aberdeen. The minister died in 1790, after serving for 42 years.

Prior to this, old Elspet Michie had discovered the beneficial properties of Pannanich Wells water and when Francis Farquharson returned from house arrest in England following the '45, the wells were developed.

The admission of the next minister was disputed because of his lack of the Gaelic. The people of the three parishes were not prime movers. The Heritors, Invercauld & Monaltrie - and the Presbytery member, the Crathie minister, Invercauld's Factor, were at fault. A personal quarrel with the other Heritor, Lord Aboyne, was involved because he had not consulted them. It appears from evidence presented that people, particularly Glengairn Gaelic speakers, understood and spoke English.

Braemar was of long standing, as the original "home base" of the Earls of Mar, then as the Invercauld "village" but apart from Jacobite activity and proximity to passages to the south and north, for armies as well as for others, it was a quiet little village.

Aboyne was originally Bonty until the Earl of Aboyne created a new village, named after himself, Charleston of

Aboyne.

Dinnet, with a scattering of dwellings, did not achieve any importance until the coming of the railway.

Upper Deeside was still a backwater by the beginning of the 19th century.

Although families were generally large, not all children survived. Infant death was common. Tuberculosis ravaged the ranks of teenagers. Women often died in childbirth and the man married again, to raise a second family.

The naming of a child was of pre-Christian origin, but even to modern times an unbaptised child was considered to be a heathen and could not be buried in consecrated ground. If the kirk or minister were too far away, the weather was harsh or the baby was delicate, a howdie or midwife carried out a baptism with three drops of water. It was usual to name the first baby after paternal grandparents, the next after maternal and the remainder had family names or names of the laird or a particular friend. The birth was not always a happy occasion for mothers frequently died of puerpal fever. Normally baptism took place in the church or the manse. As long ago as 1690 the General Assembly had decreed that baptism should be at public worship, in front of the congregation, but this was often ignored.

Perhaps the most interesting event for the area was the building, at the end of the eighteenth & the beginning of the nineteenth century of the Centrical Church to replace dilapidated buildings at Tullich, Foot of Gairn and Glenmuick. It was to be the focus of all new development in the village. That was well on the way when the Bridge was swept away by flood and there was no bridge until 1809. It too was washed away in 1829, in the Muckle Spate, to be replaced by a wooden bridge that was demolished in 1835 on completion of the present structure.

By May 1817 the 51 year old Rev.Hugh Burgess was minister - assistant to Mr.Brown. A bachelor, he was said to be kind-hearted but stern when necessary. This was a period of expansion in Ballater. In 1800 there had been only a couple of houses. Building went on steadily for by 1822 Ballater was a village with a Savings Bank (probably in advance of its time for in 1842 there were only 50 depositors).

By 1817 postal services had been transferred to Ballater from Tullich, the old ecclesiastical and trade centre of the district.

By 1845 a new official, Inspector of the Poor had been appointed and he relieved the Session of the distribution of the "Poore's Money".

The Rev. Hugh Burgess was succeeded by the Rev. John Middleton who began a ministry of 35 peaceful years. The outstanding event in his ministry was the removal of the Centrical Church and the erection of the present building

An early sketch of Ballater

XVIII. TRAVEL & TRANSPORT

PASSES OVER THE MOUNTH

In early times Deeside was isolated and little frequented. The Grampians formed a natural barrier and the routes across were from earliest times of vital importance. With modern means of communication there is little difficulty, but in times gone by there was a considerable problem. The 'Water Poet' John Taylor had visited but it was not until Queen Victoria came in 1848 that Deeside became well known.

The Mounth routes were the principal lines of communication between the Highlands and the south. There were originally thirteen passes but weather conditions made some impassable. Eight passes were really important and of these five are situated in Upper Deeside. Mounth is an English translation of the Gaelic monadh (pronounced mon-a) and means a moor, heath, or range of hills, not necessarily a pass. "The View of the Diocese of Aberdeen" written about 1732, uses the manuscript of Sir James Balfour of Denmilne to list all the Mounth routes. According to purists, Cairn o' Mounth is incorrect.

Three passes are now in regular use by vehicles, - the Cairnwell from Perthshire to Braemar via Glenshee, the Cairn a'Mounth from Fettercairn to Kincardine o'Neil and the Elsick Mounth from Stonehaven to Drum.

The Causey Mounth to Aberdeen by way of Banchory Devenick, the Fir Mounth from Edzell to Mill of Dinnet, the Capel Mounth from Clova to Glen Muick and the Tolmounth from Angus to Braemar by Loch Callater were all regularly used by those on foot or horseback. The Fir Mounth led from Edzell to Glen Tanar. The road crosses the Tanar by a single arch (military) bridge. A branch went to the Dee, crossing at Aboyne while another went right to cross the Dee at Glen Tanar Church. The main road crossed the river by ferry or ford slightly to the west. The Roman legions used the Elsick coast road to keep contact with their ships and armies and also used the others at various times.

The highest of the routes over the Mounth was the Mount Keen route from Innermarkie to Canakyle (ceann-na-coille), Woodend or Deecastle on Deeside. This was a route used by thravers or harvesters who went south for the season.

The Capel Mounth linked Clova to Glen Muick. Capel was an indication that once there had been a chapel there. The Bishops of Aberdeen established a hospice at Spital of Muick and it would have had its attached chapel. Remains can still be identified. This too was a thravers or harvesters route.

The Tolmounth route led from the Cairnwell road in Glen Clunie into Angus. It too was an old droving road. The Cairnwell from Perthshire went by Glenshe to Braemar, then to the uplands of Aberdeenshire and the north. "The View of the Diocese of Aberdeen" records 'there was an Hospitall at Carnwall called Shean-Spittal or Old Hospital'. It became of great importance when the road became a military road.

The section from the Cairnwell to Braemar was reconstructed in 1864 when the Clunie Bridge at Braemar was rebuilt. These were the main lines of communication between Highlands and Lowlands and where they crossed the river, fords, ferries and eventually bridges were to be found, and larger settlements grew up.

Historically the most important of the Mounth passes is the Cairn a' Mounth - the B974. In 1057 Macbeth came north by way of it and in 1296 Edward I marched south.

FORDS & FERRIES

Where the Mounth routes crossed a river, there was a ford. At one time there were over 30 fords over the Dee but the important ones were those near the Mounth passes. The Ruthrieston ford near Aberdeeen was important for the Causey Mounth, Tilbouries for the Elsick Mounth, Kincardine o' Neil for the Cairn a'Mounth, Mill of Dinnet for the Fir Mounth, Tullich for the Capel Mounth and the ford near Braemar Castle covered both the Tolmounth and the Cairnwell.

There was a ford east of Braemar Castle and to the west, Inverchandlick, where there were also stepping-stones. Braemar had another ford at Mill of Coull and there were fords at Ardearg, Dalmore and Delavora.

Dalmochie is an example of the importance of river crossings in the district. East of modern Ballater, a road on the line of the present one ran along the edge of the fields past the present Aberdeen Cottage. A field to the north west was named Cobletoun Park and this connected with the ferry over the Dee. The Cobeltoun of Tullich was near a house occupied at one time by a man called Smith and was opposite to Cobeltoun of Dalmuickeachie on the opposite side of the Dee. There are some granite blocks near Aberdeen Cottage that may have been where the ferry 'docked'. Since the time of the ferry crossing from Cobeltoun to Dalmuickeachie the river Dee has meandered considerably. There are traces of an abandoned settlement, date uncertain, According to old records, the spelling was Dalmuickeachie, meaning the meadow of the pig field. When one remembers that Glen Muick was the glen of wild pigs and that acorns, food for pigs, were available from the Hill of Oaks or Craigendarroch, it seems likely.

The name Dalmuickeachie (Dalmochie) continued in use until the ferry ceased to be used about 1890.

Near many of the fords were ferries. These were not entirely satisfactory because they suffered from the vagaries of the weather and spates so eventually bridges were a better option.

The important ferries for Upper Deeside were the Inchbare Boat at Potarch, in use until 1814: the Kincardine o'Neil Ferry; Waterside Ferry to the east of the present Aboyne Bridge with the associated Boat Inn; the Boat of Ferrar west of Aboyne; the Kirk Ferry at the old church of Glentanar; the Dinnet ferry below the present bridge; Cambus o'May ferry used until about 1903; the boat of Dalmuickeachie at Tullich; Abergeldie, out of use since 1891; the Polhollick ferry, used until around 1892 when the foot-bridge was erected. The boat of Crathie. west of Balmoral Castle was the Boat of Monaltrie and a ford. The boathouse stood near the mouth of the burn, but it was eventually demolished.

In 1564 a Mar charter referred to a croft, called "the cowbill (cobble) croft" which had attached to it the boat of Castletown. (Braemar). There was a right of way from west of the kirkyard to the ferry. The ferry became a private one, for estate use, and was moved about 25 yards down stream. Invercauld Estate and Mar Lodge also had ferries for estate and family usage.

In all these locations, some stones from a little pier or a flat stone for passengers to stand on can be located - with a bit of a search!

BRIDGES

Fords and ferries had their uses but they were often out of commission because of high water. Bridges were necessary but they were costly.

Bridges played an important part in transport development. The first bridge over the Dee was a wooden one, erected in the thirteenth century by Thomas the Durward (Door-ward) at Kincardine o'Neil.

ABERGELDIE CRADLE & BRIDGE
(OS 287953)

Many years ago there were two hamlets of considerable size, Torgalter and Greystone, between Crathie and Braemar, on the other side of the Dee from Abergeldie Castle. Both had a miller, carpenter and weaver.

The ford at Abergeldie was an important crossing for wheeled traffic. Michie in "Deeside Tales" suggests that this was the only ford for wheeled traffic between Braemar and Ballater. It does not appear to have been used in the 20th century.

About 1744 George Brown was born in Greystone. The

Brown family had for generations had a small portion of land there. In the hamlets there was little education, the mother usually teaching what little was learned, but even 9 or 10 year olds did not know the alphabet. George was different. He read avidly as a young boy, mostly the Scriptures, the Shorter Catechism, Bunyan's Pilgrim's Progress and one or two other books. At 17, he became a member of the Church at Crathie. The minister at the time was the Rev.Murdoch McLellan, the author of the poem about the Battle of Sheriffmuir in 1715. He wrote-:

"There's some say that we wan,
Some say that they wan,
Some say that nane wan at a' man:
But ae thing I'm sure,
That at Sheriffmuir
A battle there was, that I saw, man."

The minister let George read his books. In the district only the minister and the laird took a newspaper, or read it, but George read the minister's Aberdeen Journal from beginning to end. It was the time of the American War of Independence and he was keen to learn all he could about America. Mr.McLellan taught him Scottish History and Celtic legend and song. In 1830 all families spoke Gaelic. By 1850 most folk spoke English as well. By 1870 Gaelic was dying out. George usually recited in Gaelic. His company was sought by neighbours and he learned to communicate. He collected a great deal of Deeside lore and passed it on. He also wrote poetry. George had a reputation for high moral standards as well as intelligence.

George was a skilled weaver and had a comfortable home. Once a year he walked to Aberdeen to buy books. He stayed a week and stored up material for future reflection. One stormy night he was given shelter by a family in Culter, outside Aberdeen. He formed a close friendship with the family that lasted all his life.

George had a family of sons and daughters. One in particular, Barbara, was noted for her beauty and was usually called "The Flower of Deeside". She had many suitors, some of considerable social standing, including a high ranking army officer. Barbara, or Babby as she was called locally, decided to marry Peter Frankie, her senior by a number of years, but still reasonably young, with no children. He was smart, handsome and had a good job that at the time was considered a prize situation, - gamekeeper at Altanuisach.

Babby and Frankie were married in 1824. They stayed a few days at her father's house until the keeper's house at Altanuisach was renovated. Babby was very popular and she and Peter were invited to many houses. On a Sunday they were invited to the Smart's at Mains of Abergeldie. Early in the afternoon they left George's house and crossed the Dee. The only river crossing of the Dee between Crathie and Ballater was near Abergeldie Castle. It was a wooden 'cradle'. A strong cable was wound round a windlass on each bank. On it ran the cradle. This was just three narrow planks held by iron hoops, curved as in the rockers of a cradle. At each end was an upright, linked by a crossbar. Under it two grooved wheels ran along the cradle. The cradle could hold two or three people, and the whole contraption was usually worked by the Abergeldie gardener. When the couple made the crossing the water was high, but not in spate.

A pleasant visit over, the couple set out for George's. It seems something went wrong with the windlass and the rope broke. The passangers were thrown into the water. It was a dark night. People could be seen running along both banks with lanterns. The search continued for hours over a wide area. Old George was very distressed and spent over three hours searching that night. Finally the search was called off until daybreak. Next morning Babby's body was discovered in shallow water and recovered. It was a week later before Peter Frankie's body was discovered by John McRay. It was draped over a stone in the river, near Coilacreich. There was mourning over the whole area, Babby particularly being much missed.

There was an investigation, but no reason was discovered for the breaking of the cradle rope.

George Brown died in on 9th February 1828 and was buried in Crathie. No stone marks his grave.

A similar accident had happened many years before. There was smuggling of whisky in progress at Clachanturn on a night when the Dee was in spate, and a gauger (excise man) called Bruce was anxious to cross the river from Crathie. The Monaltrie cradle operator had insisted crossing was not safe, as did the Abergeldie operator. However, he was persuaded to go, or rather, was forced to go, for Excise men were authoritarian figures. They crossed safely, but after a search no smugglers were found. There were many places of concealment in the area. On the way back, a post snapped and both men were thrown into the water. Bruce was a good swimmer but the current was too strong for him and he was swept down stream. His body was not recovered for some weeks and then it was found about 6 miles down the Dee at Polcholaig (Polhollick). The cradleman was more fortunate. Although not a swimmer, he had managed to hang onto a rope and was swung into the bank, from where he was rescued, bruised but safe.

In 1885 the cradle was replaced by a foot bridge, to link the little village of Balmoral with the Crathie folk. It is now in a poor state of repair.

BALLATER'S BRIDGES
(OS 372956 inter alia)

At Dalmuickeachie, formerly called the "Kirke of Tilliche", according to the "View of the Diocese", there was a very important boat. Tullich ford was used for Pannanich. A 1676 charter to Charles, Earl of Aboyne, from Charles II refers to the coble-town and coble-croft of Tullich, at the ferry.

Ballater had its boat, but it was no longer necessary when the Bridge was built in 1783. However, it had a renewal of life for it had to be used again when successive bridges were destroyed. There was a ferry at Polhollick, but this ceased to be necessary when the foot bridge went up in 1892. The boat house is still a dwelling house and an oval stone structure used by the ferry remained at the south end of the bridge.

There have been four bridges in Ballater.

When Pannanich Wells developed and there was no bridge over the Dee, the ferry just could not cope. Bridges were important to the life of the area. They linked the drove roads as well as making life easier for the little communities.

The first abortive attempt to build a Ballater bridge in place of ford and ferry was in 1726. Money was requested locally and churches throughout the country were asked for help. The response was poor.

Another attempt was made in 1776 and with private subscriptions, a grant from Forfeited and Annexed Estates after the '45 and considerable help from the Feudal Superior, the bridge went up in 1783, about 100m. east of the present bridge. Constructed of granite, it cost £1700 and was described as 'beautiful and useful'. It had three middle arches and two side ones. It was swept away by flood on 30th August 1799.

Once the building of the bridge over the Dee was started in 1783 and the 'Centrical Church' erected on the bare moor, feus were granted for the land in 'Ballater' by Francis, then by William Farquharson of Monaltrie. The whole area by the Dee, known as Sluievannachie, (OS 361959) was covered with heather and broom and was a public resting place for droves of cattle on their way to southern markets. On the north west corner of the moor there was a ford for cattle to cross as they went in the direction of Mount Keen or the Capel Mounth.

Settlers took up the offer of feus. The need for a new village had become obvious when folk taking the waters at Pannanich required accommodation. Ballater developed slowly and it was not until the 1850's and 60's that the boom came. In 1840 Ballater had 271 residents: by 1871 the number had risen to 694, with 154 inhabited houses.

When Queen Victoria came to the throne in 1837, Ballater was still a little village, far from the madding crowd. When she died in 1901 it was a prosperous centre with a population of 1256, attracting visitors from all over Britain and even further afield.

The 1783 bridge was washed away in 1799. It was replaced in 1809 by a Telford granite bridge of five arches built by Simpson (one of the Caledonian Canal contractors) and costing £3,800. Half the money was raised by The Commissioners for Roads and Bridges and half had to be raised locally. Work began in 1807 but there was no accommodation for the 40 or 50 workmen so three or four houses had first to be built for them, probably in Dee Street. The foundation stone was laid by William Farquharson of Monaltrie and a plan is in Register House in Edinburgh in Latin, English & Gaelic. There were five arches, the middle one having a span of 60'. In spite of difficulties the bridge was finished earlier than expected. On 22nd September 1809 the Earl of Aboyne, Provincial Grand Master for Aberdeenshire, drove in the key-stone. The Freemasons marched from Pannanich Lodge - the old inn. Seven shots were discharged from canon on Craigendarroch. There was dinner at the Lodge and fireworks and dancing in the village. Approach roads were also made.

That bridge too went down the river in 1829, in the "Muckle Spate". This flood, ten years after Victoria's accession, caused much hardship in the village. Imagine the inconvenience for the Ballater residents when there was no bridge linking the north and south sides of the Dee! The "boat" was used, and in some places the Dee could be forded, but not when in spate.

The Muckle Spate of 1829 did a great deal of damage. Apart from the fact that the bridge was washed away, much property and stock was lost. Water is a violent force and we can only guess what distress the Muckle Spate of 1829 caused to the inhabitants of Ballater and district. There had been earlier spates in the area but the flood of 3rd & 4th of August 1829 was the most spectacular. May, June and July had been excessively hot and the aurora borealis seen frequently at night. The floods were caused by a very heavy downpour in the Cairngorms, resulting in spate on nine rivers.

As well as Ballater Bridge being destroyed an arch of

Invercauld Bridge was carried away. The Dee at Banchory rose 27' 4" while further up the valley the garden at Mar Lodge was swept away and mud deposited in the house. There were drownings in the Don and loss of good land there too. When the rain came, 1/6th of the annual rainfall fell in 24 hours. Animals and birds, especially game birds, perished.

The noise of Ballater's Bridge breaking up must have been fearsome and no doubt people living near to the river got away as fast as possible. Even so, property and livestock was to be found in Aberdeen harbour and the whole valley was devastated. A fish was said to be swimming in the plate rack at Cut-away Cottage

Sir Thomas Dick Lauder, 7th baronet of Fountainhall, Edinburgh, settled on his wife's property in Moray and there he saw the devastation at first hand. He wrote an account of it.

David Grant who was a six years old at the time of the Spate later wrote about it in verse as did David Rorie whose verses began:-.

> "The burn was big wi' spate
> An there cam' tum'lin doon
> Tapsalteerie the half o' a gate
> Wi' an auld fish-hake an'a great muckle skate
> An' a lum hat wantin' a croon".

About an acre of the minister's Glebe land by the Dee was washed away and it was necessary to strengthen the embankment. Some accounts survive to give an indication of rates of pay at the time. Charles Paterson who was probably the overseer, worked a 10 hour day for 2/- Others earned about 1/6. Four women also worked for 10 hours each day, but their day's wages were only 10d. Three of them, and perhaps all four, had on at least one occasion appeared before the Session on a charge of haughmagandy. Men with a horse and a flat-board cart also worked a 10 hour day. Five of them earned 5/- per day but the Manse servant seems to have earned 6/-. Alexander Riddell, the blacksmith who was in attendance received 1/10 for sharpening tools. The costs were shared by the Heritors - Aboyne, Invercauld, and Abergeldie.

There was delay in replacing the bridge. Heritors had to pay half the cost and a great deal of money had already been paid out for bridges.

A third bridge, of Braemar timber was erected in 1834 to the west of previous bridges. There were four arches, each with a 70' span. The fact that the bridge appeared at all was due to the exertions of the schoolmaster, the Rev. James Smith. The contractors were the Aberdeen firm of Gibb of Rubislaw. The total cost of the timber was £1957 which included improvement of the parapet railings and the road. No disaster overtook this bridge although eventually it was beginning to show signs of wear.

Ballater had risen in the world and needed to show that it was modern and up to date, so the Royal Bridge, opened by Queen Victoria on the 6th November 1885, was erected, alongside the timber bridge, and bridge number four still stands today. It was the work of Messrs. Jenkins and Marr, architects and engineers and was built by John Fyfe, Kemnay. The timber bridge was then demolished but its stone foundations are still visible over the east parapet.

The commemorative plaque was renewed in 1998 and re-dedicated by H.M.The Queen.

Inscription on Ballater Bridge

CAMBUS o'MAY BRIDGE
(OS 421976)
(camas mhaigh - the bend in the plain)

A little west of Cambus o'May railway station was a ferry, but it ceased to be used when the foot bridge was erected in 1905. A little sandy beach where the ferry operated can still be seen. The old railway line is now a walkway and the Camus Station now a private house. The path leads down to the bridge across the river, built in 1905 with money provided by Alexander Gordon of Little Mill, Girnoc, who had made a fortune as a brewer in London. He was also responsible for the bridge at Polhollick and contributed generously to the building of the Church and the Victoria Hall in the village.

Over the years the bridge deteriorated and repairs were to prove very costly. So the Cambus o'May Bridge was rebuilt in 1988 at a cost of £80,000 and opened by the Queen Mother. This is not a stone bridge, but it has stone supports. The inscription on the original Cambus Bridge read:-

This Bridge
Was presented
To the public by
Mr.Alexander Gordon
Southwood, Hildenborough, Kent
Erected 1905

CLUNIE BRIDGE, BRAEMAR
(OS 151914)

By 1831 there were comments that the bridge was too narrow and unsafe.

In 1862 the Heritors, Farquharson of Invercauld and the Earl of Fife paid for a new bridge. The Road Trustees agreed to re-imburse them a little each year. The granite bridge was completed in August 1863/4. The architects were Reid of Elgin and Knight of Aberdeen while the contractor was Fyfe of Kemnay.

In 1980's the bridge was replaced by one more suited to traffic today but not so attractive.

CRATHIE CROSSINGS & BALMORAL BRIDGE
(OS 262949)

There was from early days a boat at Crathie, near Milltown. The clachan here was a very busy place. Ford and ferry linked with the south by the Capel and Clova routes. The population at the time of the Poll Boook in 1696 was considerable. By 1801 the mill had disappeared although the name remained. After ford and ferry ceased to be used, probably about 1834 when the suspension bridge was erected, the boathouse became an inn. It was later abolished as a nuisance.

Elderly people living in Crathie now remember, as children, their grandparents speaking about a very elderly lady, dressed in black, who was always referred to as 'Old Boatie'. It was here, near the 'Milne' that Montrose crossed with his troops in May 1645 before the battle of Auldearn.

Crathie Suspension Bridge by J. Justice in 1834 had slender pylons and wooden flooring. It was partly renewed by Blaikie Brothers in 1885. The Royal children were fearful about crossing this unsteady bridge so Prince Albert commissioned the Girder Bridge in 1856. This bridge at Balmoral links the north and south roads. It ensures privacy for the estate for the south road had passed through the policies. The public road was closed and this more substantial bridge was more robust than the suspension bridge. Isumbard Kingdom Brunell was the designer of this single span wrought iron bridge with fancy perforations on the girders. The two piers at each end are of granite. The bridge span is almost 40m. Some name plates of the iron founder, R. Brotherhood of Chippenham can be seen.

Queen Victoria made no reference to the bridge in her Journal, from which it might be inferred that she was not impressed by it.

A plaque was placed on the bridge in May 2006 in the presence of H.M. Queen Elizabeth to mark the bridge's 150th anniversary.

THE PACKHORSE BRIDGE AT CRATHIE
(OS 352971)

The original packhorse bridge at Crathie, at the foot of the road to Glengairn is only a few feet wide, and of uncertain date but it was still in use towards the end of the eighteenth century.

FRASER'S BRIDGE
(OS 148865)

Fraser's Bridge over the Clunie, erected about 1750, was one of the three bridges built in the area for the Board of Ordnance after the Jacobite Rising of 1745. Although they may have been suggested by General Wade, they were not erected by him. This bridge has been attributed to General Blakeney but the officer in charge or the company concerned may have been called Fraser.

Fraser's Bridge

GAIRN BRIDGE
(OS 352971)

Near the bridge there used to be a shop and a branch of the Town & Country Bank. There were two earlier bridges, one a Packhorse Bridge that continued until fairly late in the 18th century.

A new bridge was constructed about 30 yards down stream, then in 1855 the present bridge was planned some thirty yards further down stream, to carry the Turnpike Road. The foundation stone was laid in November 1856 by James Ross Farquharson with full Masonic ceremony conducted by the Brethren of the St. Nathalan's Lodge. Coins of the realm, newspapers and a written statement were buried in the foundations. Since then there have been 'modern' improvements to the bridge.

People pass over, never seeing the excellent masonry of the bridge. Two granite supports are visible. These were built when it was planned to take the railway line to Braemar but when Queen Victoria objected, the already placed bridge was removed and taken as a road bridge to Daldownie where it gave access to a farm, and Loch Builg.

GAIRNSHIEL BRIDGE
(OS 352971)

Gairnshiel Bridge carries the old military road across the Gairn. It was one of the three bridges erected after the '45 and dates to about 1751. Although often referred to as a Wade bridge, he did not build it although it may have been based on his expertise.

A local tradition connects Fox, an army officer, with the building of the bridge. A cairn on the hill is said to have been erected in his memory by his men. A larch tree at the end of the bridge is also said to have been planted then. This, with one at Abergeldie, is reputed to be the oldest larch on Deeside.

Gairnshiel Bridge

145

GIRNOC BRIDGE
(OS 326957)

Near the confluence of Dee and Girnoc there was a ford, considered to have a very rough approach road and generally used by empty carts or pedestrians.

The present Girnoc Bridge on the South Deeside Road is a Victorian erection, but a predecessor had a chequered history and played its part in the feud between Gordon of Knock and Forbes of Strathgirnoc.

Forbes' people needed a bridge across the Girnoc to get to their peat 'moss', but because Gordon wanted to deprive them of the peat he refused to allow a bridge to be erected, for one end would be on his property. Nevertheless, Forbes put up a bridge of strong logs, in spite of Gordon protests. Such action could not be tolerated by a Gordon, so at night the latter's men threw it down the burn. The two Lairds met, in an atmosphere that was anything but harmonious. Threats and counter threats were made, and then Forbes, in a rage, said that with only one man to help, he would build a bridge that even four Gordons could not move. Gordon, sure it was impossible, said if Forbes could actually do that, the bridge could stay.

Forbes had for a long lime had his eye on a great flat stone on Creag Phioabidh. It would make a wonderful immovable bridge if only he could get it down and in place. He had a great friend, a sparring partner in a type of wrestling, who was as opposed to the Gordons as was Forbes. This Fleeman, a Fleming, and a weaver, was a man of exceptional strength who had many times assisted Forbes, often against his better judgment. A reluctant Fleeman was finally persuaded to help his friend when told that of the four men likely to pull down the bridge for Gordon, one was Johnny o'Scurrystane, a rival weaver. Forbes was a bit of a psychologist!

Fleeman buckled on his indispensable plaid and set off up Creag Phioabidh. Presumably he had some companions.

By morning a great stone spanned the burn. Folk had started to gather at first light to see the new bridge. Gordon,

Johnny o'Scurrystane and two others tried with might and main to dislodge the stone. All their efforts were in vain. Gordon kept his word and the bridge enabled Forbes' folk to cut peat on their moss.

The bridge lasted many years, until the bank having eroded over the years, it was washed away in the flood in 1799.

Was Fleeman (plus friends, one supposes) really strong enough to bring down the hill in one night a stone big enough to span the burn?

The present bridge is a Victorian erection. Long vehicles have some difficulty because of the angle of the bridge. It is still worth a visit, even though it is now rather more than one slab of stone!

Close to the bridge is Littlemill, now a private house with a collection of outbuildings. At one time it was a large complex, a village concerned with weaving and dyeing, with cottages for the workers. It was also a farm and there were dwellings for a number of artisans. The most important and the wealthiest family there were Gordons. Gordons had been in Littlemill since the early 1700's. George Gordon of Littlemill and his wife Elizabeth Gauld had a son, also George, born in 1816 and another, Alexander, benefactor of Ballater, born in January 1818.

The family, who always claimed to be distantly related to the Gordons of Abergeldie who owned Littlemill, gave generously to the building of Girnoc Bridge.

GLENMUICK BRIDGE
(OS 366948)

The old bridge was last used on 4th June 1878 for the funeral of James Stephen to Glenmuick. It had been built in 1858 and was proving unsuitable for the traffic using it. The present bridge was built immediately afterwards.

It has interesting coping and the angles provide those crossing with wonderful views.

Glenmuick Bridge

"OLD" BRIDGE OVER THE DEE AT INVERCAULD
(OS 186909)

In the 1520's a stone bridge was built over the Dee in Aberdeen but the first Upper Deeside stone bridge was that at Invercauld in 1752. It carried a military road, built by Major Edward Cauldfield to take the road across the Mounth by the Cairnwell, over the Dee and on to Corgarff. Like many of the bridges of this time, it rises high in the centre. It has four arches, built of local stone. The bridge became private in 1859 when Prince Albert built a new bridge to the west, to retain privacy for Balmoral estate. Most of the local bridges date from the 19th century.

"NEW" BRIDGE OVER THE DEE AT INVERCAULD
(OS 185910)

In 1859 Prince Albert made a new lay-out to Balmoral Castle approaches and had a "new" bridge built at Invercauld. At that time the public road ran from the Bridge of Muick near Ballater through the Balmoral Estate to the "old" Bridge at Invercauld. To secure privacy he had an iron bridge built at Balmoral opposite the Gate Lodge. This public road crossed to the north side of the river and joined the north road at the Post

148

Office. At the other end of the private domain a new bridge was built at Invercauld, west of the old bridge, that now became private.

The Bridge over the Dee at Invercauld

THE BRIDGE AT THE LINN OF DEE
(OS 062896)

The Linn of Dee leads to two passes, the better known Lairig Ghru and the Lairig an Laoigh. At the Linn the Dee rushes into a narrow channel in the rocks of mica-slate and quartz, not much more than a metre wide and then opens out into circular pools.

The lame young Byron jumped across here but was saved from injury by a young keeper when he slipped.

A timber bridge was in use at first, but it was damaged beyond repair by the Muckle Spate in 1829. It was replaced by the present stone bridge built by James Earl of Fife and opened by Queen Victoria at the Linn of Dee on 8th September 1857. She drank a whisky toast to its future.

In 1896 there was a local outcry when the Duke of Fife had a rock channel cut above the bridge to help salmon get up the river.

There is a warning that the pools of the river are dangerous and a granite memorial reads:-

GWYN GATENBY
and
KATIE TODD
Accidentally drowned
16th October 1927

The Linn o'Dee Bridge

POLHOLLICK BRIDGE
(OS 344965)

The bridge crosses the Dee about 3km west of Ballater. This iron suspension bridge with its stone supports was donated by Alexander Gordon of Littlemill, Girnoc, in 1892. He had made a fortune brewing in London. He was responsible for two bridges, this one at Polhollick and the other at Cambus o'May

Alexander witnessed a drowning in the Dee when he was a young man and vowed to replace Polhollick ferry with a bridge when he had money to spare. He did that in 1892. An inscription records details of the benefactor

The iron suspension bridge spans the Dee at a spot where there was an earlier ford and ferry. The old ferry 'pier' is still to be seen and the boatman's house is still in use. For very many years this had been a crossing point so the facility was much appreciated by the community. Over the years the bridge has deteriorated and needs further refurbishing. It can be reached from the North Deeside Road as well as from the South Road.

Alexander Gordon was also responsible for some of the cost of Cambus o'May Bridge, but an even bigger gift was the Halls, for public entertainment and education, and a large donation of £1400 to the building of the present Glenmuick (Ballater) Parish Church.

TULLICH BRIDGE
(OS 387975)

Before the 1855 turnpike was made the Deeside road crossed the Tullich Burn a few yards to the north of the present bridge. A careful look reveals the finely squared granite blocks on both sides of the stream. Presumably it was a bridge of the old high backed type for comments about the coaching days refer to coaches making a great rush to get over.

The foundation stone of a new bridge was laid on 12th August 1857 by Charles Paterson of Milton of Tullich. He was accompanied by James Ross, Mill of Tullich and the architect, Mr. Burgess. The stone itself was a great block of Culblean granite. Toasts were drunk then followed dancing, including a reel along the narrow summit of the 'auld brig'. The bridge was of ashlar work, three metal beams forty feet long forming the span. The track was about 20' wide, about twice as wide as the old one. The old bridge remained in place until the new one was completed. A detailed report on the proceedings was carried by the local newspaper, the Aberdeen Journal.

VICTORIA BRIDGE, MAR LODGE
(OS 102895)

Originally erected in 1828, when it was destroyed by flood a temporary bridge of wood was erected, to be replaced by a new one in 1905. It is a utilitarian bridge with heavy iron painted trellis supported by four stone piers. It was the approach to Mar Lodge from the Deeside Road.

MINOR BRIDGES

In addition to the larger bridges over the Dee, Muick, Gairn and Clunie etc. there are many more smaller attractive bridges. Only a selection can be made.

AUCHALLATER BRIG
(OS 156882)

This attractive little road bridge above Auchallater farm probably belongs to the period of the creation of the road over Glenshee.

BRAICHLIE BRIDGE
(OS 3689490)

Braichlie or Brackley Bridge on the B976 road is a problem for speeding traffic, being little more than single width.

CANADIAN BRIDGE
(OS 673896)

Only ends remain now of this bridge west of Inverey, built by Canadians during World War 2.

DALDOWNIE BRIDGE
(OS 242008)

Leading virtually nowhere now, except as a track for walkers and keepers, is an iron bridge at Daldownie, on stone supports. It is a miniature of Sydney Harbour Bridge.

Its original home was near the Foot o' Gairn, to take the new Aboyne to Braemar railway extension to beyond Ballater and on to Braemar. Queen Victoria refused access through her estate, so the bridge was dismantled and re-erected at Daldownie.

THE BRIDGE AT THE DERRY
(OS 040935)

The wooden bridge over the Derry has a concrete block bearing the names of 19 men, all volunteers, who built it.

GLEN GELDIE
(OS 980870)

Where the track along Glen Geldie passes Lower Geldie Cottage and stables the remains of a bridge are to be seen, - broken pillars that held the bridge. Now walkers have to ford the river, often subject to the spates that brought down the bridge itself. Beyond the ford is a group of trees sheltering Bynack Lodge, where Queen Victoria stopped for tea on returning from a visit to Blair Athol.

An elderly lady in Braemar, now deceased, was always referred to as Meg Bynack because of her earlier residence there.

The Lodge, like many others, was reputed to have its ghost.

THE LOIN BURN BRIDGE
(OS 364982)

On Sgurr Buidhe, the Yellow hill, the Farquharsons of Monaltrie quarried lead and silver and then stone for building purposes. William Farquharson who died in 1828 built a stone bridge over the Loin Burn for access to the silver mine. A portrait of William painted by Sir John Watson Gordon for St. Nathalan's Masonic Lodge shows him with silver buttons on his jacket.

Near the bridge was a little granite fog house. It was in regular use for tea etc. until the early 1900's. Fog is moss and the inside of the little house was lined with this.

THE LUI BRIDGE
(OS 064915)

Over the Lui Water is the Black Bridge, An Drochaid Dhubh, a once tarred structure.

Another stone bridge spans a burn that comes in to join the Lui.

SPINNING JENNY BRIDGE
(OS 372952)

A very small bridge with a low parapet is on the B976 road, a short distance from Ballater. Jenny, reputed to be a witch, sat there spinning. Another tradition says she mourns her lover, killed at Culloden. At one time her stone stood below the bridge. Jenny and her stone disappeared when the road was resurfaced and modernised.

THE BRIDGE AT THE LINN OF QUOICH
(OS 115913)

Around 6 km. from the Linn of Dee is another spectacular waterfall. A red-roofed cottage is boarded up and among some trees stands another derelict building, many years ago used as a shiel by the Queen Mother.

There is a bridge over the Quoich, of wood, with stone support, built some years ago by Scotrail volunteers.

The linn is a lovely shady spot and the water has a wonderful colour, due to the rocks over which it flows.

TRACKS, ROADS & TOLLS

The fords and ferries served the routes from north to south.

Along the river, East to West, where routes intersected the Mounth tracks, settlements grew up. There was a 'Highway' East to West, most of which has gone now or been made over, but sections can be seen beyond Dinnet, at the Pass of Ballater and West of Balmoral. Some of the early settlements, close to food supplies and easily defended, were abandoned in favour of others nearer to intersecting routes.

Little settlements were linked by rough tracks. Occasionally a few stones were thrown into a boggy section. Even if carts had been available, they would have been fairly useless. Travel was usually on foot or on the back of a garron. The folk of the Glens thought nothing of walking distances, - the smith, tailor and packman walked 20 to 30 miles daily when necessary. A horse could do up to 8 m.p.h. on a long journey. Stephenson's Rocket in 1829 only managed that!

Eventually Loudon invented macadamised roads, but it was a time before they were in general use. Before the eighteenth century roads were worn rather than made. By a 1719 law, every male householder was to do 6 days work on roads in the parish. Before the Benediction in the Church, a list of those required, with day, time and place was read out. Labour was eventually commuted to money, - 6d. Parishes had to repair their own roads and schoolmasters made up lists of males from 15 to 70, excluding ministers and schoolmasters. That is how roads were made, between 1750 and 1800, but labour could only be used in summer.

To avoid bogs, roads went up hill, but the slope was often too steep. The roads were narrow, unmetalled, with side ditches. Big stones were taken out, but the roads became muddy bogs in wet weather. In 1741 it was suggested that small stones and shingle be used for a depth of 6".

After 1746 the military roads could take wheeled traffic. They had a hard bottom and were built by soldiers. Other roads were primitive. In 1756 a Highways Act was passed stipulating that roads had to be at least 20 feet wide with a drainage ditch at each side. Farmers were not to plough across a road, as they had been doing!

Nothing much was done, except on the military roads, and even in 1800 there was little more than a track through the Glens. Some roads were too narrow for wheeled traffic to pass, or loaded horses with curracks. Some were raised in the middle to let the water run off. The oldest Turnpike Act was in 1750 but it was into the 1850's before the system was operative on Deeside.

To the mid 18th century mail from Edinburgh to Aberdeen took 3 days. It came through Fife, across the ferries of Forth and Tay. The messenger stayed the first night at Dundee, the second at Montrose. In 1765 the London to Aberdeen mail took 6 days. Then letters had to go out to the Glens: not many were sent.

Horses or garrons were used for transporting almost everything when they were available. The animals were fed on dried grass and dried thistles and as a result often lacked stamina or size. Currachs or creels of wicker work hung from a crook saddle, one on each side of a horse. The load had to be balanced properly. Dung was carried, sheaves, meal from the mill. When carts did exist, the 'tumbling carts' were clumsy: the wheels did not turn round an axle, the axle itself turned. There was no grease and much screeching. Eventually, by about 1830, there were carriers' carts, sometimes with two horses. Early settlements had been selected for defensive purposes as well as for the availability of food and water, but once travel and trade increased the original sites could be deserted and new settlements made.

The old Deeside Road had originally no connection with Ballater before the Bridge was built and Ballater came into being, but it was connected to the ford and ferry. The old road known as The Crags of Ballater went from Tullich through the Pass of Ballater and crossed the Gairn by the old pack-horse bridge. It had a connection with the "church" road from

Morven to Tullich. The road was eventually superseded by the 1855 Turnpike road, on which many Skye labourers were employed.

Just over 300 yards from the Fearder burn, towards Braemar is the Inver Toll House, originally a little 'but and ben' house. It has been modernised and extended. Now a dwelling house, this was not the original Inver Toll, but it was in use about 1860. The Rev. James Crombie, writing about a journey from Braemar to Ballater in 1860 mentions coming to the Inn of Inver, then the Fearder Burn and then to a Toll Bar and two or three small houses beside it. This would indicate that at that time the Toll House was east of the burn.

Just west of Inver Inn stands Inver Cottage, or Hamewith on the right hand side of the road as one travels to Braemar. At the end of the cottage there were two pillars of granite, one on each side of the road. This was the cottage used as the Toll House of Inver and the pillars were the supports for the toll bar, as used around 1855. A few years ago as a result of an accident one of the pillars was broken so both were removed to safe keeping. As far as is known, this was the only toll cottage where the stone posts remained so long.

The toll bar had been moved to where the Toll House now stands, east of the Aberarder road. Documentary evidence, backed by local tradition says the change took place because the original Toll House was in a position that missed the Crathie traffic to Mill of Inver and to Aberarder.

From 1866 tolls on Turnpike Roads were abolished. Toll houses were to be handed over to the local landowners at mutual valuation.

ROADS

BEFORE TURNPIKES

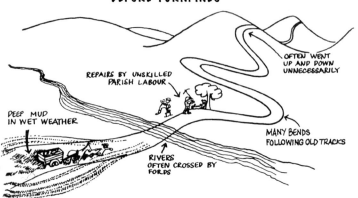

OFTEN WENT
UP AND DOWN
UNNECESSARILY

REPAIRS BY UNSKILLED
PARISH LABOUR

MANY BENDS
FOLLOWING OLD TRACKS

DEEP MUD
IN WET WEATHER

RIVERS
OFTEN CROSSED BY
FORDS

BEST TURNPIKE ROADS

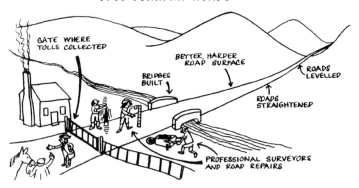

GATE WHERE
TOLLS COLLECTED

BETTER, HARDER
ROAD SURFACE

ROADS
LEVELLED

BRIDGES
BUILT

ROADS
STRAIGHTENED

PROFESSIONAL SURVEYORS
AND ROAD REPAIRS

WHEELS

 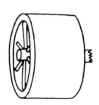 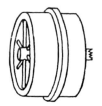

NARROW WHEELS
FAST, EASY TO
PULL, BUT MADE
DEEP RUTS —

HEAVY TOLLS

WIDE WHEELS
SLOW, HARD TO
PULL, BUT
HELPED TO ROLL
ROAD FLAT —
LOWER TOLLS

'CHEATING' WHEELS
WIDE TO GET LOW TOLLS,
BUT RAN ON NARROW
RIM FOR SPEED.

THE RAILWAY, 1866 - 1966

When a Bridge was built over the Dee at Ballater in 1783 and the influx of guests to Pannanich Wells became too great for the ferry to deal with, the 'centre' moved to the newly created Ballater. Tullich declined and Ballater prospered, helped by the Royal purchase of Balmoral and the coming of the Railway.

With the coming of the Railway, Royal Deeside was easily accessible. The Railway opened up Ballater, and all spheres of life were revolutionised. Visitors from far and near, as well as locals, enjoyed the journey through beautiful scenery. Day trips from Aberdeen became increasingly popular and whole families made the journey.

Ballater was the terminus of the Deeside Railway when it was opened on 17th October 1866. It became the "Royal" Station, welcoming many crowned heads on their way to Balmoral, many of whom were related to Queen Victoria.

The Queen herself was not very fond of rail travel. Conditions on the line had always to be checked and a pilot train usually ran ahead of the royal train with a crew of fitters and greasers.

The original line was run by a private company but in 1876 it was taken over by the Great North of Scotland Railway. Under the 1947 Transport Act it was nationalised, becoming part of British Railways. After 100 years of serving Deeside the Beeching axe fell and the Railway is now no more than a memory. The last train ran in 1966

A plaque on the building reminds visitors of the departed glories of Ballater station and its renovation in 1886 to install a Royal Waiting Room, perhaps the most sumptuous in the country at the time, with a royal lavatory in blue porcelain. Also inserted in the road are markers indicating the limits of the station property.

In the old days there had to be space for horses and carts or horses and carriages, according to social status, to turn round. Hence the space in Station Square. When the Railway came to Ballater, the village centre moved from Bridge Square to Station Square.

Most of the crowned heads of Europe and Russian rulers appeared at one time or another, so the Station Master was considered to be a man of some consequence

The old line east between Aboyne and Ballater ran through beautiful countryside, - the Moor of Dinnet and Loch Kinord, with the smaller Loch Davan behind. The Cambus o'May station was considered to have one of the most attractive settings in the country. Near the bridge is Cutaway Cottage, formerly a riverside inn. This was a favourite meeting place for the log "floaters" who imbibed freely to fortify themselves against the cold and the danger. When the railway line was constructed one corner of the house had to be cut away to allow trains to pass, hence its name.

Ordinary folk travelled from Aberdeen to Ballater for a day's excursion or alighted at o'May to picnic on the banks of the Dee. The old station buildings there are now an attractive house.

A little further along the line from Aboyne towards Ballater lies Tullich with its historic kirk yard and the eird or earth house dating to around 100 B.C. and across the river, Pannanich Wells. Beyond the kirkyard lie Craig Coillich on the left and the pudding bowl shape of Craigendarroch on the right. The track reached Eastfield of Monaltrie and from there it ran in a straight line to Ballater station. There are magnificent views of Lochnagar and other hills.

The Beeching closure in 1966 was a backward step for Deeside. Apart from serving visitors, computers to Aberdeen lost transport along a beautiful valley.

After forty four years all has changed now. The Square has been given a face lift, with marked off bays for a limited number of cars, and a 'whiter' appearance due to the foreign stone used, but that is weathering.. The Station Buildings have been repaired and redecorated in traditional livery.

Central to all the 'face lift' is the Tourist Centre, with its video and re-created platform scene in a glassed-in section.

The installation of a 'Royal Coach' as used by Queen Victoria adds interest to the existing display. The Station Square has now become the centre of the village again. Behind are houses and it will never be possible to re-open the Deeside line in its entirety for some of the land is in private hands.

The present walk and cycle track along the old line is beautified by wild flowers and the broom gives a glorious splash of colour.

The track that was planned to run to Braemar runs through leafy woodland. This is one of the most popular walks in the area, for villagers as well as for visitors, with views of the Dee. Plans had been made to carry the line to Braemar but Queen Victoria refused to have it anywhere near her Balmoral lands.

On the way the old estate boundary marker stones can be seen on the north side of the track. They indicate where Morven marched with Invercauld.

Former Railway Station as in the 1980's

XIX. THE INFLUENCE OF THE KIRK
ON EVERYDAY LIFE

People never cease to be amazed at the influence the Kirk Session had over the lives of people on Upper Deeside. The discipline exercised by the Session was at greatest strength in the seventeenth and eighteenth centuries. By 1805 its powers were slightly less strong, but it still had a great influence on the lives of Deeside folk. In four distinct areas they exercised strict discipline.

Moral issues were of course important. The male members of Session had to deal with fornication - pre-nuptial sex, known locally as haughmagandy. It was a delicate matter so the men engaged the services of matrons to help when checking for pregnancy, abortion, etc. The Elders were always on the alert to spot offences and many were reported to them. Offenders, male and female, were fined, on what would appear to be a very arbitrary scale, the money being used to benefit the poor. Most couples could cope with the fine, but that was not all that was involved. In fact the fine was insignificant. There were instances of clemency where a young mother had to support the child unaided, the father having in the interim died. Her fine was remitted as was that of a woman who accused a man of paternity to find that 'he is fled to France'.

What followed the fine was an ordeal for most people. Both parties had to appear on the stool of repentance, the "Cutty Stool", at the front of the church, facing the congregation. This was the only pre-Reformation item of furniture to remain, - a sort of double bench with arms, on a little platform, painted black. The old rhyme said

"The stool of repentance it is a black seat and those who sit on it are wonderful blate". (bashful, fearful)

Frequently further seating had to be found because there were a number of couples for arraignment.

The Church officer rang a bell and processed up the aisle before the couples. As a sign of repentance, following the Biblical account of John the Baptist, they all had to wear a sackcloth garment. It had probably never been washed and was certainly not a pleasant garment, often quite literally lousy so those who could afford to do so purchased their own, to look exactly as the original. Sitting on the stool was supposed to improve morals and show repentance. Probably all it did was to help the poor as a result of fines exacted.

The congregation looked on, critical or sympathetic (one day they could be there!) while the minister delivered a verbal lashing. After an admonishment and a number of Sundays on the Stool of Repentance, they were absolved. Sometimes the penalty ran for 26 Sundays, and as services were only held every third Sunday, the minister being at the other churches in the parish, the punishment lasted a long time. Until it was over the baby could not be baptised. Failure to accept discipline would have meant excommunication: no baptism, wedding, or funeral, and loss of all civil privileges. The practice continued well beyond the middle of the nineteenth century.

As a result of the fear of "Sessioning", to avoid the punishment, some woman had an abortion, with "Penny Royal" fairly easily obtained. Some committed suicide and some, both men and women, absconded.

A second problem was prophanation of the Sabbath. An Act of 1579 stated "na profaning na handi-labouring nor working to be used on the Sabbath day, na gamming and playing, na flytin' an scoldin', passing to taverns or selling of meat or drink on payment of fines". Many, particularly women, were fined for cursing and swearing on the Sabbath. Some appeared for 'scolding', while some, men and women, were excessively drunk. Was the excess the crime, or was the problem Sunday consumption? 'Fishening' and fighting on the Sabbath were also dealt with. That merited four public appearances.

Tulzieing (brawling) seems to have been a problem. There was a long period of punishment for the man who started a fight in church. The most serious offence was "railing on ye minister and elders". Respect was usually shown to both so this, on a Sunday, really made local news. Often whole families were involved, including the women. The Lauchlans and the Allans "trysted for a contract in a change house" (alehouse). All ten of them made public appearances and paid a heavy fine. One man drove cattle on the Sabbath, another cut up a beast that fell in the river. There were numerous cases of drunkenness on the Sabbath. There was even a fight with pistols at Loch Kinord one Sunday but the minister intervened and all the offenders paid a large fine. We have sympathy for a man whose wife was ill so on a Sunday he went to get her sister to look after four small children, one only a week old. That was considered an un-necessary journey so he was fined!

A third problem was dishauntening of ordinances, - staying away from church! A public reprimand by Minister and Session and a fine was usually sufficient to put that right.

The fourth offence involved dabbling in the occult. Charmening was the offence, - using a little bit of magic to heal someone. Punishment was heavy, - six months in sackcloth on the stool of repentance and a heavy fine. In 1665 Alex Calder was accused of consorting with a warlock while trying to recover some cattle stolen from him. He was severely rebuked, served in sackcloth for 10 months and was fined, then absolved. Charmening crops up again as a method of crime detection. Who had stolen some cheeses? The charmer, later to become schoolmaster at Migvie, near Tarland, placed a key in the Pulpit Bible at Psalm 50 v.18. The ring bit of the key had to be outside the Bible. The Bible was then closed, tied up with string and the string end held loosely in the finger tips. The charmer then repeated three times the names of those he suspected of the offence as well as the verse of Scripture. The third time the name of the guilty party was uttered the Bible was supposed to fall open. How could a teacher, a well-qualified graduate, be so gullible? A public harangue, sackcloth appearances on many occasions and a heavy fine were his punishment.

Another case involved a mother unable to breast-feed her baby. After various practices, her milk was supposed to return. She suffered numerous public rebukes, and because her elderly husband had in the meantime died, some members of the Session stood sponsor at the child's baptism. So they could show compassion! I followed that up and found that the mother died of consumption when the boy was only 10 years old. The Elder concerned took him to his own home and he was brought up with the elderly man's grandchildren and treated quite equally. The Elder had honoured the promises he made at the child's baptism. I doubt that the same would happen today.

The naming of a child was of pre-Christian origin, but even into modern times an unbaptised child was considered to be a heathen and could not be buried in consecrated ground. If the kirk or the minister was too far away, the weather was harsh or the baby was delicate, a howdie or midwife carried out a baptism with three drops of water. It was usual to name the first baby after paternal grandparents, the next after maternal and the remainder had family names or names of the laird or a particular friend. The birth was not always a happy occasion for mothers frequently died of puerpal fever. Normally baptism took place in the church or the Manse. As long ago as 1690 the General Assembly had decreed that baptism should be at public worship, in front of the congregation, but this was often ignored.

Slightly different was the problem of 'penny weddings'. Weddings were social occasions, without any fuss or special clothes. Admission to the wedding party following the ceremony was by payment of 1/- Scots (1d. English) and there was plenty to eat and much ale and whisky to drink. A piper and a fiddler were present and there was hilarity and debauchery until morning. Any money left over was used to set up the couple in their new partnership. Penny Weddings were banned by the General Assembly but they certainly did not stop.

A new home was not always necessary. No house would be needed for if the husband's father was dead his bride took over the running of the house from his mother. It takes little imagination to realise there could be many causes of friction, for the new bride was mistress and the mother had to take a back seat.

Lyke wakes or funeral vigils were also condemned by General Assembly and Session. At the lyke wake there was a Bible reading and psalms were sung - unaccompanied of course. It was not considered respectful to the dead if quantities of whisky were not consumed. Mourning became revelry and debauchery with the coffin still there. People usually met at 11a.m. in a barn or other sizeable place. On entry a whisky was offered. Seats had been placed around, - boards on turf or blocks of wood or even any useable surface. On a rough table were clay pipes and strong tobacco, together with a lighted candle to start up the pipes. The men - for no women were present, - enjoyed a smoke. When all were assembled a man served oatcakes and cheese, followed by another with a pail of beer and a drinking cup. About half an hour later more whisky was served, and plain biscuits. Then came more rum or whisky and a generous portion of black bun. Slightly inebriated, those who wished to do so viewed the corpse before the lid was screwed down. Drink was by now flowing freely. Women often came to the door as the coffin was being carried out but took no part in the ceremony in the barn. They rarely went to the church but never to the burial ground. The sorrow of the bereaved contrasted with the exuberance of the friends. The minister did his best to control the situation, with little success. He laid down rules. He would be there and only one glass of spirits per person was to be permitted. The funeral guests got round that by starting their celebrations a couple of hours before the time told to the minister!

When the coffin was lifted it was covered by a black mort cloth hired from the church and so contributing to the poor fund. It was used until the late 1800's. If a coffin could not be afforded the body was wrapped in the mort cloth, used free, and then rolled into the grave without the cloth. No burial was complete without a mort cloth. At the 'lifting' one man, usually the beadle, walked in front ringing a hand bell, a survival of the idea that it would drive away evil spirits. It was then put down at the head of the grave.

Even at a funeral so much was drunk that on occasion the coffin failed to arrive at the burial ground. Sandy Davidson was a miller's son, a man of great strength, a famous wrestler and a noted dancer. When attending a Penny Wedding in Glen Gairn he carried off all the wrestling match prizes, representing Deeside against Donside. There was jealousy and he was attacked on his way home and kicked and punched. He suffered a fractured skull and died shortly afterwards. His funeral took place on a very stormy day. Over 300 men from Crathie went to the funeral at Glen Muick about 8 miles along the south side of the Dee. Depending on the distance to the burial ground, there were frequent changes of bearers.

The bearers had to stop for frequent liquid refreshment and put the coffin down. There was even a wrestling match in Sandy's honour. After a long carry in the cold the inebriated men reached the gates of the burial ground. To their surprise and the minister's horror they had no coffin and had to go back some 5 miles to find it parked on a wall. Perhaps not surprising for even before the lifting 4 gallons of whisky had been consumed! Little wonder the Session was concerned, although I have a feeling that a number of them could have been involved!

XX. DEPOPULATION, CLEARANCES & EVICTIONS ON UPPER DEESIDE & RESULTING RUINS

"Home is the place of peace, the shelter not only from injury but from terror and doubt"

John Ruskin

Plague, source unknown, had ravaged the country from 1349 - 1350 and a second visitation in 1362 again carried off as much as a third of the population. Later the great problem was famine, which caused considerable hardship. This was largely due to poor weather conditions but the whole system of farming was to some extent responsible.

The intolerance of Roman Catholics, particularly by a Protestant Factor/Minister, caused many compulsory removals and an exodus overseas.

The consequences of improvement in farming often meant enforced removal from holdings. The land might be turned into a park land to give the 'Big House' a better view or into a deer park. Alternatively, it could be turned to grazing. The population certainly fell in the late 18th and early 19th centuries.

Shieling practices declined when farms were amalgamated or cleared although some graziers continued the practice of transhumance with stock moving to summer pasture.

Everywhere on Upper Deeside ruins of abandoned dwellings are to be seen, sad reminders of long gone homes and families.

By the middle of the eighteenth century the population of Upper Deeside was too great for the resources of the area. In a good season most people managed to exist but in a hard winter many were at starvation level. At Tullich school in 1720 nine children had only a little meal of watery gruel every day. The Lairds enlarged holdings and were not happy to subdivide holdings among children of their tenants.

Many men were unemployed and disaffection expressed itself in many ways. Some lairds served warrants of removal

Ballater Bridge

Tullich Church & Burial Ground

Crathie Kirk

Braemar Castle

The House of Glenmuick

Abergeldie Castle

Invercauld House

Kindrochit Castle

The Packhorse Bridge

Mackenzie Seat

Glengairn Kirk

Interior of Church at Harvest Festival

and when these were ignored, houses were pulled down. So a number were compelled, reluctantly, to seek foreign lands. Minor tenants had as a rule no security of tenure. They had no lease so they could legally be ejected at a term-day. If they refused to leave, the law was on the side of the Laird.

Of course depopulation occurred even without clearances or evictions. In the 150 years from 1850 the number of households dropped by about 90%.

Depopulation of the more remote areas of Upper Deeside certainly came as a result of clearances or emigration. No events on Upper Deeside could be compared with the harsh clearances that occurred in Sutherland and Ross-shire in the early part of the nineteenth century, but nevertheless clearances did take place, some for sheep but most for the creation of deer forests. It is probably true to say that the chief reason for clearances on Upper Deeside was non-enforced emigration. Much information is to be gleaned from Estate Records, chiefly those of Invercauld and Mar. Rarely is there evidence of individual evictions at various "rent days" but rather there was the eviction of all the families living in a given area, at one time.

The original of James Farquharson's 1703 map of the Forest of Mar in the National Library of Scotland shows land in Glen Lui owned by the Earl of Mar. There were four farms with associated dwellings and ruins can still be picked out. By 1715 the Earl of Mar lost his lands as a result of the 1715 Rising, with its close association with Braemar. His Hanoverian brother, Lord Grange, sold the land. According to an extant letter of 15th September 1726 he wrote to James Farquharson of Balmoral asking him to eject the tenants in Glen Lui after the harvest. He hoped to gain more revenue from felling timber than from rents. Documentary evidence exists to show that Patrick Farquharson of Inverey purchased Mar Forest from Lord Grange in 1732. From rent rolls it appears that the new owner permitted some return of tenants about that time, to increase his funds. By 1739 there were new farms, - Ryntean, Altavatagaly, Auchavrie and Dalgenie. In

1744 Delnroisick appeared in records and in 1763 Knoc Knatet and Croislish. All was well until the term day of Whitsun 1776 when an agreement was drawn up between the Earl of Fife, by now the owner and Superior and John McKenzie of Glen Lui. The latter was to leave all his houses in Glen Lui for a payment of £30 Scots. He was also to gain possessions in Allanquoich. By 1790 there are references to deer in Glen Lui but no references to people or dwellings. Other references are to ruins of buildings, proving that previously there had been habitations, but now the land was turned over to deer. The fact that there had previously been a meal mill would indicate a reasonable number of people living there. To this day Glen Lui supports a good deer population.

The Baddoch (OS 132828), a settlement in Glen Clunie nearly went the same way. In 1733 John Farquharson of Invercauld issued eviction orders against Donald Lamont, the family of James Stewart in Rienluig, and James McDonald. Alexander Farquharson of Auchendryne, a minor, whose tutor was acting for him, claimed that the land was his, so there was stalemate.

Other glens in Mar Forest where there were farms were Glen Dee and Glen Eye. The former had a number of small farm townships. Delvorar (OS 044892) in Glen Dee had a considerable stock of cattle and sheep and the area was one used for the summer shielings. It is probable that this, together with Tonnagaoithe (OS 028892) was cleared in favour of deer. A much later Factor's report of 1872 told of people in Dubrach's (OS 030888) two acres of arable land being moved down the glen because they were always ailing as a result of feeding on unripened potatoes and cereals.

Glen Ey was one of the glens where families were evicted to make way for deer. As early as 1829 five families were cleared out and resettled elsewhere. The Clearances here were not of the Strathnaver type when homes were burned and people turned out on the hill. In 1842 eight more families were turned out, with over 3,000 sheep and some cattle. The movement from the glen was further forced on people when there was a clamp down on illicit distilling. That meant that a valuable source of income was lost and tenants were not able to pay their rents.

Ruins of deserted homes can still be seen.

Originally owned by Mackenzies of Dalmore (Mar Lodge), practically all of Glen Ey (OS 090863) was Farquharson of Inverey property, having been acquired by the first Laird of Inverey at the beginning of the seventeenth century. It remained with the family until 1785 when James, the 11th Laird sold it to the Earl of Fife. As Feudal Superior, Mar still owned all the fir woods on the estate and rights of hunting and fishing. Certain areas were "reserved forest" and tenants were not supposed to have access. The upper part of Glen Ey, known as the Glen of Altanour (OS 082824) was "reserved". As well as paying his feudal dues, the Laird had other duties to perform for his Superior, including providing men and dogs for hunting and men for war if necessary. There are the ruins of an old shooting lodge at Altanour (Alltan Odhar, the dun burn). It was still intact in 1900 but seems to have been too remote for general use. Even the trees that cluster round have fallen. In addition to paying their rent the tenants had to assist with shoots, help with the harvest and undertake various tasks like carting goods. They were permitted to have timber from the Superior's woods to build or repair their homes and steadings and indeed for any agricultural purpose. There appears to be no record of numbers of tenants when the Farquharsons acquired the property but the assumption is that there were certainly tenants at the lower end of the glen and perhaps as far as Auchelie (Achery) (the field of darkness) (OS 088863). Two of the ruins there would seem to indicate houses rather larger than usual. A large settlement lay between Auchelie and Creag an Fhuathais (the crag of the spectre). A bad-tempered ghost was believed to roll stones on passers by. Near the foot of the Creag a series of larachs are to be seen, with corn-drying kiln and even longhouses.

In summer transhumance took place - tenants of Inverey and their stock moved into the area for fresh grazing and into the valleys of the Corrie & Christie. Mar lost his Superiority after taking part in the '15 and later it was bought by Lord Braco who became Earl of Fife. For years litigation went on between Farquharsons and Braco in connection with the fir woods.

Under Farquharson of Inverey ownership the arable land increased greatly probably because of an increase in population. James Farquharson's 1703 map depicts seven farms in Glen Ey. Ruins of farm buildings and shielings can still be seen.

The Millcroft of Inverey (OS 087887) was on the river bank at the beginning of the glen with the miller's house a short distance away. It needs imagination to recreate the mill but the lade can be traced. At various times there seems to have been controversy and litigation surrounding the use of the mill. The corn had to be ground at the mill but there were occasions when it was out of action because of frost or storm. The Roman Catholic Baptismal Record for 1706 records the baptism of James, son of the miller, James Harro. In the mid eighteenth century the miller was a man called Downie but by 1810 Arthur Dingwall was the miller. He was one of the men responsible for the Wrights' Friendly Society that became the Braemar Highland Society. Dingwalls ran the mill for the rest of its working life.

Another settlement in Glen Ey was Loinaveaich (OS 086888). By the 1750's William Lamond was the tenant but during most of the 19th century the occupants were members of the McIntosh family. The house was occupied until after the World War II. On the site a keeper's house was built.

Some 350m. beyond the Colonel's Bed was Ruintellich with ruins at both sides of the road. Only foundations remain. A corn kiln is built into the corner of one of the buildings on the east of the road. Farmers usually had their kiln or "killogie" for drying grain. This bit of land had two tenants, according to estate records. On the west of the road the records indicate that there were four buildings. Over the years there were numerous tenants but from the 1830's there was a preponderance of McHardies. An 1866 map shows four dwellings.

Not quite so old are two ruins at Achery (OS 088863), probably built for keepers. They appear on the 1866 map. Higher up the slope is a corn mill. In the early days there were two tenants but by the mid 19th century Angus MacDonald then his son was in possession.

Beyond Achery was Carnafea. There are a few stones and a corn mill but records make no mention of the place after the 1770's.

Across the river was the shieling ground for Corriemulzie where remains of buildings can be picked out. There was probably no farming here until the close of the 17th century. On the flat land on the east bank of the Ey were the three farms of Dalruinduchlat, Dalnafea and Alltshlat (OS 102852). Some of the best-preserved ruins are at Dalruinduchlat. There are ruins of eight or nine buildings and a kiln. This was the home of Duncan Clark, suspected of murdering in Glen Connie Sgt. Davies of the Redcoat force in 1749. By 1800 the Lamonds were tenants. Dalnafea was the home of one tenant, in the mid 1750's John Shaw, who stayed for 40 years, to be followed by a Lamont. Alltshlat lay on the south bank of the burn. The stone paved floor of the house can still be seen. Around lay shieling huts.

South of Alltshlat is Ridow with ruins that appear to be older than others around. This was Alex Farquharson of Inverey's shieling in mid 18th century. His two daughters were born here, - Marjory in 1755 & Ann in 1766 so it may have been a residence rather than a shieling. South of this almost to Altanour (OS 100843) was the meadow of Glen Ey for Farquharson cattle grazing.

Along the road is Altanour Cottage sheltered by trees after being built by the Earl of Fife in 1838. All the census records list it as uninhabited. In the 1960's the roof was removed to avoid duty. There is a feeling of desolation in the area.

A document of Clare Constat - the recognition of an heir by his Feudal Superior - refers to Riensleek and Delnabreck but little remains to remind us of the dwellers there.

There are Farquharson records of tenants poaching and

encroaching on reserved areas and causing interruptions to shooting expeditions. Many owed a great deal of rent. For the Laird, shooting lets were a better source of income than letting to tenants.

The creation of a deer forest really began in the 1830's. Little Inverey tenants lost their grazing in Glen Cristrie then soon afterwards the Meikle Inverey folk lost theirs in Glen Connie (OS 073866). Others suffered the same fate. This was a real blow. Many tenants were served removal notices and left. Compensation was paid for the value of the buildings.

The first population figures for the glen appeared in 1841. 41 people lived in the middle of the glen with 9 in the lower part. There were farm servants, female servants, a miller and a tailor. Where did the evicted people go? The Lamonts of Dalnafae moved to Inverey village and family members obtained jobs on the estate. One of the Lamonts of Dalruinduchlat became a gamekeeper and remained in the glen. At his death the family moved to Inverey. Some of the Macdonalds of Achery moved to Dunfermline and the McHardy family became farmers with a large holding where Braemar Golf Course is now. The tailor from Ruintellich seems to have disappeared. The miller was not affected and was there until the 1860's but the mill no longer brought in a living wage so he became a general odd-job man for the estate. At some time after 1861 he settled in Auchindryne. (Braemar). For a time keepers lived in accommodation built for them at Achery but the glen then became uninhabited save for a keeper at Loinaveich (OS 086888).

By 1869 all had gone and the only resident was a gamekeeper. As early as 1829 five families in Glen Ey (OS 090863) were cleared out and settled elsewhere to make way for deer and Michie recorderd that around 1830 nine families were evicted from Glen Ey at the request of the shooting tenant. They were probably settled elsewhere, perhaps in better circumstances, but loss of home and familiar surroundings is never pleasant. Little Inverey was joined to the deer forest in the late 1830's. Some tenants probably remained

174

a little longer on the fertile land of Auchelie (OS 088863) in Glen Ey but in 1842 eight more families were turned out, with over 3,000 sheep and some cattle. A number of Glen Ey evictees were given poor damp land near Braemar Catholic Chapel and they had some grazing for their cows along Clunie-side. Some evicted people emigrated, to Canada and Australia and some went voluntarily. Movement from here as well as from other glens was further forced on people when a clamp down on illicit distilling meant that a valuable source of income was lost and tenants were unable to pay their rents. Ruins of their deserted homes can still be seen.

Clearances took place in Glen Clunie (OS 147861). Dwellers of twelve farms had 500 cattle and 2,000 sheep. Two large sheep farms were created. Glen Callater (OS 175843) became a deer forest but there were no evictions although summer grazing was lost.

Sir Robert Gordon turned Glen Gelder (OS 247913) over to deer forest between 1830 and 1840 but there were few removals of tenants until after 1852 when Prince Albert purchased the estate. The entire population of the glen was moved but they were provided with better housing and employment on Balmoral Estate.

It was in Glen Gelder that a ditch was dug, about 4 feet deep and 1/2 mile long so that Prince Albert did not have to crawl along when stalking. He just popped his head up and shot.

Clearances in other Deeside glens took place to make way for deer - in Glengairn, Glenfinzie, Morven, Braemar and many others.

Although not strictly clearances, abandoned settlements are worth considering. Auchtavan (OS 204955) was an early village settlement already mentioned in connection with its "hanging-lum". Life would have been a struggle here, in this settlement that was fairly large. There are remains of a 16th & 17th century community, situated in a spectacular location. Other abandoned settlements are at Loin (OS 214957) and Dalchork, on the old road to Tomintoul that was later diverted, with remains of longhouses, enclosures and a lime kiln.

Of the townships on General Roy's map of 1745 - 1747 all can be identified except those where Mar Lodge now stands. To add to the twenty two on his map are Allt a' Sionnach on the Geldie and Croislish on the east side of Glen Luie. Up to twenty corn drying mills can be found.

By the beginning of the nineteenth century lime was being used as a top dressing. Up to twelve lime kilns may be identified.

On the Mar Lodge Estate small groups of shieling huts can be identified., together with shepherds' bothies and a couple of sheep-dip sites and some sheep-folds.

Whisky stills are hard to find, because they were originally in well-concealed places, but a number can still be identified.

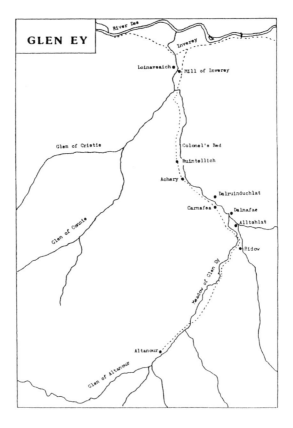

XXI. EVOCATIVE DWELLINGS & SOME OF THEIR FORMER RESIDENTS

"There is history in all men's lives."

Shakespeare

(There is room to mention only a few dwellings and again the selection is somewhat arbitrary, the choice of topics being influenced by personal interests. Spelling of place names is as in estate records. Alphatecial order has been followed, rather than geographical. Most of the Glenmuick properties have already been described in detail in the author's "The Legion of the Lost." so only a few of the most interesting ones are included here.)

The range of buildings in stone, from Inverey to Dinnet - whether in ruins or in good condition, is vast. A good number of the settings were remote yet beautiful, but life in some of the little dwellings was very hard. Precise dating is not possible, for some remains cover a considerable period. Ruins of buildings are certainly not hard to find.

ABERARDER

(OS 213937)

Aberarder lies in the valley of the Fearder and everywhere are ruins of the old settlements. This was at one time a populated area.

The story goes that a Farquharson Laird took summary action against a number of tenants. It seems that 19 of them had caused a minor rebellion and as a result he hanged all but one 'in the gryt barn at Aberardir'. One managed to escape.

About 2km. up the glen at Aberarder is the old kirk, now converted into a dwelling house. Only this now remains of the former hamlet of Knockan. At one time the Aberarder Kirk was the Free Kirk in Braemar, by the Clunie, but it was taken down, stone by stone, when the Rev. Cobban was responsible for a new Free Kirk building in Braemar in 1870 and the old building was re-erected here. After its service as a church it became a school, and then was a farmer's shelter for animals and feedstuff. Now considerably transformed, it is a pleasing dwelling. At some time

177

in the 1990's the kirk bell disappeared from the little belfry.

Aberarder is certainly a deserted glen. Middleton of Aberarder was once a thriving little hamlet. Although there are now nothing but ruins, we know that in 1810 the population must have been considerable for the Aberarder school roll stood at 120, 40 girls and 80 boys. A hundred years later only 2 pupils attended. All that remains now are the ruins of a collection of cottages. There was a smithy and a croft, where lived the blacksmith whose daughter Margaret Leys was the mother of John Brown. Among the crofters in Aberarder were a shoemaker, weavers, shepherds and wool-carders. These little communities were self-sufficient.

The remains of this "ferm-toun" in a sylvan setting probably belong to the time when farming improvements were taking place, The mill with its dam and lade can still be seen. Millers were never popular for farmers had to pay both laird and miller for mill use. When use of the mill ceased to be compulsory, many millers left for overseas. That was the case here.

The crofts of Balnoe (OS 214938) have gone. They appeared on the 1869 Ordnance Survey, but probably disappeared soon after that. The deserted farm of Balmore (OS 216943) was on the old drove road via Loch Builg.

Not far from the Fearder burn (Fearder is the glen or bog of high water) near the farm of Ratlich (OS 212947) is St. Manire's Chapel, another mute reminder of a departed population. It was here that the market that eventually moved to Clachanturn was held.

Ratlich

ABERGAIRN
(OS 355974)

Signs of the old lead mine and the extraction are still visible at Abergairn. Also in the area are possible remains of early pre-Christian habitation. There were a number of houses at Upper and Lower Corrybeg with a farm and later a grocer's shop. The thatched houses lay along both sides of the Corrybeg burn. G.M.Fraser writing in "The Old Deeside Road" records that in 1921 the place was deserted. As old folk died the houses were demolished and the ruins covered up, leaving, in 1921 only the stone walls of the gardens. Through the ages many women, probably widows, lived in the little houses. Meg Morris of Corrybeg was an early herbalist and amateur doctor and possibly a howdie or midwife.

ALLANMORE & ALLANQUOICH
(OS 138919 & 120914)

Over a mile east of the Linn of Quoich is Allanmore - the big pasture by the river, a now derelict farmhouse. The fine old house was in the 1800's the home of Col. Murray Farquharson, surrounded by a busy collection of houses.

The exterior is of somewhat irregular shape with windows placed irregularly. Inside it is surprisingly spacious with a large hall and a curving staircase. The kitchen hearth had a large lintel.

A famous walking friend of Col. Farquharson, Capt. Barclay-Allardice used to set out from Urie early in the morning, swim in a rocky pool near Allanmore house, spend a day shooting on Ben a' Bhuird and then walk back at night, across the hills to Urie. Not only was he a famous "walker" and sportsman, he was a well-known agricultural improver and established the first herd of shorthorns in Scotland. He was also a Captain in Huntly's 92nd Highlanders. Born in August 1779 his feats of strength were legendary. He succeeded his father the 4th Ury of Barclay who had made a fortune in

Jamaica and was responsible for the founding of the new town of Stonehaven.

Close to Allanmore is a derelict farmhouse and a red-roofed bothy. All around are earlier remains.

Nearby were a number of 17th century homes but by 1770 the Earl of Fife had cleared them off to give himself privacy and clearer views.

East of Mar Lodge was Allanquoich, with active dwellers - 5 tenants and 12 sub-tenants at the time of the Poll Book. They were cleared out late in the 18th century and replaced by one tenant. Others nearby were moved off on the grounds that they were not prepared to adopt new farming methods.

ALLTCAILLEACH (the burn of the women)
(OS 347 921)

At the time of the Poll Book in 1696 this was Gordon of Abergeldie property and had two tenants. By 1763 two other tenants had a cow and 50 sheep with 31 lambs. Around 1800 a Gordon family left the croft for Australia where like so many of the other emigrants from the area, they prospered. The Stewarts were in number in Allicailleach. When Birkhall became royal property Loinmuie was joined to Alltcailleachh, new buildings were added and the land drained.

ARDMEANACH (The middle height)
(OS 355 948)

In the seventeenth century Easter Ardmeanach was on the site of the present Ardmeanach and Wester Ardmeanach was where the present Dorsincilly now stands. Some 17th century cottar houses disappeared until by 1800 there were four dwellings west of Scurrystone and close to the wood. There was a labourer, a dyker, a carpenter and a weaver.

When John Cattenach was widowed he soon remarried - very soon in fact for some of the young men staying at

Abergeldie offered £10 to anyone who married while they were staying there. They wanted to join in a country wedding! With his new bride, Isobel Thomson, the wedding party, all on horseback, crossed the bridge below Birkhall. One of the party fell into the river and was badly hurt. Johnnie and Tibbie lived happily for many years.He died first. Both are buried in Glen Muick.

In the 1840's Charles Clark the blacksmith moved from Dorsincilly to a new house and smithy built for him at Ardmeanach. A shed was erected NE of 345948. By 1861 the blacksmith was John Clark. Joseph Bremner the weaver and his wife were paupers.

Sometime after 1881 the cottar houses were demolished, leaving only the blacksmith's.

There was a little group of cottar houses west of Ardmeanach, close to the wood, known as Turnamoin (about OS 354 948). By 1840 all trace had gone and the land had been joined to the farm of Dorsincilly.

ARDOCH
(OS 322009)

Catholicism was entrenched in Glen Gairn. According to the 1696 Poll Book Ardoch or Ardachie was the hamlet where all the inhabitants adhered to the Old Faith. A Braemar Catholic Register dating from 1703 refers to Ardichi and a Protestant record tells of a Hugh Strachan, a Jesuit, who resided in Ardoch which belonged to Callum Grierson alias McGregor of Dalfad, building the priest a house with a garden.

Ardoch (the high field) was one of the biggest clachans on Gairnside boasting fourteen 'fire' houses (with a chimney) a shop, and a school, probably seasonal. The shop belonged to Charles Calder: it seems to have been a little general shop but it sold tobacco and snuff. Charles was an early "rag and bone man", driving his goods to Blairgowrie. William Ritchie and James Cattenach were both weavers. The former was the Roman Catholic Sacristan

The houses were in a sheltered but muddy spot and were built at all angles. The priest's house (Father Lachlan McIntosh) was superior, with its porch and a garden or yard. Through the middle of the houses ran a little burn and every house had a tiny dam, an outlet spout and a bucket.

Most of the residents had reasonable land to cultivate and they all took part in whisky 'smuggling' - distilling the drink and then smuggling it out of the Glen once a week, for sale in the south.

Employment was at the lime quarry on the shoulder of Mammie. There is at Ardoch an excellent example of a large lime kiln and signs of the general improvements in agriculture. Prior to the nineteenth century farm complex, there had been an earlier longhouse settlement. A corn drying kiln and a horse mill were also there.

The folk of Ardoch belonged to a self contained community and they seem to have been happy with their lot. That is until the early years of the nineteenth century when Roman Catholics were evicted in favour of Protestants or sheep. There was likely to have been continuous settlement until the mid nineteenth century - yet another example of occupation through the years.

The Roman Catholic cause in Glen Gairn was supported by a Jesuit and a Jacobite mission. Three of these men were at Ardoch before 1720. The son of the Dalfad laird left his monastery in Wartzburg and came to Glengairn around 1730. The Church of Scotland tended to leave Glen Gairn Catholics to their own devices, unless something serious happened. The Manse was on the other side of the Dee and the minister, with three parishes to run, was often unable to cross the river in spate. Services were few and far between. The lower areas, nearer to Glenmuick, were Protestant. Those higher up were Roman Catholic.

Roman Catholics and staunch Jacobites, like others in the glen, the men went to Culloden.

AUCHINTOUL
(OS near 277010)

South of the ruins of the hamlet of Loinahaun in Glengairn lies the site of Auchintoul. This was the home of a succession of Flemings, seventeen in all and all named Peter. Auchintoul was really the home of a minor laird and had the distinction of having its own chapel. The Flemings were Roman Catholics and, as the situation demanded, ardent Jacobites.

The 14th Laird, Peter, was no exception and was involved with the Deeside army that went to Culloden. Like so many of the Deeside contingent, he lay wounded on the battlefield. His leg had been shattered by a musket ball and he was unable to crawl away. Not that that would have helped, for the Duke of Cumberland's forces were quickly at work, killing the wounded and taking whatever booty they could find. Peter had to fake death while enduring the agony of having his boot stripped off the shattered leg. One assumes he managed to lie quiet while the other boot was removed.

Whether he eventually managed to crawl to a cottage or he was assisted by women from the area, searching for their menfolk, we do not know, but Peter found himself in a cottage where he was cared for. His leg was amputated, and again he was lucky to survive for surgery was somewhat primitive in remote areas.

Peter fell in love with the girl who nursed him back to health and married her. They returned to Deeside in secret for after all he was branded as a rebel, and planned to set up house at Auchintoul. There they found that the government forces had not waited for a trial after Culloden, but had burned down Auchintoul and the neighbouring property of Inverenzie.

So they rebuilt the home and lived there happily, Peter not seriously hampered by his missing leg. Later Flemings were not so happy. They became embroiled in lengthy litigation and lost their patrimony.

The ruins of the chapel attached to Auchintoul were

known to my Granny who played there as a child in the early 1870's.

Today, stones are all that remain, mute testimony to yet another family's involvement in the Jacobite cause.

AUCHOLZIE (AUCHOLZIE)
(OS 344 906)
UPPER AUCHOLZIE
(OS 347 905)
MILLTOWN OF AUCHOLZIE
(OS 350 923)

Aucholie (Aucholzie) was a considerable estate in its own right, close to the Muick. The Stewarts were in strength here, - Papists and Jacobites who lost some of their men at Culloden. The estate was forfeit and then sold to the Earl of Aboyne. About 1766 Aboyne sold it to Farquharson of Invercauld. There was disagreement about a fair price, so the two experienced card players agreed that if Farquharson lost, he would pay the agreed asking price: If Aboyne lost, he would give the land to Invercauld. Aboyne thought he was probably quite safe, for he was famous for his skill and luck in cards. Both men were very drunk and unexpectedly, Farquharson won. Next morning when both were sober, they realized what had happened. Farquharson wanted to forget the deal. Aboyne said he would never break his word, no matter how drunk he was, so Farquharson got Aucholzie. When the McKenzies became owners of Glen Muick by purchase, the existing sheep pasture at Aucholzie became a deer forest.

Near Aucholzie are the ruins of Chapel Croft. Tradition places a hospice or some buildings associated with monks in the vicinity and remains would indicate that this is the case.

AUCHTAVAN
(OS 204955)

At Auchtavan there are remains of many deserted crumbling cottages, evidence of a considerable community. The name means field of the two kids and this is a reference to the rent that had to be paid to the laird. A lime kiln is close by. Some of the remains are medieval although many are later. There are longhouses, enclosures & a lime kiln. This was a harsh environment - but with wonderful views. Through it ran the old route from Aberarder to Tomintoul.

Remains of about a dozen houses can be picked out but a tiny cottage, the late Queen Mother's shiel is the only non-derelict one. Near by are the shells of 'black houses'. Of note at Auchtavan is the dwelling with a good example of a Hanging Lum -- a wooden chimney that was in a poor state, believed to be the only remaining one in the country, but now restored.

There are remains of settlements near the Fearder Burn. This was Auchnagymlinn which was washed away in the Muckle Spate of 1829. There were large deposits of sand and gravel. A giant's grave is reputed to be here and it is supposed to be 6 m. long. A story says that a family in the area were over 7 feet tall and they all died young.

Auchtavan

185

AULTONREA
(OS 364918)

Aultonrea is a farm in lower Glen Muick.

There are at least six ruins of buildings surrounded by a stone dyke. Longhouses lie there. Two kailyards can be picked out. An archaeological survey presumed the settlement to have been abandoned in the 19th century and much of the stone removed for building purposes.

BALNAAN
(OS 285005)

The farm of Balnaan (the farm town of the little ford) is only a heap of stones. The last to farm there was William McKenzie who died in 1909. There were problems getting the coffin to the burial ground because of heavy snow. The once cultivated land of the farm has reverted to nature.

BALNO
(OS 321004)

About four miles up the B972 there is a footbridge over the Gairn - the Black Bridge. Across the river is a long field and near the end is Balno (am baile nodha), the new farm town. It lay deserted, a little hamlet with its ruined meal mill, smithy and houses. Now, there is some revival.

Early in the 1900's there was a shop. John Reid, the poet of the glen, lived at Balno. He left to join the police force, first in Aberdeen then in Leith and later served as a railway detective. In his lifetime - he was a contemporary of the Glengairn writer Amy Stewart's father - the glen became depopulated.

In this little township are the remains of five longhouses and two enclosures.

BLAIRCHARRID, BALACARAIG, BLAIRCHARRID
(OS 357926)

Perhaps the most interesting settlement of all lies in Glen Muick. Blacharrage is on the 1869 Ordnance Survey map as Balacaraig.

Remains of early habitation are twelve long-houses, three enclosures and a corn drying mill that can still be identified.

Estate records show that in 1696 there was a little township of twelve tenant families on the Earl of Aboyne's land with three enclosures and the ever necessary corn-drying kiln. The patterns of the old run-rig farming are visible, where twelve oxen in the plough were turned. This is particularly obvious when the ground is snow covered

Sheep and lambs were kept in fair quantity in mid 18th century but by 1800 there were only three families there.

An Invercauld survey of 1807 showed a half acre of good field, thirteen acres of very stony land and an acre of pasture. Beyond lay another 36 acres that may have been shared with Rinlean. Plans were in hand in 1808 for amalgamation with other settlements, but they were not implemented.

Born about 1770, Meg Morris or "Fettie." lived in a very low hut and cut peats for a living. By 1841 she was listed as a pauper. By 1860 the only resident in Blacharrage was William Main, a keeper.

A track runs from here to other settlements, like Loinmore and Tombreck.

Although now difficult to access, here one can recognize most completely a village as it used to be.

CLACHANTURN
(OS 277947)

Clachanturn - Clach-na tigherna - the Laird's Village, lies about a mile east of Easter Balmoral just off the South Deeside Road. It was a large settlement with about 20 families in the nineteenth century. Now a few houses are all that remain and what had been a large farm. In the distant past it had been the site of a regularly held large market. It had too its inn, ferry & smiddy.

There was a school in the settlement about 1720, but it probably only operated in the "non-farming" periods. The ruins have gone and a handful of more modern houses remain but a little imagination can re-create a country "fair" by the river.

CRATHIE AREA
(OS 264949)

The Poll Book record of 1696 shows 16 proprietors but about 100 years later there were only 6.

Stirton, in "Crathie & Braemar" describes homes in the area, with dried mud on the walls and thatch of heather or broom. Frequently there was a dividing partition.

Crathie in the 17th century was basically controlled by the McHardies. John of Daldownie had 12 tenants, Edward had 4 and John had 3. The original Crathie was a settlement running for about a mile along the north bank of the Dee from the Mill of Crathie to Tomidhu. This busy settlement had its church with manse, burial ground and the minister's glebe. There was a ferry and a ford across the Dee which provided a link to the south by way of the Capel Mounth. At the boathouse at Milltown a little shop or perhaps a pub sold refreshments. By 1824 it was certainly an inn, then it was demolished.

CRATHIENAIRD
(OS 257958)

Crathienaird -"Crathie of the high place" - is a farm above Crathie. The name may refer to the bog above Crathie Burn.

Crathienaird too has its ruins, indicating a settlement of some size. At least 5 longhouses can be identified.

On the Crathienaird property was Bridgend of Bush, the birthplace in 1826 of John Brown whose father James had married the daughter of the Aberarder blacksmith, Margaret Leys. When John was a little boy the family, - father had been a teacher before he became a farmer - moved across the road to the Bush Farm.

In the area was the home of a family of Coutts, Pipers, who did itinerant work on farms and went south at harvest time.

DALDOWNIE
(OS 246009)

About 3km. from Braenaloin the track moves away from the river as it climbs. Here was probably the last working farm and farmhouse in Glen Gairn.. A barn remains and heaps of stones, for the building was demolished in the late 1970's.

Locals believed fairies made their home here, and a place near Daldownie is called An Sidhean, the hill of the fairies.

A rail bridge had been erected at Foot o' Gairn but when the embargo on further track-laying came, it was taken down. This miniature version of Sydney Harbour Bridge was re-erected to provide access to the remote farm of Daldownie in Glen Gairn, where it still remains, a somewhat out of place bridge leading nowhere as the area is derelict.

DALFAD
(OS 316007)

By 1863 the Church of Scotland in Glen Gairn ceased to be a Royal Bounty Mission and became a quoad sacra parish with full status for the minister. The Rev. Robert Neil then moved from Tullochmacarrick to a Manse above Dalfad, further up the Glen on Huntly land. The house had been built on the site of a thatched cottage whose gable end was retained. Life would have been pleasant and the accommodation more salubrious than that of most of the parishioners. Only heaps of stones and some flowers like doronicum are now reminders of garden and croquet green, a vegetable plot and a lawn on which strutted peacocks. Some ornamental beech trees still remain

The Manse was eventually sold for £392.10s. in 1928 and later demolished. More of the older Manse at Tullochmacarrick remains. The minister also had a small farm. The old road ran along here.

When the Rev. Neil died in 1890 he was succeeded by the Rev. James Lowe. His family, brought up in Dalfad Manse included a daughter, Amy Stewart Fraser who wrote of her early life in the Glen, with the visits of tinkers with bootlaces and matches and the Pig Man, exchanging crockery for rabbit skins. Her books, 'Hills of Home', 'Of Memory Long' and 'Roses in December', written when she was quite elderly, give a wonderful picture of a way of life gone for ever.

A path leads from Dalfad Manse to the former Roman Catholic Chapel at Clashinruich (hollow of the heather). Little remains but a heap of stones, for a larger chapel and house for the priest were built down the glen at Candacraig.

Silence reigns now where once there was the constant sound of voices.

In the birch wood lie the ruins of the uncompleted chapel at Dalfad.

DALPHUIL
(OS 316007)

On the right of the road up Glen Gairn can be seen an oddly shaped building, Dalphuil, or the "Teapot Cottage". It was purchased by the Royal family in 1938 and was a favourite shiel or picnic place.

It used to be the old Glengairn school before a new building was erected next to the church at Kirkstyle. Its last teacher was Mr.Coutts. In its early days Dalphuil was an educational establishment for lairds' sons and ruins of the dormitory accommodation can still be seen.

DORSINCILLY
(OS 354942)
(Passage way of the dripping - a wet place)

In 1696 the "Dorsinsillie" Gordon of Abergeldie property supported six married tenants with their wives - Allans, Smalls and a John Beattie. Some time later there were still a number of houses and crofts on Dorsincilly. The Small family, with associations with Aultonrie were there for a long time, as were the Riachs with similar connections. A few dwellers were cleared out about 1715, at the time when the oldest wing of Birkhall was built.

Dorsincilly became the home farm of Birkhall estate. Among other Factors were David White and William Laing. Subsequently the farm was leased to Francis Farquharson (Old Braichley) then a Mr. Mitchell, son of the minister of Kemnay became the tenant. He had married a Grassick of Donside. They lived in great style, with a nurse and a governess for the children and what was known locally as "a machine" for driving to church. After a few years the Mitchells became bankrupt. All their goods were sold off, the smaller items being disposed of at a roup which most of the locals attended. When Mr. Mitchell died hs family was in very straightened circumstances.

William Ross, son of a Ballater innkeeper, moved into the property. He too had financial problems so after a few years he left and moved to a little wooden hut erected where Dinnet Railway Station later stood. He did not survive long and his widow and children needed parish help.

About 1871 William, one of the Littlemill Gordons then moved into Dorsincilly. He had been in Ceylon for a number of years and had made a great deal of money. When he retired from Dorsincilly in 1881 his successor, a Mr. Barclay repaired all the houses. He also installed a steam threshing mill. It seems he stayed there for little more than two years when John Smith of Khantore moved in.

For many years a blacksmith carried on business at

Dorsincilly A succession of smiths worked there - among them James Smith, William Riddell and Charles Clark. Around 1843 the blacksmith's base was moved to Ardmenach and it was still there in 1900.

The naturalist William Magillivery had in 1850 written of it as a farm. In 1866 a survey was conducted for the first Ordnance survey map but beside the nine buildings that were marked was written "ruins."

Dorsincilly

DUBRACH
(OS 030888)

Below the confluence of Dee and Geldie is the site of the old farm of Dubrach (dubh bhruach - the black bank), on the south of the Dee, almost 3 miles above the Linn.

It was the scene of a murder enquiry that made history - and also had its moments of amusement.

In 1749, when feelings were still running high after Culloden, the English forces were garrisoning the Highlands. Deeside, being the headquarters of the 1715 Rising and the home of many so called 'rebels' in 1745, was given particular attention by the English forces. Many were from Col.Guise's Regiment, which had not actually fought at Culloden but one of its officers, Capt. Scott, had been involved in the later 'punishment raids'.

At Dubrach up the Dee there was in 1749 a small detachment of eight men, led by Sgt. Arthur Davies. Dubrach, the 'black bank' was a farm tenanted by Michael Farquharson. His son Donald spoke both Gaelic and English, unusual at the time in that area, and he conversed freely with members of the garrison who were delighted to find someone who spoke their language. The soldiers, apart from seeking any signs of further plotting against the Hanoverians, were also looking for offenders against the Disarming Act, - anyone carrying a weapon, playing the pipes and wearing the tartan, for these were all banned.

There was a 'conference point' twice a week with a detachment of the same regiment, based in Glenshee. The whole area was wild and lonely but Sgt. Davies enjoyed fishing and shooting and was quite happy. He did not always wear his uniform. In fact, he was quite a snappy dresser, with a silk waistcoat, a blue top coat and a fancy hat. His shoes had silver buckles, there were silver buttons on his garments, and he had a silver watch. Quite a silvery appearance! In addition to a purse for his own money and one for army expenses, he had a very ornate ring. The buckles and ring were gifts from his wife who was at Dubrach with him. She was the widow of the Regimental Paymaster. The ring had presumably belonged to him, and was engraved with the sentiment, 'Remember me when this you see'.

One beautiful autumn morning, Thursday 28th September, the patrol set out to meet the Glenshee men. Sgt. Arthur Davies went first, carrying his gun, ready to shoot deer, fowl, hare or any other quarry. Soon they came across a man hastily trying to hide a kilt. Wearing or possessing a kilt was of course a punishable offence. Davies warned this John Grewer of the danger of breaking the law and they spoke of the best places for shooting deer and game. The patrol then went on its way, eventually met the other detachment and exchanged news and views. Davies' men set off for home but the Sergeant parted from his men to go after game. They saw him in the distance, and that was the last they saw of him. He never reached Dubrach.

Sgt. Davies was reported missing on Thursday 29th September 1749. A search was mounted but this revealed no sign of Davies. Eventually the garrison at Braemar was alerted. The army organised a full-scale search, but it revealed nothing. Had he been murdered? There were only two possible suspects. Only two men had been in the vicinity at the time of the disappearance. One was a local farmer's son called Clark and the other, MacDonald, a forester for a local laird. They both carried guns to shoot deer, rabbits, etc, Macdonald having the laird's permission to do so. Clark was at the time wearing tartan, an offence for which he could have been arrested.

Donald Farquharson, son of the farmer where Davies had been lodging had a message asking him to meet a shepherd he knew, Alexander MacPherson who was at the summer shieling in Glen Connie. MacPherson told him he had been visited by a ghost claiming to be Sgt. Davies and asked that he should have a decent burial. When he refused the ghost insisted he get Donald to help him. Donald refused but eventually agreed to see the bones at a place indicated by the ghost. They found the body, badly decomposed, and then his hat and gun and brogues, minus buckles.

The only two suspects were arrested and tried in Edinburgh in 1754. Evidence was purely circumstantial at first. Clark's fiancé who became his wife was supposed to have been seen with Davies' ring and Macdonald had some items of clothing. Modern T.V. has nothing on this trial! Sandy McPherson of Inverey was called and under oath said a 'ghost' in a blue coat came to him when he was in bed, in June 1750 and said he was Sgt. Davies. He said that he had been murdered, gave the exact location, and asked that Farquharson of Dubrach would see to his burial. McPherson asked the name of the murderer but this was not revealed. The following week it came again, demanding burial. This time, in answer to the question, it said Duncan Clerk and Alexander MacDonald were the murderers. Both of them, in league? That was one odd feature, another was that the 'ghostie' of the dead Davies spoke in Gaelic, a language that Sgt. Davies did not understand. The ghost story was backed up by Isobel McHardy, in whose house McPherson was spending the night. She had been terrified and had hidden under the bed-clothes. When McPherson and Farquharson had after a search found the body in a peat moss, they buried it. There was no ring, buckles, buttons or money.

There was evidence of a body having been found before the trial. Angus Cameron, a cattle thief, claimed to have been with a friend and to have witnessed the murder from a hiding place. He said Davies, in his blue coat and fancy hat, was not far off. Clark and a smaller man came up to the soldier at the top of a hill. He said he saw Clark strike the man who put his hand to his heart and moved away. Was he stabbed? The men then followed the stranger, shot him and fled. Angus said he had hurried away.

If that was a reliable witness, the evidence was fairly conclusive. However, the "friend" could not give evidence - he had already faced the death penalty for a previous murder.

The defence council reduced the court to laughter at the thought of an English soldier speaking good Gaelic. The verdict was awaited. On the evidence, would you have said guilty or not guilty? The jury, after a long sitting, returned a unanimous verdict - "Not Guilty".

As it happened, not all the available evidence had been presented. Clark, only a year after the murder, had enough money to lease two small farms. Even stranger, the 'seer' McPherson went to work for him as a shepherd, but they quarrelled and he left. It seems he had accused Clark of murder but why did Clark employ him at all? Clark was also said to have a purse very similar to the one Davies had, and Clark's wife had a ring with the correct inscription. A very odd coincidence!

Was the 'ghost' a local Gaelic speaker, trying to persuade McPherson to inform on the suspected murderers?

The mystery will never be solved now.

Dubrach farm, where the soldiers were based was at one time the home of the oldest known Jacobite. Peter Grant had fought with Monaltrie's Regiment and was wounded at Culloden. Eventually he received a royal pardon and a pension. Dubrach was buried in Braemar.

GLEN FENZIE
(OS 320024)

Across the Glenfenzie Burn is a ruined farmhouse and out-buildings, all derelict. On a stone in the wall at the front of the house are the initials DM and the date 1879. At the other end of the wall is the date 1822.

Inside a little imagination can recreate the living conditions of the family. Some years ago the swey was in place, where the mistress of the house did her cooking. There were no ovens: everything was 'pot -roasted'. Other buildings are to be seen further down the hill - all in ruins.

GLEN GAIRN
(OS 303012)

The river Gairn, 'the rough water' runs in a stony bed from its source on Ben Avon to join the Dee at Foot o' Gairn, some 20 miles away.

The military road, made after the '45, inspired by General Wade but not built by him, winds through the glen for several miles. The Glen is now depopulated but there are in all parts ruins, some no more than heaps of stone, to show where both high and low had made their homes and lived out their lives. 150 years ago the glen was thickly populated by a hardy people. Although harvests could be damaged by harsh weather and winters were severe the people managed to subsist on their patches of cultivated ground. They had peat for fuel and everyone helped to cut and cart the peats.

Gaelic was the language of the home although English

was spoken.

At the bottom of the glen the land is well cultivated, but then it becomes wilder. Up the hill is Abergairn and the ruins of Corrybeg. Here at Christmas 1747 Malcolm McGrigor of Balmenach killed John Stewart of Abergairn. Before he died he was able to name his murderer who disappeared for 25 years. Then, calling himself John Grant, he was apprehended and tried in Edinburgh. He was acquitted but in the aftermath of excitement he was hit on the head, probably by a McGregor son, and died.

Signs of the old lead mine and the extraction are still visible at Abergairn. Also in the area are possible remains of early pre-Christian habitation. There were a number of houses at Upper and Lower Corrybeg with a farm and later a grocer's shop. The thatched houses lay along both sides of the Corrybeg burn. G.M.Fraser writing in "The Old Deeside Road" records that in 1921 the place was deserted. As old folk died the houses were demolished and the ruins covered up, leaving, in 1921 only the stone walls of the gardens. Through the ages many women, probably widows, lived in the little houses. Meg Morris of Corrybeg was an early herbalist and amateur doctor and possibly a howdie or midwife.

Over the Gairnshiel Bridge and along to Kirkstyle are heaps of stones and a derelict and a rather precarious building. At one time a shoemaker lived at Kirkstyle and a miller. There were a few small dwellings and a corn mill with a mill dam. Behind is a stone with the initials CLM and the date 1840. Tomnavey (the hillock of the deer) was in 1696 home to 17 tenant families and a cottar.

GLEN GELDER
(OS 247913)

In Glen Gelder, Rachaish, (Ruighe Chois) (OS 249923) the cattle run of the hollow, was really three townships. The remains show that the stones used for building had been large. Some gable ends can be picked out. There were at least five longhouses and a couple of enclosures.

A neighbouring township was Ruighachail, (OS 258893) cattle run of the kail. A large longhouse is visible and a kiln. The ruins would seem to show that there may have been up to 10 buildings here and a corn drying kiln.

Yet another settlement was tiny Cinn na Creige. (OS 246924) (the end of the crag.) Alex Inkson McConnochie, in his Book "The Royal Dee" tells of an old lady saying her mother had been moved out from here and settled elsewhere to make room for deer. This would have been in the early 1830's.

GLEN GIRNOC
(OS 315928)

The glen of the Girnoc lies between the Hill of the Piper, Creag Phiobaidh, and the Hill of the Firs, Creag Ghiubhais.

At the foot of the Glen, on the main road, was a school, opened by Prince Albert. This S.P.G. school continued until 1943.

This almost deserted glen was in years gone by heavily populated and was the site of many illicit whisky stills. Practically every family in the glen was involved in 'smuggling'. At least 11 illicit "stills" have been identified and there may be more.

Years before, the glen was famous - or notorious - because of the activities of witches. Further up the glen is Creag nam Ban, the Hill of the Women, where witches were burned. At the top a pile of stones and a 'stake', the reputed place of the burnings, were found.

The glen is also associated with dark deeds resulting from the feud between Gordons and Forbes

The mill at the foot of the glen was the childhood home of Alexander Gordon, benefactor of the village and builder of bridges. Little Mill was at one time a large complex, - farm, a little hamlet, cottages and a cloth mill. From the late 1600's there had been a cloth dyeing mill here and the Gordon sons were frequently called to account by the Kirk Session for haughmagandy.

John Davidson, married to Barbara Grant, was a man whose skills were much in demand. A cooper, based at Little Mill, he was kept busy producing tubs and barrels, etc., for use in the illegal trade of whisky distilling, known locally as "smuggling". When John was making the largest size of tub he usually needed 'Barby's' help in getting the staves set up and secured by hoops. It was no unusual thing when the last stave was being placed for "Barby" to make some unexpected movement and for the whole structure to go tumbling down. The work had then to be started again. John, whose English was poor at the best of times, expressed himself very forcibly. He was a powerfully built man, with some eccentric habits.

John's pet hate was Excisemen. Early in his life he had rented a meal mill at Mill of Dinnet and stored there barley, in various states of processing for the making of whisky. Whenever an exciseman made an attempt to search the mill, John disputed his right of access with lengthy and wordy arguments. The exciseman should have prevailed, with the backing of the law, but John intimidated him by a show of brute force. Working himself into a state, he grabbed the mill 'louder', - a large wooden lever or bar - and so terrified the trembling exciseman that he was ready to beat a hasty retreat.

When he was in Ballater, young people frequently tried to play tricks on John. It delighted them to see him roused, threatening all sorts of vengeance. On one occasion, a large log was placed against John's door. When he opened it in the morning, the weight pushed open the door with such force that John was knocked flat on his back. Uttering all kinds of deadly maledictions on the perpetrators, John was in a rage. They would of course be long gone!

Up the Glen and off to the left over a little burn lies the abandoned Mill of Cosh. The nearby house is still occupied. There was one occasion when the school on the main South Deeside Road at Girnoc was about to close because of falling numbers. The Laird appointed a miller who had 13 children, so the school remained open. The tiny house must have been somewhat short of space!

Two rows of houses nestled into the side of Creag Ghiubhais. The house outlines can be picked out among the stones of Na Cearr-lannan (OS 322956). Ruins and imagination can re-create the life lived here.

Further up the Glen, Loinveg (OS 316935) is a sad ruin, giving no idea of its former glory. Of all the glens in the area, this is perhaps the most depopulated.

Further on still is the Camlet (An Cam-leathad), (OS 308931) the curved slope, an accurate description. There are lost settlements all around Camlet. West of the farm are four longhouses and then a further two. There is another settlement of longhouses on the east side of the farm, north of the track. One of the best - preserved lime-kilns on Deeside is here.

A path runs down to the Girnoc Burn and crosses by what used to be a serviceable little foot bridge to eventually reach Glen Muick. There are ruins across the burn. This area was Loinn a'Choirce or Lynefork, ("the upper ploughed land.") The late Ian Shepherd the archaeologist found settlements with different styles and dates. There were longhouses, both stone & turf built and a drying kiln and kailyard.

Beyond the Camlet is another deserted hamlet, once a 'ferm toun' of considerable size, Bovaglie (OS 302920). This was once a busy place. By the 19th century the number of families in the glen had dropped drastically to 20. Bovaglie was occupied until the 1990's on a summer basis.

The Girnoc track runs through the woods of Bovaglie. Scott Skinner of Strathspey fame wrote a tune here that he called Bovaglie's Plaid. It is said that he chose this title because of a local saying that the wood haps or shelters Bovaglie like a plaid. Many of the trees are down now although there has been some fresh planting in the glen of recent years.

Beyond Bovaglie a track leads to Easter Balmoral (OS 266942) and the Distillery. From the Distillery at Easter Balmoral a track goes off in a S.W. direction to Inchnabobart (OS 310876) in Glen Muick, once a little farm, now a Royal Lodge.

The glen had its unusual character, known as "The Minister of the Camlet" but his territory was probably beyond Bovaglie. Little is known about him with any degree of certainty but it seems, like Cassandra, his prophesies were fated never to be believed.

Along the Inchnabobart road is the Builteach, (OS 277933) a former farm - 'hillock of the summer hut', where transhumance took place. A large group of people and animals would move in the summer to fresh pastures. There are remains of dairy houses or booths and bothies of cattlemen whose wives did the milking and cheese making.

GLEN LUI
(OS 063918)

Glen Lui lay on the route that linked the Lairig Ghru (the gloomy pass) with Deeside.

Many families had lived by the Lui Water. After 1715 the Earl of Mar's lands were sold. People were cleared off in 1732 and again in 1766. John Grant Michie a little later spoke of the abandoned homes. Deer replaced the villagers. All the way along the track there are the ruins of forgotten homes.

Seton Gordon in his 1925 "The Cairngorm Hills of Scotland" told of some of the characters of the area - Donald Fraser a skilled stalker who loved golf, Charlie Robertson, a "deer watcher" and John Mackintosh, a piper.

Just before the time of the '45 Rising there was a seer in Glen Lui called Duncan Calder who, like Cassandra, was destined never to be believed. On 25th July 1745 Duncan Calder told the astonished people of Mar that the landing of Prince Charles had taken place that very day at Moidart. A local Laird, in disbelief, sent a messenger to check the news. It was true. He also foretold that a thorn bush would grow in the middle of a large pool near Craig Clunie and everyone laughed at the idea. In 1752 the old bridge of Invercauld was built and at the side of one of the arches a thorn bush flourished. He also said there would come a time when the folk of Glen Ey would not be able to turn loose for grazing any of their beasts. It came true when the Duffs acquired Mar estates for the whole area became a deer forest.

Luibeg is now shut up and lifeless. It was the home of the late Bob Scott, a keeper known over a wide area. He gave shelter to hundreds of walkers in his isolated bothy behind his house. Unfortunately the bothy burned down some years ago and it has been replaced by a wooden one further down the Lui.

I knew Bob and his daughter well and they told some wonderful stories of times past.

GLENSHEE
(OS 139781)

Opposite to the the Ski Centre at Glenshee, where the ski tow in now are some old stones, remains of a little croft.

It was here that a famous bowman lived, Cam Ruadh. He was lame and red haired and no beauty.

On one occasion he took a vow not to shed blood for 24 hours. Unfortunately for him it was just at the time there was a raid by cattle thieves and his services were needed by his Superior.

At first he took no part in activities and the thieves were getting away. When the 24 hours were up he caused many casualties with his bow and arrow and the thieves retreated. Back they came with reinforcements, ready for revenge.

They came across a seemingly stupid old shepherd and promised to teach him to shoot with a bow and arrow if he would tell them where to find the Cam Ruadh. The old man threw off his tattered cloak and head covering and shouted "I am Cam Ruadh". He fixed his arrow to his bow that had been lying hidden in the heather and immediately his enemies fled.

INVERENZIE
(OS 330006)

Over the Glenfenzie Burn was Inverenzie, home of the McGregor family.

When out on an "expedition" stealing cattle, two of their sons met their deaths. One of the family had captained the Gairnside men at Culloden. after mustering them for Lord Lewis Gordon and had been killed by a Hanoverian bayonet while lying wounded on the field.

In more modern times, Inverenzie was the home of weight llifter, Robert Shaw.

LAGGAN
(OS 330006)

Viewed from the road at Lary is, in the distance across the Glenfenzie Burn, the now refurbished Laggan Cottage. About 1803 Margaret McGrigor who had been born at Tullochmacarrick moved here. She spent her time spinning strips for all sorts of uses, including tying sheep's feet at shearing time. She made wool shoes and all her own clothes. She never needed money for neighbours provided her with basic food - turnips and meal - in return for her weaving.

Well-read, she had a good number of books and was well versed in Catholic doctrine, frequently explaining it to young folk. She never went out, except to Mass, which she never missed. Known as "The Holiest Woman in the Glen", she eventually wasted away and was interred in the McGrigor burial ground at Dalfad.

Laggan was also the home of Lewis, a self taught vet. He learned from experience and was much in demand.

LARY
(OS 336002)

Lary was Gillanders territory. They were noted for their whisky produced in their illicit still, but it seems to have had too much of a peaty content to satisfy everyone. There was once a school at Lary attended by Morven children. All around what was Lary Farm are the remains of settlements, first recorded in the 1696 Poll Book. Population numbers increased considerably after that date.

LAWSIE & RINTARSIN
(OS 261960)
(Perhaps from An Lamhsaich, meaning uncertain)

At Lawsie, now with a modern house and a lovely garden, there was a farm and a considerable settlement

According to an archaeological survey the stones used in building were larger than usual. There were nine longhouses, two enclosures and a limekiln on a west facing slope, with two more at the farm of Lawsie. The footings of two further longhouses were identified according to an archaeological survey report. There was also a lime-kiln.

Slightly to the north, on the Knock of Lawsie there was another longhouse and more - perhaps three, on the east bank of the Rintarsin Burn.

Later the "township" of Rintarsin had up to thirty houses. Tradition says there is a burial ground there.

During the Napoleonic Wars there was a rifle range in the vicinity.

THE LEBHALL
(OS 299964)

The leth-bailie or half farm-town is 4 miles west of Ballater. Willie Downie was thre third generation to farm there: he died in Ballater some years ago when 98 years old, still very alert.

Everywhere, especially up the hill are remains of settlements. Bracken and undergrowth cover many of them, but they are numerous. By one of the little burns lie the ruins of a lime-kiln. These were usually round with a bowl-shaped drying chamber and a drying floor and were built into the slope of a bank or against the wall of a barn.

LOCH KANDER
(OS 190809)

One of the loneliest lochs in the whole area is Loch Kander. In the corrie above Loch Kander a heap of stomes is all that is left of a shepherd's bothy. The naturalist William MacGillivary wrote about the building, with its hearth, stone benches and pipe niches. The roofless ruin still has a bench and a niche. It had a place for a fire, two stone recesses, and two stone alcoves for storage.

LOINMUIE
(OS 340925)

Loinmuie, Loinnn Muigh, (enclosure of the field) was a high-lying clachan up the hill from Crofteithert. It lay under one of the three Coyles of Muick with the Alltcailleach forest near by. Kirk records indicate that up to twenty "reekin lums" were to be found there. Stewarts were in Loinmuie in numbers and indeed in the glen generally but after the '45 many left or changed their name, often to Dowie or Downie.

The small crofts of Loinmuie clachan were amalgamated with Loinmuie Farm before it disappeared. Afforestation hid it from view at one time but with more recent felling the fairly considerable remains are visible. Longhouses are scattered about. One house was larger than the others with a gable wall 2' thick. The fireplace with a recess on either side can be clearly identified. There are smaller dwellings and some round or oval shaped buildings. Loinmuie had virtually disappeared when in 1899 James Macdonald did a survey. Before that the naturalist William Magillivray had in 1850 written of it as a farm. In 1866 a survey was conducted for the first Ordnance Survey map but beside the nine buildings that were marked was written 'ruins'.

Loinmuie could be reached via Glen Girnoc. Opposite the farm of Loinveg was the settlement of Lynhort or Lynchork according to some records, and a track ran near here to Loinmuie. By the middle of the 19th century it was engulfed by trees.

The decline of Loinmuie seems to have happened between the census of 1841 and that of 1851. By 1861 it had gone from the census and 10 years later it seems to have been part of the farm toun of Alltcailleach. Yet another census and it has gone, not even linked to its neighbour.

MICRAS

The Micras is a general name for the farms lying between Rinabaich (OS 302964) and Wester Micras (OS 281954).

Tomidhu stands where the the old Deeside Road went N.W. to the Kirk of Crathie and the Post Office. There were connecting roads among the little settlements.

Remains are there, - heaps of stones. The old school was here where the Rev. Grant Michie taught before becoming minister of Dinnet. He had been born at Micras in January 1830. He recorded details of 11 houses at West Micras when he was a boy and there were further cottar houses. The whole area between Tomidhu and Rhynabaich was called Micras, but it was divided into Easter, Wester & Mid Micras.

PIPER HOLE
(OS 255965)
(Toll Phiobair, the Hole of the Pipers)
&
SCUTTER HOLE
(OS 254961)

Scutter is from the Gaelic Sgotan, a small farm. A Scuttle hole was a hole in a cowshed wall for throwing out dung.

Originally a group of houses north of Crathie, Scutter Hole is always paired with Piper and the two are called Piper and Scutter. They are also linked with Crathienaird and Lawsie.

In an old kirk record the verse used locally and well know to older people in the area was:-

"Piper Hole, Scutter Hole, Crichienaird an Lawsie

Doon below the Muckle Craig, ye'll see the Kirk o'

Crathie".

There are other less polite verses.   .

About a mile from Balmoral Castle are a few stones, remains of the hamlet of Piperhole that was a thriving community in mid 19th centuty. On the north side of the Piper burn was a little township, houses spresd out in a straight line, - Piperhole, the tinkers' home It was a collection of 'thackit clay biggins' some with a but and ben, some with only one room. The people had few comforts, but they were hardy and healthy. A self reliant group, in addition to cultivating their wee bit of land by hand many were proficient in wood and metal work. They subsisted on their meagre crops, gained by hard work from poor ground and whatever game they could shoot. They had meal and milk and their kale, raised large families and lived to ripe old ages. Their few sheep or the odd cow grazed around and some folk kept a pig and some poultry. Food had to be stored or cured for winter and butcher meat was scarce. Every home had its broth pot, on the fire every day and there was no limit to the amount of hot vegetable broth that could be supped. Queen Victoria, on a visit to one of the cottages, was told that in the soup pot there was a mutton bone, carrots and neeps, barley and cabbage.

Poaching was a popular past-time with fish in the Dee and game in the forest. The men were good shots and proud of their skill. Shooting matches were popular all over the area.

Communal events like sheep shearing, gathering in the harvest and casting peats were enjoyed to the full. There were no class barriers and plenty of the local brew ensured a happy occasion. Dances were usually held in the winter, with reels, strathspeys and square dances.

Sticks were collected in the wood, chiefly by women and children. They were usually tied in a sack and carried across the back. Fir cones were also collected to burn well and give off a pleasing aroma. There was a spring, but the burn was close by, to provide water.

Entertainment was home made, with visits to neighbours where there was dancing, singing, playing musical instruments (fiddle and bagpipes) and telling stories as well as regaling all the local gossip.

Piperhole was the camping place of tinkers. They were popular especially if they could contribute to the musical entertainment or take part in contests of strength. These of course were confined to good weather and putting the stone, throwing the hammer, tossing the caber and wrestling were always popular. The Piperholers usually took part in Braemar Games, walking to Braemar or getting a lift in a farm cart, and frequently the tinkers were prize winners. The tinkers replenished the Piperholders' supplies of tin plates, cooking pots, candle holders etc., often in exchange for food. Piperhole women spent the winter spinning and weaving. There was a hand - loom in the clachan and cloth was produced that was dyed with vegetable and litchen, ragwort and heather dyes. The men carved wood, made candles, and were skilled cobblers as well as making the breeches for themselves and their sons.

The people of Piperhole were Roman Catholics and ardent Jacobites. A number were in the Deeside Brigade that marched to Derby under Lord George Murray. They fought at Falkirk and some died on the field of Culloden.

A sturdy independent people, like many other groups in the area, they are only a memory, and all that remains are a few scattered stones.

Tinkers, who had almost permanent residence at Piperhole, Crathie, drank in the Tink bar of the Monaltrie Hotel in Ballater and frequently camped around. The Tink Bar has now been demolished, and the Hotel no longer operates as such.

At the entrance to Bush farm is a bridge. On the south side opposite the farm entrance was a cottage, the birthplace of John Brown, already mentioned.

A local theory is that a section of ground from the Bush to the Deeside road, a rather useless piece, was Balmoral land and that Queen Victoria gave it to the tinkers in perpetuity. There has been found no documentary evidence to support this.

REMICRAS
(OS 267000)

Remicras was a 'village' community abandoned in the nineteenth century, with a water mill that is well worth inspection.

This depopulated settlement has the outlines of longhouses distinctly visible. Later ruins are of a farmhouse and a 'U' shaped steading, in a style typical of the area. There is a lime kiln and a grain mill with the remains of the mill dam, the lade and the sluice. This is an interesting structure that would have required considerable physical effort to install. A considerable investment of money and labour to erect buildings to supersede the earlier settlement would probably have come from the Laird. The masonry of the two building ranges differs.

RHYNABAICH
(OS 302964)

Just after the 46th milestone on the Aberdeen to Braemar road, about 3 miles east of the present Crathie Kirk, Rhynabaich can be seen on the right, where are the deserted dwellings of Easter Micras. One building remains out of 17 "fire houses"- houses with a hearth.

RICHARKARIE
(OS 301015)
(RICHARCHARIE) (RICHRICHIE) (COULACHAN)

Most of the early documents prefer the spelling Richarkarie. This 'cattle run of the little road' lay on the north bank of the Gairn about 6 miles from Ballater. It was good arable land and included the little 'touns'of Torran and Tomnaverie.

Houses were dotted about at Richarkarie without any order but most had a little kale yard or garden. Most folk kept a few sheep or a cow. Among those who worked for the laird and cultivated a tiny bit of land themselves were a few tradesmen - in this case a weaver and a carpenter.

Ploughing was on the run-rig system, with more difficult areas being dug by the spade or cas-crom. There was an in field and an outfield. Small black cattle were grazed and these were walked to market in Falkirk by the drovers.

Farming in Richarkarie was only on subsistence level, as in neighbouring "touns". 1693 - 1700 were bad years for weather. Crops rotted. Death was frequent. Folk were desperate. Some parts of the Glen were converted to sheep runs. 1740 was another bad year with heavy snow in spring, as was 1747. Crops were ruined and nothing was carted in until December. There was a ban on use of grain for distilling. No food and no whisky! 1782 was a poor year too. Farmers were ruined: so were their tenants. Even farmers on a larger scale could not pay their rents to the laird and the 'tounsfolk' of

Richarkarie were in a sorry state. Crofts were abandoned. The army and overseas prospects beckoned to desperate folk. Houses were abandoned. The land was turned over to sheep grazing. Some Lairds were making deer forests, but Richarkarie did not fall prey to this. The Invercauld Factor, Charles Farquharson was easy on his tenants but when the Rev. Charles McHardy, the Crathie minister became factor, everything changed. Extant lists give the religious affiliation of tenants. Roman Catholics were often evicted to make way for Protestant sheep farms. It was often a case of Catholics out, sheep in.

Along with others Richarkarie fell about 1815. By 1808 James McIntosh was paying rent for 'Richarkrie' and had some sub tenants but the land was described as 'stoney'. One or two individuals remained for a few more years but the 'toun' had gone. In the 1870's a man called Grant was paying a small rent to the Laird, presumably for a small dwelling and some grazing, but then all records of Richarkrie disappear.

Richarkarie was the home of John Begg, a whisky "smuggler" who went legal and moved to Easter Balmoral when the original distillery was burned down.

RINLOAN
(OS293006)
&
MUIR OF GAIRNSHIEL
(OS 91007)

Near Gairnshiel Lodge the B976 road heads for Crathie. On the right is Rinloan (a wet meadow), at one time a dwelling house, a tavern and a shop. It is now an attractive house. In 1696 two McAndrew brothers, Donald and James, with wives and families, lived there.

Just across the Gairn was the Muir of Gairnshiel where in the late 1800's the Anderson family lived in a little cottage.

ROBERT LOUIS STEVENSON COTTAGE, BRAEMAR
(OS 150915)

In 1881 Robert Louis Stevenson was on holiday in Braemar for seven weeks in August and September with his wife and her 13 year old son and his own parents in a house on Glenshee Road. The weather was bad so to while away the time he painted for the boy a map of an imaginary island. The next step was to people the island with interesting characters and the plot of Treasure Island was born.

At the time a somewhat eccentric local called John Silver lived on Chapel Brae. Was he the inspiration for Long John? The house, now bearing Stevenson's name, has a plaque detailing events and providing a visitor attraction.

SCURRIESTANE
(OS 359950)

The name is associated with a monolith that guided travellers to the ford across the Muick but it was also the name of a little settlement. From early times a little clachan stood on the site of the modern Dalliefour, with all the usual tenants and a blacksmith. This was the home of the long-lived poacher Ian (John) Mitchell. In the early years of the nineteenth century the buildings were demolished and the land became arable. A steading was built about 200 yards nearer to the hill and the whole area became known as Scurriestane. However, in the 1870's a new house was erected on the site of Scurriestane. Some years later Scurriestane and Dalliefour were united.

SHENVAL
(OS 305017)

Shenval was an Sean-Bhaile, the auld toon. The old building at the side of the road is now derelict.

John Fleming worked on the croft and having only one

212

horse, he ploughed with a horse and a stot (a bullock) on very sloping ground.

The place had been occupied generations earlier, because the remains of at least five longhouses have been found on the south facing slope.

SLEACH (SLEOCH)
(OS 268016)

(Sleach is used for Easter Sleach for there has been no occupation of Wester Sleach for many generations)

The name Sleoch or Sleach, "the moory place", was used for an area north west of Gairnshiel, beyond Balnaan. There are ruins of homesteads, hardly visible. The last to farm Sleoch was Willie Gordon, a six-footer with protruding teeth and red hair. He had a squint that made him even more "distinctive".

The farm was reached over a little plank bridge and the area around was reputed to be the haunt of fairies.

STRANLEA
(OS 313006)

Stranlea, a house east of Gairnshiel is associated with Amy Stewart Fraser., who wrote various books recording life in the Glen. Stranlea is still the family holiday home and it has recently been modernised.

Stranlea was in existence in 1675 for it was the scene of a fight when Culum McGregor of Dalfad injured a neighbour's head, arm and eye with a sword. He had to pay a fine of £20 Scots.

THE STREET
(OS 287941)

The Street of Monaltrie was a little settlement of houses and a smithy. It lay to the south of the Old Deeside Way. The houses were built by the Farquharsons of Monaltrie, whose original dwelling was at Crathie, to house local men returning from war. Two houses are still distinguishable, together with remains of others. The old road was superseded by the 1855 Turnpike Road, on which many Skye labourers were employed.

The smithy was unusual in that it was water-powered, the only one on the Dee using the water. The power was used to drive a lathe and a grinding wheel. Unusually, the water wheel went directly into the water, with mechanism for raising and lowering it.

The Street of Monaltrie

TORGALTER
(OS 286957)

There was originally a clachan where the Torgalter burn joined the Dee. There was a mill and a boat that went between Abergeldie Castle and the north side of the Dee. The Boathouse, called Clinkums, was an ale house as well. In August 1846 the Torgalter Burn burst its banks and swept over a cottage by the water. Auld Janet, bedridden, was inside screaming for help. She was rescued through the roof but the ordeal was too much for her. She lost her mind and died shortly afterwards. At Torgalter a farmhouse sits in the middle of a ruined settlement.

TORPHANTRICK
(OS 411976)

This is an example of a typical 'fermtoun' situated by an old ford and ferry road.

Once over the bridge at Cambus o' May a track runs southwards through the wood. Left it goes to Inchmarnock and over to Etnach. On the right it goes westward to Pannanich, on a road that has been in use since the end of the eighteenth century.

After crossing the river the Pannanich track goes through the site of a hamlet known as Riphantach, often in past times spelled as Riefantrick or Riefrantrick. The 't' may come from the Gaelic reidh, a plain or level ground, and funntaich, cold. It was a well known name in the early years of the nineteenth century because the name was applied to part of Cambus o' May opposite the ferry, and the ford and ferry carried the name.

Riphantack perhaps comes from Ruighe Bhantraich the name of a former farm south of Cambus a' May. People incorrectly call the farm Trefantric but Rifantric is probably more correct. It probably refers to the 'widow's shiel (shelter). There may have been very early settlements here, but what can still be identified are longhouses and the remains of a depopulated post medieval settlement. Change came about slowly so dating is impossible. With a good deal of imagination houses can be reconstructed.

The remains of a track are visible down the middle of the settlement. This was an important route to ford and ferry.

TORRAN
(OS 307015)

This farm in Glengairn was for generations the home of the Ritchie family. Even in 1891, according to the census, there was still a family of 8 living there. The house was near the Torran burn.

January 1902 was a time of heavy rain and high winds and

even little burns were in spate. One of the Ritchie girls, Mary, had been to the shoemaker at Kirkstyle and on her return had to cross the plank bridge over the burn. She slipped and fell into the swollen water. It was three weeks before her body was recovered.

In her books Amy Fraser tells of old Euphemia Ritchie and her husband William with his pipe with the silver lid. A son, a brother of the drowned Mary, was a farmer and used to sow seeds broadcast.

TULLOCHMACARRICK
(OS 278013)

Near Gairnshiel Bridge a track runs along the west side of the Gairn. It leads to Tullochmacarrick. This was a typical village at its hey-day in Victorian times.

Tullochmacarrick former Manse stands sentinal over the meandering waters of the Gairn, a roofless reminder of the past. Ruins of cottages and a large farmhouse with extensive outbuildings are evident to the east, - all that remains of a little community whose name meant hillock of the rock.

In 1846 the Royal Bounty Missionary, the Rev. Robert Neil, arrived in Glen Gairn to take up his post as minister in the Glen. His Manse was at Tullochmacarrick. It was April but the Gairn was frozen over and furniture had to be carried over the ice. The home of the minister was the residence of someone of some social standing and a base for parishioners seeking help.

The building had just been turned into a Manse. The previous preacher had also been the schoolmaster and his home had been near the school. When the new ministerial appointment was made the Heritor, Farquharson of Invercauld, provided Tullochmacarrick, a two storey house facing south, as a Manse. It was some distance from the church at Kirkstyle. The minister was to remain there for eight years.

By 1863 the church in Glen Gairn ceased to be a Royal Bounty Mission and became a quoad sacra parish with full status for the minister. The Rev. Robert Neil then moved to a

Manse above Dalfad, on Huntly land, formerly the dwelling place of the Macgregor laird. The Invercauld Factor who was the Crathie minister began to clear out Roman Catholics. Sheep came in. By 1890 Peter Coutts seems to have been the last farming tenant there. There had been a little settlement since medieval times but by the end of the nineteenth century the life of the little township of Tullochmacarrick was over with just isolated dwellings of shepherds left.

Margaret McGrigor, "The Holiest Woman in the Glen" was born in Tullochmacarrick but later moved to Laggan, as already mentioned.

The Dalfad Manse that succeeded Tullochmacarrick

XXII. RUINED PLACES OF WORSHIP

So numerous are the Church buildings in the area that it has only been possible to concentrate on a few sites and some ruins. It is fairly easy for anyone to find an existing church building, but more difficult to locate a ruin or the site of an earlier building.

CLASHINRUICH
(OS 313014)

From the beginning of the eighteenth century there had been a Roman Catholic chapel and resident priest in Glengairn. A new chapel was built or the old one restored in 1785 at Clashinruich and at first the priest lived in a croft near by. When in 1802 a chapel opened at Corgarff, the priest had to say Mass there at least once a month. He did this until 1846. Another chapel was opened at Tornahaish in 1808.

The altar at Clashinruich was a rough table and the roof was open to the beams. There were a few kneeling boards but most folk knelt on the clay floor. Fr. Lachlan was constantly reprimanding some of the younger folk for unseemly behaviour at weddings and funerals. There was a choir, trained by a teacher from Tomintoul, James Cummings, who used a baton and a tuning fork.

The farm at Clashinruich had been leased by McGrigor from Invercauld and the priest was a sub tenant. The Factor, Charles Farquharson, a Jacobite, charged no rent for farm or house. Then came a new Factor, - a Church of Scotland minister, the Rev.Charles McHardy, whose parish was Crathie. Factor-minister and Catholics were at odds. Fr.Lachlan's tenure was insecure. The Chapel remained but by 1810 the priest had moved to a new house in Ardoch, on Huntly land, about a mile away, - a house with a porch and a yard. Huntly, a leading Roman Catholic, was easier on his tenants. The house is now no more than a heap of stones but it can still be distinguished from its neighbours by its porch. Frequently, in bad weather, worship took place in the priest's house at Ardoch.

By 1868 the Clashinruich chapel was in disrepair so a new chapel was erected nearer the mouth of the Glen at Candacraig, for the convenience of summer visitors and locals. Today the Clashinruich chapel has only partial walls remaining and is open to the sky.

Much of the information on Catholic Glengairn is from Fr. Meany, priest from 1888 -1899 who died in 1940 when Vicar General. It is supplemented by information from Fr. Odo Blundell, O.S.B. when he wrote about the Catholic Highlands.

Fr. Lachlan McIntosh the much-loved priest came to Glengairn in 1782 after studying at the seminary of Valladolid, in Spain. He followed Charles Farquharson who retired. At that time there was toleration of Catholic and Protestant ministeries. Even Clashinruich was a Protestant School on weekdays. Opposition came from the educational organisation, the S.P.C.K.

Every Friday morning Fr.McIntosh said Mass at Clashinruich and of course took services on Sundays and Holy Days. Confession was on Saturday evenings. In bad weather, Confession and Mass were in his house. Sometimes he used the Gaelic, sometimes English. He visited his parishioners regularly, going every week to Morven.

On Candlemas Day, 2nd. February, people brought candles made out of sheep tallow, for which every household had a mould. Father McIntosh was also responsible for Corgarff and when going to and from there, over the Glaschoille, he said the Rosary, the accompanying people making the responses. Some of the younger folk behaved irreverently, to the priest's anger. Life for the old man was austere: he fasted until after Mass, no matter where it was.

Fr.Lachlan was often a peacemaker among Protestants. He was however, capable of anger. One Lent there was a Protestant marriage in Corgarff. He forbade his flock to attend the wedding. They went. He lost his temper to such an extent that eighteen of them left his church for good.

Fr. Lachlan was involved in all the affairs of his flock, from dealing with young folk who stole peas (peasmeal was the staple diet) to writing letters and wills. The priest was to be seen about the Glen in his dark cloak with its silver clasp at the neck, worn over a red cravat. He always had his stick. He took a great interest in his croft and frequently took tit-bits of oatcake to the horses. The farming was actually in the hands of his niece, who also helped with pastoral work. He ate simply, like his flock.

Father Lachlan's family came from Braemar. They had their family problems. A nephew murdered a girl in Crathie and was eventually hanged. Lachlan's brother walked to Edinburgh to intercede for his son's life. (George 1V was in Edinburgh in 1822). He was not successful. The story goes that a pyat (magpie), the bird of ill omen, settled on the priest's shoulder before the murder.

Fr.Lachlan always invited a different married couple to dinner on Sunday. On one occasion when a couple was visiting their small daughter was lost on the hill. People and dogs searched for three days and nights, and then found her asleep on Donside. She had eaten moss to survive.

When the much loved and best known Roman Catholic priest Fr.Lachlan McIntosh died in March 1846, after 64 years service, Glengairn folk were not prepared to allow his burial in his native Braemar because the people there had not been willing to have him as their priest. So he was buried at Fit o'Gairn on a fine spring day, - 9th. March. (Spring must have come early that year.) He was 92 years of age. A memorial stone marks his grave

The Golden Age for Glengairn Roman Catholics came to an end. The situation changed. Unfortunately, those of the flock paying rent to Invercauld were vulnerable. Roman Catholics were often evicted to make way for Protestant sheep farms. Extant Invercauld lists give the religious affiliation of tenants. Quite early in the nineteenth century Catholics were going from Auchintoul, Renetton, Loinahaun and Tullochmacarrick (the home of the Kirk missionary). The farms of Richarchrie, Shenval and Torran fell about 1815 and Balno and several others in the 1820's. Catholic families were cleared from Remicras, Blairglass, Loinchork and Crathienaird, then Daldownie. Families were leaving Morven. Many groups went to Australia and Canada. By 1842 Clashinruich and Tomnavey were leased to Protestants for the first time. Often it was a case of Catholics out, sheep in. The 'Clearances' were taking place. By 1850 about 60 people had left the area when tenants were cleared and graziers took over the land. Around 1870 - 1880 depopulation of the Glen increased. By 1900 there were only six Roman Catholics, so in 1905 a chapel was built in Ballater and the priest moved there.

When the larger chapel and a house were built at Candacraig the Clashinruich building was used by James McKenzie as a sheep-fold. This shepherd had had three wives: the third, from Tomnavey, died soon after the wedding. Her brothers, called Brown, were concerned the husband was profiting from her death and demanded her clothes and its accompanying chest. They were told that as the woman had come to him with an old kist (chest) and he had buried her in a new one, he was entitled to keep the old kist and contents. He said they were actually in his debt!

There was a burial ground at Clashinruich chiefly for children who died in infancy. Between Ardoch and Clashinruich are a number of ruined crofts and a large lime kiln near Ardoch.

Gaelic was the language of the home well into the 1860's. It was supplanted by Broad Scots, not by English, as elsewhere. Scots speech uses f for wh, aa for au, and many diminutives.

Even in 1876 the Rev.Grant Michie was comparing the lawlessness of Glengairn to Fenian disturbances in Ireland, so it was not entirely peaceful!

Ruined crofts lie below the track that goes from Ardoch to Clashinruich. A big lime kiln north of the track to Ardoch has been the site of rubbish dumping. Kilns were to be found where there were outcrops of meta-limestone. When burned it was spread on the land to reduce the acidity. A quarry lies about 2 km. west of Ardoch.

THE UNFINISHED CHAPEL AT DALFAD
(OS 316007)

This was McGregor country. In 1603 the name had been banned by the Privy Council, for lawless deeds, so they changed to variations like Grigor and Gregor. They had been invited to the area to check lawless locals but they turned out to be worse themselves. Members of one branch of the family were accomplished cattle thieves and had their base around the Burn of Vat.

By 1696 'Macgregors' had a big set up at Dalfad. One was called Mac of the swivels because he used birch branches to guide his plough.

The family group started to build the chapel in 1744 or 1745 but then came involvement in Jacobite activities. The young men went to war and after Culloden all was lost. As a result many estates were forfeit. The property was mortgaged to Dalmore (Mar Lodge) then to Huntly.

The chapel building was never finished and presumably had no roof. The position of the altar can be seen at the east end. There is a feeling of peace here in the birch wood, far from the sound of battle, actual or metaphorical. Two upright gravestones remain, commemorating family members. They would have had to use assumed names. One bears the initials CMG 1734 while the other is inscribed "Here lies John Grierson died 2 May 1737." Presumably they had come from some other resting place because the chapel was never completed or consecrated. Other stones, with no obvious inscriptions, lie flat.

The stones are a link with a lively and active family, many of whom were freebooters

Nearby, in the wood, is a mound known as the Laird's Seat where Gregor viewed his land and presumably after 1745 contemplated a bleak future following the loss of sons and close relatives.

There is also the site of a well known as the Laird's Well.

222

Stones at Dalfad

THE CHURCH AT FOOT O' GAIRN
(OS 350970)

Tradition says the church was dedicated to Mungo, the Dear One, usually called Kentigern, from Cathures or Glasgow. There is little documentary evidence to support his work on Deeside, but local tradition called the church Cill-ma-thatha, the church of Tatha or Mungo.

So, near the junction of Dee and Gairn, not far from the track leading up the glen, a simple church was built. The wattle and daub structure lacked permanence, but other churches were eventually erected on the site. Little remains of the last pre-Reformation church except the front and gable walls. The front wall had two doors and three windows. The ruinous building prior to 1800 measured 46' by 23'. In1832 the dyke was rebuilt and the kirk walls repaired by friends of the deceased of Glengairn.

The ground is still used for burials. The church itself was superceded by a new D plan church at Kirkstyle, further up the glen, in 1801.

Foot o'Gairn Kirk (Mungo's)

Site of THE GLEN MUICK CHURCH & MANSE
(OS 365948)

Very little is known of the early building in its burial ground at the Muick Bridge. Presumably there was a Celtic foundation, re-dedicated by the Roman Church. Before the Reformation it was known as St. Mary's but we have no indication of its size or appearance. At the Reformation it may have been pulled down and another church built, or it may simply have been adapted for Protestant worship.

When the Rev. David Guthrie became minister in 1687 the kirk minutes record that 'the minister was away, not having any house to reside in'. If there had been an earlier one, the Manse was presumably not fit to live in. By 1794 it was reported that church, manse, garden and walls were ruinous. The Church and burial ground served a wide area until the Centrical Church was built in Ballater after the erection of the Bridge in 1783.

By the later years of the 18th century the churches of Tullich, Glen Gairn and Glen Muick were in a tumbledown state. The Glen Muick building was 24m long and almost 9m wide. The roof was of heather and turf, only partially seated, so worshippers brought their 'creepies'. The windows were small and the doors did not close. It seems there was no Communion Table for a new one had to be provided in 1796 together with seats for the officiating clergy. So Glen Muick church was abandoned in 1800 and worshippers went to the new Centrical Church in Ballater.

The abandoned church did not last long. Maggie Mitchell, looking for some lost hens in the building, set the thatch on fire and roofless, the building deteriorated until nothing now remains. A few stones in the garden of 'The Glebe' may bring back evocative memories, but all we have now is imagination. Maggie eventually died as a result of spilling boiling ale over herself. All traces of the 72 feet by $22^1/_2$ feet building have gone. Only the site remains.

In the ground surrounding the church, at a spot yet to be

identified, three men from Glenesk were buried after a fight involving 'cattle lifting'.

The Manse was as ruinous as the church. We do not know when it was built but it was certainly there in 1690. Part had been rebuilt in 1725, 'clay, not lime and not well done'. The walls were 3' thick: the ceilings were low. It too was thatched, had tiny poorly glazed windows and was divided internally by partitions. Around 1850 it was demolished and some of the stones were used to build Invermuick, now a private house saved from the ravages of the river. This was to be the Manse for a number of years before the Minister moved into Ballater.

THE TOWER OF GLENMICK HOUSE
PRIVATE CHAPEL
(OS 372945)

Just outside Ballater on the road to Glen Muick stands all that remains of the Mackenzie family chapel, hidden by trees. The building where the Mackenzies worshipped and buried their sons was a private Episcopal chapel built in 1875 but it was also used by locals. Marshall Mackenzie of Aberdeen was the architect. The family vault was beside the chapel. Mackenzie soldier sons were buried in the family ground, covering a period from the Boer War to Col. Eric's death in 1972.

During the Second World War, Glenmuick House was used by troops and, somewhat reduced in splendour, was demolished around the end of the 1960's. Like the House, the chapel went too, in 1961, leaving only the rather splendid tower among the trees near the entrance to the Glen. Most of the granite blocks were re-used as shooting butts on the hill. The family crypt, entrance blocked up, was reached by a sunken drive. The family still maintain the burial ground and keep the structure in repair and further improvements are planned.

THE OLD CHURCH OF GLEN TANAR - THE BLACK KIRK ON THE MOOR

(OS 426923)

Glen Tanar had been linked with Aboyne but kept its own services until 1763. The ruins of this Kirk, in its own burial ground, stand below the former Glen Tanar school building.

Glentanar Kirk was heather thatched and from very early times in its existence seems to have been referred to as "The Black Kirk on the moor, without a bell". A bell was presented in 1729 by William Farquharson and his wife Anne Gillanders. When the church ceased to be used, the bell was melted down to make a new bell, with the addition of other material, for Aboyne.

The west gable, - all that survives of the Kirk - had ivy planted round it by the church officer, John Ewen, when he was quite a young man.

The church was handy for people in the glen and for those across the Dee, with two ferries near by. A manuscript of Sir James Balfour of Denmilne, written about 1640, shows that the ferry "neir Glentanar Kirk", was a much frequented route.

The little graveyard of Glen Tanar church is surrounded by a stone and lime wall, restored at the end of lthe 19th century by public subscription, for the repair and upkeep of which some funds remained in 1908.

Tradition says that the plague raged throughout the district, but an improvement seems to have taken place on a Friday and a Monday. Out of gratitude, no ground was dug for graves on Monday or Friday, up to World War I.

The use of tombstones with inscriptions was not usual for ordinary folk. It was customary to place on the grave a headstone bearing only the initials of the deceased. The Gillanders family is commemorated in a number of stones: they had associations with the Mill of Dinnet. A member of the family was tenant of Cobelheugh. The New Statistical Account records that a Gillanders was the eighteenth successive eldest son to have been born on the same farm.

In the S.W. of Glen Tanar's kirkyard is buried Mary Robertson, daughter of the Ballaterach farmer. Lord Byron, living in Aberdeenshire until he was ten years old, probably spent three summers at the farm, on one occasion recuperating from illness. The whole area impressed him, with his Gordon ties, and he never forgot Mary, some years older than himself, writing of her later in 'When I roved, a young Highlander'. Mary married Kenneth Stewart, a Crathie Excise Officer. She died in Aberdeen in 1867, aged 81 years, but was interred with her family in Glen Tanar.

There were links with body snatching days. A granite slab, seven feet by two and a half feet and very thick was kept by the wall and placed over new burials. As it would require a number of men to lift the mort-stone, it would have been a deterrent to body snatchers.

Adjoining the churchyard were the Lochie Butts, where in the fifteenth and sixteenth centuries the local men practised archery on Sundays, at the command of Parliament. At that time the sacredness of Sunday was unknown in the area.

An annual fair or market was usually held in the vicinity of a church, and Glen Tanar was no exception. For many years a fair was held and there was a small market cross, probably removed to Aboyne Castle grounds. The wares were often laid out on the flat headstones. The fair itself, because of some dispute, details of which cannot now be found, was removed to Banchory. Associated with the fair was the selection of a 'beauty queen'.

In 1763 the new central church to serve the united parishes of Aboyne and Glen Tanar was built in Aboyne, lasting until 1842, when the present church building was erected in Aboyne. Glen Tanar church, disused, suffered a fire that reduced the building to a ruin.

The minister went round various houses, catechising his members once a year. In the early years of the 19th century, about 150 were catechised annually. This went on for 100 more years, the last record I can find being in 1904, although it may have continued longer.

Up to 1890 Glen Tanar was part of the Aboyne Lands. By 1854 almost half had become deer forest. After leasing for a time, Sir William Cunliffe Brooks of Manchester bought Glen Tanar from the Huntly Trustees in 1890. He kept about 250 workmen and rebuilt Glen Tanar House as his own home and practically every farm and cottage. He made many improvements on the estate. Everything was beautifully built, in a style more English than had previously been the case.

We have an interesting sidelight on the natives of the area in July 1593. The "Annals of Scotland " says:-

"Many are the troubles of the burghers of Aberdeen from these rude neighbours who would come sweeping down like a flight of locusts and leave nothing of value uneaten or destroyed." The Town Council met to consider "the barbarous cruelty of the lawless hielandmen in Glen Tanar, not only in unmerciful murder of men and bairns but in the masterful spolzing of all the bestial, guids and gear of the inhabitants."

Glen Tanar Church

XXIII. THE CLANS

"They claimed a common ancestor and followed the same hereditary chief"

In addition to the Farquharsons of Invercauld and Monaltrie who were Clan Chiefs and Lairds, the Gordons, represented by the Marquess of Huntly, known as The Cock o'the North, and Gordon of Abergeldie, there were two Roman Catholic families who figured largely in the area, - the Macdonalds and the Macgregors - or variations of that name.

MACDONALDS, 1696 - 1922

The Macdonalds claimed descent from the third son of John, Lord of the Isles. A disputed tradition says that the Earl of Mar granted them their property soon after the Battle of Harlaw in 1411 when Macdonald was taken prisoner. It is however unlikely that any grant of land would be made to such a clan, so related, so soon after the battle of Harlaw where the Lord of the Isles was so prominent an enemy. It was more likely to have been the Flemings of Auchintol who came to the Glen after Harlaw.

The family was of considerable importance. They had an independent lordship in the largely Roman Catholic past of Glen Gairn The little Macdonald 'kingdom' had quite a collection of dwellings in the vicinity, all of whose residents were tenants, many of the same name. It is interesting that although the property was sold to Invercauld in 1822, by 1880 there is not a single Macdonald tenant left in Glen Gairn. In the nineteenth century Roman Catholics had been cleared from Rineaton. Sheep or Protestants were brought in but the life of the 'toun' was really over.

A tributary of the Gairn, the Cossack, ran past the old Macdonald mansion house, a two-storey building probably erected in the early 1800's. As late as the 1930's the old oak beams were still to be seen in the Macdonald kitchen.

Rineaton (Renatton, Rinettan)) 'the cattle shelter among the junipers', was a township owned by the Roman Catholic Macdonalds. Also belonging to them was some land in Micras, near Crathie. Tradition says there was a school at Rineaton. Perhaps it was a sort of Catholic seminary, for Forbes of Skellater, Strathdon, a soldier of fortune in the service of the King of Portugal who eventually rose to be Governor of Rio de Janeiro, sent his son to the establishment.

Records show that in 1696 William Macdonald owned Rineaton and the Micras land. He had a wife and three servants. A John, probably a relation, was also classed as a gentleman. William had a son James who married Helen Grant of Tulloch, Strathspey. His son, also William, inherited Rineaton and bought the estate of St. Martins in 1750. A daughter died unmarried and a son who married but had no family sold Rineaton to Invercauld about 1822. Another member of the family, John, was an army captain and another, James, an army Chaplain.

The Captain distinguished himself in the American War and died around 1822. Buried in the family tomb, he has no memorial. He actually owned a little property of Gairnsdale near Micras but after war service stayed at Rineaton with his brother the Chaplain. William also had sons Allan, Alexander and Coll who all went abroad, Ronald who died young and a daughter Christian who married Lieut. John Farquharson. She had an unmarried daughter and a son who became a Colonel of the 25th. Jane and Anne were also unmarried daughters, while Helen married James Robertson of Ballaterach, one of whose children Mary was mentioned in Byron's poem. There were also a number of illegitimate children in the Macdonald family.

William of Rineaton, son of James and Helen Grant was a founder member and the Secretary of the Highland and Agricultural Society of Scotland formed in 1785. His portrait was painted for them by Raeburn in 1803. William was also a Writer to the Signet and died in 1814. It was his son William who succeeded him who sold Rineaton to Invercauld about

1822. As he was married but childless, his cousin Col. Macintosh of St.Martins and Rossie inherited the property.

Earlier, there had been a settlement with long houses. An excellent example of a corn drying kiln remains. Correct drying was vital for future requirements.

Closely associated with the Macdonalds were two settlements occupied by their tenants and tacksmen, Linchork and Loinaghoil.

When the property was sold to Invercauld many men left for the army or overseas. Soon the few that remained could not make a living when holdings were amalgamated and sheep brought in.

In 1890 John & Charles Michie were tenants at Lionchork and Loinagail (Estate record spelling) respectively. The annual rental of Loinchork was three times that of Loinagail. Another Michie, Alexander, was at Blairglass. One is tempted to assume they are all part of the same family. Surprisingly, Loinchork's rental was higher even than that of Blairglass, so there must have been a large amount of land.

At Loinchork there are the remains of three longhouses and enclosures and a later farm house. The rounded corners of the buildings, typical of rural Aberdeenshire, can easily be seen. Loinaghoil also had a settlement with longhouses and enclosures. A building with rounded ends and exceptionally thick masonry may at one time have been a kiln. There are the remains of a grain mill, with a dam and a lade.

MACGREGORS, (from 1666)

The other noted Roman Catholic family of 'McGregor' or endless variations after the name was proscribed by the Privy Council in 1603 and McGregors have been mentioned in connection with Dalfad. The family was really just a group of freebooters, excellent fighters and staunch Jacobites.

By 1630 a Thomas "Macgregor" had settled in Glen Gairn. The family may have come originally from Bredalbane. A few years later Huntly was using these 'mercenaries' in his private feuds. They were brought into Glengairn, a strongly Roman Catholic area, to keep the locals in check but proved to be even worse themselves.

The lands reverted to the Earl of Mar but after his involvement in the '15, they were bought by his brother and then sold to John Farquharson of Invercauld on 13th July 1726. They remained part of the Invercauld estate, together with the mill, grazings, salmon fishing and woods. The right to woods was later to cause problems between Mar and Invercauld. By 1735 Invercauld had purchased the superiority of the land for the properties he already held.

Dalfad was the 'Macgregor' stronghold. In the 1696 Poll Book their valuation was £160, quite high in comparison with others. The 'McGregors' also owned land in Crathie and Braemar as well as other Glen properties, particularly Inverenzie, of which one of the family was laird. They were closely associated with the settlement of Richrichie, variously known as Richarcharie, Richarkarrie or Coulachan. This 'cattle run of the little road' lay on the north bank of the Gairn about 6 miles from Ballater. Macgregor property included the little 'touns'of Torran and Tomnaverie. Houses were dotted about at Richarkarrie without any order but most had a little kale yard or garden. Most folk kept a few sheep or a cow. Among those who worked for the laird and cultivated a tiny bit of land themselves were a few tradesmen - in this case a weaver and a carpenter. The McGrigors were staunch Jacobites and were also at the centre of resistance to Presbyterianism that had followed the previous Episcopacy. This was a period of intolerance but such was the McGregor position that the Kirk Session was powerless to act against them. The Roman Catholic Calum McGrigor was a man of great strength. His property holdings were considerable, but his home was at Dalfad. Here he actively supported Catholic priests, erected a small chapel in the house and heard Mass, contrary to the law. He was accused by the Kirk Session of erecting a high crucifix for his neighbours to adore. Some members of his extended family went abroad to train as priests.

Callum died before 1715 but the family continued the resistance to Presbyterianism. One of the McGrigor family, Father Gregor McGrigor, a Benedictine, returned from Warzburg and started the building of a chapel at Dalfad. It was never finished, because of Culloden. The chapel lies across the ford or over the Black Bridge. In the wood above the river, deep among the birches are the ruins of this incomplete chapel and the family burial ground. The unfinished chapel with its waist high walls stands, a mute reminder of the effects of war. Of the Glen Gairn McGrigors, 24 men went to Culloden and only 6 returned, two of whom were badly wounded. The Laird himself, Capt. John McGregor died at Culloden and a Jesuit, Father Charles Farquharson, held the community together.

In 1746 Dalfad was mortgaged and passed to Mckenzie of Dalmore (Mar Lodge) and then to Huntly. In 1818 the Glenmuick minister wrote that of Dalfad's sons, John died at Culloden, Duncan died of wounds and Alex, Malcolm and Alpin had to flee abroad. So ended that branch of the family.

Also closely associated with the 'McGregor' family is the ground by the ford over the Gairn, near the Black Bridge, the Long Haugh. It was from here that their young men went to Culloden, many never to return. Loyalty to the Stuarts caused the Macgregors to loose everything. Sons who would have inherited and many other young men of the extended family fled abroad and what land they had left after most of it was forfeited was mortgaged.

Farming was only on subsistence level and after a series

of bad winters and poor harvests the 'tounsfolk' of Richarkarrie were in a sorry state. Houses were dotted about at Richarkarrie without any order but most had a little kale yard or garden. Most folk kept a few sheep or a cow. Among those who worked for the laird and cultivated a tiny bit of land themselves were a few tradesmen - in this case a weaver and a carpenter.

Ploughing was on the run-rig system, with more difficult areas being dug by the spade or cas-crom. There was a well, known as the Laird's Well, built in with rough stones. Cultivation was based on the Infield, Outfield system. Small black cattle were grazed and these were walked to market in Falkirk by the drovers. Crofts were abandoned. The army and overseas prospects beckoned to desperate folk. Houses were abandoned. The land was turned over to sheep grazing. Some Lairds were making deer forests, but Richarkrie did not fall prey to this. However, Roman Catholics were often evicted to make way for Protestant sheep farms. By 1808 James McIntosh was paying rent for 'Richarkrie' and had sub tenants but the land was described as 'stoney' Along with others Richarkarie fell about 1815. It was again a case of Catholics out, sheep in.

One or two individuals remained for a few more years but the 'toun' had gone. In the 1870's a man called Grant was paying a small rent to the Laird, presumably for a small dwelling and some grazing, but then all records of Richarkrie disappear. There had originally been here a very large enclosed area split into two by a moss. In the lower or NW section are the remains of several longhouses, the cruck frame construction being very obvious. There is also a corn drying kiln. Scattered over the hill are the remains of longhouses. It is hard to think of this depopulated settlement as a once vital and flourishing community

Another group of 'McGrigors' took part in cattle rustling and and other nefarious activities and had a protection racket well worked out, operating from their base at Burn o'Vat.

Richarkarie was later the home of John Begg, a whisky smuggler who went legal and moved to Easter Balmoral when the original distillery burned down.

Across the Glenfenzie burn was Inverenzie (the mouth of the white burn) also belonging to the branch of McGrigors famed for their cattle 'lifting'. Two sons were drowned when on an 'expedition'. The farmhouse and outbuildings are all derelict. On a stone in the wall at the front of the house are the initials DM and the date 1822. Inside a little imagination can recreated the living conditions of the family. Some years ago the swey was in place, where the mistress of the house did her cooking. There were no ovens: everything was 'pot-roasted'. Other buildings are to be seen further down the hill - all in ruins. One of the family had captained the Gairnside men at Culloden after mustering them for Lord Lewis Gordon and had been killed by a Hanoverian bayonet while lying wounded on the field. In more modern times, Inverenzie was the home of weightlifter Robert Shaw.

MULLACH

There was another settlement at Mullach, the high place. This was the home of the Jacobite Durwards. Like most families that supported the Stuarts, they sent their sons to Culloden. Three went. Two died on the field. Malcolm was later pardoned because of his extreme youth.

XXIV. THE ORIGIN & DEVELOPMENT OF BALLATER

THE BEGINNINGS

The land that was Tullich and the land that became Ballater had originally belonged to Farquharson of Inverey but James, the last laird, wanted land on Donside so he exchanged his Deeside property with the Farquharsons of Monaltrie.

Just before 1745, an old woman suffering from scrofula or tuberculosis of the lymph nodes, was said to have had a miracle cure. Elspet Michie had been bathing in and drinking water from the Pannanich wells. The laird, Francis Farquharson, the Baron Ban, developed the Spa when he returned from imprisonment in England following his involvement in the Jacobite cause. Jacobites were interested in Spas - perhaps as gathering places for those of similar religious & political convictions! So began the fashion for the rich to take the waters.

Visitors flocked to the Spa. The original Pannanich Lodge was on the low ground west of the present hotel. There was no bridge over the Dee and the ferry just could not cope. The need for a new village had become obvious when visitors taking the waters at Pannanich required more accommodation. Ballater would not have come into being but for Pannanich Wells, "beinn an acha", the hill beside the river. There was a certain amount of local employment there, caring for guests and their horses. Even the famous John Brown originally worked at Pannanich as an ostler.

Once the bridge over the Dee was built in 1783 and the 'Centrical Church' erected on the bare moor, feus were granted for the land in 'Ballater' by Francis, then by William Farquharson of Monaltrie. The focal point of the new village was the Church, with roads going off north, south, east & west. The whole area by the Dee, known as Sluievannachie, was covered with heather and broom and was a resting place for droves of cattle on their way to southern markets. On the north

237

west corner of the moor there was a ford for cattle to cross as they went in the direction of Mount Keen or the Capel Mounth.

EARLY SETTLERS

Settlers took up the offer of feus, but there was not really a great demand in the early days, for by 1848 there were only 36 feuars in all, the duty amounting to £40 p.a. Ballater really developed very slowly. A professional valuation of the property was for £249. By 1900 the feu duty amounted to £472.7s.9d. and the valuation was almost £6,000. The 1861 census recorded 362 adults over 16 years resident in Ballater while in 1901 the figure was 1256. Pictures of the 1840's and 1850's show very little development in Ballater, except by the river, in the vicinity of Dee Street. In the early days of the village a cow could be grazed on rough land for £1 per annum.

James Smith and Mary Kerr whose address was Bridge of Ballater had a daughter Ann born in 1793 and this seems to have been the first baptism in the new village. Very early, Isaac Bremner, the former Tullich tailor was the Church Bellman or Church Officer and his wife the village midwife. The Schoolmaster, John Smith came in 1807. Some of his pupils achieved distinction in Medicine and Divinity. He retired in 1860.

EARLY BUILDINGS

The first organised building plan involved the erection of a few thatched houses along the north side of what is now Golf Road. A few pre-Victorian cottages still remain, in Dee Street and Deebank Road. Most of the houses were fairly basic, with two rooms and a thatched roof. Feus were slow in being taken up. Basically, the village consisted of four roads, radiating north, south, east and west. In fact development was slow until Queen Victoria came to Balmoral and the Railway arrived in 1866. Then there was a boom. Retired farmers feued land and built houses, chiefly in the centre - in the vicinity of Church

Green and Station Square. In a cottage facing the later Station Square there was a Dame School where the pupils paid 1d per week.

Ford House was built in Ballater's early days and may have had foundations before the Bridge was erected. Inchley was an early building. Garranmhor, originally a school, was converted to a house about 1881 but it may have been adapted from an even earlier building. Deebank House, with its columns, may also have been updated. The "Exclusive" area developed later was tree-lined Braemar Road. A number of buildings along Braemar Road are typical of the development of the Victorian period in Ballater, known as "Balmorality." The former St. Andrew's Nursing Home, Oakhall and Glenbardie are good examples.

The early regulations allowed for one Established Church and one pub. The first public house in Ballater was kept by George Clark, actually in a room of a private house. When a proper hotel was erected in the 1830's and later up-graded in the 60's - the Monaltrie Arms, named after the feudal superior, Farquharson of Monaltrie, the estate leased the building. The first tenant was a man called Middleton. A family called Ross succeeded him, then came Charles Cook. He was still there in 1877. Following him came a family of McGregors and during that tenancy the building was enlarged. A Mr.Proctor took over and again there were numerous extensions and refurbishments.

The Square near the Hotel was a busy place. Stage coaches stopped there and the whole area was bustling, with stabling etc. where the modern Mangiatoia now stands.

XXV. VICTORIAN LEGACY

SLOW GROWTH

When Queen Victoria came to the throne in 1837, Ballater was still a little village, far from the madding crowd. Pictures of the 1840's and 1850's show very little development in Ballater, except by the river, in the vicinity of Dee Street. When Queen Victoria died in 1901 it was a prosperous centre with a population of 1256, attracting visitors from all over Britain and even further afield.

The Muckle Spate of 1829 did a great deal of damage. Apart from the fact that the bridge had been washed away, much property and stock was lost. About an acre of the minister's Glebe land by the Dee was washed away and it was necessary to strengthen the embankment. The costs were shared by the Heritors, Aboyne, Invercauld, Abergeldie and Monaltrie.

VICTORIAN REMINDERS

Ballater's rapid growth was due to Victoria and Albert falling in love with Deeside, purchasing the old Balmoral and rebuilding it, and to the coming of the Railway

The Victorian legacy is all around us. The whole Ballater area reflects its Victorian heritage, from the Victoria & Albert Halls to street names like Victoria Road, Albert Road, Queen's Road and Salisbury Road (after the Prime Minister), and an establishment like the Alexandra Hotel.

Many of Ballater's Victorian buildings are Category B Listed. A great number of buildings in the early days of the nineteenth century were erected by Alexander Sherriffs and Sons who were based in Tullich. The first mason to reside in Ballater and to carry out contracting work was Peter Mitchell. Feuing was at a standstill for a time until the passing of a new Feuing Act, then James Reid carried on mason work for a number of years. A company of Watt, Mollison and Anderson erected some buildings, to be followed in this work by James Michie and John Smith.

THE VICTORIA BARRACKS

These were built once the Royal Guard arrived for duty during the 'season'. Originally the military presence in the area was based at Braemar Castle.

Queen Victoria & Prince Albert came to Deeside in 1848, for three weeks, and again in the three following years.

In 1852 the old Balmoral Castle was bought by Prince Albert and rebuilt by 1856.

Security was minimal at the time. The Queen arrived at Church (the old Crathie Church) in a carriage drawn by white horses.

Once Deeside was opened up by the arrival of the Railway in 1866, (which she refused to allow beyond Ballater and through her property) visitors flocked in and security tightened. Worrall's Directory published in 1877 gives details of those in charge of the Barracks. The building was just a very simple erection, partly wooden, behind the present car park in Church Square, then an equally simple structure near the present site on Queen's Road. Presumably when colours were presented to the Royal Scots in September 1876 they were based in the old Barracks.

As time went on the building was inadequate for the Royal Guard. When Ballater became more 'up-market' new buildings appeared all over the village. The Royal Guard was in Ballater during 'the season' and more spacious and salubrious accommodation was obviously necessary. The Church had been removed and a more elaborate edifice opened in 1874 and the Barracks had to conform. It was decided to rebuild. The exact date of completion is unknown but it was in the 1880's. When the Czar & Czarina of Russia came to visit in 1896 (the Queen's family married into most of Europe's royal houses) the Royal Guard was certainly based in the new building. This was when the 'portico' was added to the

Railway Station. Among other splendid buildings, the Victoria & Albert Halls was being erected in Station Square by the firm of William Duguid By the time the new Hall was in use, the new Barracks was considered part of the village.

According to one story, whether true or not is not known, plans were somehow confused in the War Office and Ballater had seven single storey blocks of red granite rubble and sandstone dressing instead of a more ornate Victorian building to match the style of those in Station Square & Braemar Road. It would be interesting to find a Neo-Gothic barracks like the Ballaterr Village Hall at some outpost on the North-West Frontier!

Over the years there have been improvements and extensions. Out of season the Barracks was used for Training Courses, etc.

VICTORIA & ALBERT HALLS

The 'baronial' building of the Victoria and Albert Halls (1874 & 1895) with its imposing tower, is an excellent example of the work of William Duguid and Sons, Builders and Contractors, who built many of the fine edifices remaining today, like the former Free Kirk, now the Auld Kirk Hotel.

Alexander Gordon, son of a farmer and wool-dyer at little Mill, Girnoc, became a successful business man in the brewing industry, with Caledonian and Lyndhurst. He gave a generous subscription towards the building of the Church, but he is better known for his gift to the village of the Victoria and Albert Halls. He was born in 1818, second son of a tenant farmer and Betty Gauld, a native of Migvie. There were also two sisters. Alexander and his brother John stayed for a time with an uncle, William Gauld, teacher and preacher. They received a sound education, perhaps at Logie Coldstone. Alexander was apprenticed to a Mr. Rattray in Dundee, where another uncle was Rector of the Academy. Alexander seems to have had charge of a brewery in Aberdeen at an early date, - when little more than 18 years old. In 1838 he was at

242

Lochnagar Distillery and then went to London. The other brothers went to Ceylon. Once in London, Alexander Gordon threw himself into his work at the brewery, but became increasingly interested in engineering. In 1844 he married Elizabeth Mickle. In the course of years he built his own breweries and became very wealthy. Perhaps because Alexander witnessed a drowning in the Dee he vowed to replace Polhollick ferry with a bridge when he had money to spare. He did that in 1892. An even bigger gift was the Halls, for public entertainment and education. The Albert Hall opened in 1874, the Victoria Hall in 1895. The Gordons had no family. Alexander died in 1895, his wife some months later.

Hardly legible on the wall of the Albert Hall is

"This stone was laid by
the Marchioness of Huntly
1874"

Hotels in 1880 were The Monaltrie, Coylachreich (contemporary spelling) a thriving establishment run by Mrs. Frances Deans, and Pannanich Hotel with Mr. John Gauld. A Temperance Hotel was run by James and William Deans in the 1870's. Refreshment Rooms were run by Charles Cook, who seems to have had something of a monopoly. By 1880 too, there were eight Lodging House keepers, - three men and five women.

Worrall's Directory, published in 1877 mentions as important the scenery, the Railway and tourists for whose convenience were good hotels. Balmoral is commented on and the Royal Guard. Banks and traders are mentioned. Birkhall and Knock Castle are referred to as well as some private residences. The wells at Pannanich were discussed and and three churches - the new Church of Scotland, the church at Kirkstyle, Glengairn and the Free Kirk in Ballater, founded after the disruption in 1843, as a result of objection to patronage The Roman Catholic Church was still at that time in Glengairn and the Glenmuick House Private Chapel and the Episcopal Church had at that date not been built.

COACHING DAYS

The 'Square' near the Monaltrie Hotel was the original centre of the village. Stage coaches stopped there and the whole area was bustling, with stabling, etc. Many young village lads had jobs as ostlers, porters and general workers. In 1850 the Royal Mail Coach left the Royal Hotel in Union Street, Aberdeen, for Braemar, at 7a.m., stopping for a while at the Monaltrie. The whole journey took 9 hours, (allowing for refreshment stops), according to the diary of James Farquharson, a prosperous London merchant with roots on Deeside. Bridge Street did not exist at first. A description of Ballater in 1830, supposedly by a coachman, recorded "The inn, the Monaltrie Arms, is at the south east corner of the square, just on the bank of the river". Sketches of around 1856 do not show the building as it is today. The present building dates from about 1860, and stands on the foundations of the original Monaltrie Arms. The Hotel and the accompanying farm, Cornellan, formed a complex that provided local employment. The farm used to provide the Hotel with all its produce, including game. The kitchen garden was across the road, just beyond the present Riverside Garage. Tinkers camped by the river, beyond the old laundry and gave their name to the Bar that no longer exists but was incorporated into the Monaltrie development. Even when another bar opened, it closed half an hour after the last train, so everyone rushed to the Tink.

The new Pannanich Wells Hotel was an hotel in two halves between which the horses drawing the coaches stopped to drop off their passengers.

THE POST OFFICE

At first Ballater had no Post Office and it was not until 1830, as a result of a petition, that letters could be addressed to Ballater and not to Tullich. Donald Farquharson kept the Post Office for several years. He also had a considerable amount of property in Ballater. Donald's son John succeeded to the Post Office and for many years he also carried on a thriving business as a merchant. His daughter Elizabeth followed him in the Post Office. The Farquharson family ran the Post Office for almost a century. Some of their ground was sold and became the site of the Victoria and Albert Halls.

LIFE IN BALLATER

What do we know of the village, its dwellings and its customs in Victorian times?

Food was at first very simple, - much as it had been in the glens for generations. Breakfast consisted of porridge or sowans (meal steeped in water or milk, the solid matter at the bottom being the sowans: boiled with water and salt, it was eaten like porridge). There was brochan for lunch, - gruel often eaten with butter or honey or vegetables like kale. In the evening there would be potatoes, bread, oatcakes, milk or water and malt ale. Meat or fowl or game could be added, according to circumstances.

Once visitors flocked in, with new ideas and a more grandiose life-style, locals began to copy these trends. Food tastes gradually developed to include much of what we eat today, and advancing trends in food preservation and treatment came to the area. Nevertheless, diet was governed by financial considerations.

Reading material, - if one could read, - was usually a shared copy of the weekly Aberdeen Journal, price 7d. For many people there was little money to spare at first.

EDUCATION

Education was considered important. James Smith had moved into the area about 1807. He taught in temporary accommodation until a permanent building was erected, with school premises on the ground level and his accommodation above. A separate school was built around 1836. He was a popular and successful teacher, a number of his pupils qualifying in medicine and divinity. A Miss Logan opened a Female School and ran it for a number of years. When Mr.Smith retired he was succeeded by Mr. Murray. In 1862 Mrs. Farquharson of Invercauld erected at her own expense a girls' school. The two teachers were Miss Clark and Miss Anderson. They were followed by Miss Whyte who stayed for a very brief period, and Miss Simpson, who remained for a number of years, until she married the schoolmaster, Mr. Murray. Two sisters called Ferrier had a very successful period of teaching in what was then known as the 'Female' school. During their period of office a disagreement arose between the School Board and a section of the community. The board wished all teaching staff to be under the Headmaster of the Public School while some of the community wished to retain the services of the Misses Ferrier in the Female School. Several public meetings were held and feelings ran high. Long-standing friendships were broken and never restored. By 1879 the schools were amalgamated. After Mr. Murray's retirement, Mr. David Craib was appointed, to be followed by Mr. Lawson, who was still teaching in 1901 when Queen Victoria died.

A new school building had been erected after the passing of the Education Act in 1872, but as Ballater grew rapidly after that date extension had to be made to the building at two successive periods. By the end of the nineteenth century there were two male and five female teachers.

LOCAL INDUSTRY

As far as 'industries' were concerned, there were two in Ballater. The Bobbin Mill at Turner Hall, (hence the name) was run by three generations of Pithies. At one time they were sending vast quantities of bobbins to jute works in India, after being finished off in Aberdeen. The Illingworths ran the woollen mills at the Bridge of Gairn, with the date of 1788 on a stone.

VILLAGE ORDERLY

As early as 1832 the feuars of the village appointed an official "to reside in the village and to inspect all streets and lanes and wherever he observes any dunghills, wood, stones or rubbish, to call on feuars living opposite to remove the rubbish or pay the cost of doing so." Two shillings was levied from every feuar each year. The orderly appointment was reviewed at frequent intervals and it was constantly reiterated that no cattle, horses or swine should be loose in the streets. The same officer was to prevent vagrants from entering the village.

In 1845 an Inspector of the Poor was appointed so the Kirk Session gave up one of its functions and handed over the money that remained in the 'Poores Box'. There were still many people needing help.

THE RAILWAY

With the coming of the Railway, Royal Deeside was easily accessible. The Railway opened up Ballater, and all spheres of life were revolutionised. Visitors from far and near, as well as locals, enjoyed the journey through beautiful scenery. Day trips from Aberdeen became increasingly popular and whole families made the journey. The station was the setting for the arrival of many crowned heads and famous people, bound for Balmoral. When the Railway came to Ballater, the village centre moved from Bridge Square to Station Square.

UTILITIES

By 1877 Ballater had three banks or their agents, and a Savings Bank. This latter had actually started in 1821 but even after 20 years had less than 50 depositors.

There was a Gas Works, the Inland Revenue (Excise) Department had a Supervisor, four officers and an assistant. There was a Police Constable and a Sheriff Officer. The

Railway Station was important because of the visitors to Balmoral.

One could travel by coach to Braemar, leaving the Invercauld Arms (formerly Monaltrie which changed its name after the Monaltrie Farquharsons died out in 1858 and then back again to Monaltrie in more recent years to avoid confusion with the Braemar Hotel)) at 10 a.m. daily, with an additional departure in the summer season. The proprietor of the 'coach' business was Charles Cook. There were two carriers to Braemar, John Milne, and John Smart. Horse hirers were Mitchell, Dean, Farquharson and William Paterson.

By 1890 the Fire Brigade was using the church bell to call out its men. It seems the whole village turned out to see the horse drawn engine go by, or to follow it to its destination.

MEDICAL PRACTITIONERS

The first medical practitioner to reside in Ballater was a Dr.Clark, a young man whose father had property in Ballater. He does not seem to have been very successful in his profession. There was considerable rivalry when Dr.Robertson came to Deeside and began to practice medicine, the result being that Dr.Clark left the area. Dr.Robertson later became Commissioner to the Queen at Balmoral. Sometime later, a doctor from lower down the valley called Sherrifs gained a reputation for his skill in medicine. It seems that gradually he was called in to treat illness in Ballater. He finally decided to settle in the village and eventually owned a great deal of property. Dr. Reid practised for several years, to be followed by a succession of others, - Drs. Beattie, Spence, Shearer, Jack, Holden, Mitchell, and Hendry. The last two were probably in practice at the same time.

In the early days, local women acted as midwives. There was Margaret Wright and Mrs. McWilliam. In the mid-nineteenth century there was a basic training and midwifery was regarded as a profession. Jane Bowman or McNaughton was another midwife. She does not seem to have

248

been very successful. Sarah Brown or Cumming had a long and successful practice down to the end of the century. Her help was not only sought in cases of childbirth: she seems to have prescribed in cases of illness. When there was an emergency it was quite a usual sight to see her astride a horse, urging the animal to its greatest speed. She worked closely with Dr. Sherrifs, and as long as she was able, she made a daily round of the village. After she gave up the work because of infirmity, the overseeing of the duties then became the responsibility of the medical officer.

EMPLOYMENT

A number of men had employment in local businesses. There were tailors, shoemakers, clothiers. Millers, as one would expect, lived out of Ballater, but sold their grain in the village.

The first plasterer in Ballater was William Mitchell who carried on an extensive business on Deeside for many years, without any opposition. His sons followed him in the business which did well until Munroe and Wright then opened a rival business.

There were four stonemasons in Ballater around 1880, - and three carpenters. In the late 1870's to 90's there were four groups of wrights and a village plumber, Thomas Dick. Ballater supported two stoneware dealers, a woman flour dealer, a fruiterer, and George Smith, a saddler. Margaret Pringle was a baker and confectioner, and Francis Rae the Chemist.

PHOTOGRAPHERS

It was the fashon in Victorian Ballater to have one's photograph taken - if one could afford it.

George Washinton Wilson had become well know and was regarded as official photographer to Royalty. Robert Milne took photographs of locals and of Deeside scenes. He was born in Southern Ireland in 1865 but when he was about seven years old the family moved to Aboyne. He set up in business near Aboyne Green and did a roaring trade on Games Day. He then moved to Ballater, occupying the premises that are now Ted Emslie's.

In 1896 Milne became "Photographer to her Majesty in Ballater " As well as local photographs of events like cricket and curling he photographed all the leading heads of Europe and most of the Royal family. He took the last official photograph of Queen Victoria at Balmoral and then took very few photographs.

William Watson moved from Laurencekirk to Ballater in the 1870's. He did take a number of photographs of the Queen, her family and their guests but he never held a Royal Warrant. He is buried at Foot o' Gairn. Another photographer of whom we know little was William Reevie.

FAIRS

Markets or fairs that had been held in Tullich were transferred to Ballater. One was on the second Tuesday of May, and one on the second Monday of September for sheep, and on the second Tuesday for cattle. These markets were well attended for many years. Great numbers of sheep and cattle were brought from Banff, Elgin and Inverness areas and dealers came from Perth, Forfar and further south. A great deal of business was transacted. A view has been expressed that Francis Farquharson and then his nephew William developed Ballater for the purpose of encouraging markets and not for accommodating the overflow of guests from Pannanich. While markets were encouraged and transferred from Tullich, Invercauld records do not make this the prime reason for developing the new village.

BALLATER GAMES

Ballater Games began in July 1864, on the Green round the first church. Participation in the Games was only open to parish residents. A founding Committee consisted of Messrs. Cook, Haynes, Ferguson, A. Reid, Glennie, Paterson, Illingworth, Ross, W. Grant, W.Reid, Gordon, A. Grant, Smith, Massie, Anderson, and Stewart. The committee that conceived the idea of the Games was made up of local public-spirited men, presumably the leading men in the community, who saw an opportunity that would be of benefit to the expanding village.

THE BURGH

A Victorian account of Ballater, by an unknown author, describes the village as a place of cheerful people. It speaks of the pleasure felt by villagers when the Queen came, on her way to Balmoral.

Ballater was created a Burgh in 1891. There were nine elected Bailies and a Provost, John Brebner. The only woman Provost was Miss Barbara Briscoe in 1969. The Burgh continued until reorganisation in 1973.

The coat of arms of the old Burgh reflects the past. In one quarter is the lion of Macduff, representing Farquharson of Monaltrie, in another fir trees from the armorial bearings of Farquharson of Invercauld, their successors. A third quarter shows the key from the old legend of Nathalan locking his arm and leg together, throwing away the key in the Dee and finding it in a fish in Rome, and finally, a depiction of the well at Pannanich.

Letters exist to indicate that there was an attempt to persuade the King, George in 1822 to transfer the documents granting burgh status to Tullich from there to the newly developing Ballater. William Farquharson sought introductions through Sir Walter Scott and the Lord Chief Commissioner. William Farquharson showed the King some of the family

Stewart relics and according to an account in the Edinburgh Courier "had the honour of kissing the King's hand." The burgh document seems to have disappeared. Most authorities blame Sir Walter Scott for losing it.

GEDDES

A biologist of note who worked on zoological projects before doing research in Mexico, Patrick Geddes was born in Ballater in 1854. Hampered in his research work by failing eyesight, he turned his attention to ecology and the improvement of living conditions, but is probably best known as a "town-planner".

XXVI. SOME INTERESTING
PRESENT-DAY CHURCHES

ST. ANDREW'S ROMAN CATHOLIC CHURCH, BRAEMAR

This narrow building has buttresses at the west end. It was erected about 1839. Stained glass windows of saints and a former Bishop have been added. The stone font is of very early date.

The 1795 date stone from an earlier Roman Catholic church, presumably in Braemar, is now in Chapel Brae at what later became the Humanae Vitae House.

BRAEMAR CHURCH

By the early 9th century Celtic Christianity was firmly established on Deeside. By the 13th century Roman Catholic practices had superseded Celtic Christianity and gradually traces of the past were obliterated, surviving only as legends. At the end of the century the church was run on parochial lines, endowed by gifts in money or kind, from powerful landowners. Seemingly a good scheme, it put Church property in the lands of laymen. From the funds, new churches were build and the old Celtic foundations fell into ruin. In 1234 Duncan, Earl of Mar issued a charter "Liber Cartarum Prioratus Sancti Andree" gifting the Church of Kindrochit to the Augustinian or Black Friars at the Priory of Monymusk. Auchendryne is mentioned too.

In 1560 Parliament ratified the change from Roman Catholicism to Presbyterianism. It had little impact on Deeside, apart from some modification of interior design and some decay of older buildings. Most families on Upper Deeside adhered to the Old Faith and frequenthy supported or concealed priests. Worship went "underground" with services in private houses. Later a building on the Inverey road was used as a chapel and in 1795 a chapel was built in Braemar on the hill, hence Chapel Brae. St. Andrew's Roman Catholic building was erected in 1839.

Emissaries of the Protestant faith were soon in Braemar. We have a list, from 1574 to 1622. At that date Alexander Ferguson became minister and stayed until 1641. He was also from 1626 minister of the joint parish of Braemar (Kindrochit)/ Crathie.

Because of Charles I's introduction of a Service Book without Parliamentary approval, Civil War resulted, Crown against Covenant. Braemar was little affected. The Commonwealth and the Restoration of the Monarchy followed and the Rev. William Robertson was in 1669 ordained to the charge of Crathie & Kindrochit. A few months later he was deposed for neglect of duty. The Presbytery of Kincardine o'Neil was looking for a possible minister. They found the Rev. Adam Fergussone, ordained to the united parish of Crathie & Kindrochit in 1700. He was succeeded in 1715 by the Rev. John McInnes, author of "The Battle of Sheriffmuir". Other ministers followed, including the Rev. Farquhar MacRae.

The Deeside Lairds' involvement in the '15 and the '45 brought Braemar into the sphere of national history. The following retribution meant the destruction of many humble homes and ruined crops.

There were were two villages - Castleton around the Castle, Invercauld property and Presbyterian and Auchendryne, on the other side of the Cluny, basically Roman Catholic. The two sections were united in 1870. Statistics for 1791 show in the united parish 700 people who could not understand the sermon in English. In Braemar there were 580 Roman Catholics, 255 Protestants and 192 children.

The East or Parish Church was built in 1830, opposite the present Invercauld Arms Hotel. During the ministry of the Rev. Archibald Anderson the Disruption took place in 1853.

In 1879 Braemar was disjoined from Crathie and became a quoad sacra parish. Before that a missionary appointment was made in Braemar in 1874 and William Gordon became the first minister in the parish or East Church and served until 1906. The parish Church, the East Church, was considerably altered in the 1870's. Braemar as we know it dates from that time, with two villages on opposite banks of the Cluny, - Castleton on the East, Auchindryne on the West. The established church was in Castleton.

The split in the Church came in 1843 when there was opposition to the practise of patronage, - the right of a patron to place a minister withour reference to the congregation. In Braemar the Rev. Farquhar MacRae and two of the three elders and 80 of the 180 communicants left the Church and formed the Free Church. They worshipped in the Fife Arms and in a converted stable. The Earl of Fife gave permission for a wooden building adjoining the Cluny road. It was built in a few days and opened in late 1843. In 1845 it was replaced by a stone building opened on 6th July 1845. In 1870 a new church was built. The 1845 building was taken down, stone by stone and re-erected at Aberarder as a preaching station and school. It still remains, converted to an attractive house.

The inspiration for the new building came from the Rev. Hugh Cobban, He had come to Braemar in 1854, to a congregation worshipping in a little stone church on the same site. He was a forceful preacher and was called to preach in Canada & Paris. After 16 years of devoted work he caught a chill and died. The church he had spent so much time in planning and building saw no dedication service. There was a funeral service. Hugh Cobban is buried behind the pulpit. Minister followed minister. The congregation increased. The Free Church was known as the West Church and the Parish church the East Church.

At the end of 1929 it was agreed to unite the West & East churches of Braemar under the name of Braemar Parish Church. Both churches were to be used alternately and the Manse of the Free Church was to become the parish Manse. This came into being in February 1931. Finance was a problem. In 1938 an incorporating union was agreed. The West Church would be used for Sunday School and general purposes. By 1935 it was agreed to retain only one place of worship and in 1947 the East Church was sold to Capt. Farquharson. Later the Manse was sold and is now a private house. This was because the two congregations of Crathie and Braemar were finally linked, in spite of an appeal against it to the General Assembly. Both congregations opposed the linkage and I presented the appeal to the General Assembly. After initial uncertainty, the linkage worked well. Now yet another linkage is in the future, with Glenmuick (Ballater).

THE CENTRICAL CHURCH & THE PRESENT GLENMUICK CHURCH IN BALLATER

The three parishes of Tullich, Glenmuick and Glengarden (Glengairn) were united in 1618. King's College received Glenmuick & Glengairn (among others) by Act of Parliament in 1663

The churches of Tullich, Glen Muick and Glen Gairn were all in a very delapidated state but the dream of one large church to replace the three was not possible until the bridge over the Dee was built in 1783. The Heritors were dubious about building another church and really wanted to make repairs, but Presbytery insisted on a new building that would accommodate all the people from the three parishes, - about 1700.

The new church, "The Centrical Church", designed by Massey of Aberdeen, was 72' long and 34' wide and measured 17'6" "from the door sole to the level of the side walls". The floor under the pews was paved. Unlike early kirks, it had seats - three seating areas. There were four front and two gable windows and double doors in the gables. At each entrance a stairway led to the gallery. In the apse was the pulpit with sounding board, stair and stair rail. In the centre were square pews with seats and small tables. The dividers could be lifted and formed into a long table for Communion Sunday with communicants sitting on both sides. At such times communicants approached by the east door and left by the west. The church stood S.W. and N.E.

The square stone and lime steeple rose 12 feet above the ridge-stone of the roof and then was of wood, octagonal in shape but tapering to a point. It was topped by a weather-vane, 99 feet from the ground. The total cost of the church to the Heritors was £670.

The church opened in December 1800. Nothing remains from this time except the 'foundation stone', with the date of 1798, and some stone slabs in the vestibule.

The bell, cast in 1688, was a gift from the Cathedral at Aberdeen. The one dial clock was not installed until 1840. For 50 years the minister had no vestry but a bracket was fixed on the back of the pulpit so that he had somewhere to hang his hat! In the 1850's a vestry was built with a passage leading to the pulpit.

As Ballater prospered its residents increased in number. Royalty came to Balmoral. The "Railway Boom" brought an influx of visitors. The "Centrical Church", opened in 1800 was felt to be no longer in keeping with the more prosperous image of Ballater so Ballater's 1800 Church was pulled down and the present church erected on the site. The last service in the old building was the Communion Service on 20th October 1872. The new Kirk, designed by J. Russell Mackenzie of Aberdeen in 1873, lay at the heart of the village, and still does. It was designed to have seating for 600 with 100 in the gallery. This was usually adequate, in the 1880's and 90's, except at times of Communion Services. The foundation stone was laid by the Marquis of Huntly on 27th March 1873 and the church opened for worship on 25th June 1874 but the real opening was at the Communion service.. At the service on 28th June there was a record collection - £ 48. 8s. 1d.

In the absence of a musical instrument, the Precentor fulfilled an important duty. He led the congregation in singing. In the 1880's the Precentor's behaviour gave cause for concern. On two occasions he had been reprimanded for intoxication while on duty. On another occasion he was found fast asleep in the sick room of the Barracks. He had twice been given a 'second chance' and vowed abstinence. After considerable discussion and many promises of total abstinence on his part, the Precentor had his third chance. I gather he did not fall from grace again! The congregation was told at this time that it would stand at praise but would sit, leaning forward reverently on the book board, for prayer, - 'this being the nearest approximation to kneeling that the pews would permit of.'

When the organ was installed in 1889 and the new pulpit placed in a more forward position, with a new Communion Table, the seating capacity was reduced. The ladies of the Work Party used the proceeds of their 1890 sale to buy a Communion Table and Chair for £10.6s.6d. The pulpit cost £30 11s. In 1887 Mrs.Reid of Aberdeen presented two chairs for the Vestibule to commemorate Queen Victoria's Diamond Jubilee. Fund-raising for a Hall began and it was finally opened in 1898.

Four stained glass windows adorn the church.

The
Centrical
Kirk

The Centrical Church, Ballater

CRATHIE KIRK

Tradition says that Colm came to the area from the Abbey of Deer early in the sixth century and founded a chapel at Abergeldie but we know nothing of his activities. Manire was one of the early missionaries to the area. His was a Celtic, not a Columban form of Christianity and little is known of his activities but he baptized converts in a pool of the Dee that bears his name.

The first structure that can be clearly recognized as a church is in the graveyard, the current burial ground, south of the present church. Long and rectangular, of no great architectural interest, it was Crathie parish church. It was a pre-Reformation building, belonging to Cambuskenneth Abbey near Stirling and had originally been dedicated to St. Manire. Ministers and Readers in an unbroken line from Robert Christensoun in 1567 cared for the spiritual wellbeing of the parishioners. Although little more than names of these men is known, we do know that in June 1614 the Reader, David Sanderson was murdered by John Brabare.

1626 was an important year for the parish. The Braemar minister, Alexander Ferguson was then appointed minister of Crathie as well, probably due to a shortage of ministers. This was a vast parish, from Rothiemurchus, across the tops of the Cairngorms to the Cairnwell and down the Dee to Crathie. Little wonder that on many Sundays the minister could not get to the services. He preached in English in Crathie and in English and Gaelic in Braemar. From 1626 one minister served both parishes until in 1725 when a Royal Bounty Missionary was settled in Braemar.

For 300 years the ministers served the church by the river. Some were known well beyond the bounds, others only locally. In 1699 William Robertson was deposed for neglect of duty. Adam Ferguson served faithfully for 14 years but "could never forgive himself for on one occasion having heinously powdered his wig on the Lord's Day." John McInnes had a difficult time when he was expected to maintain the Kirk's loyalty to the House of Hanover and the local laird Francis Farquharson of Monaltrie, in Crathie, was to lead the Deeside Highlanders for Prince Charlie and the Jacobite Standard had been raised in Braemar. Nevertheless he prayed for King George but after Culloden was among those petitioning for a pardon for Francis. The Rev. Murdoch McLennan wrote a ballad on the Battle of Sheriffmuir.

In a ruinous state by 1804, the church's ivy covered walls remain in the burial ground.

The original building was replaced by one of no great distinction, costing only £820, on the site of the present church. It had four white-washed walls and a little belfry. Internally, walls and ceiling were whitewashed and the pews were narrow It was to be "the dear little church" of Queen Victoria's Journal.

Famous visiting preachers pleased the Queen, - men like the Revs. J. Caird, Cameron Lees & Drs. Norman Macleod and Campbell. After 1873 Queen Victoria took Communion, according to her Journal.

It was decided that the plain building had served its day. The last service in the old church was held on 23rd April 1893. It was a Communion Service. The site was needed for the new building so demolition began immediately. Some services were held in Balmoral Castle's "Iron Ballroom" but a "timmer kirk" was erected about 100 yards from the old building and was in use for about two years.

Queen Victoria laid the foundation stone of the present church on 11th September 1893. It was dedicated on 16th June 1895. It had been designed by Alexander Marshall Mackenzie of Aberdeen. Of grey Inver granite, it is roofed with red tiles. The building is cruciform with a semi-circular apse. The main entrance is on the west side but at the south there is a "Royal Porch" reserved for the visitors. In the north transept are the pews of the Heritors, Invercauld and Abergeldie. The congregation sits in the nave. The church is not typical of a Presbyterian building - it is more elaborate. The Iona marble Communion Table in the Apse does not permit Elders to seat around it at times of Communion. There is an hexagonal pulpit of various types of granite. Carved panels are from the School of Arts and Crafts set up by Prince Albert. Everywhere are gifts from Royals and others and there are many memorials.

There is yet another former church building in Crathie, - the United Free Church, erected after the Disruption of 1843. Crathie seceeders worshipped in a barn at Abergeldie Mains but had no minister. In 1853 they built a small church near Lochnagar Distillery. Then they built another on the north bank of the river in 1881. Union between the Established Church and the Free Church officially took place in 1929, but in practice it was later.

Early church at Crathie

THE CHURCH OF SCOTLAND AT KIRKSTYLE

Over the Gairnshiel Bridge and along to Kirkstyle are heaps of stones and a derelict and rather precarious building. There were a few small dwellings and a corn mill with a mill-dam. Tomnavey (the hillock of the deer) was in 1696 home to 17 tenant families and a cottar.

Beyond this the road climbs steeply up the Shenval and on to Strathdon.

The present Church building is the successor to the ruined kirk at Foot o'Gairn. Because of the preponderance of Roman Catholics in the glen, Protestant Heritors, backed by the

Church of Scotland built the present structure in 1801/2.

At first the annual Communion Service was held in Glenmuick Church in Ballater but for the convenience of glen dwellers it was held in Glengairn, from July 1850. About 100 members communicated.

Originally a D plan church, it was a 'Mission Station' until 1863 when Glengairn became a quoad sacra parish with its own minister. The Rev. Robert Neil who had been a Royal Bounty Missionary was then accorded the status of minister. He died in 1890, to be succeeded by the Rev. James Anderson Lowe who remained until 1918 when he moved to Dumfries. He had a glebe of a few acres and farm buildings at the Manse. Eventually these were incorporated into the farm of Balno. The manse itself at Dalfad had been built on the site of a former cottage and the gable wall retained.

Early in this ministry the floor of the church and vestry and the windows were repaired. The Heritors, Invercauld and Huntly and the latter's successor Keiller, were responsible for Kirk and Manse, a system that prevailed until 1929, when congregations became responsible.

In 1927 the General Assembly suppressed the parish of Glengairn and re-linked it to Glenmuick, to be served by the minister of Glenmuick, the Rev.J.R.Middleton with the help of an assistant or student. So Glengairn's years of independent existance came to an end. In 1928 the Manse was sold. Later it was pulled down.

A succession of assistants served in Glen Gairn until 1938, when the union of the Church of Scotland and the Free Church in Ballater took place. A series of licentiates then took services. The two parishes were then united in 1949. Much of the furniture in Glengairn was suffering from dry rot and was replaced by equipment from the closed Free Kirk. The floor was renewed. By 1967 the roll was down to 29 members.

Amy Stewart Fraser, daughter of the Rev.J.A.Lowe wrote of life in the glen and the family still visit the church. The family presented a lectern and two vases in her memory in 1954 and in 1989 two large vases and hymn books.

In 1971 Glengairn church was designated a building of Historic and Architectural Interest.

A pipe organ was gifted and rebuilt and it supplies the music for the services held from June to September inclusive, in the 'pan drop kirk', when an organist is available.

The kirk in its attractive setting is the venue for weddings for couples from all over the world.

THE SCOTTISH EPISCOPAL CHURCH OF ST. KENTIGERN

Episcopalianism owes its minority status to its association with the Stuarts and with the Jacobites. It was also 'English' in origin and so suspect by native Scots. In mid 18th century Episcopalians were an harassed minority. Their prospects improved after the death of Prince Charles Edward Stewart in 1788 and in 1792 the Penal Laws were repealed. Episcopacy recovered in the 19th and 20th centuries.

Episcopal worship took place in the Ballater area in the private chapel of the original Glenmuick House. The coming of Royalty and the Railway brought increasing numbers of English visitors to the area so it was in 1897 decided that the village should have its own place of worship. A small chapel, St Saviours, with a corrugated iron roof, was built slightly to the south of the present church after a loan of £409 had been obtained.

The present building, of granite, was designed by Marshall Mackenzie. Work was started in 1906 and completed the following year. The original structure, "The Tin Church", was uprooted and sold to Peterculter. The refurbished building still exists there, as a hall.

A number of items were gifted to the church when the Mackenzie chapel was demolished. There was Communion plate and a set of six candlesticks. A cross of 1916 from the Somme against the west wall is in memory of Captain Allan Keith Mackenzie, Grenadier Guards. Near the pulpit is the Barclay-Harvey window showing St. Machar & St Kentigern. This was designed by Gordon Webster of Glasgow. The

Gaskell window, from the William Morris workshops has two angels at the top, one with palm and lyre, the other with palm and violin, designed by Burne Jones for a window at Christ Church, Oxford. Underneath is St. John.

The Adam memorial window depicts St. Kentigern holding a fish with a ring in its mouth - one of the best known legends about this saint.

At the west window is a stained-glass panel representing St. George, dated 1907, by Alfred Ernest Child d.1939, who was manager of the 'Tower of Glass' in Dublin. It is in memory of Sir Allan Mackenzie who died in the Boer War in 1906. and was erected by Lord & Lady Aberdeen.

The middle window of the north wall depicts Bishop John Skinner of Aberdeen (1744 - 1816) whose period of office covered the years of penal restriction and then the growth of the 19th century Scottish Episcopal Church.

The altar of the north chapel came from the private chapel of Glenmuick and depicts St Margaret of Scotland, St.George, St.Andrew, St Patrick and a female saint who may be St.Monica. Also from the same source came a set of six candlesticks.

The organ by Walcker of Ludwigsburg-Wurtt did not do justice to the building for it was in a very poor state. It has been replaced by an organ from King's College Chapel, Aberdeen.

St. Kentigern's, Ballater

ST. LESMO'S CHURCH,
GLEN TANAR

The chapel of St. Lesmo, unique among private chapels, was built by William Cunliffe Brooks in 1870 on the site of the old House of Braeloine on the right bank of the Tanar. It was an Episcopal chapel. The house of Braeloin had, according to local lore, been built with stones from a ruined fort.

There was a busy little community of Braeloine and Knockieside which was flourishing in the 17th century. In the early part of that century the Gardens held lands that included Braeloine or Braelyne and they were actually living in the house there in the mid 17th century. Later the house became the property of the Marquess of Huntly. When Sir William Brooks acquired the estate he built St. Lesmo's on the site of Braeloine, the original arched doorway being incorporated.

Lesmo, to whom the church was dedicated, is a hazy character - half true, half imaginary, more hermit than missionary.

The Glen Tanar chapel was consecrated by Bishop Suther of Aberdeen & Orkney in November 1871. The chapel had originally a thatched roof. Spaces between the stones of the wall were filled with pebbles. Roof timbers were whole trees, without bark, joists were of Glen Tanar fir, as were the pulpit and seats. The roof had gilded stars with centres of silvered glass. There was stained glass in the windows. Glen Tanar granite floored the passage leading to the chancel and the same material formed the altar steps. Behind was an oil painting of the Virgin and Child. The font was of local porphyry. Later, deer antlers were fixed to the roof, with details of shooting. Seats were covered in deerskin. Illumination was by candle set in candelabra. A bell was specially cast by J. Warner & Sons, London. This was really a private family chapel however, it proved convenient for some locals of the Episcopal persuasion. In 1936 Thomas, 2nd Baron Glen Tanar, a talented musician, was given an organ by his brother-in-law Charles, Duke of Wellington. To accommodate it, a tower was added on the north side. Since then, stars and stags have gone, as have the wooden pulpit and the altar. The latter was replaced by a stone taken from the Dee at the spot the legend associates with St.Lesmo. This was a tangible link with that legend of Lesmo. In 1960 the decaying thatch was replaced by slates.

Inter-denominational services are held throughout the summer.

ST. MARGARET'S EPISCOPAL CHURCH, BRAEMAR

When numbers of English visitors arrived in Braemar a small timber church was built about 1880 to the design of J.B.Pirie. It was replaced by a Ninian Comper building in 1899. The detail is exceptional, with traceried windows, a spectacular roof, a carved rood screen, a stone pulpit, choir stalls and Tudor roses on the chancel ceiling.

Although not a ruin, the building is not fit for worship. External repairs were undertaken in 1998. A faulty mortar mix was used and this resulted in internal dampness and weeping walls, rendering use of the building impossible.

MAR LODGE CHAPEL

The private chapel of Mar Lodge is used by the Scottish Episcopal community of Upper Deeside. It is an attractive little chapel with a special atmosphere of its own.

ST. NATHALAN'S ROMAN CATHOLIC CHURCH, BALLATER

This Roman Catholic chapel was built in 1905 to the design of Archibald Macpherson. It differs in style from many of Ballater's other buildings in that it appears more bulky. It is constructed of red and grey speckled granite and it has a three-sided apse.The windows are smaller than one usually finds in a church.

Internally, the building is attractive and it has an excellent organ.

XXVII. A TYPICAL SCHOOL - GLENTANAR
(OS 426923)

Glentanar School building was in a style unfamiliar on Deeside. The architect was George Truefitt. William Cunliffe Brooks had his own ideas on architecture and the result was a very "English" type of building not popular in some quarters, as it was felt that a more 'native' type of architecture would have been better on such a site. The school log, shown to me many years ago by the late Tom Laing of Dinnet, whose father was Headteacher there, gives a good idea of Education in the Victorian Era. Other schools on Upper Deeside were similarly run.

Education was basic or non-existant for ordinary people, in spite of John Knox's sixteenth century vision of free universal education, never implemented because of cost. In the seventeenth century education was controlled by the Kirk, the local superior being responsible for the buildings. By the eighteenth century there were Dame schools, some good, some where women anxious to make a living dealt concurrently with cooking and the class. Religious bodies like the Society for the Propagation of Christian Knowledge also made a contribution. By the nineteenth century education was both secular and religious, public and private. Some schools were excellent, others deplorable.

By 1872 it was thought necessary for workers to read and for voters to be well enough educated to exercise their vote properly. So, the 1872 Act was passed. Education was not to be free, but parents who could not afford instruction in the 3R's for offspring between 5 and 13 years would have the fees paid by the parish poor fund. Attendance was not compulsory, because once a satisfactory standard was reached, there was no insistence on further instruction. School Inspectors could check at any time. Staff in 'public' schools (state schools) had to be qualified. School Boards were elected and expected levels of attainment, known as standards, were specified. At the base was the Infant group, then Standards I-VI. For study beyond that pupils were in Standard Ex VI. Once Standard IV was reached, parents could allow children to work on Specific subjects. A bright pupil with a good teacher could go from the parish school straight to University after 3 years of Specific Study. In practice, dominies offered English, Maths, History, Latin & Greek. Unlike the sciences, they needed no apparatus and no new methods.

A school year had 400 openings, a grant being payable after 250 attendances, subject to adequate staff and buildings. When the Inspector visited, up to 10/- per pupil was payable for 7 year olds. Above that age group, there was 3/- for every pass in Reading, Writing & Arithmetic. Good Grammar in Standards II & III merited another 2/- each, as did excellence in History & Geography in Standards IV to VI. Specifics could gain 4/- per subject. This 'payment by results' often led to knowledge without understanding.

By 1891 fees for Standards were abolished. School Boards could save money by employing women teachers, or use Pupil Teachers, paid under £10 per annum. Religious Education had to be provided, but fees were not charged nor was it examined by Inspectors. Lessons were based on the Bible and Shorter Catechism, with explanations, usually at the beginning of the day. Handwriting was usually taught after lunch, to get the best of the light. Slates were used until 1880 then it was pen and ink. At the end of January 1881 ink froze in the inkwells and again in 1887. Cold hands made writing difficult! Gradually the curriculum widened. Singing was introduced, then knitting and sewing. Drawing was taught with a mole and a hedgehog as models. By 1910 there were sewing machines and Cookery and Woodwork classes.

Usual excuses for absence were herding, harvesting, thinning, potato and turnip lifting, sheep shearing, peat cutting, grouse beating and the visit of the steam thresher. Acceptable absences were for feeing fairs, cattle and flower shows, ploughing matches, weddings and May Day celebrations. There were also Thanksgiving Days after the Communion and national holidays and any royal visits to the area. The summer holiday, or hirst-play, was governed by the ripening of the crops. It was usually towards the end of August until October. Christmas was not a holiday, but Auld Eil was.

Schools lacked the amenities we take for granted. Over crowding and poor ventilation increased the risk of whooping-cough, scarlet fever, measles and diphtheria and toilet provision was of a very primitive nature. Glen Tanar school had to close for three weeks in December 1887 because of an outbreak of scarletina which again reared its head the following year. The school was washed out with Jeyes Fluid and pupils were instructed not to share pens or pencils.

Bad weather was a problem. February 1806 was a dreadful time with everyone snowbound. 1810 and 1881 were outstandingly bad years.

Teachers even then were complaining of bad habits - chewing gutta percha and creating a 'pop', smoking, graffiti on walls, - and playing football in the school yard on Sundays.

An Education Act of 1803 was the basis for many future improvements. A teacher's minimum salary was £16.3.4. per annum, plus some fees, some perks and 'a house of not more than two rooms and a garden'. Such houses were built with the schoolroom on the ground floor, and upstairs, entered by an outside staircase, was the teacher's accommodation. The salary gradually improved until by the 1840's it was on average £30 p.a. with extra fees of about £20. Many teachers made a little extra money as Session Clerks or Precentors. Soon, purpose built schools were erected, with the teacher occupying the whole of the former building. Salaries were often increased by bequests, so a better type of teacher was attracted.

XXVIII. SOME OF UPPER DEESIDE'S INTERESTING CHARACTERS

"History is not just about ruins from the past. It is about people"

JOHN BROWN

Much has been written about John Brown, the Queen's personal attendant. The son of a school teacher who became a farmer, the family moved to the Bush Farm in Crathie when John was 5 years old.

John Brown worked in the stables at Pannanich then at Balmoral stables in 1842. He became a ghillie to Prince Albert in 1849, was promoted to lead the Queen's pony in 1852 and by 1855 was "upper servant and personal attendant to the Queen."

In 1863 on a trip to Loch Muick the coach overturned. Brown jumped from the top and rescued the ladies. In 1871 an Irishman, Arthur O'Connor put a pistol to the Queen's head in Buckingham Palace grounds to persuade her to sign a document. Brown grabbed the pistol and held the man down. In 1882 he captured a would-be assailant, Roderick Maclean at Windsor Station.

For Brown the Queen built a house, Baile na Coile.

The Queen was discouraged from writing Brown's life story. Instead she asked the Poet Laureate to write an inscription for the Boehm memorial stone - "Friend more than servant, LoyaL, Truthful, Brave."

John Brown died in 1883 and was buried in the old Crathie kirkyard.

JOHN & SANDY DAVIDSON & THE MILL OF INVER

Lying at the Inver west of Crathie, the Mill changed little over the years until in the 1970's it was remodelled as a house. It retained much of its original attraction and was an award winning development.

In the days when mills played a great part in the life of the surrounding area the miller was a key man. For many years the millers were Davidsons: the family had originally come from Donside. They are inextricably tied up with the mill building.

In 1767 John Davidson was the miller at Inver. A man of great strength, he worked hard at the mill. On one occasion he had had several hard night's work drying grain and was weary. He told his assistant to keep an eye on the kiln and let him know when the grain was ready for turning. He lay down on some sacks behind the door and fell fast asleep.

The assistant was a conscientious fellow, totally reliable, so John had no qualms about leaving the drying grain to him. Still keeping an eye on the kiln, the assistant started to trim his beard. All mill doors of that period had a round hole in the centre, for ventilation, and for use by the mill cat, - an early type of cat-flap!

Without any warning, and with no sound of approaching footsteps, from the hole in the door a large weight dropped onto the sleeping miller. When it happened a second time, he awoke to see a black hand withdrawing from the opening. His first thought was that it was a practical joke. Then another stone dropped, and yet another. He jumped up and rushed outside. There was nothing there. Puzzled, he was about to re-enter the mill when he heard a voice saying, 'Follow me'. As he looked around he saw his assistant, white as a sheet and quivering with fear. The miller advanced further into the dark night. He was conscious of a dark shadow in front of him as he crossed the mill stream. On they went to a flat field where the 'aparition' stopped. The miller, greatly daring, grabbed it.

The spectre said that when he had been alive he had stolen

271

a few things. Among them had been a sword with an iron hilt. He had buried it nearby, but because iron was involved he was precluded from finding rest in the spirit world. That was the end of the conversation. The miller went back to the mill alone. We are not told what he said to his terrified assistant or how he explained his night-time walk.

The next morning he asked his son to bring a spade. He too was mistified, but father's word was law. The lad went with his father to a kale patch and was made to dig under a rowan tree. It was hard work and took a long time. John Davidson was beginning to think he had made a mistake when they struck metal. It was the sword hilt They took it back to the house and for many years it remained above a bed, the souvenir of the encounter with the 'Black Hand'.

Presumably the spectre could now rest in peace! The story circulated in the area for a number of generations and the sword was regularly displayed. Unfortunately, I have never been able to find it, or indeed anyone who has seen it!

Sandy, son of the miller, was also a man of great strength and was always wrestling. He was very friendly with Capt. Gordon of Abergeldie for both of them were expert dancers. In Aberarder there was on one occasion a 'Penny Wedding'. The newly weds invited friends to a 'party' the admission fee being one Scots penny. This bought locally brewed beer and whisky and a very good time was had by all. There was so much debauchery that the Kirk condemned such wedding arrangements. Sandy and Captain Gordon were both there, Sandy being 'governor of the feast'. Gordon complained about the drink shortage. Sandy said 'If I were Gordon of Abergeldie I would order another anker of whisky'. Gordon did.

There were frequent wrestling matches which Sandy usually won. Up Glengairn there was another 'Penny Wedding'. Over 200 men from Dee and Don were there. The aim was really enjoyment and celebration, but there was a great deal of rivalry to see which district or hamlet could produce the strongest man. Sandy represented Deeside. He won. There was much jealousy and after the event, on the way home Sandy was attacked by a group of men and kicked and punched. Among other injuries he had a fractured skull. He was carried home, where he lingered for a few months then died, leaving a widow, two sons and two daughters.

Sandy was buried in Glenmuick kirk-yard on a day so snowy it was remembered as 'the day of the great storm'. Over 300 men from the Crathie area attended the funeral. The funeral procession crossed the Dee and went along the South Deeside road. There was a rest and refreshment stop at Corbiehall, about a mile below Abergeldie. To enable refreshment to be imbibed and to give the bearers a rest, the coffin was put down. It was very cold and as always on such occasions, the refreshment was liquid, - very many drams. It was considered only fitting that Sandy should be honoured by some wrestling and this took up quite a time. This was in the days when only the menfolk attended funerals. The result of the drink and the fighting was that the procession arrived at the Glenmuick burial ground to find they had no coffin. So they had to go back for it. Perhaps the whole episode is not so surprising for it was reported that four gallons of whisky were imbibed by the bearers before the 'lifting'!

CHARLES DAVIDSON

Charles Davidson and his wife lived in Albert Road, Ballater. He joined the railway service in 1883 and ten years later he became signalman at Ballater. A keen Free Mason, a musician and a poet, Charles Davidson was a mild man, of quiet speech. One situation showed him in a rather different light.

When he had to deal with the Tsar's arrival in 1896, the Russian language and the mountains of luggage were too much for him on a pouring wet day. So Charlie put some 'immediately needed' luggage in a horse-drawn vehicle. He ignored, or deliberately did not hear incomprehensible shouts by a Cossack. The latter, in a rage with this inferior stupid Aberdeenshire peasant was about to hit Charlie with his stick. "Stop" yelled Charlie at the top of his voice, "That's maybe a' richt in Russia, bit it winna work in Ballater". Locals were lining up on Charlie's side when a Russian detective stepped in, spoke to the Russian and pacified Charlie in what a local referred to as 'Christian Scotch'. Charlie's later comment, - 'I suppose I micht hae been shot in Russia'.

MEG GRAY & THE HOUSE IN CHURCH SQUARE

One eccentric inhabitant of Ballater with a little house in Church Square in the 1860's, unfortunately not identified, was Meg Gray. Anyone who attempted to wage war with her was sure to come off second best. Some lodgers staying in the house objected to the hen that was allowed the freedom of the house, often roosting on the table. They were informed that the hennie had been a lodger before them and would still be a lodger after them.

Meg had a well in her garden, now gone. It was always left uncovered and a stranger had a narrow escape. A complaint having been made to the authorities, a representative called on her, remonstrating about such a danger being uncovered. Meg's reply was "I am sure there is plenty of room in Ballater for folks to fall, without coming to my garden to do it".

MAGGIE GRUER, THISTLE COTTAGE, INVEREY
(OS 087894)

Maggie Gruer lived at Thistle Cottage, Inverey and was known the world over to climbers and walkers. She befriended countless Gairngorm climbers to whom her house was a place of shelter and hospitality as it had been when her mother was alive. She gave bed and breakfast to numerous walkers and climbers in the 1920's and 30's and if there was no room in the house there was always a barn with clean straw.

There was a roaring fire in the cottage and Maggie always had a cheery greeting. The invitation "Ye'll tak' an egg?" meant several. There were oatcakes and scones. Her charge was an old 1/- (5p) for bed and breakfast, but she reduced it for the hard-up. Her 'takings' were kept in a bucket.

Maggie's scones and oatcakes were famous. I remember as a child of about 6 years old being taken by my Granny to see Maggie who was an old friend, and eating her oatcakes. I can still conjure up the taste, but I have no recollection of the scones. Perhaps I was not given any!

Because her brother was employed at Mar Lodge Maggie was up on the local gossip. She was a good story teller. She loved her cats - Ramsay Macdonald and Morris Cowley. I remember sitting on the floor stroking the cats.

Maggie died in 1939 at the age of 78.

Maggie's Visitor Book was packed with names from all walks of life. On her death it went to the Cairngorms Club. I particularly like one comment:

> *"Weary and thin we wandered in*
> *Happy and stout we staggered out."*

WILLIAM LOGAN

William Logan was a well-known Ballater watch-maker, with an excellent business. A number of his clocks still remain in Ballater. He acquired a great deal of property in the area. One of William's delights was to engage in an argument, which he usually won. He was an Elder of the Kirk but had gone out to the Free Kirk

WATTIE PLANTS

People on Upper Deeside, particularly men, often had nicknames. These were often references to some physical characteristic but sometimes they had a bearing on the person's job.

Wattie 'Plants' or Walter Stewart lived in Crathie, behind the old school. After a life of hard work and scrimping and saving, he retired. Of his little cottage in a birch wood behind the then Crathie School, only a few stones now remain. Wattie was a bachelor who lived a hermit - like life. No woman was allowed in his little house, but it was always kept spotlessly clean and tidy.

Once he had retired, Wattie was still fit and could spend all his time on his real passion, - his garden. It was a large garden, and he grew fruit and vegetables of excellent quality which he sold locally, hence his nickname 'Wattie Plants'. Local boys were always tempted to steal the fruit but were generally afraid to do so because rumour persisted in the village that although this was an enchanted garden there were traps hidden everywhere waiting to catch those who entered uninvited. Wattie of course encouraged this idea.

Wattie had few visitors, but a regular caller at the house was George Brown, who also lived in Crathie. Wattie was a frequent visitor at George Brown's, and he also visited the Schoolhouse and the Manse, and the farm of his greatest friend. In spite of the fact that Wattie and George Brown held different theological views, they were the best of friends. Wattie was probably illiterate but that did not stop him from arguing on every topic imaginable. Apart from the fact that he had most unusual views on most things, Wattie was a firm believer in water-kelpies, ghosts and witches. He loved telling stories and was fond of entertaining his friends with such fancies. These stories were generally told at his friends' houses and at the end of the evening one of them always escorted Wattie home. Perhaps he was frightened to return home alone with his mind full of all his spookie stories!

Wattie and his farmer friend often had discussions on life and death and what the other world was like. Life went on for a number of years, with Wattie gardening in the daytime and spending evenings in story telling and discussion.

In due time, Wattie died. After the funeral Wattie's farmer friend told of a pact the two of them had made. The first to die would return to give the other details of the after life. It seems they had agreed that at 12 midnight exactly a year after the death of the first of them, they would meet on neutral ground, half way between their two houses. They had picked the spot together, years before, - a grassy clearing sheltered by rocks.

After twelve months had elapsed, the farmer went to the appointed place, somewhat apprehensive. Wattie had not arrived. The farmer waited, becoming more anxious as time went by. He was there at 11 p.m., he was there at midnight and he stayed until 1 a.m. because he remembered Wattie always had trouble with dates and times and he was certainly no good at Arithmetic. Wattie had always had problems even telling the time. Unfortunately, Wattie never turned up, much to the disappointment of the farmer!

When friends later asked if he could suggest why Wattie had not come to meet him, the farmer said that he thought it was because Wattie's opinions had proved wrong about life in that other world, so he had not the courage to come back to report all the details!

WILLIAM ROBB

William Robb was a Deeside silversmith who worked in Ballater and Braemar from the 1880's until the late 1920's. His Ballater base was at 8 Bridge Street.

William and his wife Elizabeth had fourteen children, five of them sons. One had a shop in Pitlochry. Alice Robb married and had a daughter and a son. The daughter Eileen, born in Ballater moved with her parents to Braemar when only a small child. They were running Mr. Robb's new shop there, next door to my late husband's pharmacy. The daughter, Eileen Ford, remembers her mother cycling to Ballater each week with the Braemar ledgers.

William Robb, a keen Mason, died in 1927. Some of his work included the silver ware for Queen Victoria's Highlanders. These included kilt pins, buckles and brooches. Ordinary folk in Braemar and Ballater bought for gifts to bring good-luck, his wishbones or "sugar-nips." In addition, Robb made more specialised items, to order.

Famous all over the world for the quality of his work, he marked his pieces W. Robb in a triangle or an oblong.

XXIX. NATURAL FORMATIONS

THE BURN O' VAT
(OS 413000)

The Nature Reserve at the Moor of Dinnet extends for over 1520 hectares.

The Vat Burn is crossed by stepping stones. The track crosses a wooden bridge and then appears to end at a rock barrier. Large stones lie at the entrance to the Vat while inside is a great bowl-like cavern. Formed at the end of the Ice Age, great rocks are all around with a narrow opening to the sky. It is in effect a giant pothole. The burn running into it rushes through a gorge between Cnoc Dubh and Culblean Hill.

It was in this area that a branch of the MacGregors operated as well as in Glengairn. Brought in to catch caterans and rustlers, they remained to become even more skilled at cattle thieving. It was a case of setting a thief to catch a thief. One of their number, Gilderoy, hid behind a waterfall and escaped detection. He was later captured and hanged in 1658.

THE CHARTER CHEST, CRAIG CLUNIE
(OS N.W. of 178914)

This is a recess in the rocks on Creag Clunie, almost opposite to the House of Invercauld, across the river. It was here that John Farquharson 9th of Invercauld hid estate charters and other valuables before being persuaded or coerced into joining the 1715 Rising by his Feudal Superior the Earl of Mar. Before the days of banks and strong rooms, this was standard policy. As a good number of charters from the period are still extant, they were obviously retrieved.

THE COLONEL'S BED
(OS 087871)

Just over 2 miles from Inverey a track leads to the Colonel's Bed. This rocky shelf in lower Glen Ey is where the Jacobite Colonel, John Farquharson of Inverey, hid from his enemies, the government troops. The "bed" is formed by a ledge of rock, probably of slate. Crumbling now, it must have been in his day fairly inaccessible as it was concealed by high rocks overgrown with vegetation. It was reasonably safe from those unused to the territory.

GLEN CALLATER
(OS 175843)

The rocks in the Callater Burn, in Glen Callater (the glen of the hard water) have been moulded by nature into odd shapes. There are long splinters among the smooth stone, the result of wear by water. Most of the rocks are of granite or mica-slate which at one time was quarried at the lower end of the glen for roof slates. At the north west end of the loch limestone is to be found. Tradition says fairies were often to be found in the glen, with a piper playing for their dancing.

A priest, Peter or Patrick, has given his name to many of the features of the glen. A tiny loch, Loch Phadruig and a hill, Creag Phadruig, are named after him. Carn an t-Sagairt is the priest's hill.

THE LINN O' DEE
(OS 062896)

The Linn, with its spectacular natural rock formation, was named after the Celtic water goddess Dee or Dewa.

THE MUCKLE STANE o'CLUNIE
(OS 183912)

The Clunie Stane is a big boulder by the roadside near the Invercauld Bridge. It was believed at one time that it was haunted by fairies. The stone is said to have rolled down from Creag Clunie.

Known also as Erskine's Stone, it marked the boundary between Erskine or Mar territory and that of Invercauld.

THE RINGING STONE
(OS 300016)

Up Glen Gairn, on the B972 beyond the Kirk, on the left is the Ringing Stone. The road climbs steeply and by an old bridge now no part of the road there is an old lime kiln and just beyond is the stone. This, according to tradition, was a wolf infested area. Inverness claims the last wolf was killed in 1743 but Gairn folk say theirs was killed later. This route, over the Glas Coille, - the grey wood - perhaps after roots constantly found under the ground, was the one used by Fr.McIntosh when going to Mass at Corgarff.

The Ringing Stone is a large boulder, of uncertain age and type, but generally regarded as of glacial formation. Years ago it was considered to have magical properties. Throw at it a small pebble and it rings! Local lore says if a wish is made and the stone has rung for you, the wish is granted. Residents and visitors are frequently to be seen trying their luck!

The stone appears to have feint arrow marks. Theories abound as to origin or meaning. Some would say they are symbols of a long-forgotten rite, of meaning long lost. Others say the marks are those of heavy chains probably use to drag the boulder into place - if it was not deposited there by melting ice. If the marks happened by chance and the stone did not come as a result of glacial action, what then is its purpose? Yet another theory says this is a marker stone as a direction finder to Donside across what would have been very wild territory.

Against this theory is the fact that it differs in shape from other marker stones. It it also suggested that this is the one remaining stone of a stone circle when the others were removed for agricultural purposes, but again this stone is not the usual shape nor is there likely to have been any agricultural activity on the little slope.

In 1650 there was reference in the Kirk Records of Glenmuick Parish with which Glengairn had been linked in 1618 to a "meeting stone" just beyond the church. This could well be the stone for there is no other likely candidate. All we can be sure of is that a stone of considerable bulk stands at the side of the road and that it rings when small stones are thrown at it!

THE ROCKING STONE
(OS 409943)

The "Rocking Stone" first appearing in the 1865 Ordnance Survey, is often called The Big Stone of Carn Beag. No matter how much pressure is applied, it just does not rock! However, the Rocking Stane (OS 405965) on the hill east of Pannanich rocks with the tiniest bit of pressure.

THE SLACKS OF CARVIE
(OS 347055)

A dry rocky gully on a hill north west of Morven cut by a glacial river is by tradition associated with the old woman, Cailleach Bheathrach. Legend says that she created the gully by trying to cut with her teeth an opening in the hills so that the waters of Dee and Don would join together.

The large stone, with a cave underneath, known as Castle Wilson, was a ready-made hiding place for illicit whisky.

XXX. MEMORIALS TO THE PAST

1. COMMEMORATIVE STONES

THE BALLOCHBUIE CAIRN
(OS 210904)

Queen Victoria bought the Ballochbuie Forest (OS 210900) in 1878. Tradition says it had been sold to a Farquharson of Invercauld by McGregor of Ballochbuie for a tartan plaid. So the Queen put up a stone bearing the inscription:-

"Queen Victoria entered into possession of Ballochbuie on 15th May 1878. The bonniest plaid in Scotland."

BALMORAL - HILL-TOP MEMORIALS
ON THE ESTATE

On many of the hills on the Balmoral Estate there are memorial cairns, some large, some small.

When Prince Albert purchased Balmoral on the 11th of October 1852 a small cairn was built on the top of Craig Gowan, - the blacksmith's hill, south of the Castle. (OS 255941). Members of the family had a hand in its construction.

Princess Victoria, Vicky, the Princess Royal, married the Crown Prince of Prussia, Frederick William. He had proposed to her at a family picnic on Creag nam Ban, (OS 299946) the hill of the women or witches, near Abergeldie, in 1855. The Prince was apparently nervous and unsure of what reception he would get, but he felt he was going to be lucky when he found a sprig of white heather. So, later a cairn went up on the Hill of Canup, west of the Castle.

So far happy events had been commemorated but in 1861 Queen Victoria's mother, the Duchess of Kent, died. She was a tenant of Abergeldie Castle during the summer months for a number of years. A small cairn was erected on Creag Asp, (OS

300938), the hill of the adders, near Abergeldie Castle.

The same year Prince Albert died at Windsor Castle so the next year, 1862, the largest of the cairns was erected. To ensure that it could be seen from all parts of the estate it was built on the top of Creag an Lurachain (OS 259933). This 35 feet high pyramid cairn is an excellent example of 'dry stane' work. It is of granite, without mortar. It has on it the initials of the Queen and all her children, together with a Biblical quotation from the Wisdom of Solomon, chap.4 vv.13 &14.

In 1862 there was another family wedding. Princess Alice married Louis, Duke of Hesse. So Craig Gowan (OS 255941) had yet another cairn.

The next wedding was that of the future Edward VII to Princess Alexandra of Denmark, so in 1863 on Creag Bheag, (OS 251959) one of the Coyles of Muick, there was another cairn.

Princess Helena was the next to marry. Her husband was Prince Christian of Schleswig-Holstein, and their cairn to commemorate the event was again on Craig Gowan in 1866.

Again on Craig Gowan after quite an interval, another cairn was erected in 1879 to celebrate the marriage of Prince Arthur to Princess Louise of Prussia.

The Marquis of Lorne, later the 9th Duke of Argyll proposed to Princess Louise between the Glasallt and the Dubh Loch in 1870 and a cairn just off the path marks the spot.

There was another interval before the family had something to celebrate. In 1885 Princess Beatrice married Prince Henry of Battenburg and their cairn was on the lower slopes of Creag an Lurachain. (OS 259933).

In 1887 Princess Alice wife of the Grand Duke of Hesse, whose marriage cairn was on Graig Gowan died of diphtheria in Germany and was buried there. A memorial Celtic cross of granite was erected in her memory.

The Castle grounds have many memorials. In 1867 a granite obelisk was placed in Prince Albert's memory as well as a bronze figure by William Theed.

Prince Leopold, Duke of Albany and Earl of Clarence, a

haemophiliac, died as a result of an accident in 1884 when 31 years of age and he is remembered by a granite garden seat.

Prince Henry of Battenburg, husband of Princess Beatrice died in 1896 and his life is commemorated by a Celtic Cross.

There is also a Celtic Cross erected in 1901 in memory of Alfred Earnest Albert, Duke of Edinburgh who had married Marie, daughter of Alexander II, Tsar of all the Russias.

Queen Victoria herself is remembered. A granite obelisk was erected in 1901 in addition to the bronze figure of 1897. The same sculptor had created a bronze figure of John Brown in 1883 but this was later banished to a secluded spot in the wood.

King Edward VII and King George V were both remembered by granite seats, one in 1910, the other in 1936.

In 1947 a sundial of Caithness stone was erected in honour of the marriage of the then Princess Elizabeth and the Duke of Edinburgh.

There are dog memorials on the path to the west - Noble died 1887 & Tchu in 1890.

'15 STONE, BRAEMAR
(OS 150915)

The Deeside Field Club set up a memorial in 1953, opposite the Invercauld Arms. This commemorated the raising of the Standard of the Old Pretender in Braemar on 6th September 1715 at the start of the Rising.

Notwithstanding his Jacobite sympathies, John Erskin, Earl of Mar had been Secretary of State for Scotland under Queen Anne, but when he was dismissed by George 1st. in 1714, he left London and travelled by sea to Aberdeen and on to Deeside. He was joined by other Jacobites, ostensibly for a deer hunt but to secure agreement and make plans for a Jacobite rising.

When the standard was raised the golden finial fell from the top. To superstitious Highlanders this was an omen of doom. The defeat at the Battle of Sheriffmuir destroyed morale and the Rising was doomed.

The memorial consists of a bronze plaque set in a large stone. Mrs. Farquharson of Invercauld unveiled it on 1st. August 1953 and removed a cloth bearing the arms of John Erskine. A replica of the standard was raised by Capt. Farquharson.

A tablet in Invercauld Arms Hotel marks the actual spot where the Standard was raised.

CARN NA CUIMHNE, CRATHIE
(OS 241942)
(THE STONE OF REMEMBRANCE)

Just west of the 51st milestone from Aberdeen, along the A93 road to Braemar is the Carn-na Cuimhne, anglicised to the Cairn-na-Quheen. It lies on the south of the road near the Dee, opposite the site of the original Monaltrie House. This heap of stones, somewhat disorganised, is the Cairn of Memory, the Gaelic words representing the Farquharson war-cry. It is the Farquharson place of Remembrance, almost surrounded by trees.

This was the rallying place for Clan Farquharson. When men were called to arms the cry 'carn-na-cuimhne' brought them. The situation was excellent for it was within reach of all the passes in Upper Deeside.

There is no documentary evidence about the purpose of the cairn but the traditional story says on going to war every man laid a stone on a small heap. On his return he removed a stone. The remainder then acted as a memorial to those who did not return and these were transferred to the big pile. Hence the name Cairn of Remembrance.

The date of the original cairn is uncertain but the pile was in existence well before the Jacobite risings but it was no doubt used during the '15 and '45 and the pile considerably increased. Monaltrie House had been at Crathie before the '45 and when it was burned by Redcoats and Francis Farquharson returned from 20 years as a prisoner in England, he built a new house in

Ballater, known as Ballater House, then Monaltrie House although there is no real evidence that he actually resided there.

William Farquharson of Monaltrie, nephew of the Baron Ban and last of his line enclosed the ground round the stones and planted larches with the help of a representative youth from every house on the Monaltrie estate.

On 10th May 1972 the Clan Farquharson Association under its President Miss Margaret Farquharson, with about 20 members from all over Scotland, in the presence of the 16th chief Alwyne Arthur Compton Farquharson and his wife, visited the site. The President spoke of the history of the Clan Society, its declining membership and the desire to erect a commemorative stone. The Chief spoke of the purpose of the Cairn, saying that in case in the future the reason for the cairn's existence should be forgotten, the stone now dedicated would be a lasting reminder.

The stone, covered by Farquharson tartan was then dedicated.

Cairn na Cuimhne

CLACH THOGALACH
(OS 032934)

When the 1715 Rising was being planned Mar arranged a "Hunt" to gauge and encourage Jacobite support. Grant of Rothiemurchus was undecided as to whether or not he should join the men assembled at the Linn of Quoich. Among all the talking and the whisky drinking from the "Punchbowl" rivalry athletic activities were taking place. Grant was of the opinion that his followers were stronger than the Deesiders. A stone, "The Stone of the Lifting" was used for trials of strength. Mar asked Finlay Farquharson to lift the enormous stone. Casually he picked it up and threw it over a horse's head. Impressed, the Grants joined the Rising.

The hole for containing the whisky is now without a bottom, but a stone remains that might be the stone of the lifting, Clach Thogalach.

THE CULBLEAN STONE
(Culblean Hill OS 412010)

The battle of Culblean was fought on 30th November 1335. When Robert the Bruce died in 1328 he was succeeded by an 8 year old son, David. Edward Baliol was a rival claimant to the throne, supported by Edward 111 of England. For the boy king was the Guardian of Scotland, Sir Andrew de Moray.

David de Strathbogie, Earl of Atholl opposed Sir Andrew de Moray. The forces met near Loch Davan.

Moray outmanoeuvered Earl Davy, who according to the chronicler Wynton stood with his back "til a gret stane" and in Sir Walter Scott's words shouted "Come one, come all, this rock shall fly from its firm base as soon as I."

The stone remains, a reminder of one of the most decisive battles in Scotland's Second War of Succession and Independence.

In 1956 The Deeside Field Club set up a stone to mark the

event. Culblean was until the 1870's part of the parish of Tullich, Glenmuick and Glengairn.

THE GORDON MEMORIAL PLAQUE, 1899
(OS 366948)

At the Bridge of Muick is a memorial seat and plaque to commemorate one of Queen Victoria's last public duties

The year was 1899. Queen Victoria arrived to take the salute and the Prince of Wales presented Colours to the Gordon Highlanders before they embarked for South Africa to take part in the Boer War. Visualise troops lined up by the Muick Bridge, weapons sparkling in the sun, ready for a local "Trooping of the Colour".

An inscription at the entrance to Glen Muick, placed by Col. Mackenzie records the event.

Some years ago a person whose name is unknown cleaned up and renewed the lettering.

The Gordon Memorial at the entrance to Glen Muick

THE MILENNIUM STONE TO
COMMEMORATE MANIRE
(OS 264947)

On 31st May 2009 the memorial set up to commemorate Manire at the time of the millenium was dedicated at an after-noon gathering of members of Crathie, Braemar and Ballater Churches. It was an appropriate service for Pentecost Sunday and served to link the present with the past, when Manire preached Christianity to the people of the area.

MULLACH CAIRNS
(OS323011)

Mullach, the high place, was a busy little settlement in Glengairn. This was Durward territory, the home of staunch Jacobite supporters. Like other families in the glen, they sent their sons to Culloden. Three went. Two died, being killed by Butcher Cumberland's men as they lay wounded on the field of battle. Malcolm saw his brothers killed but was captured with only a superficial wound. After a period in prison he was pardoned.

Towering above the houses was the rounded hill of Mammie. Here there are two cairns, visible from all around. One was erected by the folk of the glen in honour of Queen Victoria at the time of her Diamond Jubilee in 1897. The other cairn is probably much older, but no one seems to know the reason for its erection.

TILLYCAIRN, Dinnet
(OS 416899)

On the Firmounth track, - the hill road leading from Deeside to Glenesk, a stone bears the inscription 'Let well alone'.

On the hill top at Tillycairn is an almost obliterated inscription on a stone

Sir William Cunliffe Brooks erected a granite memorial saying :-

Fir Munth

Ancient pass over the Grampians

Here crossed the invading armies of

Edward I of England

A.D.

1293 and 1303

Also the army of Montrose

1645

The position of the stone was changed a little when the road was altered.

The accuracy of these statements is in doubt. It is interesting to note that Edward I did not cross here but rather by the Cairn a'Mounth. Montrose was not the king's Lieutenant General until later and when he did appear at the head of a Royalist force he was most likely to have used the Cairn a'Mounth route.

QUEEN VICTORIA'S JUBILEE FOUNTAIN, SOUTH DEESIDE ROAD

(OS 323963)

Becaue of the local association with Queen Victoria and particularly as Abergeldie had been leased to the Royal family and had been the home of the Queen's mother during the summer months, tenants were anxious to express their loyalty and to celebrate the Queen's Jubilee. Many of them felt they had a personal interest in the event.

Queen Victoria Fountain, Abergeldie

QUEEN VICTORIA'S JUBILEE FOUNTAIN
nr. PANNANICH WELLS
(OS 395967)

This stone trough with its spring was erected to commemorate the Diamond Jubilee of Queen Victoria in 1897. Provided by residents around Pannanich (at that time there were little settlements) and by the Mackenzies of Glenmuick House, it indicates the respect felt for the aged Queen.

At the front is a traditional inscription:-

VICTORIA

RI

1837   JUBILEE   1897

On the left is :-

> Drink weary traveller in the land
> And on thy journey fare
> 'Tis sent by God's all giving hand
> And stored by human care.

On the right is:-

> From Earth I flow: Seaward I go
> Refreshing the world on my way
> My duty done, my guerdon won
> I rise on celestial ray.

Queen Victoria Fountain, Pannanich

292

2. STONES ASSOCIATED WITH PERSONS

A number of stones have close associations with people.

FARQUHARSON MEMORIAL OBELISK, BRAEMAR
(OS 158929)

James Farquharson 12th Laird of Invercauld, 1808 - 1862, was the son of Catherine, only surviving child of the eleven children of James Farquharson and Lady Sinclair. James was the laird when Queen Victoria first came to Balmoral.

James was a popular laird who did much to improve conditions on the estate and develop it. He planted trees and developed agricultural methods.

During his lifetime Braemar Castle was restored to the family.

Shortly after his death in 1862 the estate workers and his many friends erected an obelisk on the left bank of the Sluggan Burn, at Invercauld.

THE FARQUHARSON NEEDLE, 1836
(OS 400978)

The Aberdeen granite obelisk in William Farquharson's memory stands on a knoll of birch west of the site of the old Cambus o'May Railway Station. The monument was erected in 1836 by the widow of William Farquharson of Monaltrie, the last of his line. His uncle Francis Farquharson of Monaltrie was an enlightened laird, interested in estate development. Francis had fought at Culloden and been captured. On his return from English captivity 20 years later he had the waters at Pannanich analysed and built a 'Pump Room' and Inn. When he developed the Spa at Pannanich and realised that the ferry boat could no longer cope with the influx of visitors he began to develop a village on the land that became Ballater. He devoted his energies to local development and was really the

'Founding Father' of Ballater.

When Francis died in 1791 his plans were developed by his nephew and successor William, who was responsible for much that we see today that we have inherited from the past.

William died at Vevey in Switzerland in 1828, without heirs, at the age of 75 years. Without him, there would probably have been no Ballater. His widow, Margaret Garden, died in 1857 and was buried in Tullich. After that the Farquharson of Monaltrie property reverted to Farquharson of Invercauld.

The inscription on the obelisk reads:-

In Memory
Of
William Farquharson of Monaltrie
Who died at Vevy
in Switzerland
20th November 1828
aged 75 years.
Erected
By
His affectionate widow
Margaret Garden
In 1836.

An addition reads:-
His widow died in 1857 and was buried at Tullich

FOUR LORDS' STONES
(OS 424002)

North of the Marchnear burn on the track from Loch Davan to Cambus o'May are four stones lying together. Known as the Four Lord's Stones, tradition says four lords dined together and each had a stone for a table. Who they were I just do not know. An alternative name is The Four Marys, from the old Scots ballad of Mary Hamilton.

About 200 yards away in a north westerly direction is a great erratic boulder, in a water course, known as Clashneach.

About another 400 yards away on the steep side of the hill is a glittering white quartz mass called the Witches' Stone. Again I do not know why.

FOX'S CAIRN
(OS 284018)

This cairn north west of Gairnshiel is said locally to have been built by his men to commemorate Major Fox who built the Gairnshiel Bridge after 1745. Some authorities prefer the explanation that it is in commemoration of the statesman Fox, but he appears to have had no association with the area. Local lore is more likely to be correct.

THE STONE IN THE DEE AT
INVERCAULD BRIDGE
(OS 185910)

Sandy Davidson, 1792 - 1834 appreciated the fact that God had provided plentiful fish and game on Deeside and considered it was his duty to help himself to this abundance. In an age of illiteracy he could read and write. He spoke perfect English and his native Gaelic, but never Scots. He was a hardy fellow, typical of the area. 5' 11" tall, he had a good physique, a proud bearing and a fine face.

Sandy's family had been millers at the Mill of Inver but his father, a local "strong man" had been killed when Sandy was only a child. Father had taken part in a wrestling contest at a "penny wedding" in Glen Gairn which as usual he won. Afterwards he was ambushed on the way home by jealous opponents. He died later as a result of a fractured skull.

Young Sandy, an excellent shot, had worked as a keeper for titled families, The noted young upper-class men in the area were Lord Kennedy, son of the Earl of Cassalis, Farquharson of Finzean, and one or two others. They led a very fast life.

They had shooting estates on Deeside and Donside for deer and game but their most important estates were near the source of the Tilt. Sandy's first job was there, but he left, disliking the fast life of his employer and refusing to shoot on a Sunday. He was no sanctimonious young man, for he attended ceilidhs and parties and other functions but drew the line at excessive drinking. Like many men of his time, he was full of highland superstitions and had a strong belief in the supernatural. He was brought up on the story of the Black Hand that involved his grandfather, John Davidson, miller at Inver and his head was filled with similar stories from babyhood

Sandy was interested in making money and decided that whisky smuggling was the way to make ends meet, or even to make a fortune. In the whisky business one activity was to make illicit whisky, the other was to transport it to market, - more dangerous but more lucrative. Sandy took part in the latter activity carrying the liquid gold to market further south and had many brushes with the excisemen. In spite of this he was very successful.

There came a time when the Earl of Mar, one of the feudal superiors in the area, needed money. To raise it he sold trees in Glen Derry. Sandy used his 'whisky' money to buy the timber. The speculation gave him great excitement. In a glacial area he built a dam, the result being that he had a large lake. By ingenious means he managed to use water power to float his timber to the Dee. This was the age of 'Floaters' who had a hard life and a dangerous one, disentangling logs with crowbars. There were fatal accidents, sometimes attributable to the drink taken to keep out the cold. Sandy always worked with his men.

Sometime before this the Invercauld Factor, Mr. Roy, had accused Sandy of taking game. Sandy was probably guilty, but his reaction to the charge was to poach some more! Mr. Roy was not amused!

Not far from the Invercauld Bridge was a great rock. It caused many a log-jam. Sandy decided that with hard work one night would see a blasting operation complete. He had of course not asked Mr. Roy's permission. The job was bigger than Sandy had thought and by morning it was unfinished. The Factor arrived on the scene. There was anger and the threat of violence.

Without letting Sandy know, his men planned to get Mr.Roy on a temporary gangway of logs from the river bank to the stone and then to slip a log and let him fall into the river and likely death. Sandy perhaps guessed the men were up to something but he had no part in the plan. He was on the rock when the Factor came. The water was swirling angrily. Although advised not to, Mr. Roy was determined to cross to the rock. Sandy shouted to him not to cross, as his life could be in danger. No one ever told the Factor what to do! On he went. A floater slipped the log. At that moment Sandy realised what was happening and shouted a warning. He rushed onto the log bridge, grabbed the Factor and carried him to the bank. The logs went rushing down the river but the Factor was safe.

Everyone thought Sandy a hero, - except the Factor, who tried to add attempted murder to the earlier poaching charge!

Next time you see the stone in the Dee, think of Sandy.

THE LAMONT MEMORIAL, INVEREY
(OS 087895)

The Lamonts were distantly related to the Farquharsons by marriage.

There is documentary evidence that a John Lamont was in Braemar in 1661. One of his descendants was Robert, forester to Duff, Earl of Fife.

Robert was twice married, his second wife being Elizabeth Ewan. Their son John was born in the forester's cottage at Corriemulzie in 1805. Afer his early education at the local school in Inverey he went to the Scots' College in Regensburg, Germany, to be educated for the priesthood of the Roman Catholic Church.

John was a brilliant scholar but it seems he decided against entering the priesthood. Instead he entered Munich

University in 1828 when 23 years of age. He left theology behind and studied his real love, astronomy. This led to a career in the subject and he became Director of the Royal Observatory near Munich and the University's Professor of Astronomy. He gained a world-wide reputation, determining the position of over 80,000 stars in his charts. Appointed Astronomer Royal in Bavaria in 1835 and then decorated by the Bavarian Crown, he became Johan von Lamont. Johan was awarded many Degrees from European Universities and Orders of Knighthood. Even to this day his name is perpetuated by a spot where the Apollo mission landed in the Sea of Tranquilliy being named Lamont and a mountain on Mars bears his name.

John was a prolific inventor and one of his magnetic theodolites is in Marshal College, Aberdeen. He died in 1870, far from Deeside to which he never seems to have returned in a life of 65 years. He is buried near Munich. He left his wealth to provide grants to students at the Academy of Science and his property and workshops to Munich University.

Victoria, the Princess Royal who by marriage was the Crown Princess of Germany, sent the obituary notice to her mother, Queen Victoria. The latter had some enquiries made and discovered relations still lived in the area, so those in Braemar and Inverey had a visit from Queen Victoria.

It was not until 1934 that the Deeside Field Club erected a monument to Johan von Lamont, Bavaria's Astronomer Royal whose early life and education had been in Inverey. Members of the Clan Lamont Society attended and a Piper played "The Green Hills of Tyrol" and "My Home."

The monument stands on rising ground in Muckle Inverey and was unveiled by the Duchess of Fife, yet another of Queen Victoria's daughters.

The inscription on the front of the stone reads:-

This stone commemorates John Lamont 1805-1879
Who was born at Corriemulzie
His name is written in science as
Johan von Lamont
Astronomer Royal of Bavaria.

On the back of the stone is the Biblical quotation
"Day unto day uttereth speech and night unto night showeth knowledge."

This is repeated on the two other sides, in Gaelic and in German.

Another Lamont of Inverey was reputedly hanged by the Farquharsons of Invercauld. His mother cursed the Farquharsons, saying that the tree on which her son had been hanged would still be green when Farquharsons had gone from Deeside.
"This tree will flourish high and broad
Green as it grows today,
When from the banks o'bonnie Dee
Clan Fhionnlaidh's all away."

The male line of Farquharson failed in 1805: the tree survived as a tree into the twentieth century and is now supported.

ST. LESMO'S STONE, IN BOBBIE'S GIRNEL, GLEN TANAR
(OS 426923)

Glen Tanar, the glen of the river, had a long tradition of Christian work along its banks. Although there is no firm historical foundation, local legend associates St. Lesmo with the area. He is reputed to have lived a hermit's existence near Hermit's Well, at the foot of 2058' Clachan Yell. Stories tell of St. Lesmo preaching to the tiny population of the glen and ministering to folk crossing the Mounth. His well was reputed to have magical restorative powers and it continued as a place of pilgrimage up to the Reformation.

Most authorities consider St. Marnoch to have been the saint of the area and the only evidence for Lesmo is from a Belgian publication of 1838. It speaks of' Lesmo, a hermit 'in Glentanar, Scotland'. In 1600 a Thomas Dempster wrote that 'the 9th December is the festal day of St.Lesmo, Abbot in Argyll, later a hermit in Glen Tanar'. Lesmahago is named after him.

Many tales are told of St. Lesmo's ministry in the glen. Perhaps the most fascinating legend is the story of the Stone of Evil. In the 1902 edition of Lloyd's Magazine reference is made to a stone found in one of the Dee's pools, - Bobbie's Girnel - the Devil's Meal-chest. On the stone, about 12" square, is what might be the shape of a human hand. Legend has it that Lesmo, after having 'tamed' the locals and satisfied himself about their progress in Christian matters, left them for a few months while he went off on pilgrimage. The Devil (Bobbie) seized his chance to undo the good man's work and placed a rough stone on the narrow track to the shrine the inhabitants had promised faithfully to visit every day. This was no ordinary stone. Misfortune befell anyone who passed it. Milk spilled over, eggs broke, clothes tore, legs bruised. Even trying to by-pass the stone caused problems, the briars and thorns causing hurt. Most visits to the shrine ceased, to the delight of Bobbie safe in his girnel. Husbands forbade wives to make the attempt ever again. Two or three pious women disobeyed their menfolk and made the attempt, only to find the stone had grown to enormous proportions. The surrounding area was so thick with brambles, thorns and nettles that it made passage quite impossible. One morning all the menfolk, urged on by their women, took picks and shovels to remove the offending stone. Great disagreements had taken place. Was it the folly of attempting a daily visit to the shrine that had caused the evil? When that folly ceased would the evil cease?

Half-hearted attempts to dislodge the stone were

interrupted by the arrival of a stranger who said he had come from far off lands to bring news of Lesmo. Somehow he didn't ring quite true. He didn't ask any intimate details such as their own Lesmo would have known. In fact, he seemed just too saintly! They attacked the stone again, but picks and shovels broke, and they could make no impression on it.

Moreover, the stranger actually laughed at each new disaster! He then produced a flask of liquid, reputed to have in it the juice of berries picked by Lesmo in some foreign land. The result of drinking the liquid was that the men turned what implements remained against each other. Those who could, staggered home in a very battered state. Those who had been left to fish or till the land, chiefly children and women, had had a bad day too.

The next day the men went back to the stone. The stranger had gone, but his flask was there, - full. Drawn there by curiosity came the women. They all drank of the flask. Lesmo's teachings were forgotten. Robbery, murder and vice reigned supreme. The stranger appeared most days, much amused. The stone was the centre of all evil activities.

Far away, Lesmo heard of these goings on from travellers and pilgrims and hurried back to Deeside. He saw corn unharvested, fire sweeping through trees and drunken orgies throughout the glen. So upset was he that he turned away, to leave the backsliders to their fate. Then he heard a child calling "St. Lesmo, if you are our saint, help me". It was his favourite pupil, a six year old girl, alone by the stone, deserted by all. She had wild flowers in her hand and had been on her way to the shrine, but she was scratched and torn and beating her hands against the stone. Full of compassion, he lifted her up and comforted her.

Then, he moved to the Stone of Evil and uttering a prayer, he lifted his right hand and struck it with all the power he could muster. It immediately shrank to its original size. Lesmo then picked it up and flung it as hard as he could into the waters of Bobbie's Girnel.

As the stone disappeared, so did all the evil ways.

Hundreds of years later the stone was brought up from the river bed, but it was no longer evil. It was said that it bore the imprint of Lesmo's right hand!

I've found one stone in the river that just might be the one Lesmo threw in but you certainly need to use your imagination!

THE MACKENZIE SEAT

Looking down on the village and approached by the track from the end of Ballater Bridge is the "Seat" in memory of Allan Mackenzie, 2nd Baron of Glenmuick, who died in 1906.

Also associated with the Mackenzies is ALLAN'S PROP (OS 368931) a cairn that is visible from the bridge at Ballater and from the road along Glen Muick. Allan's Prop is in memory of Sir Allan Mackenzie, a former owner of Glenmuick Estate. (A prop is the local name for a marker or landmark.)

THE EARL OF MAR'S BREAKFAST STONE
(OS 428005)

A big flat stone lies on Culblean on a hillock known as Earl Mar's Hill, west of Loch Davan. In a cavity in the bank there used to be a stone known as the Earl of Mar's Breakfast Stone where he was supposed to partake of refreshments after the Raising of the '15 Standard in Braemar. According to Milne writing in 1912 it refers to an incident that took place in 1431. The stone was broken up for building material and only a fragment remains.

Downhill from the Breakfast Stone is a boulder thought by some to an inscribed stone. There may be something, but it is indecipherable.

THE EARL OF MAR'S PUNCHBOWL
(OS 114913)

About 6 km. from the Linn of Dee on the south side of the Water of Quoich is the Linn, or waterfall of Quoich. The 'punchbowl' is a circular hole in rocks that lies in ridges over the Quoich.

It is forever associated with Jacobite preparations for the '15 for, as was often the custom, Mar arranged a period of 'hunting' for guests. The Quoich was remote, a hunting area, and suspicion would not be aroused, - unless of course the guest list had ben examined. Had the powers that be had a look at the guest list, they would have surely suspected something was afoot, for all were noted Jacobites.

To toast the success of the venture Mar is reputed to have filled the bowl with whisky for all participants to drink. Since then the bottom of the bowl has disappeared and it is no longer a whisky-tight bowl for now water runs through.

On the other side of the Quoich is a ruined building which used to be one of the Queen Mother's shiels.

A bridge of wood near the Punch Bowl was rebuilt by Scotrail volunteers. The water here is a beautiful blue green colour, due to the rocks over which it flows.

MEG' S CAIRN
(OS 263985)

The steep hill on the Crathie road from Gairnshiel Bridge is the Sron Ghearrig. One New Year when Meg Andrews worked in Corgarff she set out for Crathie to spend a few days with her parents. Walking was of course her only option.

When Meg set out, it had started to snow but there were only a few lazy flakes. However, before the journey was half over, the snow storm had turned into a blizzard. There was a "white out". By the time she was approaching Glengairn she was lost and completely exhausted.

Meg never reached her parents' home and day-long searches, hampered by drifts, revealed no sign of her. It was not until some weeks later that her body was found where the cairn now stands.

MURDOCH'S CAIRN, CRAIGUISE
(OS 316959)

A tramp was murdered around 1880 on the south side of the road east of Abergeldie. A cairn was erected to mark the spot but most of the stone was removed in the 1940's when road improvements were undertaken.

HUGH ROSE FOUNTAIN, BALLATER
(OS 370960)

An imposing fountain sits on the Green opposite to the front door of Ballater Parish Church. Quite a land-mark, tasteful and not too ornate and originally useful for residents and visitors alike, the Fountain arouses curiosity, even though it is now dry. It was the gift of a public-spirited man to the village he served.

Hugh Rose was the first Provost of Ballater and he took a leading part in all village activities. Originally from Coull, he began as a backsmith then turned to farming. He became a farmer with large properties, rented and owned. He settled in Ballater and by 1884 he was retired. He was particularly interested in the erection of a stone bridge that replaced the timber bridge of 1834. George Washington Wilson, the well-known photographer, has a picture of Hugh Rose laying the first arch stone of Ballater Bridge. He and the Laird, Farquharson of Invercauld, owner of the land on which the village was built, worked closely together. Provost Rose had ensured the streets of Ballater were well kept, that the people had a good water supply, good drainage and an efficient railway system. He was noted for his benevolence and helped a great many poor families.

Hugh Rose worked hard for the village and the fountain was for the benefit of Ballater and its visitors. The fountain (now dry) cost £200 (a great deal of money at the time) and was gifted by the Provost to the people of Ballater in appreciation of his election as their first Provost. The fountain is after a design by Messrs Macdonald of Aberdeen, the mason work being carried out by Mr. Reid, Ballater and the plumbing by Thomas Davidson of Banchory, The fountain was to be enclosed by a rail and seats were to be placed in the enclosure for the benefit of visitors. If erected.they have long gone.

Made of granite, the 'water-bowl' had water delivered by way of a green rose-shaped fawcet. The tower-like erection with a hollow centre dominates the Green and is in excellent condition. Some inserted metal work at the side might indicate a barrier or even a fixed seat. The back has a square of different stone inserted, with a small central hole. Although without water now, it is still imposing and must have been a convenience to the village when amenities were not as plentiful as now.

The presentation ceremony took place on 8th October 1884 at 4p.m. Lieut. Col. Farquharson who gifted the feu was welcomed by the Ballater Volunteers commanded by Lieut. Duguid. Col. Faequharson turned on the water and drank from a silver quaich, wishing long life, health and happiness to all. A half-holiday was observed and the village was decorated with bunting. The whole event was rounded off by a splendid dinner at the Monaltrie Hotel with much ceremonial.

The inscription on Hugh Rose's fountain reads:-

PRESENTED
TO
LIEUT. COL. FARQUHARSON
AND THE
INHABITANTS OF BALLATER
BY
HUGH ROSE
1844

TAILORS' STONE -Clach nam Taillear
(OS 983965)

In the Lairig Ghru there is a group of stones.

According to the legend, three tailors took a wager that they would be able to dance a reel in Rothiemurchus and another in Tullich on the same day. Unfortunately there was heavy snow and they all perished.

3. HEADSTONES & GRAVES

"Tread lightly lest you stir the dust of forgotten men, at rest within their sepulchre."

Lady Margaret Sackville

From earliest times people have commemorated their dead so scattered around the area are burial sites, to reming us of our heritage. The poor had no headstones so there is no way of checking the number of burials. Tradition tells of the sites of a number. Before about 1500 there were no gravestones as we know them, Grounds round the church were the sites of "wapinshaws" or display and practice of weapons as decreed by Act of Parliament in 1457, to be held in every churchyard four times each year. Important personages were frequently buried within a building with a memorial plaque inside or outside. Ordinary people were buried without stones, Everyone had a right to a burial plot. Those who could not afford a funeral plot were interred by the church using the "Poores Fund." The coffin was re-usable, having a hinged bottom that opened to deposit the corpse. Even the wealthy often hired the church coffin and returned it on completion. Soon relations marked the burial place with a stone and headstiones as memorials appeared. At first there were only crude carvings of initials and sometimes date of death. There could be motifs appropriate to the deceased including symbols of immortality or trade symbols. Because granite was so hard and skills and finance lacking, in many cases only initials are to be found on stones. It was well through the seventeenth century before names appeared here.

Later in the nineteenth century headstones could be mass produced by monumental masons but until then each stone was unique, the work of a local man who also had a full-time job. Many of our local stones are tributes to their skill but the hardness of the granite prevented flights of fancy seen elsewhere.

Families tended to be buried in the same part of the burial ground and a family area can span many years. Women were usually buried under their maiden names.

The Heritors, (feudal superiors) were the Gordons of Abergeldie so Charles Gordon of Abergeldie (1796) and his wife have a railed ground with a square monument. Some ministers of the kirk are also buried in Glen Muick near their former church

Many headstones commemorate the lives of people well-known in their own time.

BALNOE, ABERARDER
(OS 217943)

In Chapel Park there are a number of graves, the burials unidentified.

CARN SEUMAS na PLUICE
(OS 082823)

This cairn (and probably a burial) in Upper Glen Ey for "James of the fat cheeks" is in memory of James Mackenzie of Dalmore (Mar Lodge) who was killed by Lochaber caterans in 1727.

CATERANS GRAVES
(OS 139782)

From the Battle of the Cairnwell in 1644 there were a number of burials. Hollows are all that now remain, the site of the Ski Café cesspool.

CHAPEL PARKS, GLEN GAIRN
(OS 339996 & OS 341995)

In two fields, not far from a former chapel, are a series of burials.

CRATHIE KIRKYARD
(OS 264949)

The burial ground is by the ruins of the old kirk dedicated to St. Manire.

Just inside the gate is an impressive memorial to the D'Albert-Anson family (D'Albertancon). Francois, from Alsace was for many years Queen Victoria's Steward and his wife Housekeeper.

Francis Clark was in the Queen's service as a ghillie for many years. He is actually buried in Braemar but a wall plaque in Crathie burial ground records "In memory of Francis Clark Highland attendant to Queen Victoria whom he served faithfully and devotedly for 25 years b. Belmore, Aberarder 1Sept.1841 d. Buckingham Palace 7 July 1895."

Also interred in Braemar were John Grant and his wife Elizabeth Robbie. A wall plaque in their memory is at Crathie burial ground. Born in Braemar in 1810, he was head keeper to Sir Robert Gordon at Balmoral and he stayed on with Prince Albert. He had been head forester and keeper for 26 years. The inscription reads "Much beloved by Queen Victoria and all the Royal Family. Erected by Her Majesty Queen Victoria."

Peter Coutts who died in 1885 was a ghillie for the Queen and later Invercauld Piper. Another ghillie and keeper was Charles Duncan, born in 1826. He excelled at Braemar Games but after a run up Creag Choinnich he had permanent lung damage. The Queen then requested that the run be stopped. John Macdonald, who died in 1860 was an Invercauld keeper but from 1847 he was Prince Albert's Jaeger.

The Balmoral nursery gardens at Corbieha' were run by John and Annie Simpson. He had served under Nelson at the Battle of Copenhagen, 1801. They are remembered as well as William Duran, a later gardener there.

Similarly remembered by the Queen were William Thorpe for 26 years working in the stables, who died in 1873, Thomas Hall for 18 year's service in the kitchen, Daniel Burgoyne, under-butler and Peter Farquharson for 27 years a gamekeeper. An under-gamekeeper, John Morgan had served for 39 years. Another gamekeeper with 17 years service was James Bowman who died as a result of an accident in the Ballochbuie forest in 1885. A wardrobe mistress for 31 years and in the royal service for 41 years was Annie McDonald neé Mitchell who died in 1897. James Bruce was the farm manager at Abergeldie Mains.

Other faithful servants remembered by the Queen and buried in Crathie kirkyard are John Spong, upholstered to Queen Victoria for 19 years. He died at Balmoral in 1870 aged 49 years.

John Brown gave long and devoted service to Prince Albert then to Queen Victoria. Born at Crathienaird in 1826 he died at Windsor in 1883.

The Queen was advised on what should go on his headstone in Crathie kirkyard that she was responsible for erecting and the result was:

"This stone is erected in affectionate and grateful remembrance of JOHN BROWN the devoted and faithful personal attendant and beloved friend of Queen Victoria in whose personal service he had been for 34 years. Born at Crathienaird 8 Dec. 1826 d. at Windsor Castle 27 Mar. 1883. That friend on whose fidelity you count, that friend given you by circumstances over which you have no control, was God's own gift. Well done good and faithful servant."

John Brown's Headstone

Queen Victoria was responsible for the erection of another ten headstones in memory of staff.

Although stones were not erected by the Queen, sixteen servants are remembered like Alexander Profit the Queen's Commissioner for 22 years, and servants like the upholsterer, attendants, head gardeners, gamekeepers, foresters, stablemen, footmen and Clerks of Works.

A number of Crathie ministers and Queen's Chaplains are buried here. Murdoch McLellan wrote the Ballad of the "Battle of Sheriffmuir". He was in Crathie from 1749 - 1783. On his flat stone is the symbol of the minister's Bible. Mr. McHardy was minister and Invercauld Factor. Inducted in 1789 he immediately planned a new Manse - now part of the older section of the present Manse. It cost £243. He insisted on a new church, with whitewashed walls and a belfry. It was replaced by the present church in 1893. Mr. McHady had great plans for Invercauld estate. He did not like Roman Catholics and as Factor, he evicted many and put in sheep or deer. He died in 1822 and was succeeded by the Rev. Alexander MacFarlane who instituted health regulations. He died in 1840. His "table-on pillars" headstone also remembers his 18 year old son. The Rev. Archibald Anderson, 1840 - 1860 followed him. During his tenure the Queen came to Balmoral. The minister's dog Towser sat on the pulpit steps and if the sermon was lengthy, he got up and stretched. Thinking the Queen might not appreciate a dog in the pulpit, Towser was left at home. The Queen sent an equerry to see if Towser was ill. So he returned to his usual place. Mr. Anderson officiated at the laying of the foundation stone at the new Balmoral Castle. Another minister remembered is a Queen's Chaplain, the Rev. A. A. Campbell who died in 1907.

Near the west gable of the old church is a stone in memory of the Queen's fiddler, Willie Blair from Balnacroft. He died in 1884 at the age of 90. His most noted tunes were "Craigowan Reel", "Lochnagar Whisky", "Abergeldie" and "The Brig of Crathie".

Local people are of course commemorated. Headstones remember Samuel Page, the Crathie Church organist for 56 years, Scots Guardsman C.S. Campbell who died in 1917, the Thomsons who ran the Post Office - Charlie had been Head Forester - and the Rev. James Halliday, minister of the United Free Church in Crathie who died in 1923.

Locals of all walks of life are remembered, together with their wives and families as well as those men who fell in military actions.

THE DUBRACH STONE
(OS 152917)

In St. Andrew's burial ground in Braemar, on the site of the old St. Andrew's Kirk is a table headstone immediately to the left of the Farquharson Mausoleum. This is the grave of Peter Grant of Dubrach, 'Old Dubrach', the last survivor of the '45.

He died on the 11th February 1824 at the age of 110 years. Peter, born in 1714, was the son of a Glen Dee tenant farmer and was educated by the priest in Inverey. Apprenticed to a weaver and tailor in Auchindryne (Braemar), he eventually took over the business and was there at the start of the '45.

He was only a baby at the time of the '15 but he grew up

an adent Jacobite. In the first wave of 'recruiting' he joined up in the Mackintosh batallion, raised by "Colonel Anne", the Farquharson Jacobite wife of The Mackintosh.

Dubrach fought at Prestonpans in 1745 and was promoted to the rank of Sgt. Major. The following year he fought at Falkirk and marched with the Jacobite army to Culloden. Captured, he was imprisoned, first in Inverness, then in Carlisle Castle to await trial and execution or deportation. He managed to escape and made the long walk back home to friends in Auchendryne.

When home, surprisingly unmolested, he attended the baptism of a neighbour's daughter, Mary Cumming. Sixteen years later he married her.

Although his old home and indeed the whole area was under the control of government troops who were garrisoned at Braemar Castle, he was, somewhat unusually, allowed to return to his old occupation of weaving and tailoring. Peter and Mary had three sons and three daughters, one called after Col. Anne. When he retired the couple went to live with a son on the Panmure Estate. Mary died in 1811 and was buried in Lethnot. By that time Peter was 96 years old. A new minister was appointed to Lethnot whose wife, a keen Jacobite, was the daughter of Peter's commanding officer from the past. By 1814 Dubrach was 100 years old, the last Jacobite survivor of Culloden. The minister made the facts known and when George IV in Edinburgh in 1822 heard of the old man he granted the 107 years old man a pension of £52. per annum, for life - quite a large sum.

In May 1823 Dubrach went to stay with his elderly son William in Auchendryne and died there the following year, aged 110.

The funeral was a great occasion. There were pipers and vast numbers of Highlanders. As was the custom, much whisky was imbibed, but the coffin was safely buried, to the tune of 'Wha widna fecht for Cherlie's richt?'

The political climate had certainly changed!

THE MACDONALD AISLE
(OS 269003)

As a duinewasal or gentleman farmer, McDonald was entitled to a private burial ground. About half a mile west of the old mansion house, tucked away among the trees but near to an old drove road is the Macdonald burial place, known as The Aisle. Roughly half an acre in extent, it is enclosed by a stone wall with an iron gate. Central is a square vault with two headstones. One is built into the west wall and the other beside it. One has the inscription "Within this tomb is laid the remains of Jas. Macdonald Esq. of Rineaton, who died the 9th of May 1776, aged 63. Likewise of Helen Grant of Tulloch, his wife and several other Descendants."

James Macdonald and Helen Grant of Tulloch in Strathspey had a daughter Christian who was also buried at Rineaton. Her inscription reads "Within this sanctuary are deposited the mortal remains of Christian, wife of Lieut. John Farquharson of the 79th Regiment and eldest daughter of James McDonald of Rineaton Esq. She departed this life on. 29th August 1791, in the 49th year of her age, leaving one son and one daughter. This stone is erected to her memory by her son Colonel Farquharson of the 25th Regiment." The stone was erected sometime between 1814 and 1817 when the son was Colonel of the 25th.

A right in perpetuity was granted to the Macdonalds for their burial ground at Rineaton on payment of a nominal feu duty of 1s. per annum.

DONALD MACKINTOSH
(OS 426923)

Around St. Lesmo's Church is a small graveyard where a number of interments have taken place. Sir William Cunliffe Brooks, 1819 - 1900, has his memorial not far from the church door. A large rough stone bearing a cross is a memorial to a stalker, Donald Mackintosh and his wife. At the foot of the grave a 6' boulder stands, a reminder of a pact between Sir William and his keeper, that whoever died first should have as a grave marker a huge stone they used to see in the Tanar. The keeper died in May 1876 and the Laird honoured the arrangement.

IAN MITCHELL, GLENMUICK
(OS 366948)

All the burial grounds on Upper Deeide were close to a kirk, scenically sited and usually close to a river.

Locals were often long-lived - both men and women survived to be well over 90.

The most interesting stone in the burial ground at Glenmuick is at the entrance, a small upright stone on which are carved the initials I.M. 1596 - 1722. It marks the grave of John (Ian) Mitchell who lived a few yards along the road at Dalliefour. He was a noted poacher and had a pool in the river (where the Dee joins the Muick) named after him - Mitchell's Redd. (A redd is a spawning area). He was married twice but there appears to be no stone to commemorate either wife. He lived through stirring times and was a young boy when James VI became King of England as James I. He also lived to see the Union of the two crowns of England and Scotland in 1707. Did he really live as long as that? From Kirk Records appearing when younger contemporaries would have known him, or have heard parents speak of him, it appears so. He was the longest lived of those who were buried in Glen Muick, although there were others of 100 and many in their 90's.

A poem is attributed to him, but I think that while it is about him, it is from another pen, for it would appear that he was cunning but illiterate.

> "Full forty years a bachelor life I went
> And twenty six in wedlock next I spent.
> Then twice three years I passed a widowed life
> And fifty nine lived with a second wife.
> Betwixt my cradle and my grave I wean
> Seven monarchs and two queens have been.
> I saw the union of the British crowns.
> Twice Presbytery gave way to Stewart gowns

As oft again thrust out prelatic towns.
Eight times I've seen my fellow subjects try
If law or princes which should bear the sway.
I've seen the Royal Stuarts bold ancient race
With Scotland's freedom, state, name to cease.
Such devastation in my life hath been
That I the end of families great have seen.
But those were safe who kept from faction free,
Served God in truth and sound sobrietie.

The last line is an interesting sentiment from a man who was over-fond of his whisky!

Also reputedly buried in the vicinity of the Glenmuick kirkyard are victims of a fight between Glenesk men and locals over cattle 'lifting'. Glen Muick men had stolen Glenesk cattle and were nearly home with their spoils, approaching Iverton when the owners of the stock caught up with them. A fierce fight ensued in which the locals were victorious. Three Glenesk men were killed. They were buried in what is now the garden of the house by the Muick. There was ill feeling between the two Glens for many years, the Glenesk folk condemning the Glen Muick people for not coming to the help of the innocent.

The Gordons of Abergeldie, heritors of the area, are also buried in Glenmuick, as are some of the parish ministers.

John Mitchell's Headstone, Glenmuick burial ground

THE TINKER'S GRAVE
(OS 269989)

Beyond Meg's cairn, a little further on towards Crathie, two stones mark the top and bottom of a tinker's grave.

Unfortunately, nothing is known of him, not even his name.

THE TINKER'S GRAVE, - THE BLACK KIRK ON THE MOOR, GLENTANAR
(OS 426923)

To the north east of the burial ground is a water-worn stone with a barely decipherable letter. Tradition says this is a T, cut into the flat side. The stone, taken from the Dee by a local farmer, marks the grave of a murder victim in the 1880's. The woman was killed by her common law husband, a tinker, as they came to the glen by the Fir Mounth. Both had drunk too much. The T presumably stands for tinker. The Edinburgh trial, during which the accused condemned himself by contradictory evidence, was a nine day's wonder in the glen. Some of the local women called to give evidence of identification were thrilled to visit the capital. They each bought a shawl, known locally as 'Tinker's Shawls'. My Granny had one, given to her by an aunt. Where it is now I have no idea.

BURIALS in ST. MUNGO's CHURCH, FOOT o'GAIRN

(OS 303012)

The earliest grave slab commemorates the Grant family of Abergairn and is dated 1714.

The next oldest is in memory of Elspet MacDonald who died in 1719. A stone is in memory of three persons called McAndrew, 1729 & 1738.

Jervais, who wrote at length on headstones was convinced that John Michie, farmer Tomanraw, d. 1870 and his wife Ann Coutts, d. 1876, were the uncle and aunt of the Rev. Michie, minister of Dinnet. The family came from Micras, at that time in Glenmuick parish and later transferred to Crathie. The Coutts family were farmers at Tullochmacarrick and were noted for their longevity.

There are stones for the 18th century MacKenzies of Dalmore (Mar Lodge). William MacKenzie, minister of the united parishes and previously missionary minister at Braemar died in 1790 at the age of 79. The inscription reads "A pastor vigilant beyond his strength over the flock committed to his charge: of courteous behaviour and beneficent life: a pattern of charity in all its branches: a man adorned with many virtues."

Also buried here is Rodolphe Christen, born in 1859 to a Calvanist shoemaker in St. Imier, Switzerland. He was apprenticed to an engraver but then moved about and was in Paris painting buttons for dresses, then became an engraver. His real interest and skill was in painting and he taught art students and ran summer schools in Aberdeen. He was unhappily married to a rich American lady and there was a divorce. He travelled widely and in 1900 married Sydney Mary Thompson, a water-colour artist.

The couple built a house, St Imier, at Foot o' Gairn, later called Delgarno and then Glengarden.

Rodolphe died in 1906 and was buried within the walls of the ruined Church. His wife died in the early 1920's. A bequest was set up for children of Ballater School and a number of local people were recipients.

317

TULLICH BURIAL GROUND

Tullich was a burial ground from very early times and it is still in use today.

Among very old stones are those featuring the skull and cross-bones.

Skull and cross-bones on an old headstone at Tullich

WAR MEMORIALS

In every village on Deeside there are memorials to those who have served their country and never returned to their homeland. One memorial at Crathie, as one approaches the South Deeside road from the bridge is taken as a representative of all others.

War Memorial, Crathie

XXXI. STONES ERECTED FOR SPECIAL PURPOSES

1. INDICATORS

CAIRNGORMS NATIONAL PARK INDICATOR, DINNET
(OS 461982)

Close by the Highland Boundary stone at Dinnet is the Osprey Emblem marking the beginning of the National Park at Dinnet.

Below the Osprey are the words:-

"Cairngorms National Park."

HIGHLAND BOUNDARY STONE, DINNET
(OS 461983)

The Deeside Field Club proposed that the line of the traditional Highland Boundary line be commemorated. Fenton Wyness designed a massive Craigenlow granite stone. It was unveiled on 2nd October 1965 by Lady Muriel Barclay Harvey. It stands just west of the Dinnet Burn, the traditionally accepted Highland boundary.

The inscription reads :-

"You are now in the Highlands."

MORRONE INDICATOR
(OS 125904)

In Morrone Birchwood above Braemar a stone is visible, almost hidden by trees. It is An Car, or as called locally, Car Prop.

Through the old Birchwood (Birkwood) of Morrone and the Nature Reserve lies an indicator, identifying the peaks of the Cairngorms. It was erected in 1960 by the Deeside Field Club on its 40th Anniversary and was unveiled by Major David Gordon on 3rd. September 1960. On the side of the indicator a plate gives the names of the first four Presidents of the Deeside Field Club together with a four-line verse by George Stephen, Lord Provost of Aberdeen:-

> "Upon this vantage ground I fain would stand
> The prospect with delight my spirit fills
> How oft in glowing rapture have I scanned
> The waving outline of the distant hills."

The stone enables visitors to locate surrounding peaks and add interest to their climb.

2. WELLS

There are on Deeside many small wells that are part of the local story.

THE ARROWMAKER'S WELL
(OS 208838)

This well on Lochnagar was named after an arrowmaker with associations with Lochnagar in the mid 16th century.

WELL & DRINKING CUP, CROFTS
(OS 359944)

At the roadside just before the Crofts is a little well and a drinking cup. A track left goes past the walled garden that once belonged to the old Glenmuick House, reputed to have a window for every day of the year.

GLENTANAR
(OS 426923)

There are numerous wells on the Glen Tanar Estate. The owner, William Cunliffe Brooks was fond of adding little quotations, some criptic. He used his initials -WCB all over the estate and even created a road, the Wilcebe Road.

Initials and sayings are to be found on stones, walls, and seats as well as wells. On the Wilcebe Road there are seven wells. At a water trough opposite Braeloine Bridge the Gaelic "Ceud Mile Failte" wishes a hundred thousand welcomes.

A second well is known as the Snakeswell because the inscription states "The worm of the still is the deadliest snake on the hill". This is a reference to the considerable trade in illicit whisky distilling. There is a wall seat near the well.

Another well, still producing water, with a drinking cup attached, is a partly overgrown well near Tillycairn Farm. The inscription reads "Well to know when you are Well off".

Beyond Newton Farm, at a field gate is a pile of twisted stones. They are built round a well, now without running water. The inscription invites "Drink, Think, Thank".

A well was built into the wall of Glen Tanar school, created in a definite English style, to celebrate Queen Victoria's Jubilee. It advises "Shape thyself for use. The stone that may fit in the wall is not left in thy way." There is an uncut stone among the dressed ones. This was Brook's way of pointing out that one imperfection spoils the whole.

Another well is built into the wall of Fasnadarroch House and says "The Well of Grace."

322

A well at Dinnet Bridge, an unusual place to hace a well, is difficult of access. It is on the Dinnet or west side of the river and has the inscription "Alike, yet so different."

INVEREY, THE WELL OF ST. MARY,
Tobar Mhoire
(OS 084892)

In the days before Christian missionaries came to the valley an old man, obviously foreign, appeared on Deeside and was not made welcome. Eventually he reached Inverey and started to tell the locals of a new religion. Locals refused him food and even a drink of water. Weary and thirsty, he crossed the Ey burn and found a refreshing spring. Concerned by his lack of welcome and failure to introduce his religious message, he failed to hear a man approaching.

He had just dedicated the spring to the Virgin Mary when a voice ordered him to curse the spring. Of course he refused so the newcomer picked up a nearby handful of mud and threw it into the clear spring water. The water ceased to flow.

When questioned, the newcomer said he was a Druid priest and resented anyone speaking of a new religion. The old man replied that his was the true religion and to prove it the spring would bubble up again. It did. The Druid was so impressed that he begged forgiveness and supported the old man in his task of introducing Christianity to the area.

So, according to legend, that is how Christianity came to the top of the valley.

MUNGO'S WELL
(OS 354970)

Mungo, the Dear One, or Kentigern of Glasgow fame, came to Glen Gairn, according to tradition, in the sixth century.

Legends about Mungo abound, particulatly one involving a fish, which is depicted on Mungo's banner.

Early documents refer to his church as Cill-ma-thatha, the church of Tatha. No trace of this wattle and daub building remains and little of the later pre-Reformation church although the ground is still used for burials. Even this building was superseded by one further up Glen Gairn at Kirkstyle, still in use.

A well near the original site was named after Mungo who died c. 603. It was believed that a drink from the well would bistow a blessing on all who sought refreshment. The well was for many years a local trysting place.

Every year until World War I a market-cum fair, with a shooting match then a dance, was held on 24th January, old style calendar. This Feill Macha was a time of great merriment and superstitious folk said if you were well and did not go to the Feill Macha you would not be alive when next year's event came round.

Mungo's Well

324

PANNANICH WELLS
(OS 395967)

One immediately thinks of Pannanich Wells in connection with the topic of wells, although the thereputic interest in wells is comparatively modern.

Across the River Dee from Tullich is the hotel building of Pannanich Wells and the hill and surrounding woodland of Pannanich - beinn an acha, the hill beside the river, is well named.

The situation is ideal, with the hills of Culblean and Morven to the North and Craigendarroch Hill and the Coyles of Muick on the west.

Just before the '45 old Elspet Michie, probably from the neighbourhood of the little settlement of Cobbletown of Dalmuchie who had scrofula or inflamation of the lymph notes was said to have recovered as a result of drinking and washing in the well water.

If it had not been for the development of the 'Spa' at Pannanich by Francis Farquharson after he returned following imprisonment in England as a result of leading the local men at Culloden, there would be no Ballater today. The Spa attracted many visitors. The boat to take the visitors across the river from Tullich just could not cope with the traffic, so once the bridge was erected at Ballater in 1783, a village could be created to accommodate those "taking the waters." Ballater was born. The first simple "Spa" building was not far from the bridge but later a larger building was erected, - a hotel in two halves. Between the two the coaches stopped to enable the health-hunting passengers to alight.

The wells became popular over the years.

There were four wells, rich in iron according to the analysis. In the early days, the poor had a dip in a bath but the wealthy went to the indoors bath house. Queen Victoria visited in 1870 and commented on the outdoor bath. John Brown had been a stable boy there before going to Balmoral.

John Oglivey wrote:-
"I've seen the sick to health return,
I've seen the sad forget to mourn,
I've seen the lame their crutches burn
And loup and fling at Pannanich."

PETER'S WELL
(OS 184840)

At Loch Callater there is a well, Peter's Well, where a priest called Peter put an end to frozen water due to a long period of frost in the Braemar area.

3. MILESTONES

Milestones were introduced into Aberdeenshire in 1776, with references to distances appearing about 1780. They really came into their own in the Turnpike period at the end of the eighteenth and the beginning of the nineteenth century. Distances from Aberdeen were measured by a wheel and chain. Lists were produced in 1913 and revised the following year. It seems that the first milestone was not found and measurements were taken from the second.

Deeside's milestones are not always consistent. The old road ran through the Pass of Ballater but when Ballater village came into being a new road was created. The 42nd milestone used to be in the Pass not far from its junction with the Braemar Road at the Craigendarroch end, but according to 1776 maps the 42nd milestone was about $1^{1}/2$ miles west, midway between Bridge of Gairn and Coilacreich. After the Turnpike Road was taken round by Ballater, according to the 1855 Act, the 42nd milestone was at the Bridge on the Braemar Road, near the station.

4. ROYAL SHIELS

The royal family had its special haunts, where they enjoyed picnics. They were known as shiels, from the old Scots word for a temporary or summer shelter. In the early days of Victoria's reign the favourite place was "The Hut" or Alltnagiubhsaich - the burn of the fir tres. About nine miles south east of the Castle is a little cottage that climbers know well, for the path to Lochnagar starts in the area. It is sheltered by pine trees and looks south across Loch Muick. Victoria and Albert often stayed at Alltnagiubhsaich and other more modern members of the family have done the same.

A private road from Alltnagiubhsaich ran along the west of the loch to the Glasallt Shiel. The Glas Allt, the green burn, forms a delta as it goes to the loch. The scenery is beautiful and this was a favourite spot for picnics. Seven years after Albert died his widow built in 1868 the Glasallt Shiel - the shiel of the grey burn - on the picnic site, frequently calling it her "Widow's House"

In 1878 Queen Victoria purchased the Ballochbuie Forest. Through the forest runs the Garbh Allt, - the rough burn, with its beautiful falls. Nearby is the Danzig Shiel, built by Prince Albert. It is on the site of a sawmill that used to be run by a Danziger, hence the name. When during the First World War there was anti-German feeling, the name was changed to the Garbh Allt Shiel, the Garrawalt.

There was a shiel on the Gelder, about half way up the glen of the white burn, south of Balmoral Castle. It was here at the Ruidh na Bhan (the Queen's Shiel) that Queen Victoria entertained the exiled Empress Eugenie of France in October 1879. On the menu was brown trout in oatmeal, caught and cooked by John Brown. The original stables near by are used by climbers as a bothy. From here climbers can go to the summit of Lochnagar by way of Meall Coire na Saobhaidhe - the hill of the Corrie of the Foxes' Den. A Foxes' Well is also on the way up to Lochnagar from Allt-ne-Giubhsaich.

Other favourite places were Connachat, the mossy place,

on the Queen's Drive.

The Linn of Dee was popular and also the Queen's Cottage that overlooked the Earl of Mar's Punchbowl at the Quoich. By the time of George VI, Dalphuil, "The Teapot Cottage" in Glengairn was in use, having been bought for the two Princesses in 1938.

The late Queen Mother favoured a tiny cottage as her shiel. This was at Auchtavan, Field of the Two Goats, perhaps a survival of the days when rents were paid in kind, two goats being the rent for the ground. Near by are the shells of 'black houses'. Auchtavan lies at the head of Glen Fearder, the Glen of High Water, with a wonderful view of Lochnagar.

As Queen Victoria said "All seems to breathe freedom and peace. It does one good as one gazes around, and the pure mountain air is most refreshing".

The Glasallt Shiel

XXXII. SEMI-PRECIOUS STONES & METALS

CAIRNGORMS

A variety of stones can be found on Deeside. Quartz crystals or Cairngorms come from the mountain of the same name, Culblean Hill and the Pass of Ballater: Cairngorms can range in colour from dark brown to the rare pale yellow

Garnets can be found in the granite and mica-schists in Glens Ey and Callater.

The Cairngorm found by Effie Morragh or Murray on the Invercauld Estate in 1788 is one of the best examples of smoky quartz ever found in Scotland. Hexagonal in shape, it measures 12" by 9". and weighs 52 lbs. It was on show at the Crystal Palace Exhibition in 1851. It was the usual practice for locals to dig for Cairngorms at the top of Ben A'an. Meagre incomes were supplemented in this way and there was a ready market. On this occasion the woman was given £40 by Invercauld, - a considerable amount of money in 1788.

In the collection of stones in Braemar Castle is green beryl from the top of Beinn a Bhuird found in 1960, a two inch square topaz, fluorspar crystals, green and blue, white marble, a cinnamon stone that is a type of garnet from Crathie limestone quarry and many others..

Pearls can be found in a number of the quiet stretches of the Dee and in some of its tributaries. Mussel type shell fish, like oysters, deal with any tiny intrusion in the shell. The foreign body is covered with a mother-of pearl substance. Tinkers used to spend hours searching, but the returns were fairly good.

GOLD

Gold can be found in a number of streams if a careful search is made. While the quantity is not sufficient to make the finder a fortune, a good number of young men have managed to find enough to make wedding rings for themselves and their brides.

SILVER

Among the crags of Sgurr Buidhe, the Yellow Crag, the Farquharsons of Monaltrie quarried silver. The quantity was not sufficient to make mining viable and after test extraction by specialists the project was abandoned. However, a portrait of William Farquharson by Sir John Watson Gordon shows him wearing a jacket with silver buttons from the estate "mine". There was also a silver mine in Glengairn, on the southern slopes of the Craig of Proney, and in the Pass of Ballater..

LEAD

According to a an indistinct Invercauld document, a Mr. Jeans or Jones of Avon who was an expert in searching for precious stones in the hills discovered in 1806 on the Monaltrie Estate a vein of lead on the perpendicular face of the "Rock of Grunel" (?) Traces of mining operations can still be seen west of Abergairn Castle.

In 1806 lead was extracted on Sgurr Buidhe but as in the case of silver, quantities were found to be commercially non-viable.

Only stone for building, found in the Pass of Ballater as well as in other parts of the estate, was in sufficient quantities to be a viable proposition.

XXXIII. EPILOGUE

"'Tis man's worst deed to let the "things that have been"
run to waste, and in the unmeaning present sink the past."

Charles Lamb

Ballater, as the "capital" of Upper Deeside reflects the social history of the area. There were three phases. From early times to the Union of the Crowns the whole district was a hunting forest or playground for kings and nobles. From the seventeenth to the nineteenth centuries it was the scene of some political and military activity but basically the people were involved in subsistence agriculture. Then came a new type of hunting forest or natural playground, at first for the royal and the wealthy, then for everyone to enjoy the beauties of nature and the associated activities.

We are what our past has made us. The traits we inherit, our attitudes and our education have all contributed to what we are today.

So ends over eight thousand years of history in the area, where the past is always with us in the present and the stones of our area are a link with those who have gone before.

> *"Of ancient deeds, so long forgot:*
> *Of feuds, whose memory is not:*
> *Of dwellings, now laid waste and bare:*
> *Of towers, which harbour now the hare:*
> *Of manners, long since changed and gone."*

Sir Walter Scott

TIME LINE

c. 6000 B.C. - 4000 B.C.   Mesolithic Era
c. 4000 B.C. - 2000 B.C.   New Stone Age
c. 2000 B.C - 700 B.C.   Bronze Age
c. 700 B.C. - 300 AD.   Iron Age
   300 A.D. - 843 A.D.   The Picts
       late 5th century Christianity comes to the valley
c. 1120   Feudalism introduced by David I & Anglo-Norman barons settle on Deeside
c. 1220   First bridge over the Dee at Kincardine o'Neil
1275   Tullich Church mentioned in "Bagimont's Roll"
c. 1300   The Feudalisation of Deeside complete
1323   Last mention of serfdom in Scotland
1335   Battle of Culblean
1336   Edward III on Deeside
1390   Sir Malcolm de Drummond granted a licence to build Kindrochit Castle
1505   James IV at castle on Loch Kinord
1596   Aberdeen witchcraft trials
1618   The "Water Poet" on Deeside
1639   Covenanters on Deeside
1644   Deeside plundered by Argyll
1654   Battle of Tullich
1689   Braemar Castle burned by the Black Colonel
1715   Jacobite standard raised by Mar at Braemar.
1745   Jacobite Rising. Deeside houses burned.
1748   Braemar Castle leased to government.
1783   Ballater Bridge erected
1829   The "Muckle Spate."
1831   Government troops finally left Braemar Castle
1843   The Disruption & formation of The Free Kirk
1866   The Railway comes to Ballater.
1878   Queen Victoria bought the Ballochbuie Forest
1881   Robert Louis Stevenson in Braemar
1893   Foundation stone of Crathie Kirk laid by Queen Victoria

1953	Severe gales and trees down
1966	The Deeside Railway line closed.

"Study the past if you would divine the future"

Confucius

Sheila Sedgwick, M.B.E. PhD. left Aberdeenshire as a child for the Lake District.

She returned to her roots on Deeside with her husband, after a career in Colleges & Universities in History & Theology.

She has always been interested in the way people lived in the past and has undertaken considerable research on the people of Upper Deeside.

Her books include:

The Curious Years (Churches)

Abandoned Glories (Tullich)

Recalling Glengairn

The Legion of the Lost (Glen Muick)

The Grue and the Glory (Stories from Deeside)

Variorum (Stories from Deeside)

Then & Now (Customs & Superstitions)

The Story of Ballater